IMPLANTED

"Lauren C Teffeau brings us a fully-realized world filled with conflict, drama, and insight."

Walter Jon Williams, multiple-award-winning author of Hardwired *and the Praxis series*

"*Implanted* takes readers to the bleeding edge of a hopeful future and dives headlong into the risks required to make that future real. Emery is a character I loved from the start for her skills and flaws both, and Teffeau takes this ultra-high-tech future to new heights and depths with incredible skill. Such a great adventure!"

Fran Wilde, Hugo and Nebula finalist and Andre Norton-winning author of the Bone Universe series

"Futuristic intrigue solidly rooted in intricate, multi-level worldbuilding spiced with just a touch of romance singles Lauren C Teffeau's *Implanted* out from the cyberpunk pack."

Jane Lindskold, New York Times bestselling author of Through Wolf's Eyes

"Teffeau serves up the future and it's entertaining and scary! The arms race of hackers and blockers goes to new heights, in an intriguing tale of life in the non-utopic automated cities of the future."

S M Stirling, New York Times bestselling author of Black Chamber *and* The Sky-Blue Wolves

"Imaginative and thrilling, *Implanted* features a truly unique premise, characters you'll want to root for, and a fascinating, fully-realized future."

Lori M Lee, author of Gates of Thread and Stone *and* The Infinite

LAUREN C TEFFEAU

IMPLANTED

ANGRY
ROBOT

ANGRY ROBOT
An imprint of Watkins Media Ltd

20 Fletcher Gate,
Nottingham,
NG1 2FZ
UK

angryrobotbooks.com
twitter.com/angryrobotbooks
Recalibrated

An Angry Robot paperback original 2018

Cover design by Argh! Nottingham
Set in Meridien and Avant Garde by Argh! Nottingham

Distributed in the United States by Penguin Random House, Inc., New York.

ISBN 978 0 85766 799 1
Ebook ISBN 978 0 85766 800 4

Printed in the United States of America

9 8 7 6 5 4 3 2 1

To Eric, who has given me everything

PART ONE
BREAK

CHAPTER ONE

My implant, working in concert with the arcade's rec suite, mimics the sensations of fists striking flesh and bone. The pain reverberates back to my brain, but I don't bruise, I don't bleed, I certainly don't break. And I don't feel the crawling animal need to survive – or fear that I won't – the way I would in real life. Fear I know firsthand.

Considering all that, beating the shit out of computer-generated thugs is only so satisfying, but I take what I can get.

The immersive generates my next wave of opponents, and anything goes. That's the whole reason I chose this particular street combat scenario to complement the hours of martial arts training I've logged. When your life's on the line, form and philosophy can hinder as much as help. Setting up kicks or chaining together moves burns time you may not have. With the arcade's AI tweaking the level of difficulty each round, I have to draw on every technique I've picked up over the years.

The fear found in the arcade may be a simulation, but it's still a good way to learn how to stay on your toes. Especially down here.

The abandoned warehouse has rows of cargo containers I can hide behind or otherwise use against my opponents, but I try not to resort to that if I can hold my own in the open area toward the center of the building. Ancient fluorescent lights buzz overhead, adding to the derelict ambiance.

Anticipation blazes bright and hot as the two gangbangers circle me. There's a story mode about infiltrating a drug ring, but I'm just here for the realistic fight mechanics. The taller one on the left is the first to oblige. He steps forward, leaving his buddy to watch on. After a few more rounds, the AI will make it so they fight in teams, but for now I have the luxury of taking them on individually.

My opponent's gaze sweeps over my avatar, and he smirks. He sees a petite woman – not far off from my true stature – and assumes he knows what he's in for. But he's wrong wrong wrong.

His eyes widen in surprise when I duck his first swing and follow up with a quick jab to his side. Whatever else, at least the game gets character reactions right. He throws a wild punch. I knock it aside, then catch him in the chin with an uppercut, driving into him with my shoulder. He sags to the floor.

His friend wastes no time and charges after me. I barely have a chance to reset when he wraps his arms around me in a bear hug. My implant hijacks my olfactory system, and all I can smell is his cheap cologne. I tell myself I can handle the swamping claustrophobia, the choking sense of being smothered.

It's a lie, but a practiced one. One that allows me to kick out, my foot catching him in the knee. Lucky. He groans, and his grip loosens enough for me to slip out from underneath him. To land a solid punch along his temple. He falls, and I fall with him, pummeling him with my fists.

Anything to feel, to inflict pain tenfold, even if he's not the true recipient of so much rage.

||| Level complete. |||

A harsh cry rips through me as I stagger to my feet. I give my opponent a kick in his soft belly for good measure. Dull, gnawing pain radiates up from my toes. Still worth it.

||| Would you like to continue? |||

I'm tempted, even though it's a struggle to slow my breathing. But I have an appointment I've gotta keep.

I log out of the game. Gone is the industrial, early twenty-first century warehouse. In its place is a capsule-sized room scented with lilac, housing the latest cutting-edge tech for superimmersive simulations and games. The arcade provides a much-needed escape from everyday life in the domed city of New Worth, but some days I need the ritual more than others.

With sleepwalker precision, I pry myself out of the harness that lets me interact with the game's augmented environment. The feedback mitts are next, and it takes a moment for the sensation to return to my hands as the data receptors embedded in my palms and fingertips disengage from the tech. My implant projects messages and alerts that arrived while I was at the arcade into my field of vision. I scan through them with a series of eye movements, trashing a reminder for Brita's party tonight. As if I'd forget.

Rik pinged me while I was under. For a moment, I want nothing more than to reach out and have his consciousness brush against mine, a connection fostered by our implants. But I don't dare. Not with the risk of emotional bleed from what I've tasked myself with this afternoon. He'll have to wait.

With a hard blink, my implant's ocular interface recedes into the background. I fit my day gloves over my hands, grab my bag, and exit the suite.

Kenzie, the jockey on call, gives me a nod. Feeds from all the recreation suite rentals scroll across his monitors, tracking account balances, vitals, and hardware performance. Although arcades in the Canopy are closer to my dorm, this is the one I grew up going to, only a few blocks away from my parents' apartment in the Terrestrial District. The jockeys all know me and ensure I get the best functioning suites. They tend to do a better job cleaning up after the previous occupants, too, when I have a reservation on the books.

I drift toward the exit but hold off on joining the late afternoon crowds that always plague New Worth's lower levels. I'm a few minutes ahead of schedule. Just as well. I try to shake off the brawl from the game – I need all my focus for what's next.

With the Promenade – the biggest thoroughfare that traverses the length of the Terrestrial District – only a few blocks away, the bustle and hum of people are everywhere. Down here in the perpetual twilight, streetlamps burn day and night. Holographic projections and bioluminescent paint cover every flat surface with advertising. I adjust my ocular boost accordingly to help me make sense of the chaos as I search. Not everyone gets the night amplification filter – only the lucky few in the Terrestrial District who can afford it. My father never got one, but he worked overtime for a year to ensure I had it by the time I started middle school.

"What are you doing, Emery?" Kenzie asks, suddenly at my side.

I whirl toward him, fist at the ready, then relax at the sight of his startled, pale face. Guess I'm still amped up after my session.

"Whoa." He holds up his hands, faux leather wristlets protecting his data receptors. "Sorry I scared you, but you looked a bit lost." Up close, I can make out the metal plates along his forehead and cheeks, just under the skin, where he can magnetically mount different accessories. Anything from devil's horns or reptilian frills to carved bone ornaments. But he's just himself today.

"Oh, I was just…" I tap my temple, signaling preoccupation with my implant, and hope he'll drop it.

"Well, don't let me interrupt a conversation with one

of your blink buddies. Or maybe a confidant?" He waggles his brows suggestively at the idea of me having an implant contact I share *everything* with, but to trust someone with that much of myself? There's an extremely short list of potential candidates. "You know I'd calibrate with you any time," Kenzie continues. "Just say the word. Isn't that why you started coming round again?"

He usually doesn't let me leave without some form of banter, but I'm not up for it today. Perhaps sensing that, he saunters back to the desk. "Put you down for the same time tomorrow?"

"Nah. Sunday," I call after him.

"You're taking a day off? What's the occasion?"

"I have a life outside the arcade, believe it or not." I keep my gaze trained on the crowd, scanning for a very specific shade of brown hair.

"*Sure* you do."

"Jealous?" I say over my shoulder. But before I can give as good as I get, a guy with the exact tint of brown hair comes down the street.

For a moment, all that aggression from the game flares up at the sight of Breck Warner. It's him all right. His easy stride camouflages his lean strength. The mop of curls hanging into his eyes softens his slightly beady gaze as he tracks his surroundings. By day, he's a mild-mannered assistant tech at an implant clinic in the Understory. Decent job, good benefits. He doesn't need to prey on the people down here. That he does anyway…

Death-gripping the shoulder strap to my bag, I make my decision. Actually, I already made the decision when I came here today. I just keep expecting it to get easier. "Gotta go," I tell Kenzie.

I brace myself for not only the increase in humidity as I pass through the arcade's automated doors but also the crowded stink that permeates everything dirtside. Leaving the arcade behind, I walk the cramped streets of the Terrestrial District. Mile-tall towers hulk overhead, blocking any possibility of natural light filtering down.

New Worth's just one of the domed cities around the world shielding humanity from the elements that rage on the other side of the glass. After too many years of storm-leveled towns, receding coastlines, drought, flood, pollution, and devastating fighting over food and resources as governments tried to provide for their people, domed cities became our only option to escape the ravages of a world that had finally turned against us after so many years of abuse.

While everyone in New Worth is granted equal protection from the hostile environment outside, our lives *inside* the dome are dictated by status, credit balances, and career potential. Those with the right credentials have every advantage as they literally ascend through society, living out their lives in the city's luxurious upper levels. Everyone else remains landlocked in the Terrestrial District – choked off from light, constrained by space, and constantly inundated by others tied to the same fate.

The one bright spot on the horizon is Emergence – the day when the glass can finally come down, and we return to the land of our ancestors. So, as we wait for our rehabilitation efforts beyond the dome to take root, implants not only help us pass the time, but also make our lives a bit more bearable.

With a simple eyecast command, I can filter out the incessant noise down here. No more crying babies or shrieking feral children. No more desperate pitches from beggars with homebrew credit transfer devices clutched in their bare hands. Or the aggressive advertising jingles piped out of every storefront. No windy grumble from the maglev tracks crisscrossing overhead or the creaking drone of air ventilation shafts that pump cool air into the Canopy.

The resulting relative silence gives you the space to think – something I didn't know I needed until I got outfitted with my implant at age ten.

The smells are harder to get rid of, requiring expensive implant add-ons or body modifications. Most people learn to live with it. There was a time I was noseblind to it all, but my time in the Canopy has since put an end to that.

Crowds trickle along, eddying at intersections or swirling around busy storefronts, as garbage bots and far too many people fight their way through the constant gloom. The government keeps saying they want to clean things up, but with buildings constantly being appropriated to better support the Understory, and by extension the Canopy above, instead of something useful like retrofitting them for capsule residences to accommodate the waiting lists, life in the Terrestrial District can only continue to degrade.

There are too many people stuck down here for it not to.

Following someone through a crowd, especially in the lower levels, isn't difficult with the sheer numbers of us out and about. But when the people thin out and there's less of a buffer between you and your quarry, it's a lot harder to go unnoticed. Something I've learned the hard way shadowing Breck these last few weeks.

One wrong move, game over.

But this is no game. My first unencumbered glimpse of him through the press of bodies sends a wash of cold down my spine. He's shouldering a large pack. It's going to be today. Intellectually, I've known every time I follow him he might act. Moisture floods my gloved palms, and a knot of panic coils tight in my sternum. But I know what I need to do. Can't lose it now.

His target, a girl in her late teens, wrestles a canvas bag full of groceries from the corner market. She's as unaware of him as he is of me. We navigate the twisting streets, moving further away from the more populated blocks that feed off the Promenade. In the Terrestrial District, there's a certain safety in numbers. A safety we're forgoing with each step.

She's barely aware of the danger, probably lost to her implant to pass the time. She should know better. But it's impossible to go through life always on your guard. It's unfair that's what's required of those of us who live dirtside instead of the lofty heights of the Understory or beyond in the hallowed upper levels of the Canopy.

That's one of the reasons why I vowed to get out of the Terrestrial District as soon as possible. Growing up on the fringes of the Bower, a rough neighborhood only a few blocks away, I watched my parents do everything they could to create careers that would let them rise through the ranks – to no avail. I was lucky enough to get accepted to the College of New Worth in the Canopy and didn't look back. I thought nothing could make me return. Not after experiencing the golden light and fresh air of the upper levels.

But that was before I realized scum like Breck use the Terrestrial District for their hunting grounds.

There's hardly anyone about now. I fall back, sticking close to the shadowed façades as best I can. The girl turns left toward an abandoned construction site just a few blocks away. Supposed to create some much-needed new housing for the area, it has been stalled by permitting issues and lawsuits, while the rest of the neighborhood rots around it. Making it the perfect cover for his purposes.

And, coincidentally, mine.

He glances back once, and I busy myself with a secondhand clothing store's sidewalk display in just the nick of time. The racks are full of cheaply printed fabrics that'll only withstand a few wears, but most people down here can't afford to be picky. I wait three painfully long breaths, then ease back into the street.

They're both gone. For a moment, my heart jackhammers in my chest. I could simply return to my dorm in the Canopy, levels upon levels above, and forget whatever happens here today. No one would know the difference.

Except for me.

My gloved fingertips toy with my throat for a second before I realize what I'm doing. I force my hand back to my side. Swallowing my doubts, I approach an emergency kiosk. Not everyone in the Terrestrial District can afford the subdermal implants that make life under glass worth living. Thankfully it's still functional – not always a guarantee down here.

"Hello. I'd like to report an attack. I heard screams at the 100 block of the Bower. I saw a man with a knife."

"Who am I speaking–"

"Please hurry!"

I end the call before things go any further. Hopefully that'll be enough to bring the police. If not, there's still me.

The next block over, I catch up to them. Breck's yet to touch the girl, but she's picked up her pace, throwing nervous glances over her shoulder. By now she'll be trying to use her implant to send synch requests to friends or family members. Maybe even the cops. But Breck's close enough for the implant-blocking device he no doubt has in his pack to put an end to that.

I want to tell her not to run, to stand her ground, to fight back, but she yelps instead. Her grocery bag rips as she takes a turn too hard, scattering day-old produce across the ground. Running scared.

Breck's there in two strides, his painful grip on her arm propelling her toward the dark alley alongside the empty construction site. We're on the outer edge of this sector's police coverage, something he no doubt factored in. What if they don't come in time?

Stealing myself, I follow. The arcade sessions are supposed

to psych me up, file off the edges of my anger so I don't do something foolish, thoughtless, *reactive*, whenever I'm down here. But instead of calm poise, I sound like I've run a marathon. I try to get control of my breathing as I reach into my messenger bag. All those arcade scenarios I've thrown myself into over the years won't matter if I don't get this right.

The taser's awkward in my hands, slippery on account of my gloves. I should've practiced this part more. The construction site rears up in front of me, skeletal I-beams and rebar. It disappears overhead into the underside of a concourse that links it to another building.

A shout pierces the air, then it's quickly muffled, but it's enough to guide my feet. I find Breck crouched over the girl, a hand clamped over her mouth.

Before I make a conscious decision, the taser recoils, and a jolt of blue slams into his back. He seizes up, eyes rolled back in his head. He never even saw me.

With a sob, the girl pushes him off her. Tears track down her cheeks, the pale skin of her neck rubbed red where he put his hands on her. "Thanks. How did you–"

"The cops are on their way," I say as I help her to her feet.

"My implant–" Her hand reflexively covers the small square on the back of her neck where the device lives under the skin.

"Don't worry. It's temporary."

"No, I mean I thought he wanted…" She trails off with what's better left unsaid, and gestures to his pack and the surgical tools and miscellaneous tech from the clinic that have spilled out of it. "But he was after my implant, wasn't he?"

I nod, not trusting my voice. A scrapper dealing in black-market, gently used implants taken from people he could easily overpower. Some of the Disconnects down here are so desperate for the implant tech they could never afford legally, scum like Breck have turned that desperation into a lucrative cottage industry.

He moans. Oh no. What if he wakes up before the police get here? The taser needs more time before it'll be able to discharge another blast.

The girl ducks behind me. "What do we do?"

I hand the taser off to her. I'm moving before I even register the action. As though he's just another thug I need to end in an arcade scenario, I snatch up a discarded brick and slam it into his head. The impact rattles up my arm, buzzes into my shoulder. Definitely not a simulation. But that doesn't stop me from doing it again.

"Hey." The girl grabs my arm, gives it a shake, and I drop the bloodied brick. "Pretty sure he's out after that, if you didn't kill him outright."

Hands shaking, I take a step back, trying to look anywhere except for the trickle of blood oozing from his scalp. The alley presses closer, moldering brick and old flyers, the stench from a nearby dumpster wreaking havoc on my stomach. This isn't what I planned. I thought–

Police sirens peal, and I practically jump. Get it together. I turn to the girl. She's stopped crying. That's good. "I was never here, OK?"

She nods slowly, then gives me a look that bruises. "I get it."

Some of it perhaps, but not all. Not enough. I don't bother correcting her. She'll have enough to worry about when the police arrive.

"But tell me, how did you know?"

I squeeze her forearm, as if by touch alone I can impart as much fortifying sympathy as possible before I bail. "Doesn't matter after today."

CHAPTER TWO

A complicated sort of lightness fuels my steps toward the train station, boiling over with commuters making their way to the lower levels after a long day spent in the offices and businesses overhead. Fewer of us are traveling to the city's upper reaches. A security gate pings my implant and deducts the fare as I pass through. The other passengers are lost in their own little worlds, their eyes half-closed, rolling through eyecast commands.

I grab a seat in a deserted train carriage, and the weight of what happened this afternoon comes crashing down. Self-righteous victory burns in my heart, but it comes with a cost. I'm exhausted, mentally and physically. I couldn't stand if I tried.

Advertisements crawl up the windows on pinpoints of light as the train glides out of the station. Beyond, the gloom of the Terrestrial District slowly gives way to the merely drab Understory as we climb. The train spirals between buildings connected to one another by a network of concourses and skybridges. I'm glued to the window, waiting for that ineffable moment when we breach the Canopy and true daylight shines down.

With Breck arrested, the Terrestrial District is saved from another scrapper. Then I remember the comforting weight of the brick lodged in my fist, the wet thump it made against his skull, and I'm no longer sure of anything.

The right thing done for the wrong reasons has a way of poisoning everything around it. But he won't hurt anyone else again. Not after the cops took the girl's statement and bundled him away in handcuffs. Isn't that what matters?

When I get off the train, I'm tempted to hurry back to the arcade and drown myself in another simulation to work out my frustration. But no. Sunlight's the only answer for today, and I know just where to go.

Whenever I pass through Skychapel, a little ache blooms in my chest at the unknowable expanse beyond the dome. For a moment, I can forget all the things clamoring for attention and simply look up at the largest span of uninterrupted glass in all of New Worth.

No synch requests. No news alerts. Nothing but me and the vermilion sky.

For a moment, I can even forget what happened down below before my implant's proximity sensor protests at the sudden surge in the evening crowds. Tourists from the lower levels and Canopy-dwellers alike flock here for the sunlight, spreading out on the manicured swaths of sweet-smelling grass or commandeering the benches that line either side of the walkway. Usually, I come for the thunderstorms. Nothing's more exhilarating than the lightshow or the hammering of rain against glass. The heartbeat of the city.

Right now though, the sunset slides into twilight, but it's enough to clear my head as I work my way against the current. Most people are shuffling toward the lifts in the opposite direction, ready to descend after a day spent shopping at the Canopy's high-end boutiques or dining at the best restaurants the city has to offer. I should know better than to come here at this hour, but I can never resist the opportunity to see the sky through the clear panels.

Finally, I'm able to dart through a gap in the press of bodies. Personal space regained, I take a deep breath and hold it in my chest. Instead of the overly recycled air of the lower levels, in the Canopy everything's fresh and clean, touched by the plants that cover nearly every surface with frothy tendrils. Even after four years, the air up here's still a marvel to me.

Rik pings my implant. I jump guiltily, knocking into the woman walking next to me. "Sorry." Still cringing at the accidental contact, I lengthen my stride and open the connection to Rik with an eyecast command.

<<Let me guess. One of the gardens, a park maybe?<<

Perceptive as always. I don't know why it still surprises me. We've grown as close as two people who've never actually met can be. >>Something like that. How did you know?>>

<<Like clockwork, Liv. Some of that… delight bleeds through.<<

>>So? I get some of the same thing whenever you take a shower.>> A slight tingle along my forehead nearly every morning. >>But at least I have the good manners not to mention it.>>

Somewhere out in the city, he laughs, the sensation across our linked implants effervescent, as though bubbles fizz against my skin. I rub my arms to banish the sudden goose bumps.

<<Point taken.<<

Giving the sky one last look, I cross the columned boundary separating Skychapel from the rest of the city. The massive things tower overhead, terminating in hyperbolic arches that mimic an actual forest canopy. Or at least as far as I can tell from my ecology modules at school. The architecture in the Canopy's supposed to evoke nature, but one of my professors said once it's more like an epitaph. A mere copy of what was – like so much else in New Worth – to hold us over until Emergence, the day we can finally leave the dome behind.

All I know, fake or not, the Canopy's better than the Terrestrial District in practically every way.

I angle for a small overlook, my steps slowing as the city of New Worth spreads out before me. Terraced rooftops overflow with leaves cascading like waterfalls. Elevated concourses and skybridges link various buildings together, lined with vine-covered handrails. Further down, maglev trains glide along guideways connecting the different sectors of the Canopy to the levels below.

Growing up in the Terrestrial District, I never really appreciated the design of the domed city. The poor light and cramped conditions hide so much from view. But from up here, I'm always amazed at how the engineers were able to construct the skyscrapers and chain them together, all the while keeping us safe from the elements that seethed on the other side of the metallic glass.

As with anything, I guess it all depends on if you're the one looking up or looking down.

<<You're awfully quiet today,<< he says with a laugh.

>>Don't mean to be.>>

His amusement dissolves, leaving only a slight tremor of uncertainty. An unconscious transmission from him, but it doesn't change the way my stomach lurches in response. <<I wouldn't have suggested finally meeting if I'd known how much it would upset you,<< he says, finally putting words to the one thing we've been dancing around for a while now.

Biting my lip, I veer toward the railing. Below, the green of the Canopy eventually gives way to the gray cement of the Understory, then darkness. No help there.

I'm taking too long to answer, I know it. Just as I know I can't blunt all the anxiety I feel – have felt – since Rik first proposed an in-person meet. And after that thing with Breck today… >>I'm not upset. It's just that things between us are fine the way they are. More than fine, even…>>

He sighs, a slight ruffling that fills my ears. <<Then pretend I never suggested it, all right? We'll keep things as they are.<<

>>But that's just it. You can't take it back.>> Through my gloves, I run a thumbnail over the ridges of the handrail, made to look like a tree root emanating from the trunk-like column at either end. Back and forth.

<<I'm not going to apologize for wanting to finally meet you.<<

I push back from the edge and start walking again. >>Part of me really wants to. You can feel that much, right?>>

A smile this time. A slight tug at the corner of my lips tells me as much. <<Yes. But it's the rest of it that worries me.<<

My neck prickles, and this time it isn't Rik. I glance back at the concourse, but no one's paying undue attention to me. Not that I can be certain since everyone's preoccupied by whatever their implants pipe into their field of vision.

<<What's wrong?<<

I face forward once more, still unable to shake the crawling sensation of being watched. >>Nothing.>>

<<You sure? I've come to have a healthy appreciation of your gut after *Partners in Crime*.<<

The immersive online game we met in a few years back. I was desperate to play the detective thriller after it won all kinds of awards. The only catch was I needed a partner since it wasn't configured for solo missions. Rik and I were paired up, and the rest is history.

>>I don't think my gut's very reliable today.>> Going down to the Terrestrial District always makes me paranoid. That's probably all it is. Rik's familiar presence hovers at the edge of my awareness. Patient as always. >>Sorry I got distracted. You were saying?>>

<<I was trying to convince you I'm not a psychopath.<<

Right. Not everyone finds someone to let into their mind. To formalize our relationship as confidants, we have to calibrate the data receptors on our hands, which means finally putting the face to the person we've been synching with for years.

There's no guarantee we'll actually take things that far, but meeting face to face is the first step on that path.

I breathe out slowly. >>I just don't want to break what we have.>>

<<We won't break anything, Liv.<<

>>I've heard too many stories of people who can't reconcile the person they've constructed in their head to that of flesh and blood standing before them. Connections severed just like that because of unrealistic expectations. I don't want that for us.>>

Rik simply lets the silence build, the connection between us alive with feeling. Synching can be surprisingly intimate, depending on how a user customizes their implant settings. The length of delay between thought and message. Whether or not nonverbals should be broadcast. The priority of the interaction over other tasks and contacts. We've become so attuned to one another over the years, now our connection practically vibrates with what's left unsaid. My doubts, his certainty, yes, but also a desire for more – a strange sort of friction as we run up against the limitations of our current configuration, like a snail that's outgrown its shell.

<<*This*. This is why we have to meet.<<

I feel it too. It's why I took a chance and started talking to him outside of *Partners in Crime*. It's why we've grown as close as we have despite all the very good reasons not to. You don't let someone into your mind with no safeguards in place.

The next step, calibration, will further bolster our connection through shared feedback from our paired data receptors, making it even more immediate than synching. I'll still be able to set limits on our interactions, define what Rik can or cannot see, as can he. But given how close we already are, calibration will make it harder to hide from one another. And goes against the whole idea of having a confidant in the first place – someone you can share practically everything with, good and bad, the awkward and the amazing too.

<<I can be patient,<< Rik says at my continued silence. <<Remember how long it took for me to convince you to move things outside the game?<< The teasing lilt to his voice puts us back on more familiar ground.

>>Can you blame me? The arcade attracts a certain subversive element.>>

<<Subversive, huh? I've got this all wrong. What if you're the one who's going to corrupt me?<<

I am, I nearly say, but manage to tamp down the impulse. >>Look, I gotta go.>> Then like a coward, I shut my eyes to close the connection, both welcoming and mourning the resulting emptiness in my head. But I wasn't lying. I do have to go. I promised Brita I'd come to her party tonight.

The crowds ease up as I cut through a neighborhood built around a lavish courtyard brimming with palm trees and orchids. The sensation of being watched flares back to life just as a man, thirtyish, with olive-dark skin and a satchel strung across his torso, steps out from one of the doorways in front of me. "Miss Emery Olivia Driscoll? I'd like to speak with you."

How does he know my name? Only law enforcement and anyone I've designated as an acquaintance should be able to read that off my signal. Even though he's not broadcasting any signal info himself, between his tailored clothes and the cut of his gloves, he could be anyone who lives in the upper levels of New Worth. But it's the crafty look in his eyes that sets off alarm bells.

Immediately, my guilty conscience plunges me back down to the Terrestrial District. What if he's a cop, following up on what happened with Breck? No, that's ridiculous. I was careful. I'm always careful. Besides, the police wouldn't approach me like this. They tend to round people up first and ask questions later. This is something *else*. "What do you want?" My underused voice doesn't sound nearly as forceful as I'd like.

"To discuss a mutually beneficial opportunity."

I keep moving. "Yeah, right." Though scammers are rife in the lower levels, they usually steer clear of the Canopy, with its frequent security checkpoints. But clearly not always.

The man arches a brow. I glance behind me. Sure enough, he has a friend. A Hispanic twenty-something with muscles I'm certain are the real deal, not mods. What have I gotten into? "We'll be happy to explain everything in a more secure location," the first man continues.

"Not interested," I say sharply, despite the fluttering of panic sweeping through me. By the time the police respond, it'll be too late, even in the Canopy. But I'm not helpless. I've made sure of that. Instead of giving into my shaking limbs, I focus on my breathing – deep belly breaths – and try to recall everything I know about the area.

"I'm afraid I must insist," the first man says.

His partner strides toward me, determined to cut me off from the walkway leading back out to the main concourse. Can't let them corner me. I hop the knee wall separating the walk from the large planter bed dominating the courtyard. Kicking up pea gravel, I sprint across it, intent on a set of stairs on the opposite side that should take me up to the next level.

One of the men curses. My world narrows to the thudding beats of my heart as I take the stairs two at a time. Then dash down another walkway. I slam into the evening crowds filing down the concourse, but at least I know where I am.

And what I'm going to do about the two men following me.

With a sequence of hard blinks, I turn off my implant and dart through clusters of commuters. Then I do something

I haven't done in years. In the automated cart lane, I find one only partially loaded down and vault on. I crouch so I'm hidden by the topmost crate.

In the Terrestrial District, it's often a game to see who can hitch a ride on the carts without upsetting the cargo. Such antics are frowned upon in the Canopy, but so many people are using their implants to escape rush hour, I only get a few exasperated looks as the cart whisks me down the walkway.

By the time I reach Brita's apartment complex, my pursuers long gone, it's hard not to feel mildly victorious. But the weirdness of it all lingers, something I can't quite vanquish even in friendly territory as I push past the guests already crowding the small courtyard. The door security has been disabled for tonight, which makes it that much easier to shoulder my way in.

I've been going to Brita's legendary parties since we met in freshman Biology at the College of New Worth. She knows precisely how many people can be crammed into her offcampus apartment. How long it takes for the police to respond once guests start spilling onto the concourse. How loud the music can be before the neighbors complain. And then there are the decorations.

Tonight, she's outdone herself. Streamers cascade down from the ceiling, shuddering through all the colors of the rainbow in time to the bass that vibrates the room. Luminous paint has been spattered against the walls, so artfully it looks accidental. She's also done something to the filters. The air tastes of lime with an herbal tang. Invigorating enough to keep the party going all night.

Brita's eyes widen when her attention lands on me. "Emery! You made it." She tosses back her curls, dyed silver and glinting like metal links in the dim light. "I was beginning to worry about you."

Her concern's a knife-twist in the chest. I would've

been here sooner if I hadn't been detained. All the anxiety I managed to bury on the way over surfaces in full force. "Sorry. Something came up."

She's shed her gloves for tonight, revealing fingernails that reflect the colors swirling across the wallscreen opposite us. She catches me looking and lifts her chin defiantly, daring me to say something.

I don't see the appeal of calibrating with random strangers, but Brita claims it's a fun way to pass the time without having to let someone into her mind. Managing a potentially intimate situation by setting limits. All body, no brain, by augmenting a hook-up through shared physical impressions. The reverse of what I have with Rik.

But last time... I don't need my implant to recall her tear-streaked face, desperate to clasp my hand after a handshake gone wrong. Something about the person in question spooked her, and she needed a palate cleanser, and fast. You wouldn't know it looking at her now. All cool confidence, the eye of the party's storm.

"Come on." She takes my arm and leads me to the drink table. "Try this." She picks up a pitcher of... something, and pours it into my glass.

I take a careful sniff. Raspberry? "What is it?"

She waves her hand vaguely, the lights sparking against her nails. "No idea. But don't let that stop you." It's fizzy with an alcoholic tang. "Atta girl. Come on."

Brita tugs me deeper into the luxurious apartment her parents secured for her freshman year. She's practically Canopy royalty since her father runs New Worth News, the biggest infotainment company in the city. "Eleni, love your dress! Asher, thought you swore off parties after last time." She leans in. "What's wrong? I can't find your signal."

Even though I'm pretty sure I wasn't followed, I'm not taking any chances. With my signal still dark, I'm only receiving the highest priority notifications. My un-enhanced presence is all I can offer her tonight. "I was feeling overwhelmed. Needed to upgrade anyway," I fib.

Thankfully, that in itself isn't so strange. Every so often, you have to go dark to install the latest release or to troubleshoot config settings. I've had my share of malware and privacy glitches too. *Everyone* on the New Worth network has at some point. It's part of the reason why a person's implant has so many different settings to accommodate a wide range of interactions and manage the potential abuses that can result. But for most, the inconvenience that viruses and occasional reformattings pose are worth the connectivity and convenience.

Brita takes my arm again, this time heading for the stairs. On the way, she waves to a cute underclassman. He bobbles his drink, spilling it down the front of his shirt, as he tries to wave back. When we reach the second floor, still giggling, she pulls me into her bedroom and shuts the door. "I've been pinging you for the last hour."

Only one thing would be that important. "Did he go for it?" I ask. She's been desperate to convince her father she'd be perfect as a junior correspondent for New Worth News.

She shakes her head.

"Oh no. I'm sorry."

Her shoulders droop slightly. "Don't be. We both knew it was a long shot."

"But still. I know how much this meant to you." She lives and breathes the news feeds. Keeping her away from New Worth News is just cruel. But her status-conscious father's never forgiven her for being a bit of a handful growing up, nearly getting kicked out of high school. Since then, she's worked hard to turn things around. Perfect grades, glowing recommendations from her journalism professors. I guess that wasn't enough.

Her flawless, pale face wavers, then turns defiant. "And if not, his loss, right? I can go work for any of good ole Dad's competitors. I've already started brainstorming new pitches. Here, what do you think?"

She shuts her eyes briefly and rolls back her shoulders on a deep breath. She told me once the trick to believable reporting is to look into the camera like it's the most fascinating thing in the world. Her mouth parts, her hazel eyes sparkling-wide. "It's hard to believe there are people out there who don't want neural implants. Who are these so-called Disconnects shunning the connectivity that keeps the city running? And what are they hiding from?" Her focus returns to me. "Well? What do you think?"

"It sounds great. I just never realized there were actually people out there who relish being disconnected." You can't pass through the lower levels without running into your fair share of people who don't have the neural implants that make life worth living. Lots of people simply can't afford the tech. That doesn't mean they wouldn't jump at the chance to get it – not when it would make things so much easier on them.

To be disconnected in New Worth means having a digital handicap that follows you everywhere and affects *everything*.

"Well, that's just it," Brita says eagerly. "Some of them have given up hope of being able to get implants and have found ways to justify not having them to make them feel better about missing out on such an integral part of society. But some people *really* believe it. Those are the people I want to focus on. See how they tick, you know?"

"Your dad's bound to be jealous when he sees it on another channel, too."

"Let's hope. Anyway. Enough about me." She gives me a critical once-over. With a mischievous smile, she goes to her vanity, rummaging through her makeup.

Now I'm in for it. "Brit, this isn't necessary."

"House rules." She looks up from a compact with the same blue-green bioluminescent glow that rims her eyes and flares out toward her temples, then discards it for a peach and purple one. "Besides, I need *something* to cheer me up. Now hold still."

I groan but dutifully set my drink on the floor and sit on the edge of her bed as she gets to work. She knows enough to go slowly, that sudden movements will scare me away. I'm jumpier than usual, especially after what happened earlier. Starting with my eyelids, her steady strokes of the makeup brush calm me enough to unclench my hands.

Something flashes red in the periphery of my vision, and I start. Brita swears as I pull up the priority message. From an actual police detective. Uh oh.

||| Your signal was logged at the 100 block of the Bower at 16:13 this afternoon. We need you to provide a statement as to your whereabouts and anything you may have seen. We have taken the liberty of scheduling an appointment for you first thing tomorrow morning. ||| Then the address for the Specialist Investigation Division in the Upper Understory.

Breck, the brick in my hand, all that blood... Shit. I thought I'd done enough to mask my signal. That's why I used a kiosk instead of my implant to call the police. I also memorized a map of all the cameras that I knew of in the area, but I could have missed some. If they put two and two together, my days in the Canopy could be numbered. Even if I'm not formally charged, a criminal complaint would risk everything I've achieved. Graduation's next week, and after that, work at a prestigious curation firm. They would never hire an employee with the barest hint of impropriety. We take a pledge to be objective in all our decisions related to the preservation, disposal, and discoverability of data.

Deep breaths. Maybe it's just a routine follow-up. But I'm numb with the possibilities as Brita finishes up. "There." She puts the compact away, and I rescue my drink from the floor. She rests her hands on her hips as she inspects her handiwork.

In the vanity mirror, the peach and purple whorls make my light brown skin glow. My lavender tunic matches perfectly. I never could've pulled this look together without her help. Would Brita have bothered if she knew what I was doing in the Terrestrial District earlier today?

My conscience rears its head. "You've always been so generous to me. Why?"

Her surprised gaze snaps to mine in the mirror. "What do you mean? We're friends."

"Yes, but you're... you, and I'm just some upstart from the Terrestrial District tracking dirt through the Canopy." In the mirror, she's tall where I'm short, elegant in cool, jewel tones where I'm playing pretend in contrasting warm colors. "Admit it, that's what you thought when you first saw me."

"Yes, but when you opened your mouth and took down that obnoxious TA in freshman year, I decided then and there I'd love you forever."

"Did not."

She crosses her arms, pretends to consider it. "Well, maybe it was after we were paired up on that lab final." She watches me, slightly puzzled. "Hey, what's with the memory lane tonight, anyway?"

I shrug and paste a sheepish smile on my face. "Sorry. It's just an end of an era, that's all."

"Well, I'm not going anywhere. I mean, I'll be working my way up through the ranks at some second-rate infotainment firm, assuming Daddy hasn't blacklisted me, and you'll be sifting through decades of digital refuse."

"You make data curation sound so glamorous."

"*You* picked it. Anyway, what I'm trying to say is we'll still have each other up here," she says, tapping her temple. "Blink buddies for life. So stop acting like graduation's the end of the world. You'll make me weepy. And if you ruin my makeup, I'll never forgive you."

I hold up my hands. "I take it all back."

And truly, I wish I could. I thought I could eliminate someone like Breck Warner from the world and face no repercussions. All the scenarios I logged at the arcade made me feel invincible, above the law even. And now my appointment tomorrow with the New Worth police department could jeopardize my future in the upper levels.

And not just mine. My family. My friends. Brita, standing before me. I'd be dragging her down with me through association. She gives me a brilliant smile, which only deepens my guilt. "Glad that's settled. Come on, we should get back downstairs," she says, and tows me back to the main floor.

The first cocktail was to appease Brita; the second, my nerves. With our drinks refilled, we take up position in front of the living room holoblinds. Our classmates churn around us. Many of them are graduating seniors like us, along with a number of underclassmen. A heady energy's in the air, but I can't tap into it tonight, not with the uncertainty of tomorrow now hanging over my head.

Brita elbows me in the ribs. "Stop brooding, Em. This is supposed to be a *celebration*."

I manage to muster up a smile. "Sorry. Don't mean to."

"Well, try harder. Forget who you are, Emery Driscoll. Tonight be who you *want* to be – no constraints. God knows New Worth has enough of them already."

I raise my drink to her in mock toast and take a sip, relishing the languid warmth flowing through me. Desperate for anything that'll take the edge off the paranoia that's cropped up in the wake of the detective's inquiry.

The music cranks higher, and there's no more talking. Brita tugs me towards the dance circle that soon takes over the main floor of the apartment. The heated press of so many bodies competes with the arctic A/C on full blast. Kaleidoscopic color and sound burrow under my skin. My blood demands I move, delirious with the need to be a part of the collective throng, the beat pulsing everywhere in time to my heart, this moment in time that will never come again.

I tell myself it doesn't matter what they ask me in the interview tomorrow. Then I reach the bottom of my drink and know that's a lie.

All my doubts and renewed fear bubble up, cresting like a wave, propelling me into the next song. If I don't dance, I'll drown in the anxiety of tomorrow. There is only tonight. Faces of friends and strangers flash by, any nuance to the music reduced to the bassline that buzzes in my chest. I may burn up from the inside out. I dance until I can scarcely breathe. Stumbling, I push past two girls as I make my retreat to the hallway.

Clumsy, shaking, barely able to see, my eyes are still adjusting to the strobing lights. The tears don't help either. Damn.

The bathroom's miraculously empty, and I lock the door behind me. Then I do what I promised myself I wouldn't.

Rik answers swiftly to my summons. I try not to think about what that means at this time of night. Thinking at a time like this can only be bad. <<I'm surprised to hear from you again. Usually…<<

>>Don't say it.>> Usually, I keep this part of myself from him, the irresponsible, emotionally needy part that can only threaten the delicate balance we've struck. Brita's always told me I'm foolish for holding myself back from him. Maybe she's right. In any case, no matter how many people she's crammed in here, there's only one person I want to spend my last night of freedom with. >>Starlight Lofts, level 4 of the Canopy.>>

Shock, anticipation, confusion. All of it whirls dizzily between us as the party rages beyond the door.

<<What are you saying?<<

I stare at myself in the mirror. It takes a few seconds for my reflection to stop spinning long enough to focus on my face. I take a deep, centering breath. Straighten the drape of my lavender tunic. Inspect the makeup Brita helped me with one last time. Thankfully she also ensured I didn't make a complete mess of my thick hair.

I'm the best possible version of myself. That's what matters, right? No matter what happens tomorrow.

>>Can you get there? Here, I mean?>>

<<Yes, but–<<

I squeeze my eyes shut, desperate to ignore the roiling sensation cascading through my body. >>You wanted to meet, didn't you? Then come find me.>>

CHAPTER THREE

Even though I know Rik's mind almost as well as my own, it doesn't mean I'll recognize him in the flesh.

When *Partners in Crime* ended and we decided to stay in contact with one another, I insisted we refrain from sharing too many personal details. No names, places, specifics. All of it verboten between us as a way to protect us from each other. Now, I wish I hadn't been so adamant about the rules that shielded me from the full force of his identity. Clues litter our game discussion logs here and there like bugs in old code.

But I know nothing about him. Not really. Not nearly enough to make this work.

I don't even know what he looks like. Each person who passes by me in the living room is considered in my mental calculations. Too old, too feminine, too attached to someone else. As I keep trying to fit the partygoers into my conception of Rik, I worry the edge of my evening gloves.

At that perilous moment where I debate refilling my glass again to keep my nerves at bay, Rik pings my implant. <<I'm here. Where are you? There're way too many signals to disambig.<<

He's right. My proximity map blazes with the concentration of implant signals in the apartment complex, making finding one akin to a needle in a haystack that's been set on fire. >>Marco...>>

<<Have you been drinking?<<

>>Doesn't matter. *Marco…*>>

He sighs. <<Polo. Where–<<

>>Meet me at the garden overlook.>> And then I cut the connection again.

I battle my way outside, my eardrums grateful for the reprieve. The cool night air's a shock after the cramped interior. The garden overlook's a few doors down. Brita lives in one of the most exclusive housing complexes in the Upper Canopy, topped only by the Echelon, which the real elite of New Worth calls home. Each unit has a private balcony off the second floor with railings curved like bleached, bisected ribcages, making it feel like you're standing in the belly of some long-extinct creature.

I lean against the overlook's railing, staring into the cluster of trees spangled with spotlights. I can do this. Even though I jump every time the door opens as more partygoers come and go. The door to Brita's quarters opens again, and it takes everything I have to not whirl around and see who it is.

Approaching footsteps, then a heartbeat of silence. No turning back now.

"Hello, Liv."

My ribs ache from holding my breath as I let the sound roll over me. My implant did a surprisingly good job of mimicking his real voice. Not too deep, with appealing mellowness.

Reluctantly, I let go of the railing and face Rik. He's a couple of years older, tall like his avatar in *Partners in Crime,* with the same black hair and brown eyes. But otherwise the real-life expression of the same elements is completely different. Who knew so much personality could be captured in eyebrows and cheekbones? Or a glance unmediated by the arcade? I'm eternally grateful I've kept our connection minimized so he can't know what I'm thinking right now as anxiety settles in my already nauseous stomach.

"Uh, hi. Glad you made it." My brain crashes. I have no idea what to say. I force myself to smile. "You *are* Rik, right?"

He nods. "My full name is Randall Iverson-Kemp. RIK for short. It also sounds less pretentious that way," he says with a wry smile.

"I'm Emery Driscoll. You know, in the flesh?" Could I sound any more ridiculous? We've been friends for years, and yet I've suddenly turned into a blithering mess.

He cocks his head. "So why did you choose Liv as your handle?"

"My middle name's Olivia." And when I created my profile for *Partners in Crime* all those years ago, I wanted to be anyone but me. I thought I was so clever, creating an alter ego to hide behind. And now that the big reveal is here, all I want to do is run away.

"Emery." The way he says my name – as though trying it on for size and finding it a perfect fit – raises goose bumps on my arms. "Do you live here?"

"Ah, no. My friend Brita does."

"I remember you mentioning her once or twice."

For a moment, we simply stare at one another. "Second thoughts?" I ask, to break the tension.

Randall's dark brown eyes widen in alarm. "No." He says it quickly, then frowns. "But your implant..."

"Oh. Right."

With an eyecast command, I restore our connection. Randall inhales sharply beside me. When he first appeared, I acknowledged to myself he was attractive in an abstract way – a data point to be filed away for later – but now I *feel* it, as every conversation we've had via our implants is irrevocably mapped to his face, the cadence of his voice, the look in his eyes as he watches me process, well, everything.

Feedback from our connection converges with the overwhelming sense of recklessness that has defined the evening. *No constraints*. The possibilities make me flush, something I've tried so hard not to indulge until tonight. But the dark look on Randall's face brings me back to reality.

"Why are you frowning?"

He forces his gaze away from me. "This isn't how I wanted to do this."

"What's so wrong? You're here, with me, and..."

"And you're drunk."

"It's a party, Rik. You know about those." I tap my temple. >>I know you do.>> An awful thought occurs to me. "Or maybe it's me."

"Liv–"

My nightmare come to life. "Now that you've seen my face, our connection doesn't mean anything to you anymore?"

"*No*, that's not it at all."

I throw up my hands. "Then what's the problem?"

"All I know is you were dead set against meeting before tonight. What changed?"

"A little liquid courage."

"Bullshit. Something's been off with you all day. I didn't say anything because I didn't want to fight, but..."

Breck. Subconsciously he must've picked up on my preoccupation. And now, the threat of tomorrow...

"*There*. What were you thinking just then?"

I don't dare answer. Instead, I hold out my hand. There's no way to misunderstand my intention. Calibration of our data receptors lurking underneath the fabric of our gloves. He stares down at my hand, frozen. Shock and anticipation rumble between us at the magnitude of the next step.

>>OK... let's start with something simpler.>>

Instead of holding my hand palm out, customary for calibration, I rotate my wrist so now I reach for his hand, palm up. He takes it automatically, something we simulated hundreds of times in *Partners in Crime* at each save point. A tremor leaps through him and is absorbed by me, but he doesn't pull away.

While our gloves prevent calibration, they don't protect me from the weight of his hand or the heat of his fingers. In the game, his firm grip told me he always had my back, no matter what we faced. Now, it's telling me the same thing, despite the doubts reflected across his face.

"Liv–"

"Shh. I'm making a memory."

He groans and tugs his hand out of my grip. "This isn't the time or place," he says with a glance at the rest of the apartment complex. For the moment, we're still alone.

"We're finally talking to each other, not synch chatting. Doesn't that mean anything to you?"

"It means more to me than to you, apparently."

"*What?*"

"I thought I meant more to you than a drunken hook-up."

"You do. Calibration will prove it. That's what you wanted." Clumsily, I feel across our connection, searching for snippets of emotion before the limitations kick in. "What you still want."

Longing swamps the connection before he bottles it back up. "This was a mistake, coming here tonight." He turns away.

I lurch after him. "No. You don't understand. If we don't do this now…" We might not get another opportunity. What if the police learn of my involvement with Breck, and, instead of a routine inquiry, I end up on the other side of a jail cell? No, worse. What if Rik finds out what I did and wants nothing more to do with me?

"What? What happens?" He faces me once more, gripping my arms. "Tell me what has you so scared."

I rear back. "I'm not–"

The distinct chime of the lift heralds more party guests, and I leap away as though burned. Seconds later, a new wave of people files down the concourse. If the bash isn't at capacity yet, it will be soon. A particularly… energetic thrash metal song starts up, rattling the walkway.

Randall scrubs his face with his palm. "Look, you wanna get out of here?"

I give him a hesitant nod, but… "I don't want to fight any more tonight."

"Then it's a good thing it's tomorrow."

Rik refuses to synch with me, and Randall refuses to speak, as we make our way to a twenty-four-hour caffeine bar. Nighttime in this part of the Canopy has a reverent quality. Most residents have already retired for the evening. A furtive few keep to themselves as they pass by, the lush vegetation absorbing their transient sounds. As a result, our steps seem obscenely loud as we walk, the soles of our shoes slapping against the tile.

I'm not sure why I've even agreed to come. But the connection's still alive between us, a complicated, snarling tether threaded with equal parts affection and annoyance. The cool, clean Canopy air clears away my lingering drunken fog, leaving behind recriminations and an appalling self-awareness of just how foolish I've been.

Randall leads me to a table by the window so we can look out, instead of at each other. Thoughtful of him, since at this point all I want to do is vanish.

"Let's start over. What do you say?" Randall asks with forced calm.

"I'd like that."

We stare at each other in silence until I finally look away. Beyond the window, a lavish courtyard full of tropical flowers. Before we left the party, I pinged Brita. Her Do Not Disturb auto-response assured me she'd be all right. One less thing for me to worry about as I try to salvage this evening with Rik, Randall, whoever he is.

A waiter comes and goes, leaving behind a foamy latte for me and a traditional macchiato for Randall. I stare down at my drink in surprise. He must've ordered remotely for us. "How did you know?"

"I seem to recall a conversation about dairy to caffeine ratios, and your misguided belief that the bigger the better."

"That was years ago."

He shrugs and takes a sip of his drink, all nonchalance.

"What else do you think you know about me?"

"Only what you told me. What I could figure out on my own."

"Like?"

He shifts uncomfortably in his seat. "Like... you probably attend the College of New Worth. Some of the partygoers were proudly chanting the school motto when I arrived."

"Graduating next week, actually."

"Congrats. I graduated from there three years ago."

I grimace. "Tonight must've seemed so... immature to you."

He hides his grin behind the rim of his cup. "You make me sound like an old man."

"I just meant..."

His amusement skips across the line. "No one said this would be easy."

"I just didn't expect it to be so awkward now that I know who you really are."

"You've always known who I am on the inside. Think of it like this: it's the same signal, but now there's even better resolution." And the fidelity can only improve once we calibrate. At some point between now and when we met earlier, his reserve has melted away. He stares at me with such openness I'm afraid to look into his eyes, to see what I'll find there.

"New subject?" he asks. I nod gratefully. "All right, let's see. I grew up in the Understory. What about you?"

"The Terrestrial District." I hold my breath, waiting for the recoil, the disgust that most people have for the lower levels, but it doesn't come.

"That must have been hard." At my disbelieving stare, he ducks his head. "I know, because I live down there now." A College of New Worth graduate, now with dirt underneath his feet? "I work for Vector Agronomy," he adds.

That explains it. Some companies like Vector, no matter how prestigious, need to set up shop down there because of economies of scale or the access to certain resources the lower levels provide. "You're the ones rehabilitating the land beyond the dome?"

"That's right. We're responsible for monitoring the soil and the plants," Randall says.

"Have you, you know, been outside?" I ask, genuinely curious. After all, he's helping us work towards Emergence. When the glass dome finally comes down, and we can return to the land we left behind.

Randall chuckles. Probably gets that question all the time. "Yep. In fact, I just got back from a planting trip."

My eyes widen. "What's it like?" Everything in the Canopy's meant to evoke the outdoors, the nature we took for granted for so long. But compared to the real thing?

"Different, but in a good way. You can see so much…" He shrugs. "And the air is sweeter than the Canopy's."

"Is it true what they say? That Emergence is finally here?"

When humanity first took refuge in the domed cities spread throughout North America and the rest of the world, no one was certain when we'd be able to return to the land. Scientific models disagreed on how long it would take for the harm done to the climate by global warming, warfare, and pollution to settle out. While we wait, each city has the responsibility of cleaning up the surrounding region. But there's no denying the green beyond the dome that's grown in intensity each year.

"Well, technically I'm not allowed to say one way or the other."

I nearly laugh at his shift into formality, so at odds with our usual irreverent banter. "Oh, come on. I heard there's supposed to be an announcement in a few days."

Every couple of months, the city uploads a new vid to the network documenting the rehabilitation of the land. Disconnects do most of the work, but scientists and engineers like Randall guide their efforts. You can always tell when a new video hits the network because performance slows down dramatically as everyone scrambles to take a look.

But network chatter says *this* announcement will be different. To think my generation could be the one to step beyond the glass… I've always dreamed of being outside.

He gives the bar an uncomfortable glance, then leans in, like he's about to impart a secret. "All I can tell you is the land wants balance as much as we do. The rest's politics."

"I've toyed with the idea of doing something like that. You know, doing my part to reclaim our future outside," I say, echoing the narrative that's been drilled into us since birth. "But…"

"But?"

"Data curation seemed more sensible. There'll always be demand for people who can make sense of the explosion of digital information created every second."

Competition for jobs across New Worth is fierce since there are so many of us trapped under glass, even with limits on how much automation each industry can have. One way to succeed in a city full of constraints – spatial, social, and economic – is to get a degree in an in-demand field like data curation. It takes a precise set of skills to determine what's important and what's not, measuring current usage against future needs.

"Tell me about it. At Vector we have metadata for our metadata. But…" He trails off with a shake of his head.

"What?"

He hesitates, then says, "It's just not what I would've expected. Curation, I mean."

"Why not?"

"The job feels a bit stifling compared to who you are up here," he says, tapping his temple. "That's all."

I shrug. "It's not exciting, but the steady work means I'll be able to help my parents move out of the Terrestrial District one day." That's all that matters.

Three AM flashes in the periphery of my vision. I can't quite stifle my groan. Or the rebounding of my anxiety which thankfully stayed out of the way during our conversation.

"Time to go?" Randall asks.

"I'm afraid so, if I'm going to have any hope of accomplishing anything tomorrow. Today. You know what I'm trying to say."

I walk him to the train station in a strangely companionable silence. A maglev bound for the Terrestrial District hovers over the guideway as Randall files through the security gate. Our connection's placid for the moment, but I know we're both disappointed in our own ways by the evening. "I didn't mean to mess things up between us," I call after him from the other side.

"You didn't."

"But…"

His mouth quirks. "Baby steps. Next time will be easier."

Next time. >>I'll hold you to that.>> I'm rewarded with a smile, our connection humming between us. Despite making a fool of myself earlier, I wouldn't trade this moment for anything.

"Rik–"

The maglev doors flash and chime. All aboard. Startled, Randall steps back just before they slide shut. <<What is it?<<

>>Nothing that can't wait.>> I hope.

I watch his face through the window, looking for that instant when my thought reaches him. He smiles, and a bit of that resulting warmth filters through. A tangle of emotions, too scattered to settle on any one for more than a second, haunts our connection as the train goes gliding off into the night.

CHAPTER FOUR

The next morning, the crippling sensation of being watched deepens with every checkpoint I pass on my way to my appointment. A slight prickle on the back of my neck that morphs into stifling self-consciousness as my signal's tracked throughout New Worth.

When I first ascended to the Canopy, the sight of all the checkpoints mounted everywhere was a relief. Nothing would go unnoticed up here, and such transparency meant safety, something that was never guaranteed in the lower levels. But today everything sets me on edge. The checkpoints, the crowds congregating around the lifts, and whatever it is that's waiting for me at the Specialist Investigation Department in the Understory.

A few minutes ahead of schedule I reach the designated office suite, located in one of the corporate plazas scattered throughout the Understory. Sandwiched between an accounting firm and an ad agency, the office is gloomy with heavy plaster columns flanking tinted glass doors. Inside, a bright atrium decorated with air plants greets me. Water tinkling in a nearby fountain interrupts the otherwise hushed atmosphere.

Not quite what I was expecting. No criminals waiting their turn for processing or uniformed police officers pacing the floor. A mid-forties white man in a suit gets up from the receptionist's desk. "Emery Olivia Driscoll?"

"That's me."

"Right this way." He gives me a bland smile as he leads me through a set of double doors and down the lifeless hallway. The receptionist stops me with a hand on my arm at the entrance to a small conference room. The physical contact makes me want to bolt. I have to force back my initial impulse to tear my arm away. Too many years of protecting the data receptors embedded in my hands from incidental or unwanted contact from others. Besides, we're both wearing gloves. And based on his benign bordering on haughty expression, I'm pretty sure calibration's the last thing on his mind.

"This is an implant-free room," he says. "Do you understand?"

They're not kidding around if they want to prevent me from synching with anyone. The instantaneous sharing of thought-text is the one thing exempt from the transparency laws mandating that the majority of digital information can be monitored for security purposes. A necessary evil of living in such a constrained environment. Thought-text, by its very nature, is temporary, lasting only long enough for the recipient to acknowledge it. An imperfect compromise to keep citizens' lives private. But I guess privacy has no place in a police inquiry.

The receptionist doesn't let go of me until I say, "Yes, I do."

As I cross the threshold, my implant's snuffed out like a candle. Usually, Rik and I keep our connection open but minimized, so he's always there, reassuringly, in the back of my mind. Any other day, I'd be pinging Brita with a joke or something from the feeds, and vice versa. As I'm cut off from my implant's network-dependent functions, even passive features like calendar notifications, proximity alerts, and simple messaging are silenced.

It's a complete mental amputation that immediately gives me a headache.

The receptionist follows me into the room as I take a seat at the conference table. The sooner I know what they want from me the better. Do they know about Breck, or is all this an exercise in formality? And just where is the detective that contacted me?

The man from yesterday and his musclebound friend enter the room. I nearly leap out of my chair as my skittishness goes into overdrive. "What the hell is this?"

The receptionist raises a hand for calm. "Forgive me for underestimating you, Miss Driscoll. Normally these conversations aren't quite so protracted."

"I take it you're no secretary." I glance over the room. "And the message? This was all a scheme to get me alone." I should have crossreferenced the address with the network to ensure I was headed to the *real* Specialist Investigation Department instead of this... ambush. But how could I have known the message didn't come from the police in the first place? My stomach drops. Just who are these people?

He gives me a self-satisfied smile as he takes a seat on the edge of the table. "Please, allow me to introduce myself. My name's Thomas Harding." He gestures to the first man from yesterday. "You've already met my colleague, Tahir Ahmed. And this is Diego Martinez." He must mean the muscle.

"How nice. Can I leave now?"

"I'm afraid not," Harding says. Diego adjusts his stance, ready for me if I try to bolt. I reluctantly settle into my seat. "In fact," Harding continues, "we're here to offer you a job with Aventine Security."

Me? My petite stature's not particularly threatening, as I well know. There's no way I'd cut it as a security guard. "Is this some kind of joke?"

He acts as though I didn't say anything. "So you can be trained as a courier."

"All this, so I can deliver packages and pizzas? No thanks."

Harding spreads his hands, a placating gesture belied by the uncompromising cut of his gloves. "Nothing so commonplace, I assure you. You won't simply be carrying information on behalf of Aventine," he replies. "You'll be carrying it inside you. In your bloodstream."

A wave of nausea rises up. My hands clench, squeezing the seams out of my gloves, as I force myself to keep breathing.

He smiles, but nothing about it puts me at ease. "You see, you carry a very rare trait in your DNA that allows you to hold encrypted data in your blood cells. Given the digital transparency laws..." He lifts his shoulder, an elegant gesture. "We have a number of government and corporate clients who want a more *secure* way to transfer data than across the New Worth network. That's why we're only interested in the best of the best, so to speak. That's why we want you."

He watches me expectantly as I process this truly bizarre turn of events. "Seems a bit extreme. The network's not *that* bad," I finally say.

In the beginning, the network and the implants connecting us were the only things holding the city together. People had given up their homes and independence and in some cases much, much more to come to New Worth – built on the battered foundations of Fort Worth, Texas, after a series of violent tornadoes ripped through the region – and the instant connectivity and the camaraderie that came with it was a relief in a time of so much uncertainty. Sure, the network's not perfect, but the city wouldn't be what it is now without it.

"Where to start?" Harding leans forward, hands on his knees. "New Worth has millions of users in a highly concentrated area and endless ways to connect, customize, and create new content. Taming the network's growth has become virtually impossible – too much of the city's infrastructure relies on it. Which has made data security increasingly difficult. We had to come up with a new way of doing things. The government and business sectors were sinking so much money and manpower into chasing down bugs and backdoors and staying on top of new advances, actual work ground to a halt." He smiles, looking rather pleased with himself. "We had to go back to basics. With a twist, of course."

Physical instead of digital delivery of information, the twist being the DNA-encoded blood cells as the new format.

He taps his temple. "Surely you haven't been immune to problems."

Inwardly, I shudder. My implant picked up a virus last month. The thirty-six hours I was offline repairing the damage were the longest of my life. I can only imagine such inconveniences are so much worse for businesses and their bottom lines. That, combined with the difficulty of keeping information private and free of incursions, snooping, and security flaws… no wonder something like Aventine Security exists. But why does it have to be blood? My stomach lurches.

"Then why isn't everyone using data vampires?"

"We prefer the term blood courier. But to answer your question, for some businesses, it's financially prohibitive. For others, overkill. No one cares about a beauty parlor's financials or a restaurant's internal communications. And some industries require transparency as a result of regulations or the need for public oversight. But the rest? Those competing for consumer dollars or on the cutting edge? Pockets of the government dealing with classified information or data they've been entrusted with? That's where we come in."

"This is all very interesting," I say, implying just the opposite, "but I already have a future."

He leans back, looking almost smug. "Ah, yes. Your data specialist degree from the College of New Worth. A respectable field, but it cannot compare to your new role with Aventine Security. Isn't there part of you that's always wondered if there's something *more* out there?" he continues. "Something

I guarantee you'll only find at Aventine."

Harding waits for a reaction that I struggle not to give, biting my lip against his words, too insightful and infinitely more persuasive than anything else I've heard so far. Data curation was a safe choice, not my first choice. But I don't have the luxury of choosing anything else, not if I want to get my family out of the Terrestrial District.

He spreads his hands wide. "This is a once-in-a-lifetime opportunity, Miss Driscoll. In addition to the fiscal rewards that come with the position, I can assure you, you won't want for intellectual stimulation."

"If working for Aventine's such an honor, why haven't I heard of you?"

His brow wrinkles ever so slightly. "We wouldn't be very good at our job if you had."

"Still not interested."

"I'm sorry. Perhaps I wasn't clear. You'll work for us because you aren't in a position to say no."

"And how's that?"

The look he levels makes it seem like he already knows all my secrets, like he's simulated this conversation dozens of times and knows every possible contingency to any argument I might have. "Because we know what *really* happened in the Terrestrial District yesterday."

And that's why they bluffed their way into this meeting after I bailed on Tahir and Diego's initial summons.

Harding smiles. I think he means it to be kindly, not the pedantic stretch and flex it really is. "Your... deliberation in catching the subject in the act the other day without his notice was truly impressive."

He holds out his hand, and Tahir produces a touchscreen. He momentarily retreats into his implant, his eyes shuttling back and forth under their lids. A moment later, a vid plays on the screen. Spliced surveillance from the Terrestrial District.

The only thing that keeps it from looking like realtime footage is the brightness settings filtering out the dim conditions so I can see where I'm standing in the shadows between a bodega and a payday loans center. Breck's in the opposite corner of the frame.

Months ago, an item in the news feeds caught my attention. A girl attacked near the Bower, her implant ripped from her body. After weeks of searching, I learned his name, the innocuous-sounding Breck Warner, and started making plans.

My breath catches as he darts past the cameras, and the past-me moves out of the alley to follow a few seconds later.

"We have a wide set of parameters we use to determine aptitude of potential couriers since simply having the DNA trait isn't enough. Things like intelligence and physical ability aren't always reliable indicators," Harding explains. "So we have to keep an eye out for that little something *extra*."

"And Aventine found out about this?"

A new clip, this time of me pretending to shop in a second-hand clothing store as the guy goes past, his quarry clueless. Yesterday's footage.

"Stop the playback." I don't need to see any more.

"But we haven't even gotten to the good part yet."

"Now."

He sighs as though I'm spoiling his fun. "Very well." He waves to Tahir, and the playback's halted. Breck's oily good looks still fill the screen. I force my gaze away.

Tahir watches me steadily. "After some sleuthing, we were able to reconstruct the way you targeted him, shadowed his movements for weeks before you were able to get the police involved, catching him in the act. When we saw that, there was no question you would work for us."

"And now you're going to blackmail me into becoming one of your couriers? Your evidence is circumstantial at best."

"I wouldn't be so hasty, Miss Driscoll. Thanks to Mr Warner here, we've done some additional investigating." Harding then reads off a list of seven more names I know by heart. "All scrappers operating in the Terrestrial District who the police found conveniently incapacitated over the last four years."

"At first we thought you were one yourself, looking to eliminate the competition," Tahir adds.

Never.

Harding grins as if he can divine my thoughts. "Ah. You think of yourself as some sort of vigilante hero, yes? Or should I say heroine? Is that why you targeted them?" He pauses invitingly for my response.

I'm no hero. A hero wouldn't feel so much exhilaration in the moment, so guilty afterwards. But my reasons are my own. Maybe the *only* thing they don't know about me. And it needs to stay that way.

He busies himself with adjusting his shirt cuffs. "No matter. Please know you're welcome to spurn our offer of employment, Miss Driscoll, but if you do, we'll be forced to turn over this evidence of serial stalking and assault. Not only would you be risking jail time, but it could also affect the case against Mr Warner and all the others you've brought to justice in your own way."

Undoing all I thought I'd accomplished. The malice of it robs my breath. "No," I whisper. "You wouldn't."

He finally meets my gaze. "I'm afraid we would. But keep in mind that you will be well compensated for your work with Aventine. Enough to move your family out of the Terrestrial District."

"The Understory?"

A gloved fingertip points to the conference room ceiling. "Higher."

When I received my acceptance to the College of New

Worth, my parents were thrilled. I was too, but I also knew it would fall to me to help them ascend with me. And it's so damn tempting to no longer have that hanging around my neck like a millstone if Aventine's as good as they say.

"What assurances do I have you'll hold up your end of the bargain?"

"Well, we've already settled your school loans," Harding says. "Of course, that can easily be undone if you choose not to cooperate."

He waves to Tahir, who pulls up the interface for my bank account on the touchscreen. The obscene balance is gone, and it's no illusion. The digital watermark ensuring no fraudulent activity or faked transactions shimmers over the screen like a protective glamour. Thousands of credits, wiped clean just like that?

"We view all our couriers as an investment," Harding says at my open-mouthed shock. "We ask much of you, it's true, but we reward you accordingly. Now, if there are no more objections..."

My stomach's full of ice cubes. This whole conversation could've been lifted out of a storyline from one of the arcade's espionage-tinged immersives. Recruitment into a secret organization by any means necessary. If I can't be bought, blackmail always does the trick. With what they have on me, I can't say no, and the smug look on Harding's face tells me how well he already understands that.

"Please know we look forward to working with you," Tahir says.

The good cop/bad cop routine's really getting old. "Aww, that sounds almost sincere. It'd be easier to believe if you didn't have to strong-arm me into working for you."

"There's nothing wrong with a mutually beneficial arrangement between adults," Harding says.

I squeeze the hem of my shirt in a fist, as if I can disintegrate the nanofilaments through sheer will alone. "Whatever helps you sleep at night."

"So that's a yes, then. Excellent." Harding gets to his feet. "Aventine started out as a government initiative spearheaded by the secretary of Economic Development. But we became an independent contractor approximately eight years ago. Our charter comes all the way from the City Council itself." A rotating body of elected councilors tasked with governing New Worth until the day when the dome comes down.

Given how deep Aventine's reach is, that doesn't surprise me, but I'm still relieved we're not operating beyond the city's purview. Aventine may have forced me into joining up, but at least they aren't asking me to do anything illegal now. I hope.

"I don't like your methods."

Harding chuckles, then sobers. "When I was tapped to replace Aventine's founder a few years back, I soon realized I wasn't put in this position to make my employees *like* me. I'm here to create an elite group of couriers who are more reliable than anything the New Worth network can offer." He adjusts his gloves. "And I'm very, very good at it."

Tahir clears his throat. "Now, there's one more piece of housekeeping we need to take care of. By necessity, we need to wipe your implant. *Now.* Because of the nature of the position and the proprietary training you'll be receiving, all our employees must have their identities reset for the duration of their contract with Aventine."

"But losing my identity–"

He holds up a hand for silence. "Is necessary to keep you safe, an asset to Aventine."

"An asset, not a real person."

Harding sighs. "A small sacrifice in the grand scheme of things, I assure you." He begins to pace, his movements as precise and controlled as a dancer's. "Indulge me for a moment. Think of every person you've come in contact with over the course of your implant's life, however fleetingly. Now, consider all the entities you've interfaced with across New Worth. Arcades, restaurants, your school. Every train ride, every checkpoint you've passed. Each interaction a potential security threat."

He pivots on his right foot to face me once more. "From our standpoint, the only responsible choice is to reset our employees' identities. We back up everything, of course, should you wish to revert to your old life once your obligations to Aventine are met. Once we're satisfied with your progress, you'll be able to reestablish contact with those dear to you on a case-by-case basis, if that's what you want."

I inhale through my mouth. But to give up my identity and my connections for who-knows-how-long to my family and friends? And Rik? I held off contacting him this morning – we both needed time after last night – but now I'm regretting that decision.

Tahir's gaze remains unreadable. "We give our couriers a clean slate so they can become who they need to be without interference from old attachments," he says. "It's not an easy process, I know, but once the shock wears off you'll quickly find out which people from your old life still matter, and which ones are just noise."

In other words, which ones are really worth the effort of securing Aventine's approval for. "But the emotional trauma.... It's so cruel."

"What good's a new identity if you're still beholden to your old life? Haven't you ever thought about starting over? It can be quite freeing, escaping the expectations other people place on you," Tahir says.

It can be. There's even a procedure for it called digital fugue, where you voluntarily purge all your old contacts and start over like some kind of mental cleanse. But I never expected to do one myself.

Tahir steps toward me as Harding watches on. "What we do is not without risk. Not only to yourself, but to anyone close to you. Think of it as protecting your friends and family by disappearing. That way they can't be targeted to get to you and the data you'll be carrying."

Spycraft 101. No attachments.

Harding waits until I give him my full attention. "I'm sure I don't need to remind you of the consequences if you fail in holding up your end of the bargain. Diego here would be happy to escort you to the nearest police station, if you wish it. No? Well, remember this. We only take the best, and as such we expect the best from you. If at any point we feel you are not living up to your potential, we reserve the right to terminate this arrangement."

"Terminate how?"

"You'll be downgraded to the Terrestrial District, for starters." I inhale sharply. I won't go back down there. Not willingly. "You'll be given a job that'll keep you out of our hair," he continues, "and I'm afraid we'd be forced to alter your implant to ensure you retain no knowledge of our operation."

"And what's the success rate on that?"

"It's not very good, admittedly." Which probably means the procedure incurs lasting damage of some kind if they don't kill me outright. "That's why it'll be best for all concerned if you simply embrace this opportunity. If nothing else, remember your contract lasts for ten years. After that, you're free to pursue your own interests with our blessing *and* a significant retirement package."

He holds my gaze as if daring me to voice any more complaints. They haven't laid a hand on me, but they don't need to. Impersonating the police, implant interference, blackmail, smuggling secrets through the city.

And blood. Can't forget the blood.

My mind churns with it all.

"Well, I think that covers everything. I'll leave you in Tahir's capable hands. He's your point of contact going forward." Harding moves towards the hallway and gives me a wink. "Oh, and welcome to Aventine."

Diego looms in the doorway, blocking any possibility of escape from a nightmare of my own making. Though I'm not sure where in New Worth I'd be out of Aventine's reach. For a moment, I wonder if having to work for them is fitting punishment for helping the system along in bringing scrappers to justice. But I never dreamed I'd have to give up my implant.

Tahir pulls out a touchscreen. The display bathes his face in a blue-white glow, making him appear older than he really is. ||| Are you sure you wish to strike Emery Olivia Driscoll from the public registry? |||

The words await an answer. All that I am, all that I've achieved, folded up neatly into the characters of my name: *Emery Olivia Driscoll.* I can only stare. At the letters separating me from the men from Aventine Security.

Tahir's finger hovers over the screen for a long moment.

"Wait–" But it's too late as his index finger stabs the "Yes" button.

My birth and school records, places I lived, physical description, GPS check-ins, handles and content for my linked profiles, connections with all my friends and contacts. And Rik.

||| Action complete. |||

All gone in three and a half seconds. I count. The system allows erasure so easily. I never knew that before today. And I never expected it to *hurt* with the twinging awareness of a phantom limb.

When it's done, Tahir looks at me grimly. "Note your implant's signal."

My implant flares back to life, whatever hold the room had on me now gone. My digital death's nearly as devastating as the real thing. It would've been kinder if Aventine dug my brain out of my skull with an ice cream scoop. I'm hollowed out, devoid of everything that matters. My old life – everything that made me *me* in the eyes of others – gone with the press of a button. The magnitude of what I've given up surges hot and choking in the back of my throat as I gingerly run through my implant's settings.

My signal's scrubbed of any identifying info. I assumed I'd get a new, Aventine-approved ID. Without one... "How am I going to go anywhere like this?"

He wags his index finger at me. "Precisely. Think of it as our insurance policy. Because your signal isn't assigned to an identity, you'll draw plenty of attention from checkpoints and security personnel."

I'll look like someone with something to hide at best. At worst, a criminal. "How will *that* help me be a courier?"

"Ah, that's the beauty of it," Tahir says. "When you're on official Aventine business, your signal will cycle through a randomized set of identities, making it impossible to track you. But if you deviate from protocol, the anonymous setting, which isn't anonymous at all in practice, will be all that's available to you."

His voice softens. "Remember: in this business, you can be anyone or no one, but regrettably not yourself."

CHAPTER FIVE

With my digital identity dismantled and put into cold storage, I am but an empty vessel, my mind stripped bare, so I can be remade in Aventine's image. I should be angry at the loss and the manipulation – and I am – but it's buried under a layer of icy shock.

Tahir watches me for a long moment, then turns to Diego. "I'll handle things from here." After a sharp nod, Diego disappears down the hall after Harding.

"So you're my official babysitter?" My voice scrapes slightly, but I'm grateful that's the only indication of how upset I am.

"I'm your handler," Tahir says mildly. "Here to make your transition a smooth one."

I snort. "You've done a stellar job so far."

His brief wince cheers me slightly as he taps something into the touchscreen at his side. Now my implant broadcasts the identity of Gennifer Armstrong, age nineteen, from somewhere in the Understory. "This ID'll suit our purposes for today."

"No credits?"

"Issued only if you'll have need of them on assignment." His eyes cross momentarily, and he transmits a new message. "Next order of business is to pick how Emery Olivia Driscoll dies. I've sent you a selection of scenarios to choose from."

The message blinks red in the periphery of my vision. My

stomach heaves. "A rather morose way to start the day," I force out.

"But the easiest way to financially assist your parents is through an insurance payout."

He has me there. A sequence of eye movements pulls up the different options. Slipped and fell off a concourse, knocked in front of an oncoming maglev, implant-induced stroke after a malware attack. "Really? If I have to die, I at least want it to be memorable." One last chance to leave my mark on the world. Doesn't Aventine owe me that much?

He half-turns toward me. "Mundane's more believable. Less questions that way."

I settle on a nasty fall and submit my choice back to Tahir. I try not to think about how my friends and family will take the news. I'm still not sure how *I'm* supposed to take it. Sure, the credits are nice, along with the prospect of helping my parents, but faking my own death?

Cruel, unusual, and completely my fault.

Automatically, I seek out Rik's signal only to remember too late he's gone. Just when we were beginning to explore the fragile thing between us. What will he think? Brita and my parents too… The most life-changing thing to happen to me, and I can't even share it with them.

"Harding said something about reconnecting with my contacts after training. When will that be?"

Tahir's jaw works. "Let's not get ahead of ourselves. We have a lot of ground to cover."

A wave of helplessness rises up, but I push it down. I have to play by their rules. For now. "Any other major life changes Aventine's going to force on me today?"

The look in Tahir's eyes shifts slightly, as though he suddenly finds me as dubious a prospect as I find him. "Nothing major, no."

He escorts me out of the office and onto the concourse. He

wades into the crowds of morning commuters, leaving me in his wake. I'm no stranger to peak travel times, but he's a master as he charts a course through the throngs, dodging people intent on the lifts and slipping past the slower-moving sections of traffic at walkway intersections. In comparison, my steps are clumsy, off-balance, as I trot after him. Understandable, considering the morning I've had.

The commuters finally abate enough that we can walk next to each other. "I should have a handle or something, right?"

"All couriers are given an alpha-numeric identifier." He sounds like he's reciting from a textbook. Couriers 101.

"Could you be any more dehumanizing?"

He gives me a sharp look. "It's just how we do things."

"Well, do I at least get to pick my *identifier*?"

"No." Why am I not surprised? He casts about the sparsely populated concourse, then leans toward me. "You are M-37."

"Sure rolls off the tongue."

He wags his index finger at me, the white fabric of his gloves unbelievably pristine. "M for short."

M, close enough to Em, which is the closest thing I have to Emery. "Better."

The corners of his mouth curl up. "Thought you'd approve."

"Do you have an identifier?"

"Just call me Tahir."

"Why do you get to keep your name?"

"Because using the real name of your handler carries positive psychological associations that help us work together." Me working with him, not the other way around. At least he's honest.

"You've wiped me out of the system, but what about people I see in passing? What if I run into someone from my old life?"

Tahir tips his head. "It *could* happen, but we'll be teaching you techniques on how not to be noticed. Besides, surely you've heard of the Law of Digital Recency?"

I nod. When all information's immediately accessible, what's the incentive to retain it when your implant can bring up anything in fractions of a second?

Tahir taps his temple. "Over-reliance on digital infrastructure. If you don't exist in the infrastructure, where do you exist?"

And technically, I don't anymore.

"I know what you're thinking. How could this be? But humans are fallible. Fallible for putting all their trust into the network. Fallible for not believing what they see with their own eyes. And we at Aventine use that to our advantage."

My parents wouldn't forget me, nor my friends. At least I hope not. But Tahir's not wrong about the implants being so integral to how we see the world. I myself often rely on approaching signals to tell me who's in my immediate vicinity, only using my eyes for backup confirmation. Usually because I'm using them to do something else with my implant.

Tahir leads me to a large bank of lifts that'll take us to the Understory. We file into an available elevator with a large group of passengers and join in that awkward little dance as we arrange ourselves just so to maximize the number of occupants but still preserve a precious inch of space between everyone. It can take some doing, and today is no exception – we're just lucky it's early enough in the day that people are predominantly ascending to the Canopy, not descending.

The doors close, shuttering the sunlight. A few minutes later, the lift dumps us onto a bustling plaza. Natural light filters down to the Understory, amplified by mirrors, but it can't match the intensity of the Canopy even with the sunlight simulators worked into walls and ceilings to provide supplemental illumination. It's not so bad though. When I was a kid and my parents first took me up to the Understory, it was so bright I thought we *had* to be in the Canopy. I know better now, but for a lot of people the Understory is good enough. Good enough restaurants, good enough apartments, good enough light.

At least it's not the perpetual twilight of the Terrestrial District.

Pushing along the crowded concourse, Tahir leads the way toward Fountain Center. There, the wider spacing between buildings makes it the brightest part of the Understory. I smell the fountain before I see it. Sculpted trees and pastoral woodland creatures linked together by water fanning out in arcing bends of light.

"Wait here for ten minutes," Tahir announces, then he pings my implant. Reluctantly, I let him through. <<When time's up, you'll need to find the entrance to Aventine's headquarters. It's on this level, but that's the only clue I can give you.<< With the barest hint of a wave, he vanishes into the crowd.

>>But how–>>

<<It's not accessible on your digital map. You'll have to find it on your own.<< I can almost hear his grin across our connection. Because he's sharing some of his nonverbals with me, I have a more nuanced sense of him compared to talking face-to-face. He's not nearly as straitlaced as he presents himself to be. <<Think of it as your first test.<<

First test? Meaning there'll be more of them? This just gets better and better.

<<Couriers are expected to navigate all of New Worth. You're no exception.<< He says it crossly, but I catch flashes of his underlying amusement.

But without an accurate map? Or a workable address? >>Should I do it with my eyes closed and my hands tied behind my back as well?>>

<<We'll work up to that, don't you worry.<<

Tahir disconnects from me, and I swear aloud, earning a

glare from a mom with two kids in tow. Don't know why she cares – their glassy-eyed stares tell me they're way more invested in whatever they're doing with their implants than with me.

How to find a place that doesn't exist? I start with a basic search, unsurprised there are no results for Aventine Security. I suppose I could review every business on this level and compare it against its physical location, but that would take forever. There has to be a better way.

I perch myself on the rim of the fountain. People fade as I pull up my map of the area. Buildings are prepopulated with business and tenant names. Nothing jumps out until I reach an old pre-dome building located a few rings out from Fountain Center.

My grandparents remembered being outside and their sweltering childhoods in Texas – they were part of the generation that built the domed cities and consolidated society inside them until the time when it's safe for the glass to come back down. The building in question was originally part of the Fort Worth metro area, constructed in the late twentieth century, and somehow survived the terrifying windstorms that plagued the region. It needed all sorts of special permits to then convert it into a multipurpose Understory tower.

But there isn't anything the network can tell me about the current tenants on the floors that extend into the Understory. Strange. Suspicious even. But only noticeable if you are actively looking for it. Did Aventine erase itself from the public registry like they did me so it wouldn't show up in search results? There's only one way to find out as my ten minutes elapse.

My stomach protests as I stand. When I get there, they better feed me.

Abandoning the fountain, I file down another walkway. The multipurpose tower's revealed after the next turn with its concrete façade pitted and stained by exposure to the elements before being enclosed. Unsurprisingly, there's no signage telling me this is the place. Everyone else unthinkingly walks past as if the building didn't exist. Seems to be a trend with Aventine. I slowly approach and run my hands along the exterior. Grit sloughs onto my gloves.

I ping Tahir. >>I'm here, I think.>>

<<Very good, M. Let this be another lesson for you. Even if something doesn't officially exist, it still leaves digital echoes in the absence of information. It also means no matter how many precautions our couriers take, the job isn't without risk. Never forget that.<<

>>Are you always so encouraging on a courier's first day?>>

<<I'm only being honest. Now, take a look around you. The next time you walk the city's concourses, you'll be a different person.<<

I do as he says, memorizing the sunlight dappling the concourse, the lingering humidity from Fountain Center, the feeling of being at the city's heart as countless people pass through the Understory on their way to… somewhere.

In the Canopy, it's easy to forget all the people living on the lower levels. Here, the weight of humanity's everywhere, above and below, energizing in its own way compared to the crushing bulk it becomes in the Terrestrial District.

<<There's an access door up ahead coded to your new signal.<<

Scanning the wall, I almost miss the metal door painted the same color as the old concrete. >>Got it.>> With one last look at the Understory, I step toward it, and it whooshes open, revealing a small vestibule. Cameras and body scanners embedded in the wall come to life as the door shuts behind me. Aventine really doesn't leave much to chance.

Seconds crawl past, long enough for a cold sweat to

break out between my shoulder blades. It's a relief when the interior door flashes green and finally slides open. Tahir stands there with his arms spread wide. "Welcome, M-37, to your new home."

He whisks me through Aventine headquarters, pointing out the common areas – gym, training rooms, and the medical bay – all on the main floor. "On the second floor are Aventine staff apartments, while the third is administrative offices and meeting rooms." He flashes me a smile. "We even have recreation suites you're welcome to make use of in your free time."

"Free time? How civilized."

Tahir doesn't take the bait as he escorts me to the medical bay, consisting of a small pharmacy, examination rooms, a surgical suite, and lots and lots of lab space. He bypasses the glassed-in laboratories where two mousy techs work and comes to a stop in an examination room that screams hospital.

"M-37? So nice to meet you," a woman says, coming in behind us. Her reddish-brown hair is pulled into a low knot and freckles smatter her nose. "I'm Dr Finola, hematology specialist and Aventine's in-house physician." A med tech wheels in a cart full of surgical tools. A mockup of a human head has a mask of lace-like circuitry.

My gaze locks onto the tools. Another layer to be stripped away by Aventine, and it's only my first day. "It's not enough for you to take my identity, you want to cut me up, too?"

Tahir shakes his head. "We're only going to have some enhancements made. For starters, we need to strengthen the blood vessels in your arms."

I swallow hard. I had almost forgotten that crucial detail.

He gestures to my eyes and the line of my cheek, making one half of a parenthesis with his hand. "You'll also be outfitted with a retina simulator and facial projector."

The gear on the dummy. They want to surgically modify

me? My hands go to my face, every part where it ought to be, warm and solid and mine. An involuntary shudder rolls through my frame. "I thought you said people won't remember me?"

"That doesn't mean we don't have to help them along," Finola says gently.

"But I like the way I look," I say to Tahir. "You never said–"

"Relax, M. Your face will stay the same. We're only changing the digital perception of you, not the physical." He raises an index finger. "When you pass through checkpoints or encounter other security measures, the modifications will activate, creating the illusion you are who your implant says you are at any point in time."

He places a hand on my shoulder. He means to be comforting, but it just highlights how wrong everything is. "You will still exist as you, but digitally, you'll be a ghost. Transient and ever-changing."

Dead… barely a step up from being a Disconnect.

"Will it hurt?" I hate how small my voice sounds.

"Of course not. We're regimented, I grant you. But we're not cruel. Remember that."

Before he can say anything else, Finola lifts my chin and peers at me in such a way it's like she's trying to analyze me from the inside out. Maybe she is. Who knows what mods she's added to her ocular boost?

She says something to the tech, who jots the medical-speak down on her touchscreen. "It'll be over before you know it," she says with a wink.

I don't have the energy to tell her that, for me, it's just beginning.

"M? How do you feel?" Tahir hovers over me as I blink back drugged sleep, my arms weighing down the bedsheet draped over my body.

"The anesthesia should be wearing off," the med tech says from the other side of the bed, eyes on the digital readout on her touchscreen. "The procedure went beautifully."

My hands go to my face. Tahir holds up a mirror for me. Brown eyes, brown hair, brown skin. All normal. I can't even see where they sliced into my face. Everything's smooth and unblemished. Maybe they threw in a facial for free while they were at it.

Dr Finola bustles back into the room and pushes up the sleeve of my right arm. I jump. She gives me a smile. "Sorry, cold hands. But I work better without gloves." She takes a subdermal scanner from the table and runs it along my newly exposed forearm. Grunting to herself, she moves on to the left arm.

Tahir peers over her shoulder. "Well?"

Dr Finola straightens. "The fistula looks good." At my questioning look, she continues, "While you were under, we reinforced the blood vessels in your arms." She gives my right wrist a squeeze. "Data goes in, and travels through your body on a closed circuit until," she squeezes my left wrist, "it's time for the data to come out."

She lets go and takes a step back. "Aventine employs a proprietary hemocryption process where data's encoded onto the protein strands of your immune cells in your bloodstream. When you get an assignment, encoded blood's injected into your body. When you arrive at the drop-off location, your blood needs to be scrubbed – essentially a type of dialysis where the encoded cells are separated out from the rest of your blood."

My cheeks grow hot, the rest of me feels numb as though I've been paralyzed from the waist down.

Tahir clears his throat. "We keep a strict accounting of people who have a very rare HLA type – a set of genes that encode proteins on cells responsible for regulating the immune system." He sends me a reference file that's way too technical for me to parse at the moment. "The proprietary hemocryption process Aventine employs for data encoding is geared to a specific HLA type that you and the other couriers have. In other words, you are immune, unaffected by the encoded blood, where people with different HLA types would become sick, with something akin to anaphylactic shock, if injected. But don't worry, M. We'll cover all the specifics over the course of your training."

He thinks that simply learning more about the process will settle whatever anxiety he sees reflected on my face, but he's wrong.

"Oh, I almost forgot," Dr Finola says. "We need to administer a booster."

"As in a shot?" I ask in a small voice.

She nods and opens up a refrigerator unit that has been built into the cabinet. Inside, a dark red vial awaits. "Vitamins, primarily, along with vaccinations to most diseases. Since you'll be operating throughout the city, you'll be exposed to exponentially more microbes than you normally encounter, and this'll help combat that." She gestures to my arm. "If I may?"

Holding my breath, I brandish my arm so she can fit a medical cuff to it. With the press of a button, a small sensor within the cuff locates a vein while the doc lines up the booster to the cuff's needle slot. When the cuff chimes, I squeeze my eyes shut as she depresses the plunger, doing my best to hold still and keep my breaths even.

"There. All done," she says briskly, as she puts the equipment away.

Tingling warmth travels through my blood vessels, then the sensation slowly fades. But the queasy sensation in my stomach lingers.

"You may feel... uncomfortable over the next few days as

your body gets used to the booster's properties, but that's to be expected," Tahir says.

Dr Finola picks up her touchscreen and looks at Tahir. "I'll have her back to you in an hour, maybe sooner."

"Very good." With a wave, he leaves the room, pulling the door shut behind him.

Dr Finola turns back to me with a smile. "All right, M. To start, I'd like to get a sense of your overall physical condition so we can tailor a diet and exercise plan for you..."

I've about had it with "orientation" by the time Tahir leads me to the second floor after my examination. Décor from another decade is everywhere in warm, neutral tones. Inoffensive to a fault. I hate it. They must've designed this place to deliberately distract from the fact HQ's just a dressed-up isolation ward.

When Tahir codes open the door to a small apartment, I like my quarters even less. He waves me in, and the sunlight simulators that stud the ceiling turn on, slowly growing in intensity. Each wall has a large vid screen mounted to it to make up for the fact there are no windows. The lack of personality just highlights what I've lost. Nothing from my old life is here except for the clothes on my back.

Tahir gestures to the wallscreens. "You can customize them to display whatever you want." Right now, the Aventine logo's emblazoned on each one. Steel gray letters against a burgundy background. The first thing to go.

I suddenly wish Brita were here to make everything light and bright and less lonely. Freshman year, she helped turn my teeny-tiny dorm room into a breathtaking escape from the Terrestrial District. She knew all the stores to find the latest trends. I could barely afford the updates, but for the first time I felt like I belonged in the Canopy. How could I put a price on that? And the friendship that followed? A friendship

I've so easily destroyed. But my new place could certainly use her sprucing-up.

Blinking back tears, I half-heartedly follow Tahir through a tour of the space. A small sitting area, kitchenette, separate bedroom, and bath. Tahir stops in front of the bedroom closet and opens it for me with a flourish. A rack of austere clothes hangs in monochromatic hues ranging from midnight black to beige, navy to gray. Underthings all in white.

"Color not in the budget?"

Tahir shrugs. "Your job from now on is to blend in. Your wardrobe's an essential part of that."

If that means my face will stay my own, I'll take it. "Hasn't someone figured out by now that the people in boring business wear are couriers?"

"You'd be surprised. Most people are appallingly unaware of their surroundings, particularly if their implants tell them there's nothing irregular going on." The Law of Digital Recency in action. "Besides, if there's a need to deviate from the basics, Wardrobe on the third floor can help. But you won't be assigned those jobs for a while."

He plucks a shirt at random. "The technical properties of your clothes provide protection to your core and can even shield your temperature from heat scans if necessary." He holds up the sleeve. "An added feature: when synched to your implant, your clothes will discharge an electric shock to anyone trying to attack you. You'll be trained on how to customize the filters so you don't zap everyone you happen to brush by in rush hour."

I examine the fabric carefully. Looks normal enough. I guess that's the point. "And how often do couriers get attacked?"

"Hopefully never." He drops the sleeve and shuts the closet door with a snap. "In security, you plan for all outcomes, not just the most likely ones."

"Do all the other couriers stay here too?"

"Over a dozen couriers live and work out of HQ. Many are already out on assignment, which is why things are rather quiet around here."

I follow him back to the sitting room, eager to investigate the fridge. Breakfast was a lifetime ago. Literally.

"You have the rest of today to settle in." With an eyecast command, he transfers the door security controls to me so I can pair it with my implant's signal. "The next few days'll be rather intense, but I look forward to working with you, M."

I'm not sure how to respond. Even though we lived in the Terrestrial District, ignored by the rest of the city, my parents drilled good manners into me. But I'm no longer a Driscoll. And while that may not be Tahir's fault, he's easiest to blame.

I take a half step toward the door to see him out. "We'll see how it goes."

He makes no move to exit. Stripping off his right glove, he holds up his hand, palm out. I freeze. He tries on a smile. "From here on out, we're a team, M. This'll help me help you."

Calibration's not something to enter into lightly, even for platonic contacts. Tahir probably knows that better than I do, and yet he still stands before me, offering his hand.

"No way."

"You're allowed to refuse, of course. But couriers who don't calibrate with their handlers earn extra scrutiny from Harding. He's not a bad man, but as you might be able to tell, he does live up to his namesake."

A hardass in both name and deed. "I don't suppose he improves upon closer acquaintance?"

Tahir merely shrugs.

"You're really selling it."

"I'm only being honest, Emery."

"Not M?"

He grimaces. "I won't force you, but this might help with all you're feeling right now."

That makes me laugh. "You have no idea." For so long, I assumed the next person I'd calibrate with would be Rik. Not some spook with an agency I've never heard of until today.

Tahir inclines his head. "Maybe not. But at least you'll know I'm committed to your success with Aventine."

"If I do this, I'll keep you on the most restrictive setting."

"Naturally. I'll be doing the same thing on my end. Trust still has to be earned. From both of us."

If I'm going to succeed here, I'll need Tahir's guidance. And there's only one way to find out if he sincerely wants to help me. I hate that I'm already starting to think like Aventine.

I undo the small pearl button at the top of my right glove and ease it off. My hand feels hot and cold at the same time, as though I can't decide if I'm in danger or not. That's a lie. I haven't been safe since Aventine entered my life. But I don't have any other choice in this – in anything – do I?

With a deep breath and deeper misgivings, I fit my palm against his and wait for our implants to do the rest.

CHAPTER SIX

The next morning, Tahir's awareness presses against my mind, insistent as a buzzing fly. Groaning, I gain my feet and give him the mental equivalent of the middle finger – a heavy dose of static – before settling in for a long shower.

I slept well, though I'm pretty sure that's courtesy of my exhaustion after all the upheaval from the last two days. Formalizing my connection with Tahir helped too, not that I'll tell him that. I could feel his earnestness as soon as our data receptors calibrated – a whirling, undirected sort of goodwill – but the ease I had with Brita or Rik is missing. Something I never noticed until it was snatched away. Tahir and I won't be best friends, but maybe a functional working relationship will be possible.

So long as he doesn't take it upon himself to be my personal alarm clock every morning.

I dry off and dig through the closet. Can't help the color choices, so I settle on mixing and matching a navy shirt with beige trousers. The new clothes are unbelievably comfortable, but they still feel like a uniform.

By the time I'm dressed, Tahir's deigned to approach my quarters in person, pressing the doorbell with fervor. At least he hasn't tried to override the new security settings I implemented after he left yesterday.

I make him wait a few minutes longer as I brush my unruly

hair and braid it away from my face. Finally, I open the door.

"How are you doing?" He sweeps into my apartment, doing his best to hide his annoyance at having to wait behind a smile. Gotta give him credit for that.

"I'd be doing better if you'd let me sleep in. It's not even eight o'clock."

"We have a lot to cover today."

I sigh. "So long as there's time for breakfast."

He chuckles. "Fair enough." He holds out a packet of croissants from J'amie, an Upper Canopy delicatessen. My scalp pricks at his sudden focus on me. "You approve?" Tahir asks.

I blink up at him. "These are my favorite. How did you know?"

"Your profile suggested this might help you… adjust." He sets the packet on the counter and takes a seat.

Once a month or so, my parents would visit me in the Canopy. I'd take them to J'amie, and we'd sit at one of the bistro tables overlooking a slightly overgrown English garden. With flowering ornamentals scenting the air, we devoured the decadent pastries and sipped luxuriant cups of espresso. That Aventine was watching in those unguarded moments…

My chest squeezes. But this is actually the first time Tahir's seemed human. Better not waste it. I join him at the counter on the opposite stool, snatch up a croissant, and take a bite, nearly moaning as buttery flakes dissolve in my mouth.

Tahir wolfs down his own pastry. "Today," he says between bites, "we'll be reviewing best practices for courier missions. Simulating skills, situations, and so forth."

I savor the last few bites of my croissant and lick the remains off my fingers. When I'm finally done, he stands, brushing crumbs off his hands. "All set?" He sweeps back into the hallway.

A twenty-something man of mixed East Asian descent, with dark hair and chiseled cheekbones, is just exiting his apartment. He's wearing gray slacks and a white dress shirt with the top two buttons undone. A small tattoo lurks at the bottom of his throat. Maybe there's still room for personal style.

But then the man sees me and Tahir, and deftly does up the last two buttons. Guess not.

He nods to Tahir. "Ahmed. This our new recruit?"

Tahir smiles. "M-37, please meet D-19. He's been with us for five years now."

D-19 looks me over thoroughly, then turns back to Tahir. "Did I look that young when I first started?"

A surprised chuckle escapes Tahir. "No comment."

"Hmm." D-19 gives me a wink. "Cheer up. It gets better. Promise." He saunters off in the opposite direction. I'm not quite sure what to make of him, but I suppose it should be encouraging that it doesn't seem like he hates it here.

"This way, M." I match my stride to Tahir's as we go down to the main floor.

For the next few hours, he has me read through some material covering courier basics. There are even a couple of vids illustrating the different concepts. Then it's thankfully time for a more intensive demonstration. We enter a white training room, maybe half the size of a basketball court, with a small console embedded into the wall next to the door.

"Couriers travel all of New Worth, and we pride ourselves on identifying the most effective routes through the city." Tahir inputs a new program, and a projector transforms the room into a block somewhere in the Understory. With another set of commands inputted into the console, the scene is populated with holograms of people.

Satisfied with the parameters, he faces me. "Right now, I want to see you walk. Your goal is to get to the other end of the room without disrupting the projections. Cameras are trained on your movements to model the holos' adaptive behavior." He turns back to the screen. "Ready?"

As I'll ever be. The program chimes, and the room animates, wrenching away my certainty in perspective. My stomach sloshes at the projections hurtling toward me as though they're hitching a ride on a conveyor belt. Before I can react, one of the holograms barrels into me. As the lights warp and wrap around my body, my implant buzzes with feedback.

"You'll have to do better than that, M," Tahir calls out.

"Getting there." I step through the narrow gap between a young man and a simulated planter against the railing.

"What are the best ways to navigate crowds?" Tahir asks.

A headache flares, and my mind blanks. "I don't know. I guess stay on the edges if at all possible."

"Yes. Usually people maintain more space than is strictly necessary between themselves and walls, railings, and other obstacles, leaving room enough to bypass them in a hurry."

"If it's really bad, I try to find someone bigger than me who's making progress against the crowd." Tall people can usually see over the others and find gaps to move along more quickly. Unlike me, all five feet and barely three inches.

Either way, my calf muscles will get a workout speedwalking through New Worth.

"Good. Another thing to think about is the act of walking itself," Tahir calls out over the projections. "The shoes you've been provided with are non-squeak on most surfaces. But if you find yourself in an area where sound carries, you should walk toe-first, not heel-first, to minimize noise."

I hop back and dodge left to avoid a woman with a stroller.

"Every new location you walk into," Tahir continues, "ask yourself how do I avoid attention in this space? What's my exit strategy? And–"

An old man steps right into me, and the simulation ends

with feedback rattling my teeth. I made it three-quarters of the way across the room, on a setting I'm pretty sure is harder than what I've actually experienced walking around the Understory. But somehow I doubt that excuse will cut it with Aventine. The perfectionist in me wants to start over, determined to reach the other side now that I know what to expect. Whenever an arcade simulation kicked my ass, I played it over and over until I mastered it. I never expected the New Worth crowds to be just as challenging.

When I turn back to Tahir, a slight frown mars his face. "And where's the nearest location for emergency scrubbing. That one's just as important as the other two, maybe even more so."

I rub my face, surprised by the sweat on my brow. "OK, OK, I got it. Avoiding attention, exit strategy, scrubbing."

"Now, avoiding attention doesn't mean you have to avoid being seen. Remember the Law of Digital Recency. Most people are too invested in their implants to pay attention to their surroundings overly much. They see what they *expect* to see. Your job is to avoid extra scrutiny. Walking quickly down the concourse avoiding other people won't necessarily inspire questions from passersby, but walking quickly through the biopark when you're supposed to be taking in the scenery might."

"Code switching," I say. That's something you pick up early in the lower levels to navigate the intersection of so many different kinds of people. What's normal in one neighborhood can get you gutted in another.

Tahir gives me a genuine smile. "Yes, exactly. Matching your behavior to the setting. Also, keep in mind that sometimes the most prudent path is around, through, up, or down. Rarely a straight line. Don't forget to think in three dimensions as you so aptly demonstrated the first time we met. I won't say it's something you'll need in every job, or even one out of five, but it *will* come in handy."

I cross my arms. "I think Aventine likes to unnecessarily complicate things."

"When you're approved for active duty and have to deal with corporate espionage firsthand, believe me, you'll come to appreciate it. Now..."

My stomach heaves in spite of the contentment in my progress radiating from Tahir. We still have the whole afternoon to go, but I don't think I'll make it. "Can we take a break? I'm not feeling so good."

"We'll cut things short for today." I almost don't believe my ears. Tahir, my taskmaster, going easy on me?

He focuses on my face and grunts after a second. "Looks like you're running a low-grade temperature. Probably just a mild reaction to the booster you received, but I'll have some medicine sent up."

As I make my way to my quarters, the stairs prove to be more of a gauntlet than the simulated concourse. Finally, my door whooshes open. I don't bother with the prepackaged, nutritionally calibrated meal waiting for me in the fridge and collapse on my bed, welcoming darkness.

I feel even worse the next morning. I'm not sure how that's possible since, at some point last night, I found the pills Tahir slipped under my door and downed them. My limbs feel like lead weights, heavy and awkward. Still have a headache too. I can't seem to beat it even with my implant tweaking my neurotransmitter levels.

Could be withdrawal. I'm so used to having my friends and family a blink away, the absence of their connections and the relative silence in my head is jarring. No communication, no emotional feedback, no status reports.

They are as dead to me as I am to them.

A brief obituary hit the feeds late yesterday, reducing my

life down to a few impersonal sentences. Seeing my parents named as survivors sent a fresh wave of guilt crashing down. But I have to believe that I'm doing this for them. To pay them back for all their sacrifices to give me the best start possible.

Tahir's chipper voice is an ice pick against my skull as he meets me downstairs. I follow him as he codes into one of the rec suites. Just like a rental at one of the arcades across the city, this one suspends me in a harness, leaving my legs and arms free to interact with my environment. He gestures for me to gear up. My implant pairs with the rec suite interface as I settle into the harness.

||| Please select which module(s) you would like to experience. |||

Tahir stands in front of a small console by the door, his fingers skating over the screen. "Today's simulation integrates all the techniques we've introduced so far. That's all I can say about it since I don't want to color your reactions and responses."

"Sounds good." My headache wraps tighter around my head. Hopefully the simulation'll distract me from the pain.

"I'll be monitoring your progress in the next room." He taps his temple. "But if you need anything, you know how to reach me."

I dart down a tight alleyway somewhere in the southeast quadrant of the Terrestrial District, a cold sweat running down my back.

The simulation's so good it almost hurts. On the air, I can taste the slight tang of trash. There's too much of it produced down here for the cleaning bots to keep pace, and it doesn't help that they're usually cast-offs from the upper levels.

The low light's perfectly rendered as well. When the simulation started out in front of a dirtside train station,

I didn't think. I simply reacted, switching on my ocular boost's night amplification filter to make it easier to navigate the tight streets. The simulation's AI congratulated me for that move since the NAmp filter's apparently a new mod for most recruits. Growing up in the lower levels, I've been the proud owner of one for years, for what good it's done me.

All my senses tell me I'm back in the Terrestrial District, but I cling to the stubborn voice in the back of my head reassuring me it's just a *very* sophisticated simulation. No need to flinch at every shadowed doorway or tense up at each intersection. I tell myself nothing down here can hurt me, not really, as I follow my map, closing in on the location for the data drop.

The ambush, when it comes, takes me by surprise. Not because I wasn't expecting one – there was bound to be one in the scenario somewhere – but because it's so brazen. Two men stumble out of a bar as I go past. As soon as I dismiss them as your typical dirtside degenerates more interested in my breasts than my blood, the first one tackles me to the ground, punching the air out of my lungs.

The thug yelps as my shirt zaps him, momentarily shocking my NAmp filter. Somehow, my fist manages to connect with his solar plexus. I swing my leg up and around, twisting the rest of my body out from underneath him – a handy move I picked up from the arcade.

I get to my feet just in time for his partner to take a swing at me. I dance away, minimizing the hurt he intended, and grab his wrist before he can pull back. I give his overextended arm a ruthless twist, then take off running, his pained cry chasing my steps.

We're not supposed to be drawn into altercations if we can possibly avoid it. The risk of failure's too high. Evasive maneuvers it is. As I take the next turn down a twisting alley, my NAmp filter flickers, then goes dead, and no amount of eyecast commands can reset it. Other functions are hashed too. Déjà vu so sickeningly fresh hits me with maglev speed as darkness bleeds into my vision, blurring with memories better left buried.

Steps tramp closer. This AI doesn't like downtime. I back myself deeper into the alley, hating the effortless way my mind fills in the gaps. It was the rear of a half-empty mod parlor, not a rowdy bar four years ago, though the dumpster and its position are roughly the same. This time it's full of rotten food and broken glass, not stinking bags of medical waste.

That doesn't matter, though, as I find myself retracing my steps, retreating at a half-crouch, tears stinging my eyes, my breath coming in hiccupping gasps. Darting behind the dumpster, I tuck into myself and breathe slowly through my mouth, mentally willing the thugs to pass by.

I close my eyes, but my ocular interface is gone. A whimper escapes me, breaking the memory's hold long enough to hear footfalls echo off concrete. A muttered curse. Then, eventually, silence. But I know silences can lie.

History won't repeat itself. I won't let it. I won't–

||| Simulation complete. |||

The dark alley fades, replaced by boring rec suite walls. My heart's still struggling in my chest when Tahir breezes into the room. "How did it go?"

I can only manage a lopsided shrug, feeble like a stroke patient's. I keep my gaze on the ceiling, determined not to see the disappointment on his face when he realizes just how royally I screwed up in the simulation. They're going to send me back there. To the Terrestrial District.

I should've known I couldn't escape it forever.

My headache redoubles in intensity as he goes to the console screen and scrolls through the simulation readouts. Then he grunts, breaking the painful silence. "Most recruits run and get caught when they start to flag. You chose a good tactical position and didn't get spooked as you waited them out, giving the backup team time to intervene," he says over his shoulder. "That's very good."

I blink back a sudden wave of vertigo. Is that what he thinks happened? I was locked into my own simulation with a completely different set of parameters. I'm still breathing through my mouth to avoid the rotten meat smell of medical waste. I can still hear the drip of a water pipe somewhere behind me. Feel the bruising grip on my wrists as I was pulled out from behind that stinking dumpster.

Tahir gives me an apprising look. "Those kinds of instincts don't come easy."

No. They certainly don't.

I don't know what's more upsetting. That I froze up, or that Tahir, through some twist of fate, views my performance as a success. My shame compounds, but I dare not say anything.

He turns back to the readouts and frowns. "But your emotional readings are rather..." He looks at me, questions pressing at the edges of our connection as though he's trying to see past the restrictions keeping him at bay.

Mentally, I'm still in that alley, curled in on myself with stale beer and grease clinging to my nostrils. But he needs an answer, one that will get him off my back. I shrug, more convincingly this time, I hope. "Not a big fan of the Terrestrial District, simulated or otherwise."

"I see." He sets the screen down. "If you want a break before we move on–"

"That won't be necessary."

"Excellent. I've reserved the training room for the afternoon." He's already headed for the hallway.

I wrestle out of the rec suite harness and fall to my knees. Light-headed, sick to my stomach, and full of self-loathing. I've never had an arcade hangover like this. At least Tahir didn't see. I get to my feet and stumble after him like a drunken sleepwalker.

The rest of the day passes in a blur. It feels like I've just fallen asleep when my implant wakes me up the following morning. I lay there for a moment wishing I didn't have to meet Tahir and start the process all over again. My head still hurts, my body aches all over, and if so much wasn't riding on me keeping Aventine happy with my progress, I'd seriously consider throwing in the towel, even though I've never quit anything in my life.

When I finally go downstairs I wonder if I'm hallucinating when Tahir tells me, "No modules today." He leads me to the training room where a young woman, maybe mid-twenties, with a kind face and copper, chin-length hair, waits for us. "This is K-29. She'll be your sparring partner," Tahir says. To K, "It's M's third full-length day."

Her eyes widen. "Oh, I see." She gives me a smile. "Welcome to Aventine. It'll be nice to have another girl around."

It's a struggle to smile back. "Thanks. Wait. Sparring? I'm really not up for–"

"We want to ensure our couriers have the tools to protect themselves," Tahir says.

"Can't you just access my old arcade profile? I've logged plenty of..." A tremor runs through my body. I mentally scream at it to hang on a little bit longer. Any weakness Aventine will use against me.

Tahir sounds like he's underwater as he speaks. "Impressive as that may be, all the training in the world can't compare to the real thing. Now–"

K puts her hands on her hips. "Sorry, but I'm out. She's so far gone, she doesn't even realize she's bleeding," she says with a nod in my direction. Tahir gives her a look I can't decipher. K ignores him and catches my eye. "Come find me when the curdle's over."

What is she talking about? I check over myself for cuts, then see the drops of red pattering to the floor below. My hand finds my nose. Warm wetness that glistens red on my fingers. I'm bleeding. A lot. Just like before. I can't...

Oh *no*.

The room shifts, and everything fades away.

CHAPTER SEVEN

"M."

"Mmm." Skimming the surface of sleep, I clutch at fragments of a half-remembered dream. Rik was there, only–

"M, wake up." I throw up my arms at Tahir's voice, needle-sharp in my ear, desperate to call back the dream, but it recedes until only a vague sense of loss remains. "Hold her down," Tahir says to… someone. "M, open your eyes. Come on. Focus."

I turn away from his voice. "Leave me alone."

"Emery, please."

At the slight catch in his voice, something mentally clicks into place, and I stop fighting him. Squinting, I can just make out Tahir looming over me. Past him, instead of the walls of the training room, or those of my Aventine-issued quarters, stainless steel paneling and air scented with antiseptic surround me. "Where am I?"

"The med clinic. How do you feel?"

My body twinges at his words. "Shitty."

"Do you know why?"

I shake my head, but that only makes the clamp around my skull squeeze tighter.

He gives me a patient smile. "Remember why you're here."

"Seriously? Another lesson? Just fix me already."

"Your blood. You're rejecting the encoded blood that was injected into your body three days ago."

I hear the words, but it takes a while for my mind to make sense of them as I struggle against sleep's grasping fingers. "The booster shot? You knew this would happen?" I should be angry, but I'm too exhausted to muster up the energy.

"That's right," he says, calmly. "What you're feeling right now is what couriers call 'the curdle.' It's important to experience it yourself so you'll recognize the symptoms." My implant pings with an incoming message from Tahir. It might as well be an air horn. "I've sent you a more technical explanation for reference when you're feeling better."

I groan. "Great. More homework."

"M, listen. Three days. Three days is all you have before you have to get your blood scrubbed." Removing all trace of data from my bloodstream.

Dimly, I register someone changing out the port on my arm. "Wait. What happens if I don't?"

He pats my hand. "We'll get you fixed up and talk later."

At some point, they bring me back to my apartment. I sit up in bed gingerly, keeping my eyes shut until I'm certain there's no more blood oozing out of my body. After fumbling about in the bathroom, I discover Tahir, sitting trance-like on the couch, communing with his implant. How long has he been here?

He blinks, slowly coming back to himself. "Feeling better?" Nodding, I take a seat on the opposite side of the room. "You faint at the sight of blood?" An amused smile tugs up the corner of his mouth.

I cross my arms. "It's not funny."

"On the contrary, M. I've been doing this a long time. Never seen someone with such a… strong reaction."

"Leave it alone, OK?"

At my sharp tone, his brows raise. "Does this have anything to do with your history in the Terrestrial District?"

"Why don't you tell me? You were Harding's right-hand man at recruitment. You already know everything."

He frowns, lines creasing his forehead. "Not this."

No, I guess he doesn't. I glare at the wallscreen opposite. Haven't had a chance to purge the Aventine logo yet. It stares back at me, cold and unyielding.

"Emery?"

At his words, I can't stop my hand from going to the delicate skin at my throat. It's impossible to feel the threadlike scar there through my gloves. But all I have to do is close my eyes to recall the thick, coppery, somnolent sensation of my lifeblood siphoning out of my body.

>>I was attacked on my way home from school, senior year.>> Verbalizing what happened gives it too much power, so I stick to synching instead. >>Nearly bled out in an alley in the Terrestrial District.>>

<<I see.<< Some things are better left unspoken. Tahir, at least, seems to understand that much. <<That particular hospital stay four years ago is in your file, but I didn't realize the cause.<<

>>Wasn't something we wanted advertised. I fought back, managed to protect myself long enough for help to arrive.>>

Tahir clamps down on his reaction, but I catch bits and pieces of it – his horror, his sympathy, and a sudden surge of anger. <<Did the police catch your attacker?<<

>>No. All I know is he wanted my implant. In the struggle, he nicked my carotid by accident and ran off.>>

He inhales sharply beside me. <<That's why you targeted all those scrappers in the Terrestrial District. I wondered what was driving you. Did you find him?<<

>>No. With each one, I kept hoping... But it turns out there are a lot more scumbags in the Terrestrial District than I thought.>> And the police weren't terribly interested in putting a stop to them, not with their ballooning caseloads and

general disdain for anything remotely related to Disconnects.

Our connection churns as he processes everything. "You have my apologies for not better preparing you for today's scenario," he says with painful formality.

Intellectually, I know I got off easy when too many before me haven't. It was just a scrapper, not an even more dangerous kind of predator. But there're always moments, ones that often creep up on me, where I'm back in that alley, my muscles screaming, my mind in shock.

"I've worked hard to not let that day define me," I say, slowly. Same for all the people I saved from other scrappers over the years. That sustained me even when my search for the man who attacked me kept coming up empty.

"I know. That's why you're here. We take people with potential and make them strong, stealthy, strategic. Prepared to face anything. I'm certain you'll find a way to channel that day into your work for Aventine. You can't rewrite history, but you *can* rewrite your reactions to, shall we say, less-than-agreeable stimuli."

True. I thought if I learned everything I could to protect myself, I'd never find myself in a situation like that again – or if I did, I'd know how to get myself out of it with better results. Endless arcade sessions helped me rebuild confidence in myself, but it wasn't enough. I vowed to hunt my attacker down, just as he had me. I shake my head. "I wanted revenge. I wasn't thinking about any of this."

Tahir nods slowly. "Understandable. But I have to ask, why risk your future on one degenerate scrapper?"

Any advantage I gained from graduating from the College of New Worth would be wiped out by a criminal complaint. But I convinced myself the risks didn't matter. "Because he needed to be caught."

That he's still out there somewhere, Tahir thankfully doesn't point out. Instead he leans forward. "I promise you'll have more notice for any training scenarios that might be uncomfortable for you. But believe it or not, your experience just makes our job easier. You already have the situational awareness to monitor your surroundings. Not everyone comes to us with that healthy distrust of their environment already built in."

Tahir sounds so weirdly pleased I guess things like this are features, not bugs, as far as Aventine's concerned.

I flop back into the chair, running my hands along the armrests as Tahir watches on. "What about the curdle?" I finally ask, desperate to change the subject. "Didn't you say the whole reason you want people like me is because we're supposed to be immune to the hemocryption process?" If that's true, we shouldn't present any rejection symptoms.

"You're certainly immune. However, the curdle's something Aventine adds in as a failsafe. The encoded data has a finite lifespan, and as it degrades, a toxin builds up in the courier's bloodstream. Not only does it encourage swift and orderly transactions, but it gives our clients assurances that their data's protected at every stage of the process."

"Can the curdle kill me?"

"Not right away, but the side effects are incapacitating, as you've already experienced." No shit. "Basically it's to ensure couriers stay on task and stay loyal. In the event of failure, if they're abducted by an opposing force or are otherwise prevented from doing their job, the curdle helps neutralize them."

Every time I think I'm starting to understand how things work around here, Aventine upends my expectations. "All this was conveniently left out of training."

Tahir spreads his hands helplessly. "A necessary evil, I'm afraid. It's important you understand the limits to your ability so you can manage them responsibly." He gives me an approving look. "You should feel proud. Most recruits are a mess at the end of day two. Day three, and you could still function."

"Up to a point."

"Up to a point," he agrees, tenting his fingers.

"You should've told me."

"Standard procedure not to."

"I'm really starting to hate how things are done around here." I back off on my implant's emotional filter momentarily and enjoy Tahir's slight wince. "Intensely."

He gets to his feet. "Well, the good news is the rest of your training's fairly straightforward from here on out. No more tricks, I promise."

He means it, and I give him a slight nod. "I'll hold you to that."

"I'm sure you will." A disturbing gleam lights up his eyes as he sets a briefcase onto the coffee table. "Now, how about a lesson in scrubbing your own blood?"

My stomach lurches at the remembrance of all that red leaking out of my nose like a faucet. "You're kidding."

"We have to break you of your squeamishness some time," he says with a wag of his index finger. "And for you, the sooner the better."

He displays the contents of a scrubbing kit for my inspection: on one side of the divider, clear plastic tubing wound together, gauze, medical tape, and a medical cuff. The other side must be the scrubber unit – where my blood enters, the encoded blood is filtered out, and then the cleaned blood exits the other side so it can be pumped back into my body.

He swings the medical cuff around and around his index finger. "These make the process extremely manageable."

Once the cuff's mounted to my forearm, it automatically locates the appropriate blood vessels for dialysis, one for exit and one for reentry. Easy enough, I can do it with my eyes closed.

He slides the cuff into his pocket. "That's why you're going to practice the backup method." He opens up a side compartment, revealing individually-wrapped catheters.

"You're really going to make me do this?"

He gives me a patient nod. "We need the assurance that every courier we send out into the field can take care of themselves." He gives me a considering look. "You need the assurance too."

He passes me the kit, and I take it, willing myself not to dwell on the needle hidden inside the catheter's plastic cap. If Aventine's going to deem me unfit, I won't let it be because I can't conquer my aversion to blood.

"You remember how the process works from the modules?"

"Yes."

He makes a small gesture with his hand that says go ahead. But I can't. Not just yet. I sit there, measuring the weight of the kit balanced on the tops of my thighs. It should be a small thing, and yet it feels as though I stand at the edge of a concourse, staring down into the deep, dark heart of the city, with nothing to keep me from falling.

>>It didn't always bother me, you know.>>

Tahir shifts in his seat, but doesn't say anything inane like, "I understand," when he really doesn't, or "You'll get used to it," when I'm pretty sure this is something I *shouldn't* get used to.

<<Take your time.<<

I inhale deeply and finally look down at the kit. Tahir points to the scrubber unit. "In the field, you'll need at least a half hour to ensure the encoded data gets out of your system, but an hour's preferable." He points out the small slot where the tubing's inserted into the unit. There's also a button I'm supposed to press at the end of the process to push bleach into the scrubber, destroying the encoded blood cells once and for all. "For now, we won't worry about the actual scrubbing process. Just focus on locating a proper site."

"Why can't I have a permanent port placed in my arm?"

Tahir's mouth purses, but he doesn't accuse me of stalling. "Early on, we did that, but after a rather… unfortunate incident, we decided it put our couriers at risk if their ports were discovered." If someone knew about the process, I guess it would be fairly easy to look for otherwise healthy individuals with ports, blowing a courier's cover.

From the case, he pulls out a stack of medical patches, individually wrapped. "These wound-heal patches will rapidly repair your skin and hide the damage the injections and dialysis can do over time and, in turn, protect your identity."

I slowly push up my left sleeve. Left for scrubbing. Right for encoded data injections.

"Don't be afraid to take off your gloves for this. It's better to ensure you find the right area than guess wrong."

I know that. I just want that little extra layer between me and the reason I have to do this. Without the safety net of my implant and the people it connects me to, it's harder to stem the flow of memories that makes blood so treacherous for me. But for better or worse, I'm a courier now.

Biting my lip, I strip off my glove. My arms might still look like they did before I knew anything about Aventine, but as I press down on my flesh, the branching veins resist the pressure slightly, as though they've become small plastic tubes embedded in my arm.

"An artificial fistula was created there – essentially a section of reinforced blood vessels." Tahir hands me a catheter. "That's what you're aiming for."

In the modules, they talked about how so much of the process is keeping your hand steady and letting the needle do most of the work. Just have to slip it in and tape it into place. One-handed. Yeah, right.

I breathe through my mouth, fighting waves of nausea as I search out the right spot. *There.* My hand aches with the effort of holding the needle straight and true when all I want to do is fling it across the room. I can't look away, though, as I bring it down, pricking skin.

It doesn't hurt at first, not until it bites into the vein. Then, I can't be sure if it actually hurts or it's just my brain telling me so when all that red bubbles up in the plastic housing. Like the gorge in my throat. I'm going to lose it.

But I'm not alone here. Tahir's statue-still beside me, our connection alive with as much reassurance as the settings allow. I shift my focus to him, drawing on his strength – one of the advantages to emotional bleed. I orient the catheter just so and tape the unit to my forearm as I drag air back into my lungs.

Beside me, Tahir radiates a quiet sort of pride at my work. "I know how difficult that was for you." He gestures to my blood sloshing around in the plastic container, but I don't dare look down. "Remember. This is a process you control from start to finish. I won't say it'll be any easier the next time, but it *will* be more manageable. You'll look back on this moment and know you can do it again when the time comes."

I pull in a shuddery breath. "How often do couriers find themselves in this situation?"

"It's very rare. But we did have one case earlier this year. A courier got chased away from the drop-off location by competitors and found himself in a part of the Terrestrial District where we couldn't provide logistical support. Curdle symptoms were coming on, and he needed to act."

"But that's the exception, right?"

"Most definitely. The scrubbing kit'll usually be on hand at the drop-off location, mailed in advance of your arrival. If not there, then the location will be revealed to you following a successful data transfer. Only in rare cases will you have to perform an emergency scrubbing in the field."

I slowly nod. "Can I take this out of me now?" I manage to gesture to the port in my arm without looking at it.

"I'm afraid not," Tahir says, gently. "Since you went to all the trouble to put it there, we might as well make use of it and draw your first pint so we can start building up your blood supply."

With the constant wear and tear of dialysis, having extra blood on hand will help with anemia and other potential complications. It makes sense, but I still groan.

"Just when I think I'm starting to like you, Tahir, you go and ruin it."

CHAPTER EIGHT

There are a million reasons to keep my head down and follow the rules Aventine's laid out for me. Good reasons, sensible reasons, reasons that'll pay off handsomely in the end, so I've been told. But I've tried telling all that to my heart, and it refuses to listen.

I find myself huddled up in my quarters between never-ending training sessions, remotely accessing the arcade's network, piggybacking off enough signal relays to hopefully disguise the ghost account I've just set up to get a message to Rik. Not Randall. That would be too obvious, too easily tracked by Aventine.

The arcade's better. Not only is there a certain symbolism to it, but there's also so much spam and malware, what's one more account in the digital sludge traveling through the arcade's veins? Anonymity through obscurity.

||| Rik, you told me once you didn't care how it happened, so long as we kept talking after *Partners in Crime* ended. Even though I'm officially dead, the Liv you know is alive and well. It's hard to explain, but if anyone deserves the whole story, it's you. |||

The doorbell to my quarters rings. I start guiltily. With a hard blink, I trash the message and log out of the fake account. Did Aventine figure out what I was doing and send someone to put a stop to it? But thankfully it's not Tahir; his signal places him somewhere on the third floor.

Biting my lip, I get up to answer.

"Hello, M." My neighbor D gives me a wink and wipes away my paranoia. "Tahir finally gave you a break?" He peers around me and finds my untouched lunch on the kitchen counter. "Why don't you come down to the mess instead of staying holed up in your room? I'll introduce you around."

These past few days, I've subsisted on the bland meals Finola's been keeping my fridge stocked with. I've seen other couriers in passing, but I've either been training with Tahir or sidelined by the curdle. "Come on," he says. "It'll be fun."

Any relief at not getting caught reaching out to Rik fades almost instantly at D's earnest face. I'm not free. It's unfair to even consider shackling Rik to Aventine just because I'm not strong enough to give him up. He's probably moved on already; I'm the one who can't. When will I learn? This whole situation's like a bruise I keep pressing down on, convinced this time it won't hurt.

But it always hurts, even if it's only the memory of pain.

D patiently waits for my answer. Ten years *is* a long time to go it alone. Might as well see who else is imprisoned with me here. I follow him into the hall. "What do I call you?" I've already forgotten the numeric part of his identifier.

He snorts. "Yeah, the code names leave much to be desired. So we've taken to giving each other nicknames based off our letter designations. Officially, I'm D-19, but you can call me Dash," he says. "Everyone's curious to meet you. It's not fair Tahir's been keeping you too busy to make formal introductions."

"I'm not that interesting, believe me."

Dash chuckles. "Maybe not. But you're a new face around here, which is almost as good."

In the half-empty dining hall, Dash leads me to a table of couriers. Two men and a woman, all in their late twenties. "I present to you our newest arrival, M," Dash announces. He gestures to the taller of the two men, pale with sandy brown hair and blue eyes. "That's Bandit."

The woman, with curly black hair and olive skin, gives me a warm smile. "I'm Cache. Nice to meet you." Her voice has a pleasant burr to it.

That leaves… "Fleet, at your service," the last guy says with a smirk. Dark brown skin with neatly cropped hair and a deceptively lean frame. Crossing his hands behind his head, he tilts back in his seat, exuding a carefree sort of confidence. "What do you think so far?"

"Ask me again after I get used to all the lies and manipulation that's apparently Aventine's MO."

Bandit and Dash exchange a look and erupt into laughter. Dash finally calms down enough to say, "Well, now we know why Tahir's been in such a good mood this week."

I give them a bewildered look. "What do you mean?"

"Tahir likes his couriers with an independent streak, that's all," Bandit explains.

"Could've fooled me."

Dash shrugs. "He just plays things close to the chest. Think it comes from his time in law enforcement."

"Really?" I file that away for later.

"Yep. Detective of some kind. He doesn't talk about it much."

That probably explains why I'm so transparent to him, even before we calibrated.

Cache catches my eye. "Didn't enjoy the curdle, I take it."

"Among other things," I reply. "So, uh, all of you like working here?"

Nods all around. I watch their friendly, relaxed faces carefully. Did they buy into Aventine's recruitment pitch or were they blackmailed into signing up, like me? Or maybe they've been here so long the distinction doesn't matter anymore. The work *is* fascinating, but can that make up for all the restrictions Aventine places on us? My emotional barometer's been fluctuating so wildly since coming here; one day I'm hungry to learn more courier secrets, the next I'm full of caustic remarks and desperation. Like today and my message to Rik, written for all the wrong reasons.

"Most of the time, sure," Fleet says. "Though if I get caught up in a Disconnect demonstration on a job, I'll need to have a talk with management." He points to the ceiling.

Cache gives him a sharp look full of sisterly concern. "You said it wasn't that bad."

"It wasn't, but it *could've* been."

With a quick eyecast command, I find what he's talking about on the feeds. A demonstration in the Terrestrial District that turned violent, putting a couple of bystanders in the hospital.

Disconnects have always been the minority in New Worth, running in the background, but I didn't realize just how dissatisfied they've become. Because they've shunned the implant technology linking the city together, they're often eyed with suspicion. There've been clashes over the years, pitting them against the rest of the connected population, but growing up in the Terrestrial District I've interacted with enough of them to realize they're just people. Disgruntled perhaps, with limited options for ascending, but that's all. Not the pariahs that people who've only lived in upper levels see them as.

"What were they protesting?" I ask.

"Who knows?" Dash shakes his head. "Not enough jobs, not enough housing–"

"Pretty sure they'd complain about anything that's not subsidized hardware so they can catch up to the rest of us," Fleet adds with a flick to his temple.

Brita had been so certain there was more to the Disconnects

than jealousy of the connectivity they can't have. Hopefully she'll get her chance to do her exposé the way she wants to one day.

Dash's eyes cross with an eyecast command. "Wait just a minute. Kat says New Worth News just released the latest on Emergence... Wow. What a game changer."

A hush falls over the room as everyone retreats into their implants. I access the network, and, sure enough, New Worth News claims they have the scoop in advance of the city's announcement. "Are you kidding me?" I exclaim a few seconds later.

Cache looks thoughtful. Bandit gives Fleet's forearm a squeeze, and they exchange a grin at the news.

Emergence really *is* here. That's why Rik got so close-mouthed when I asked him about it directly. Pushing back the twinge of pain related to all things Rik, I dig into the story.

According to the latest research, life outside the dome's finally possible. Well, it's been possible for a while, but only in small doses. Without food, shelter, a way to filter the air, and an uncontaminated source of water, though, it wouldn't be a very *long* life. But now, the scientists tasked with rehabilitating the land are saying it's time to start planning for the infrastructure that will support the staged reintroduction of New Worth citizens to the homes they left behind, in keeping with initiatives underway at other domed cities.

As a result, the government has announced construction's underway for Vesa, a new housing development located *outside* the city. I scroll past images of five squat buildings arranged around a picture-perfect lake, the land beyond reclaimed with lush trees and vibrant green undergrowth. Must've been leaked to the media in advance of the announcement. I can't believe it. What's more, there's to be a lottery to be the first people in generations to live outside the dome. I minimize the rest for later.

I've always wanted to see outside, but my excitement dims. "I suppose we're ineligible for the lottery thanks to Aventine."

Dash shrugs. "Yes, but do you really want to go out there? Vesa's still an experiment, and experiments can go wrong. I'll wait until it's officially declared safe, thank you very much."

"We're going to change things up this afternoon," Tahir says, grinning as he ushers me toward the exit. With a pang, I realize I haven't passed through this door since my arrival at headquarters almost a week ago.

A week since I was forced to sever my connections with my friends and family. A week since I talked with Rik. A week to get used to the idea that Emery Olivia Driscoll's better off dead.

The last few days spent cloistered at HQ, I had almost managed to push that out of my mind thanks to the relentless barrage of experience modules. But to walk the concourses of New Worth again as a stranger? Knowing they're out there, grieving the old me? I have to draw on every scrap of strength I have left as the Understory settles over me, familiar and foreign at the same time.

Tahir said I'd be a different person when I passed back through the doors, and he's not wrong. He glances back at me. The connection's muted between us, but I have the distinct impression he's eager to get started. That makes one of us. "We're going to sit in on an actual courier job."

I perk up slightly at that as Tahir leads me away from Fountain Center, down a tight connecting walkway. Stragglers from the morning rush scurry past. The walkway opens onto a larger concourse with a bank of lifts a few shopfronts away. We queue up, the line taking us past a small cafe, which must be doing all right given its proximity to the elevators. Rent's often higher the closer a building is to the lifts. That holds true even in the Terrestrial District, where upward mobility's too often more myth than reality.

He taps his temple. <<Your map's only as good as the assumptions you bring to it. You'll find yourself in situations where it's impractical to consult it. Times when you need to make a split-second decision. Remembering this pattern will help you.<<

He sends me an image of a fractal built on a series of interconnecting crosses. <<The walkways and concourses are largely based on fractal architecture, at least here in the Understory and the Canopy. Routes through the Terrestrial District are too often tied to the pre-dome architecture, in comparison.<<

>>Huh. I never realized that.>> My eyes cross slightly as I look out over the concourse so I don't get too caught up on the details. Now that he mentions it, there *is* a pattern to the branching walkways. At the College of New Worth, I was trained in dozens of different ways of organizing and visualizing data, and yet I've been blind to what's right in front of me.

<<Learn to look beyond your surroundings to the structure underneath. Once you internalize the pattern, you'll be able to anticipate where to go. Your implant can be a huge resource, but if you become too reliant on its features, it can also slow you down.<<

>>Like waiting to pull up my implant's map instead of making a reasonable guess where to go?>>

He nods. <<The Law of Digital Recency. Our over-reliance on digital tools to navigate our environment makes it all too easy to discount physical cues, even common sense.<<

At his words, the hushed crowds of the Understory drifting past us have new meaning. Practically everyone's preoccupied with their implants, synch chatting, messaging, navigating the feeds. I remember my mother telling me about a group of people who walked off the edge of a concourse like lemmings when I first got outfitted with my implant. They were so caught up in their own worlds, they were simply following after one another without realizing the danger. Mom taught me how to set up navigation filters to prevent that from happening to me, even though there was little risk of falling in the Terrestrial District. But even then, she was hoping for loftier prospects for our family.

>>You make it sound like everyone with an implant is a walking zombie.>>

<<Implants are wonderful things, make no mistake, but they do change how one interacts with the world in a fundamental way. One you sometimes need to guard against.<<

We file into the next available lift and arrange ourselves amongst the other business types heading up. <<You're turning something over in your mind.<< I give him a sharp look like I always do when the perception he no doubt honed as a detective rears its head. He taps his temple. <<Sorry. I can feel a slight churn across the line.<<

I debate what to say. At this point he knows more about me than anyone else in my life. From what happened to me in the Terrestrial District to the calibrated connection linking us together, even with the limitations I've placed upon it. It should make me angry how quickly I've grown accustomed to interacting with him.

>>It's just I've never felt hindered by my implant. It's enhanced my life in so many ways…>> My parents could send me a hug any time of day, no matter how far apart we were. Being able to synch chat with my friends made me feel connected in a way that simply wasn't possible before I got my implant. I felt less alone, my daily life enriched and reinforced through our shared experiences. And all that's before factoring in my connection with Rik.

Tahir's quiet a moment. <<Tell me, did you recognize that woman who got off a level ago?<<

>>What? No. She was just some random girl.>>

<<Was she?<<

There's something infuriatingly blasé about his tone that has me pulling up my implant's cache and taking another look at a pretty Asian woman close to my age. >>I don't recognize her.>>

<<She's Christa Phan, enrolled at the College of New Worth, graduated a year ahead of you.<<

The name combined with the face eventually jogs my memory. We never had any classes together, but her dorm was on the same floor as mine. We were just scenery in each other's lives. Before Aventine wiped my implant, it held an accounting of the other college students, tagging their signals so I'd be able to recognize them as such if I ever ran into them outside of school. With those linkages now destroyed, with just my memory to go on, Christa may as well not exist to me.

>>You took me this way on purpose.>>

Tahir neither confirms nor denies it, just fusses with his gloves as the lift comes to a stop, people filing on and off. <<Just remember that you, with or without your implant, aren't infallible.<<

Aventine's certainly taught me that, in more ways than one.

We travel up three more levels, still firmly in the Understory. I start slightly when Tahir walks toward Del Floria's, a sedate drycleaners in the middle of an unassuming strip of shops and offices. With their fabric recycler out of commission, business must be slow given the popularity of one-use printed clothing and the ability to incorporate the latest trends into an outfit instantly.

A bored clerk waves us toward a door past the recycler's dark screen and behind the rotating racks, half full with high-end business wear.

"A drycleaners needs our services?"

Tahir shakes his head. "We maintain locations like this around the city in case clients want to do data drops off-site. You may also find yourself at one of these locations for scrubbing following data transfers if the client requires it."

The room beyond the cleaners has a hemocryption kit splayed out along a long counter running across the back wall. K, who I haven't talked to since our sparring session, looks up from where she's spinning round and round in a desk chair. She puts her foot down, and the chair jerks to a stop at our entrance. "You're looking a lot better," she says.

The curdle wasn't my fault, but my face still heats at the memory of such weakness. "No kidding." She's a couple of years ahead of me, but at this point, blood must not even faze her.

"The client's come and gone?" Tahir asks. At K's nod, he continues. "Good. K's going to have a thirty-second head start when she leaves here to go wherever the client has instructed her for the drop. M, your job is to keep up as she travels through the city." He gives K a wink. "You know the drill. See if you can throw her off your trail before you reach the rendezvous for the data transfer."

K's wide grin is almost predatory. "Sure thing."

"That's all I have to do?" I ask.

Tahir can't quite hold back his chuckle. "You'll have plenty to occupy yourself with for the next few hours."

I receive a synch request from a signal I don't recognize. K waggles her brows at me, and I let it through. <<Don't worry.<< An approximation of her voice runs through me. <<If you get too far off course, I'll give you a hint.<<

Tahir and I follow K back to the front entrance of the cleaners. He stops me with a hand on my shoulder, and we both watch as she effortlessly merges into a cluster of businessmen and women.

"Memorize the precise shade of her hair."

I keep my eyes glued to K's back as she gets further and further away. "That's it? That's the only hint you're going to give me?"

"She must avoid attracting attention in the spaces she moves through. As should you, but there are ways to use that to your advantage." He presses his lips together, and I know that's all I'll get out of him.

He holds out his hand, counting down. Anticipation twines through me. Three, two... one. At his nod, I step out onto the concourse and open up my connection to K.

>>Ready or not, here I come.>>

CHAPTER NINE

A flash of copper-colored hair in the periphery of my vision is my only warning K has veered off the concourse and onto an intersecting walkway. My heart rate ticks upward as I move to follow. Two women holding hands stroll along, blocking my way forward. Come on, come on… When they don't give way after a few moments of dogged tailgating, I give up on politeness and finally squeeze past them, ignoring the dirty look the woman on the left flashes me.

I won't let them be the reason I can't keep up with K. My pride's on the line. How many arcade missions have I played where I had to follow someone? Scrappers, too, in real life? This is no different, but I should know by now nothing's straightforward where Aventine's concerned.

In the central Understory, concourses radiate out from Fountain Center, with tighter walkways that function as connective tissue. They aren't always straight or evenly spaced, but they get the job done. Unless of course your job is following someone down them. Then you're screwed.

Tahir's fractal cross flashes to life in my mind. Even though there's supposed to be a pattern, it's a lot more wild and woolly in practice with all the branching possibilities. Already, the strain of speedwalking twinges in the tops of my calves. But the rest of me hasn't been this alert – this alive – in forever as I struggle to keep K in visual range.

She glances back once. With my ocular boost, I see her wink before a stocky man shields her from view.

<<How did they find you?<< K asks.

>>If you're trying to distract me, it won't work.>>

Her laugh shivers across our connection. That she's allowing me access to her nonverbals suggests she wants an honest interaction, but my competitive streak keeps me cautious. This whole thing might feel like a game, but with Aventine keeping score I can't let down my guard.

<<You don't have to answer. Just thought it would be good to get to know one another since we still have a ways to go.<<

I bite my lip. I've closed some of the distance between us, but then again, her progress through the Understory has been pretty straightforward so far. What happens when she decides to really make me work for it? Still, it can't hurt to have someone to talk to who isn't Tahir for a change.

>>Witnessed a crime,>> I finally answer. >>You?>>

<<Arrested for an attack on a classmate back in middle school. Didn't do it, but the group of girls I was running with were trouble. Shoplifting, vandalism, you name it. But not battery. DNA evidence cleared me.<<

>>But it didn't keep you safe from Aventine.>>

She's quiet at the bitterness in my voice. That, or she's deciding her next move at the upcoming intersection. Right will turn us back toward the drycleaners. I can't imagine she'd go that way, given how often Tahir harps on efficiency. So it must be left, taking us further away from Fountain Center, toward the outer edge of the northeast sector of the city. From there, she could take the lifts, or maybe the client's in one of the corporate plazas along the way.

I lengthen my stride slightly. Don't want to miss which direction she actually chooses.

<<It's not so bad, you know.<<

>>I'm withholding judgment for the time being.>>

I crane my neck to see over the eddying crowds that always pop up at intersections. The food carts and shopping stands don't help. A woman with bright red hair scurries left, but after zooming in on her, I realize she's not K. Too many freckles, hair more carrot than copper. Frantically, I quicken my steps. Did she turn right then? Does taking the most efficient route go out the window if you're being followed?

The concourse opens up, but even more people bustle along the wider corridor that cuts through the heart of two buildings ahead. Finally, I spy K's copper hair working against the current on the left-hand side of the concourse. I haven't lost her, but why is she backtracking?

With an eyecast command, I pull up my map of New Worth, translucent enough to still see where I'm going. Nothing on this level stands out as a potential destination. But just as I scroll to the level below this one, a slight rumbling *whoosh* shakes the concourse. Just for a few seconds, but it's enough for me to put it all together: a maglev station must be below us.

Across the way, K makes a beeline towards a stairway. My map displays the train's realtime schedule as K disappears down the stairs. Crap. Train's leaving in three minutes.

I zag left to avoid a family unit, then zig between two clerks guiding their automated hand carts loaded down with packages. Their swears chase me to the stairway. Holding onto the railing for dear life, I charge down them, trying very hard not to remember what it feels like to sprain my ankle.

<<Still with me, M?<<

>>Gloating doesn't become you.>>

She's still laughing by the time I reach the bottom and rush toward the queue of laggards hoping to board in time. K passes through the security gate and turns back, taking only a second to locate me in the line. She flashes me a smile, then boards the train, all cool confidence. <<Clock's a'ticking.<<

I don't answer as the line moves forward, quickly, but not quickly enough for my nerves. As the gate creeps closer, I remember all the modifications and changes to my implant. This will be the first time I put them to the test. My palms itch as the fabric of my gloves absorbs the extra moisture there. What if it doesn't work?

<<You should see your face right now.<<

I grit my teeth. >>It's not funny. What if I can't board?>>

<<Relax. Look around you. Four security gates and only one guard in a booth at the very end of the platform. He's not looking at individual boarders. He only cares about his digital readout first, then chastising the occasional troublemaker who doesn't queue up properly second. A very distant second.<<

The man in front of me moves through the gate. It flashes green as he heads toward the maglev. My turn. Time slows to a crawl as I wait for the gate to cycle to green. When it finally does, I practically run to the train.

||| Thank you for traveling on the New Worth Magna-Rail. One ride has been deducted from your account, Ms Ana Gonzalez. Have a nice day. |||

Ana, huh? At least at this particular moment in time. My body limp with relief, I grab the first seat I can find. K's not in this carriage, but I can see the back of her head in the next one through the glass.

<<See, what did I tell you?<< she says, breezily.

>>I didn't realize I'd be putting all my new gear to the test today.>>

<<Well, if it's any consolation, I tripped the system my first time up against New Worth security.<<

>>What happened?>>

<<The guard told me to step out of line, that my account was non-compliant, and would I please see a bank at the earliest opportunity.<< She's quiet a moment. <<Turned out to be a configuration error, easily fixed.<<

The train doors close, and it glides out of the station, quickly picking up speed along the rails mounted to the sides of buildings. With a slight lurch of my stomach I realize we're descending. I was so frantic to keep up with K, I didn't even notice our direction when I boarded.

>>So what do I call you?>>

<<I go by Kat.<< She practically preens. <<You've done good so far, but I won't go easy on you when we get off.<<

>>You think you can shake me?>>

<<Positive. But don't worry. When, not *if*, you get lost, just ping me with your location. I'll find you after I make the drop. We'll get something to eat on our way back to HQ, OK?<<

For a moment, I wonder if she's just as lonely as I am. >>Sounds good. But you won't lose me.>>

She laughs, not unkindly. <<Famous last words, M.<<

She leaves me alone after that, and I split my time between watching the city slide past my window and keeping an eye on Kat so I'll know when she gets off. The train makes alternating half circles as we spiral down the sides of the dome, only to straighten out as we bisect the city. Stations located along the diameter are often carved right out of the sides of the buildings that happen to be in the way.

Finally, we reach Ashton Depot, the last stop in the Understory, before the train continues into the Terrestrial District. Mentally, I will Kat to get off here. She stands, and I do too, working my way closer to the end of the carriage. She doesn't turn around, but something about her stiff posture makes me wonder if she knows the only things separating me from her are the double doors between carriages. She falls in behind a cluster of other people waiting to disembark. Just as I'm about to get off, she continues past the exit and up the aisle. She takes a backwards-facing seat where she can smirk at me.

The man curses behind me as I push myself out of line and find another seat of my own. >>Nice try.>> I realize I'm grinning, so focused on winning this little game with Kat, it's easier to overlook how I came to work for Aventine in the first place.

She shrugs. <<You won't believe how many others fall for that.<<

>>So we're heading into the Terrestrial District then?>>

For a moment I wonder if she'll answer, then I catch her nod, slightly distorted through the glass. Part of me's annoyed I have to go back down there. The rest's grateful for the change of pace, even though I had to leave Emery Driscoll back at HQ.

The train slows to a stop at Randolph's Corner, an elevated station near the heart of the Terrestrial District. Kat remains seated as the doors open. Passengers clamber on and off, Kat blocked from view. When the aisles clear, she's vanished from her seat.

No. Can't lose her now. I jump up and force myself through the doors just as they start to slide shut.

"Doors are closing. Please stand clear. Doors are..."

The automated voice fades as I find myself surrounded by people milling around the platform, Kat's copper locks nowhere in sight. A woman struggles to wrangle her two kids toward the security gate. A trio of teens pushes through the crowd, insulting everyone in loud, braying voices about their clothes, their connectivity, their cluelessness. But only a few barbs hit home since too many people are using their implants to block out the ambient noise. That or they know better than to engage Disconnects en masse, given the tensions of late.

The lifts and train stations are actually the most dangerous places in the Terrestrial District – pinch points where so many people are trying to get through, no one notices someone who's there one second and gone the next.

It cuts both ways down here.

The old claustrophobia rises up, swamping me with unwanted sensory impressions, but I fight it back, searching for Kat in the crush. Just have to rewrite my reactions to… how did Tahir phrase it? *Less-than-agreeable stimuli*. But that's easier said than done.

The government keeps saying it wants to reinvigorate the Terrestrial District, that the city can only thrive with strong roots, but I see no evidence anything's been done besides maybe a few extra trash bots dutifully navigating the crowds. I'm nearly ready to call it when I spy Kat on the other end of the platform, pushing her way past folks content to merely stand as the escalator rolls down to the next floor. Across from me, a set of stairs is cordoned off for maintenance. How much maintenance can they really need?

Arcade games always rewarded aggressive, out-of-the-box solutions. Aventine's the same way, considering how they select potential couriers. The stairs it is. Reluctantly, I let go of my glimpse of Kat, hop the barrier, and hit them at a sprint, something I've been practicing in my parkour sessions. At the landing halfway between this floor and the next, orange cones are set out where the grating's been removed to get at the pipes underneath.

I'm going fast enough that a hard stop will do more harm than good. But the hole beckons. Too wide to jump easily. Deep enough to break something if I guess wrong.

I lunge toward the railing, barely clearing it before I pull my knees into my chest. I slide down the rest of the way along the polished metal banister, finally reaching the bottom no worse for wear except for the few seconds it takes me to regain my sea legs.

On my right, Kat flashes past, heading for the Promenade. If I don't catch up to her now, I won't have a chance in the seething afternoon crowds. Kids killing time after school, shift workers just finishing up for the day, and everyone else with the misfortune to get caught up in the crush.

All the techniques Tahir's drilled into me for navigating crowds don't really work at peak times in the Terrestrial District. There are too many people trapped down here for me to make headway in polite, orderly fashion. As much as I hate it, there's no way to avoid being touched. Gotta go on the offensive. I whip out my elbows, shouldering my way through like a linebacker, uncaring who I have to squeeze past. At least down here, this kind of behavior goes with the territory.

Jostling past two matrons clutching their purchases to their chests, I see Kat up ahead and her brief glance over her shoulder to locate me. A burst of adrenaline floods my body. All my arcade-honed instincts scream. She must be getting close to the drop. I can't afford any more mistakes. She stays ahead of me as we wade into the crowds along the Promenade. One second I have her locked in my ocular booster's sights, then she's gone and no amount of craning my neck changes that.

Frantically, I scan the thoroughfare. So many people… then I see a flash of copper fleeing toward a tight alley ahead on my right. I let the crowd buffet me along, bringing me close enough for me to break through the bodies, ricocheting like a ping-pong ball.

In the sudden quiet of the alley, there's no Kat. Just a dumpster set against the exterior wall of a pizza parlor. Where…

I pull up my map. A dead end. The bricked-off wall's very real under my hands. Kat's long gone. Along with any chance of possibly catching up.

I failed. What if this delays my training? Or worse. What if I'm stuck down here thanks to my poor performance? I clutch my forehead.

<<M?<< Tahir's voice breaks through. <<What's wrong? Your vitals are fluctuating.<<

>>I'm OK. I …>>

I swing back toward the crowd shuttling past. It's too much. Too many people. Too many smells, so horrid yet achingly familiar at the same time. I want to crawl inside myself and disappear.

<<Take a minute. Breathe, M. Breathe.<<

My back's against the wall of the pizza parlor. I put my head between my knees and breathe in through my nose, out through my mouth, desperately trying not to choke on the smells of freshly baked pizza dough. >>Sorry. Just light-headed.>>

<<Liar. You were enjoying yourself up until now. What changed?<<

I was, but I'm so not dealing with this right now. >>If you hadn't interrupted, I might've had a chance to catch K.>> Another lie, but I don't care.

Tahir's quiet. Either unwilling to call bullshit or unable to without more proof. <<She'll be back in an hour's time, maybe less. Wait for her across the street. The diner there carries a nice chamomile blend. Drink some.<<

Across the way, the twenty-four hour diner beckons in the semi-darkness like a beacon in the everlasting night of the Terrestrial District. I push off the wall, glad to feel something other than panic, even if it's fury at Tahir. >>Is that an order?>>

A burst of annoyance jumps across the connection before he can battle it back. Like static quickly squelched. <<A suggestion only. But a good one.<<

>>I'll consider it.>> Then I disconnect from him entirely.

I'm on my second pot of tea when Kat wrenches my stool around to face her. "There you are. Still feeling sorry for yourself?"

I shrug. "You got away fair and square."

The lavender chamomile *did* take the edge off, not that I'd ever tell Tahir that. The aching pressure on my chest eased up after just a few sips, the cold paranoia in my gut vanquished after the first pot. A second steep seemed to be in order to motivate me for the walk back to HQ.

She smirks. "Not exactly. Come on. I'll show you."

I follow her out of the diner. The crowds have eased a bit, losing some of the frantic energy from before, as we cross the thoroughfare and enter the alley she vanished from earlier. She gestures to the grimy walls and the boarded-over windows. "You've only been with us, what, a week? What do you see?"

I clamp down on my wayward mouth before I say something I can't take back. Why does every damn thing with Aventine have to be a teachable moment?

Her eyes flutter with an eyecast command, and a moment later she sends me a zoomed-in map of the alley with a small rectangle highlighted on one of the walls. Squinting, I cycle between the map and my normal sight, struggling to find the exact spot. "What is it?"

"A door." She waves me closer, toward a section of wall. "These maintenance corridors are all over New Worth. Supposed to blend into their surroundings for aesthetic reasons," she says with a roll of her eyes, "but they come in handy if you know where to look."

The door opens, revealing a tight corridor of cement-block construction, ancient cleaning bots charging against a powerstrip running along one wall.

Kat taps her temple. "Aventine can override the door security and," she points to the end of the corridor and the other door there, "most of them cut through city blocks or levels if you need to switch things up in a hurry."

"Huh." I never really thought about how the city of New Worth kept things clean – all I know is they try a hell of a lot harder the higher up you go.

She closes the hatch. "So cheer up. I almost didn't have enough time to secrete myself away in here before you caught up to me."

I feel slightly better at that and Kat's friendly smile. "But the hatches don't show up on my map."

"They will. Once Tahir's satisfied with your grasp of the city's geography, you'll move on to these types of shortcuts and receive an updated map as well."

The two of us retrace our steps back toward the train station. "I know a place near headquarters that has the best spring rolls in the Understory. Winner buys on these little excursions," Kat says, "so, my treat."

"That sounds gr..."

I trail off at the sight of a large group of people marching toward the train platform. Their voices follow. "Don't Cut Out the Disconnects" and "New Worth Isn't Worth It" reverberate off metal and concrete. The teens I saw earlier are in the thick of the protest, thumping their chests and shouting to the Understory.

"Just another Disconnect demonstration," Kat says with an exasperated sigh. "Nothing to worry about."

My steps slow at the raw anger reflected on the protestors' faces. A team of reporters is already capturing the rally for the next update of the news feeds. With so many people with implants and the ability to share what's going on instantaneously, true breaking news can get lost in all the noise on the New Worth network. That leaves the outlets to weed through the digital morass, vetting the stories that are really newsworthy for the general public.

A black reporter gestures to the seething crowd behind her, her flawless dress gloves hitting just above the elbow. A New Worth News press badge swings from her graceful neck like a medal.

A lump fills my throat at the thought of Brita. I still feel bad I didn't have a chance to talk to her after the party before Aventine disconnected us, abandoning her so soon after her father's refusal to let her work at New Worth News. But I tell myself I wouldn't be able to help her from the Terrestrial District. With her goals of becoming a reporter, she'd be risking too much to associate with me, marred by scandal. Disappearing's the only way I could help her, as much as I hate to admit it.

Kat watches my face. "What's wrong?"

"Nothing."

"Come on." She directs us toward the far side of the platform, away from the Disconnect demonstration.

I bite my lip. Give the Disconnects their space, and nine times out of ten they'll leave you alone. Live and let live. But I don't think that's the case today. >>I've never seen them this angry.>>

Kat glances over at the protestors once more. <<True, though they've been getting angrier and angrier the last couple of months. Maybe the latest broadcast about Emergence spooked them.<<

For years, they've spoken out against the discrimination they've faced. The more militant ones have always advocated leaving New Worth and starting over, away from the high-tech city, despite the unfeasibility of living outside the dome. But now that Emergence is here, suddenly their renewed anger makes sense. >>*They* want to be the ones to go. The Vesa trial.>>

Kat nods. It's no secret Disconnects have been disproportionately forced into the jobs to help return the land to its former glory. High-risk, disposable positions. For people who shunned the New Worth network or had it taken away. The unspoken assumption that they aren't fit for anything else.

>>They think they've earned Emergence for the rest of us. But what about the decades of scientific research and engineering that have made it possible?>>

She shrugs. <<Well, if you went through years of backbreaking labor to bring about Emergence, how would you feel?<<

CHAPTER TEN

Kat nearly moans at her first bite of spring roll. "Now *that's* what I'm talking about. So many places trick you with exotic proteins but forget the most fundamental part – the fresh mint leaves that turn an ordinary roll into a transcendent one."

I dunk mine in the accompanying peanut sauce, with the perfect balance of spice and crunchy nuts.

Kat licks the remains of the translucent wrapper from her fingers and sighs happily. "If I could, I'd get a whole entrée of them, but the pho here is pretty good too."

"You like working for Aventine?" I ask, as we wait for the rest of our order.

She nods. "I do. I get to see all the different parts of the city. The work's constantly changing but… how to describe it…" She plunks her elbows on the table. "Regardless of how straightforward a job is, I still get an illicit thrill out of it all, carrying secrets through the city."

I get it. The exhilaration of making a successful drop, with no one the wiser, too wrapped up in their own concerns, clueless of the larger world around them. A rush I've only found in an arcade game. I take a sip of my iced tea. "But don't you miss your old life? Friends? Family?"

"Parts of it, yeah, but I like working for Aventine more. Giving up my identity was worth it for me. Digitally, I may be a ghost, but I got permission to synch with my dads, which helps."

That would be something. If I've learned anything this week it's that it's not healthy for me to stew in the relative silence of my head. My friends, family… I'll do almost anything Aventine asks of me to have those connections restored. But they already think I'm dead. Could they forgive me for putting them through this?

Kat looks thoughtful a moment. "It's OK to grieve, you know. We've all been through it. You don't have to act tough all the time."

The lump in my throat is back. "That's the only way I know how to cope." By forcing everything deep down where it won't interfere.

The expression on her face has me gritting my teeth. Brita looked the same way when I finally told her the story behind the scar on my neck. "You're not alone as you go through this process," Kat says.

But I am. "There's not a minute that goes by where I'm not reminded of what I've lost."

Memories, like shrapnel, lodged in my mind, ready to rend at a moment's notice. Yesterday, scrolling through my apartment's wallscreen settings, I came across the ocean channel my parents favored for their holoblinds. I had to change it to a mist-shrouded forest before I lost it. Hell, just seeing one of the training room projections that had dark brown hair like Randall was enough to send me over the edge. Because thoughts of him inevitably lead back to Rik.

And that's something I can't handle right now. Perhaps that's a sign I'm better off leaving things as they are. It's certainly easier that way, for everyone who's not me.

The waiter brings us the rest of our meal. A steaming bowl of pho for Kat, and a faux-pork and vermicelli dish for me.

She takes her time mixing in sprouts, cilantro, jalapeños,

and enough hot sauce to make my eyes water before she's satisfied with the flavor of the broth. Then she stabs her spoon toward me. "So who'd you leave behind that's making you so miserable? I'm betting it's not your parents."

A bitter laugh escapes me. "Not exactly."

Kat taps her temple. "What about up here?"

I stare at my plate. "I was considering calibration with someone before all... this happened."

I want nothing more than to synch with Rik, for him to reassure me that I'm still *me*. Without him or Brita around, I fear I'm losing a bit of Emery every day. Aventine's determined to chip away at the letters of my identity until only M the courier is left.

Kat slurps at her pho for a long moment, then sets down her spoon, frowning slightly. "Well, confidants are tricky. Cache got permission for someone on the outside, but she really had to work for it. That's why Aventine likes to get us while we're young and unattached."

She's quiet a moment while I half-heartedly push noodles around my plate with plastic chopsticks. "I know you're still getting used to everything, but," she leans in, "some would say we lucked out. Even with the sacrifices Aventine requires, you have to admit we have it better than most people. You were in the Terrestrial District today. You know what the alternative is."

I do, but at least I'd have my friends, my family. At least I'd have Rik. I used to think I could face anything with him in the back of my mind. Now, I have to figure out who I am without him.

The following morning, Tahir has filled the whole training room with doors. Locked doors, each frame mounted on rollers.

Armed with a standard-issue pick kit and the techniques

I learned from one of the training modules, I'm tasked with undoing all manner of locks. Some snap open after a few seconds, others need to be coaxed by my pick and cajoled by my torque wrench into giving up their secrets. And the last one seems determined to withstand every trick I throw at it.

Tahir hovers over my shoulder. "Picking locks is a defensive measure only. You're a courier, not a criminal, but this skill can come in handy should you find yourself in a situation where you need to, shall we say, make your own path."

"Got it." I hold the pick between my teeth as I give the doorknob a hard yank. Still nothing. Damn.

Tahir puts his hand on my shoulder. "That's enough, M. Let me show you something."

With a blink, he sends me an updated map of New Worth. Aventine requires all their couriers to run a local copy on their implants, supposedly more reliable than the New Worth network – subjected to outages, traffic slowdowns, corruption, and intrusions. "You remember the maintenance access point K used to elude you yesterday?" How could I forget? "This version includes all maintenance hatches and utility right-of-ways across New Worth. We have an... arrangement that provides our couriers access to these spaces."

He gestures to the lock I've spent the better part of an hour trying to break. "Aventine worked with the city to get these locks installed on most maintenance portals. Largely tamperresistant tubular design with a small receiver unit embedded inside." He flares out his hands, outlined by his ever-pristine gloves. "And the tip of your middle finger transmits the encrypted key."

He waves me back to the lock. "Now, try again."

I shake my head. "Have to get my gloves."

"Then what are these?" He snags my wrist and upturns my hand.

"They're *my* gloves." I pull away. This morning I woke up, wanting to wear something that was mine. Not bought and paid for by Aventine.

Tahir frowns. "The clothes we've provided all perform essential functions. You cannot pick and choose which elements to wear. What if you were on a job and needed the protection a maintenance hatch provides? What then?"

"I'll wear them next time, OK?"

Tahir shakes his head. Disappointed. Well, that makes two of us. "What's wrong?" he asks. "You've been rather subdued all morning."

I cross my arms, staring down the line of open doors. All leading back to Aventine.

"If this is about yesterday," Tahir continues, "no courier-in-training has managed to keep up with K. The fact that you stayed with her for so long–"

"It's not that. At least not wholly. But talking to her reminded me of how much I've lost. Ineligible for Emergence and dammed-if-I-do, dammed-if-I-don't, when it comes to reconnecting with my contacts. All so I can get paid to play hide and seek across the city."

"Ah. Well. If you are concerned about your parents, know they've recently secured quarters in the lower Canopy with funds we were able to disguise as death benefits."

I saw, thanks to the alerts I set up for all the people I care about. I'm tracking changes to just their public profiles since that's all I have access to now, but I tell myself that's better than constantly sending out search queries into the ether to appease my fragile, always-fluctuating emotions. Brita's status also changed a few days ago, indicating she's taken a position with the NW Signal – a respectable but small media outlet. Not what she wanted, I'm sure, but I'm glad she's not abandoning her dreams, given all that's happened. Rik's profile has remained the same. I didn't expect it to change, but it does reinforce just how meaningless a glimpse the profiles provide into someone's life.

"That *is* what you wanted for them?" Tahir prods.

"Yes, but–"

"You may grumble, and sometimes your attitude's truly appalling, but I know," he says, tapping his temple, "how well you've taken to the work. It's the perfect marriage of the arcade scenarios you love with many of the principles from your data curation program. Do you deny it?"

I can't. "But the cost–"

He sighs. "If you wish to reopen communication with some of your contacts, you must first secure approval from management once you are cleared for active duty." Which I'm not yet. "Keep in mind some people *think* they understand what it means to be connected with someone with a high-security clearance, but fail when they're put to the test." I'm suddenly aware of just how tightly controlled the sensations he's broadcasting across our connection have become. As in hardly any. "Sometimes it's... unfair to ask that of others."

His face remains inscrutable, his tone even, but the absence of anything else makes me wonder if he's speaking from personal experience. Dash said Tahir's background was in police work. I wonder if something happened to him, a case gone bad or a rough transition when he started working for Aventine. That would explain some things, but does me no good when it comes to Rik or anyone else from my old life.

"Now, as to Emergence," Tahir says, briskly, "it's true your arrangement with Aventine prevents participation in the trial."

"But Emergence changes everything, doesn't it?"

"You mean what happens if people begin moving out of the city before your contract is up?"

I nod.

"Regardless of how New Worth evolves, our services will still be needed. Data security must be maintained while the infrastructure's being built up. Besides, it'll take years of coordinated effort until developments like Vesa are truly independent of the city, even if the recent reports about the air quality and soil remediation efforts are accurate." He flashes me a boyish grin. "I know the idea of Emergence is exciting, but don't get your hopes up. I've lived through a couple of these announcements now, and nothing's changed. Life will still go on in New Worth and will continue to do so, even once the outside's habitable."

"But all that green beyond the dome cannot be denied."

"Maybe not, but it'll still be waiting for you once your contract's up. It's a few years before your time," he continues, "but you should read up on New Sacrament." That's a domed city in California. "They were so eager to push back outside despite the risks, they had too many people they couldn't support living outside the dome and not enough people *inside* to keep things up and running."

A situation that only got worse when they realized the land wasn't ready to sustain them.

Tahir shrugs. "Regardless of what the reports say, the City Council isn't going to let New Worth make the same mistake." I can feel him mentally shifting gears. Trading the lecture-y approach for one slightly more playful. "Now, if you'll indulge me, I have a surprise for you."

"Aventine doesn't have the greatest track record for those."

He chuckles. "This is *my* surprise, not Aventine's." He beckons me over to his side.

"And that's supposed to make it better?" But I still look over his shoulder, at the video he's queued up on his touchscreen.

I get a wave of something across the line, and his

amusement drops away. "I took the liberty of looking into your case."

That throws me, but only momentarily. "And?"

"I think I found him."

There's no question as to who he means. A tremor works through me. Not fear. Fury, along with a jolt of anticipation. "Show me."

Like magic, he pulls up the live feed of a cramped, crummy little apartment. Dimly lit, walls dirty with the patina of previous tenants, and hardware of all kinds scattered across every available surface. Then the male figure on the couch gets up and stretches his arms overhead with a jaw-cracking yawn. He's scruffier than I remember, gray peppering his stubble, lanky instead of the hulking monster he turned into in that alley. I don't know how Tahir managed it.

"That him?"

I can only nod.

Tahir goes completely still next to me. Synching. "Keep watching," he tells me distractedly.

I force myself to look upon the man who tried to steal my implant and ended up taking something even more valuable from me.

His head suddenly rears up, and a police officer bursts into his apartment. Another police officer follows, and in seconds my attacker is marched out of there in magnetic handcuffs.

Tahir studies my face. "I called in a couple of favors with some old associates of mine. Turns out he's wanted in almost a dozen cases. The combined sentences will put him away for a long time."

Tahir did all this for me?

"I can tell you his name, about his personal life..."

"No," I say with a shake of my head. "Not yet. I need time to process all this."

"Very well." His eyes close briefly. "I just sent you the sealed case file for you to look at when you're ready."

In truth, I'm not sure when that will be. Just knowing he's caught might be enough without having to dwell on the details of such a small, cruel man. I don't want to waste any more of my emotional bandwidth on him if I can help it. But at least I'll have Tahir's file to fall back on if I can't. I store it in one of my rarely accessed directories.

"What's wrong?" Tahir asks gently. "I thought this would please you."

"Oh, it does. Immensely. I cannot thank you enough for…" I wave at the now-dark screen. "How did you find him?"

"I wasn't half bad as a profiler before Aventine secured my services," he says with a selfdeprecating shrug. "In addition to courier oversight, I help identify potential candidates."

I shake my head. "I never had a choice, did I." Not if Tahir can close a years-old cold case in mere days.

A slight grimace contorts his face. "You always had a choice. Just not very good options."

For the next week, training sessions are interspersed with actual forays into the city. Sometimes I accompany other couriers on a job, learning by example. Other times, Tahir will assign me a destination, and I'll have to make it there before one of the other couriers catches up to me – in a reverse of my expedition with Kat.

The relentless pace of training nearly succeeds in drowning out the insistent voice in my head that the old Emery wouldn't abandon her friends or family so easily, regardless of the circumstances. But there's no denying my work for Aventine's an escape from my conscience. Just like my implant helped me escape from the realities of the Terrestrial District growing up.

A willful sort of blindness to cope with things out of my control.

Two days later, Tahir comes to my quarters bright and early. I don't bother to hide my scowl as I admit him. "What is it today? Sparring? Simulations?" More lies of omission for my own good?

He shakes his head, a slight tremor of anticipation vibrating along our connection. "No. Instead, you've been assigned your very first courier job."

"Oh."

"What's this? No sarcastic remark? No frowny face?"

"Give me time. It's still early."

Tahir chuckles and props himself on a bar stool. Our dynamic's grown easier since he helped tidy up my unfinished business in the Terrestrial District. If I doubted his commitment before, I don't now. "For your first mission, you'll be shepherding data for one of our government clients. The Department of Economic Development's main office is located in the Canopy, but the data drop's in the Terrestrial District."

The Terrestrial District again? It's been over a week since Kat and I went down there, but I'm not eager to return. Tahir gives me a knowing look. "Like blood, you need to get used to operating dirtside." Despite what most people in the upper levels think, most of the Terrestrial District's covered by concrete or asphalt. Only below that do you actually find dirt. "Aventine does not discriminate. We have clients operating out of every level of New Worth."

"They're too cheap to get a direct line between the physical sites?"

Tahir glances my way. "Do you have any idea how many permits would be required to run a dedicated cable from the Canopy to the Terrestrial District?"

"Not really."

"Well, it's expensive. Prohibitively so. The construction costs alone would be..." He shakes his head. "Not to mention the labor required to keep miles of line in good working order, secure from surveillance and vandalism."

"I get it. And I guess it doesn't make sense to invest in New Worth's infrastructure if the dome's going to come down anyway."

"That remains to be seen. The Vesa housing development won't be complete for another couple of weeks, and then its inhabitants need to live there independently for at least a year – though some are arguing for a longer trial period in keeping with the efforts of some of the other domed cities. As a result, the timeline for Emergence for everyone else is still yet-to-be-determined, with many adopting a wait-and-see attitude." He winks. "It also means business is booming."

Makes sense. We might have the ecosystem back in some semblance of working order, but without infrastructure – plumbing, power, communication networks – we'll be doomed before things even get underway. A government taskforce has started planning how to expedite the process, in secret of course, assuming Vesa succeeds.

And Aventine's on hand to facilitate communication between stakeholders.

But in a way, everyone is a stakeholder. Including the Disconnects who've gotten increasingly vocal since the announcement, fearing they're being left out of the process. Reports of pop-up demonstrations have become practically a daily occurrence as the lottery drawing creeps closer.

On our way out, we pick up the hemocrypt kit for today's job. Similar to the scrubbing kit, in convenient briefcase size. <<Our goal's to look like any number of New Worthians on our way to a business meeting in the Canopy.<<

I glance at Tahir out of the corner of my eye. >>Will you babysit me the whole way every time, or is today special?>>

A grin struggles against his otherwise sober expression. <<Today *is* special. I'll introduce you and ensure everything's all set for your first job. You'll be able to synch with me at any time, but otherwise I'll await your return to HQ afterwards.<<

>>I already know about the party. Kat let it slip the other day.>> She has made it her mission to get me up to speed on the more social aspects of Aventine.

He arches his brow. <<I see.<< Then he wags his index finger at me. <<Then you should know if you're late, you'll never hear the end of it from the other couriers.<<

We make our way to the lifts, queuing up behind other business types tapping their feet or endlessly adjusting their gloves as the different carriages fill up and launch skyward. Five minutes later we're ascending ourselves. My ears pop as we pass the levels for the Lower Canopy, then, as the lift reaches Level 10, Tahir indicates we're next. The middle levels of the Canopy are Corporate Central. Of course the Department of Economic Development would want to be located near the city's more successful businesses. Sliding doors off the concourse lead into the Department's modest atrium.

"We have an appointment," Tahir announces to the receptionist sitting behind a long console desk. She has light brown skin like me. An intricate set of braids frame her face. Most certainly mods but stylish ones. I feel drab in comparison with my hair simply brushed back from my face and my plain Aventine-issued clothes. All the better to blend in, I suppose. I can just imagine Brita's upturned nose at that.

"One moment, please," the receptionist says, even as her eyes roll back into her head, presumably an eyecast command to alert whoever's waiting for us that we're here. After a moment, she straightens. "Right this way."

>>Will it always be offices like this?>> The secretary takes us down a hallway, past doors with brass nametags, shut tight. Portraits of past department secretaries line the walls, each having served the city for a two-year term. My father always grumbled that wasn't time enough to do anything worthwhile once appointees got staffed up and fully briefed on their role and responsibilities. Maybe for the other parts of the city, but certainly not the lower levels.

<<In many cases, yes. But factories and warehouses are common as well.<<

>>And for clients above my clearance?>>

His stride falters a second. <<K *has* been telling tales. But to answer your question, nothing is out of bounds. It all depends on the client's needs.<<

Past an empty conference room, the hall terminates at another office for Joan Sheridan, aide to the secretary of Economic Development. The receptionist gives it a quick rap, and moments later the door swings open to admit us.

A fortyish white woman greets us. Sheridan must be a high-ranking aide considering the spacious office. Brittle blonde hair brushes her shoulders and an assessing glint lights up her blue eyes as she looks us over. "You must be with Aventine," she says in a nasally voice.

Tahir nods and gestures to the briefcase with a snap of his wrist and a flourish of his gloved fingers.

"Well, come on then." Unceremoniously, she clears a space on a small worktable adjacent to her desk. Tahir places the case on it. Inside, one half of the case is crammed full of processors. The other side's preloaded with a small pouch of my blood and the actual hemocrypt unit, which has a slot for data input from the client. The attached empty pouch will be filled with encrypted blood at the end of the process.

The blood I'll then have to inject into my body.

I feel her watching me as Tahir turns the unit on. He waves her forward, and she inserts a datakey into the slot preloaded with whatever info I'm supposed to transfer. With a chime and a chugging whoosh, the hemocryption gets underway.

"I have to prepare for a briefing for the secretary this afternoon," she says to Tahir, her tone resonant with command. "I'll be in the next room. Ping me before you leave."

"Of course," Tahir says.

Ten minutes later, the empty bag of blood is filled. My turn. Tahir gestures for me to take a seat. I'm suddenly glad Sheridan isn't here to witness this part. Doesn't seem to be the type to tolerate squeamishness or really any hint of incompetence. With a slow exhale, I push up my sleeve. Tahir fits the medical cuff around my right arm and lines up the injector to the needle slot.

I close my eyes. I've simulated this a dozen times. The way the cuff clips around my forearm, the brief pinch of pain as the needle finds my vein. The cold burn as the encoded blood fills me. After a minute, it's all over. The cuff disengages, and I unsteadily get out of the chair.

Tahir busies himself with putting the case to rights. "That should do it."

Sheridan returns and pockets the datakey she provided. With a nod to me, she sends me the address and location code for the drop, an apartment complex along the perimeter of the Terrestrial District. Clients can choose to keep my final destination a secret from Aventine if that makes them more comfortable. Security feature. But apparently that's not necessary for today's job.

"Got it. Anything else I need to know?" Both Tahir and the woman shake their heads. She taps her foot impatiently as Tahir bids her a good day. She shuts her door with a crisp snap behind us, eager to get on with the rest of her morning.

Tahir accompanies me back out to the concourse. "You know how to reach me."

"Right." Pushing down the sudden wave of nerves, I start down the walkway. If all goes well today, I'll join the ranks of active couriers. I'll also have to decide just how badly I want to reconnect with my friends and family. A question I keep cycling through on an infinite loop.

Risk. Reward. The selfish need to quash the bone-deep loneliness of an empty mind. The crushing guilt at the unforgivable pain I've already caused. And the queasy knowledge I'd do it all over again.

"M?" Tahir calls after me. "Don't be late."

CHAPTER ELEVEN

A half hour later, I'm waiting for a lift down to the Terrestrial District. Unlike the section I visited the other day with Kat, the apartment complex is located on the outskirts in a more industrialized area of town. Rougher crowd, too.

Even though I'm not thrilled at descending to terra firma, I have to remember I'm way better equipped to face it now than when I was actually living there. Evasion and defensive skills to scare off the street urchins, and clothing that'll zap anyone who wants to get too friendly with a young woman unescorted.

How bad can it be? But as the lift closes, and it travels downward, I wish Kat were making this trip with me. On the other side of the glass doors, the light wanes until it's nearly dark, leaving only the glow of the elevator's operating lights.

So long as I get past the crush at the base of the lifts, I'll be fine. Pinch points like this are prime targets of roving gangs. I'm used to the gauntlet though, and it helps that what I'm carrying is *inside* me, not something that can be easily stripped from my person. At least I don't scream victim like the two guys who got on the elevator with me in the Canopy. Looking for cheap thrills? Or maybe they just want to feel morally superior for a few minutes as they take in the local color. Either way, I'm pretty sure they've never seen dirt – the slight curl of their lips gives them away.

"Terrestrial District, Northwest Sector," the lift intones as the doors open.

I let the two gentlemen go ahead of me – anyone watching the lifts will see them as easy pickings. That's something Tahir taught me once. If you can't avoid attention, try to set up an unwitting decoy. Then I ease myself into the crowd, stick to the shadows, and don't make eye contact with anyone.

When I was tailing Kat, the Terrestrial District got in my head with an ease I never expected. Today, I'm better prepared for the memories clamoring for attention, along with the stench of too many bodies, frying oil, and sewage. Thanks to all my training, I'm more confident in how to handle myself. To evade, to defend, to hurt if I have to. A heady feeling I've yet to grow tired of.

Tahir's words come to mind, about rewriting my reactions to stimuli. Starting today, I vow. Most people pay me no mind as I travel past market stands selling secondhand goods and leftover produce. Past carts selling knockoff Canopy brands and greasy street foods. Troops of children, who should be in school but for some reason aren't, dart down the alleyways, all shrieks and laughter.

I can't remember a time when I was that carefree. Not down here.

The further out I go, the quieter the streets, the wider spread the street lamps. People are still out and about, but I can't expect them to step in and help a stranger if things get bad. Not that I'd blame them. Keep your head down and keep going is the Terrestrial District motto.

Despite all that, some businesses make a go of it down here – those with infrastructure tied to the land before the dome went up, or more often, manufacturing and engineering firms that would be unseemly in the upper levels of New Worth. In the distance, I can just make out the greenish glow from the windows of one of the city's vertical farms, reaching up into darkness. They often span dozens of levels to make distributing food more efficient. My parents' apartment used to face one of them, a stripe of windows running down its side. From our living room we could see the robotics shuttling back and forth as they harvested plants, and even the condensation of water vapor and nutrients that inevitably collected against the glass. The grow lights in the distance always helped me navigate to and from home before I got my implant.

But the familiar sight doesn't help my nerves as the streets get less crowded, checkpoints further apart, and rent-a-cops guarding storefronts increasingly visible. Concrete transitions to packed dirt. I forgot how different it feels underfoot. Solid, in a way concrete can't replicate.

Finally, I can make out the apartment complex in the gloaming. Well, more like a stylish capsule residence. But it looks like a ghost town at the moment. Empty storefronts on the ground floor wait to be leased out for essential services for the tenants. Surprising, given the demand for housing down here, even if it's a bit off the beaten path. A good twenty-minute walk to the lifts and even further for the trains.

Through the front gate and across a courtyard in desperate need of landscaping, I find the rental office. I'm swiftly ushered into a conference room by an unsmiling woman in a business suit way too nice for the lower levels. Probably thinks this job's beneath her in some way. Rik works down here too, but I can't imagine him acting like such a snob. Actually, it's probably better I don't imagine him at all.

A male technician of some sort has the scrubbing kit already laid out for me.

I take a deep breath. No one here needs to know this is my first job. I push up my left sleeve and fit the medical cuff over my arm. The tech carefully connects me to a modified scrubber unit. Unlike the one Tahir made me practice on, this one includes another piece of equipment that converts the data-encoded blood back into digital info they can access while I'm scrubbed. As the tech turns on the scrubbing unit, I try not to think too hard about the blood being pulled out of my body. At least it doesn't hurt – it feels like more the constant suction of a tiny drinking straw.

The woman moves to the tinted window overlooking the street, arms crossed, sentry-like in her silence. A few minutes later, the tech grunts, "First bit's decrypted. Should be in good shape."

The woman turns back to the table. "Excellent." She looks in my direction, somehow managing to avoid my eyes as if she wants as little to do with me as possible. Despite my training, I suppose some people will only see me as someone in the service industry. A very rare and expensive service, but a service nonetheless. "Once the scrubbing's complete, someone will come by to see you out."

Her lack of interest in me is mitigated by Tahir's approval as I report in. <<Congratulations, M. You're officially an Aventine courier now. Stay out of trouble, and we'll see you back at headquarters.<<

My stomach swoops as scrubbed blood loops back into my body. Now for the hard part – sitting quietly for an hour of hemodialysis. Thank goodness for implants.

I must've dozed off because I jump when the scrubbing unit chimes and automatically shuts off. The tech flashes me a smile before returning his attention to the data readout.

"Everything as it should be?"

He nods, and I happily disconnect myself from the machine. "You know your way out?" he asks.

"Yes, thanks."

I retrace my steps, eager to get back to HQ, but when I reach the courtyard hundreds of people have gathered in front of the complex. My implant's proximity sensor would've told me there was a concentration of signals so close, but this...

Then it hits me. Disconnects. Hundreds of them. Someone sees me and points. That can't be good. I turn on my heel and duck back inside. The woman in the suit's nowhere to be found, but the tech's where I left him in the conference room.

"Umm, did you know Disconnects have the entrance surrounded?"

He groans. "Again?"

"What do you mean, again?"

He gets up from the table, and I follow him down the hall. "Management refuses to lease to Disconnects. We can't afford to since they have a higher risk of defaulting on the rental agreements. This place needs seven years of full occupancy just to break even. So they've been picketing and harassing our residents and any potential renters that come this way."

"Not every Disconnect's a degenerate." They're hurting themselves by not renting to even the highly motivated ones who've found steady work despite not having implants. "Besides, this location isn't particularly desirable, even if it's brand new." Making it harder to recruit the type of renters they want.

"I know, but I don't make policy." He nods out the window, where the demonstrators are lined up. "We hoped all the updates would convince people to move out of some of the more central slums, but it hasn't happened yet. And the protesters have made it that much harder to get things up and running."

And probably why the complex has been working so closely with the Department of Economic Development. It isn't good form to get *too* curious about the clients we work for. Tahir always says curiosity killed the courier. As a result, our focus needs to be on completing a secure data transfer, not the reasons behind whatever secrets we're ferrying. But there's no rule forbidding me from using prior or freely available information.

"I usually just camp out down here until they leave," the tech says with a shrug.

"Well, *I* can't do that. Is there another way out?"

"Guess you could cut through the basement." He leads me to a flight of stairs and down a hallway scented with damp and construction dust. "Keep going, and you'll exit on the far side of the complex. Good luck."

When I reemerge on the street, no one's in the immediate vicinity as I dart down an intersecting alley. Voices from the crowd reach me in snatches: "Don't cut out the Disconnects" and "New Worthians no longer." The chants grow stronger with every footfall. Along with my resolve. I won't let this demonstration ruin my first courier mission for Aventine.

Ahead, the faceted bank of lifts resolves out of the gloomy distance. My escape valve to the Understory. But my relief's short-lived. An even larger group of protestors congregate there like a blood clot, the pressure growing as more of them pour into the street.

>>Tahir, I have a problem.>>

Immediately, his attention snaps to me. <<Location?<<

I tell him and take a few pics of the rally with my ocular boost. Already an animated exchange between one of the onlookers and a Disconnect has morphed into a shouting match. I don't want to be here when it graduates to shoves and punches.

Tahir curses to himself. The sudden jump in intensity across our connection a dead giveaway. <<The closest maglev station is on the other side of the demonstration.<<

>>You want me to hole up in a maintenance area?>> I open my map and start scanning.

He sighs. <<No. The nearest one's in the middle of that mob. You'll have to take the access stairs.<<

Immediately, my mind rebels. >>You're kidding.>>

<<I don't like it any better than you, but we don't have a lot of options.<< He sends me a new route through the Terrestrial District. <<Report your status every two minutes until you reach the Understory, clear?<<

>>Clear.>> There's no point in arguing. I can feel how closed off he's become, like a door slamming shut. Now it's just a matter of finding the old access stairs that connect levels, usually located near the lifts. The set Tahir's routed me to goes through a warehouse that transitions into an apartment building a few levels up. Mandated for public use, which means anyone can use them at any time.

Two minutes elapse. >>I'm coming up on them now.>> The warehouse comprises the whole block, the doors shut up tight. One of them has a placard that reads, "For public stairs, use south entrance."

I creep along the edge of the building, but luckily I haven't been followed. A rally this large will hit the feeds big time. Best to be gone before live coverage catches up. Empty hinges and a busted streetlamp herald the entrance to the access stairs. Only emergency lights at the base of each step illuminate the dark passage. At least I have my NAmp filter.

I climb. Any access to the warehouse has been closed off, the brick now covered in luminescent paint and old-school flyers. Sour air surrounds me, sweat and urine and something else I don't want to think too hard about.

Given the housing waitlists and the overcrowded shelters that have been carved out below ground, access stairs are often used as a temporary – or not so temporary – safe haven for people with no place else to go.

The police supposedly keep these spaces clear, and the first couple of levels are. But the further I climb, the more evidence of hard use increases. Trash heaps up in the corners. The walls have been busted open in places by people looking for wire and metal. A shift-working cop won't come this high unless they're in pursuit of a criminal. Heck, I've probably passed into a different precinct by now, and the homeless use that to their advantage.

>>Level 4 and climbing.>>

Tahir doesn't answer, but the prickle on the back of my neck tells me he's paying attention.

Cardboard and ragged burlap cover a still-sleeping figure huddled up in the corner of the landing on Level 5. They don't stir as I pass through, walking on the tips of my toes. I double-check my map. The warehouse turns into an apartment complex at Level 6. But when I reach the thankfully empty landing, there's no concourse access. The door's been chained shut. And unless Aventine installed bolt cutters in my hands, I won't be getting through.

<<What's wrong?<< Tahir asks.

>>Door's blocked on Level 6.>>

His focus veers from me momentarily. <<Looks like residents complained about the types of people the stairs attracted and got the complex to close them off,<< he responds a few seconds later. <<I'll file a complaint with the district, but in the meantime, keep climbing.<<

>>Lucky me.>>

The apartment complex goes up thirty more levels before the building gets divvied up into smaller offices and storefronts. It doesn't get difficult until I reach Level 15. My clothes have to work harder to keep me comfortable as I climb ever upward in the darkness. Definitely working a different set of muscles than I usually do powerwalking across the city.

Rats and cockroaches scuttle out of my way. Thighs burning, I climb the last flight of stairs. Any residual fear from the Disconnect rally has been thoroughly drained out of me. Ahead, a door beckons. I try the handle, but it doesn't budge. Well, shit.

I hunker down in front of the lock. Good. I should be able to override it with the small transmitter in the fingertip of my glove. Still nothing.

>>The door on Level 36 isn't responding to Aventine's auto-override.>> If I had to say the words out loud, they'd be between pants, but synching remains as fast as my thoughts. I send Tahir the lock's signal.

<<Stand by.<<

>>Don't mind me. I'm just breathing.>>

The door lock disengages a few seconds later. I barely hear it over my gasping for air.

<<We just secured permission to open that door. How's it on your end?<<

>>Unlocked.>> I walk through, relishing the fresh air that bathes my sweaty face. I emerge into a modest Understory neighborhood. People going about their business crowd the concourses, with no throngs of Disconnects in sight. >>Should be smooth sailing from here on out.>> I hope.

<<We expect you back in twenty.<<

>>Understood.>> I wend my way down the concourse, having already identified my route to the lifts. My thighs are jelly, and it's a struggle not to limp. >>So long as I don't pass out between here and there.>>

He grins. <<Perhaps we need to adjust your workout schedule. We'll start with upping the intensity of your parkour sessions...<<

>>No! Wait, that wasn't–>>

<<Twenty minutes, M,<< he says, back to business as usual.

Instead of a party, all that's waiting for me at headquarters is an impromptu all-hands meeting in a large conference room on the third floor. Many of the other couriers file in, though Bandit must still be in the middle of the job, based on his absence. Tahir's here, along with the other handlers, and Harding, grim and gloomy where he stands in the front of the room. In the far corner, I spy Diego as he surveys the room with his arms crossed. Haven't seen either of them since recruitment.

Once everyone's seated, Harding raises his hand for attention. "Thank you all for coming. Recent events have made it clear we need to update our security protocols."

Behind him, the wallscreen fires up. A bisected map of New Worth slowly rotates through the different strata of the city. Different areas are color-coded. The blue sections match the quarantine zones on my map where a highly contagious virus of some kind has swept through, given the close quarters. There are red and green areas as well, but I'm not sure what they're supposed to represent.

"We cannot afford to look the other way any longer. We've been aware of flash demonstrations throughout the city, but today," Harding's gaze comes to a rest on me, "M-37 was chased off course and forced into a less-than-optimal route back to headquarters."

Eyes flick my way, curiosity and speculation in turn. One of the couriers I haven't been introduced to yet wrinkles his nose. My hands clench. Do they think it was simply a rookie mistake?

Harding clears his throat. "Nonetheless, it was a successful drop, and M-37 will be joining the ranks of active couriers, effective immediately. But we cannot allow the Disconnects or anyone else to upset our work." He gestures to Diego. "As some of you have cause to know, Diego Martinez manages our support cells around the city."

They're the backup teams who assist couriers who get in over their heads or clean up the messes they leave behind. At least I didn't botch things up so badly today I needed one of his teams' help.

Diego nods to the room. "For starters, we've stepped up our

oversight presence." He turns to the wallscreen. "The green cells represent our current support teams' locations." He gestures to the handful of red cells on the map, the majority of them in the Understory and Terrestrial Districts. "The red represents new locations that'll be gearing up in the coming weeks. We'll be fast-tracking new recruits and taking on a few loaners from the government security force so we won't be spread too thin for you guys out there."

Harding crosses his arms. "Unfortunately there's no indication the Disconnects' unrest will be abating any time soon. During the demonstration, a localized power outage cascaded through the Canopy, suspected to be their doing. Because of the escalation in tactics, there are some procedural changes that'll go into effect immediately." He gestures to Tahir.

He faces the room, his expression devoid of any emotion. "Reporting in every ten minutes when you're on a job is now a requirement, regardless of how routine your situation."

The couriers groan. Tahir always says a boring job is a job well done. This extra reporting just makes more work for both the couriers and their handlers, who sometimes have concurrent jobs running at any one time.

"Certain routes and neighborhoods are now off-limits, primarily in the Terrestrial District," Tahir continues. "We'll be pushing out an update for your local maps sometime this evening. You'll have to go around these areas until further notice."

Surprise, surprise. A big chunk of the Terrestrial District I was in this morning is now rendered in yellow. Off-limits.

"We're also temporarily freezing approvals for outside contacts. The people you've already secured permission to communicate with won't be affected. This is for all pending and new requests. The unit who does our background checks has been reassigned to support the government as they monitor the situation." His gaze darts toward me briefly. <<Sorry, M. I know you were considering reconnecting with people from your old life, but–<<

A sudden stab of loss streaks through me. >>How convenient.>>

<<It was an order from high up. But as soon as the restrictions are lifted, we'll get whoever you want fast-tracked. No guarantee they'll get approved – the process is rather rigorous – but we do recognize how this particular security measure disproportionately affects you.<<

That's an understatement. I've only been agonizing over this ever since my implant was wiped. And now, when I'm finally in a position to start the process of reaching out to friends and family, it's yanked out of reach, reminding me once again I'm just a puppet dancing to the whims of Aventine.

Grimacing, Tahir returns his attention to the room. "Finally, given the political climate, keep your eyes open out there. Anything remotely suspicious needs to be reported to your handlers."

"What does that mean, specifically?" Dash asks.

Tahir makes a vague gesture with his hands. "Your collective knowledge of the city is formidable. You know what's normal and what's not. We just want you to be our eyes and ears out there."

Murmurs break out at such a significant expansion of our responsibilities. Fleet and Cache exchange a look, but I can't tell what they're thinking. Kat told me that because of all the difficulties in getting permission to have a confidant on the outside, Cache always toes the company line now. Fleet was in the same boat as me, wanting to help his family ascend from the lower levels. For him, Aventine has been a godsend. Can't imagine either of them speaking up now even if Aventine's new security protocols go above and beyond.

Harding pulls the focus back to him. "I've already pledged our support to the New Worth government. Any information you can provide related to the Disconnects and their movements throughout the city at this delicate time will be of interest to them. Your handlers will instruct you how to proceed if you find yourself in such a position, but in the meantime, stay focused on each data transfer as it comes."

He surveys the silent room, then he nods. "You're dismissed."

CHAPTER TWELVE

Our waiter drops off a round of liquor concoctions at the corner booth Kat, Dash, and I've taken over. There's no way we'd be able to get in here without a reservation at night, but a late lunch on Aventine's dime at the buzziest restaurant in the Understory is no problem.

"Sorry your celebration got sidelined by the meeting," Kat says, as Dash passes me a glass full of fizzy grapefruit liquid.

I take a sip and try not to wince. A bit too tart for my tastes. "Not a big deal." Supposedly everyone gets a party after their first job, some kind of courier rite of passage, but after the day I've had, it's just as well. As a consolation prize, Kat and Dash set up an approved excursion for the three of us.

"Still," Kat says, "we want you to feel welcome." She nudges Dash's shoulder. "After all, you're one of us now."

My head thumps against the back of the booth. "I'm just glad training's over." They exchange a look. "It's not?"

Dash shrugs. "There's way less of it, sure, but there's still plenty more to learn, depending on what mix of clients you get assigned."

Different types of data require different precautions, same with different industries, whether they're corporate clients or government units. Apparently the world of fashion's rather cutthroat at the moment, requiring couriers to take extra care. Priority or highly sensitive transactions often call for the more experienced couriers. Whether it's a routine or a one-off transaction can also influence assignments. Some companies want to deal with only one courier or set of couriers. Others want assignments randomized. I've even caught whispers of occasional jobs we've done for celebrities and prominent public figures.

"Don't worry. Tahir'll give you a break," Kat adds.

Dash chuckles. "He gave me a day off after my first job."

I turn to him as if seeing him for the first time. "Wait. You're one of Tahir's couriers too?"

He nods. Being calibrated with Tahir these past few weeks and getting the bulk of his attention as he's gotten me trained up, I have to remember he has obligations to people besides me. Looking at Dash and knowing he's just as close to Tahir as I am, maybe closer... It feels kinda weird. Like we're in competition with one another, when really we aren't. We just happen to share the same handler.

Kat tousles his hair. "Apparently Tahir's *very* particular about who he brings on." She aims a smile my way. "Maybe he and I have more in common than I thought if he picked both of you."

"Sounds like you two are more than just blink buddies..."

My words hang there as Kat darts a glance at Dash. His ears pinken slightly. "We became confidants last year."

"And Aventine's OK with that?" I ask.

Kat frowns slightly. "It's not explicitly forbidden and circumvents a lot of the issues of calibrating with someone on the outside."

"You mean like freezing all communication requests the second I'm eligible to make one?"

She winces. "Yeah. Shitty timing, I know."

The waiter brings over a large platter. Golden-fried potato and yucca straws drizzled with avocado crema and cheddar béchamel, all nestled on a bed of microgreens. Cilantro and chive stud the dish.

Kat waits for him to move off. "Now do you see why we brought you here?"

"An inappropriate carb chaser like this is verboten in the dining hall," Dash says, "and Finola has cracked down on what takeout gets brought into HQ."

The aromas curl into my nose, and my stomach growls. "But we're going to eat it anyway, right?"

"Oh, certainly. The doc will fuss over our nutrient levels for the next couple of days, but it'll be worth it." Kat takes a yucca straw and stabs it at the garnish of pea shoots, baby arugula, and frizzled kale. "Besides, it has *some* green in it."

As we dig in, the late lunchgoers trickle out. Our waiter's enthusiasm starts to wane as Kat and Dash order another round of drinks instead of the bill. "Have you thought about what we're supposed to call you?" Dash asks, nabbing the last potato straw and dredging it through some leftover crema.

"Uhh..."

"We can't just keep calling you M."

"Why not?" In truth, I'd prefer it.

Kat crosses her arms. "Because *everyone* gets a nickname. We're supposed to bestow them after a successful first job, but..."

"No party, no name," Dash finishes for her.

"It's really not a big deal."

"You can't be the only one without a nickname," Kat says.

"Doesn't bother me."

"That's not fair," she says with a pout. "*I* never wanted one either."

Dash pats her shoulder in mock-sympathy. "There, there. You'll get over it soon, I'm sure." Suddenly her cheeks burn redder than her hair, and she whirls toward him. Silently, they look at each other. He breaks off first, with the corner of his mouth tucked up, victory or amusement, I don't know.

When I reach the bottom of my cocktail, I'm ready to call it, stuffed full of decadent food and sleepy with drink. It doesn't help watching Kat and Dash pretend they aren't holding hands underneath the table when they totally are. I should be happy they can share so much of themselves without running afoul of Aventine's confidentiality requirements. But it just reminds me of what I've lost. Or rather, what I could've had without Aventine in my life. Even if Rik and I had calibrated at Brita's party, I still would have lost him – all of him – when Aventine wiped my implant.

Somehow that seems even worse, knowing exactly what I'd be giving up instead of the vague loss I feel now.

"I'll see you two back at headquarters."

Kat's attention snaps to me. "You don't have to go. We have the whole afternoon."

Pretty sure I do with the way Dash looks at her, by now too buzzed to moderate his expression. "It's OK. I'm pretty tired anyway." I get to my feet. "Thanks for today. I mean that."

Just before I exit the restaurant, I glance back at our table. They're already making out. I can be happy for them even when I'm annoyed at the same time, right?

People bustle through the Understory around me. What next? Approved excursions are good because Aventine selects an ID I can use for the day, usually one flush with credits and privileges. None of the anonymous user nonsense they threatened me with in the beginning. Retail therapy, entertainment, and apparently cuisine Aventine won't import.

Perhaps an arcade rec suite rental's in order. This time of day, it's only me and the hardcore, mind-scrambled regulars. Those addicted to the experience or with nothing better to do except submerge themselves into the digital spectrum and forget their worries. As I scan through my options, deliberately ignoring the icon for *Partners in Crime*, I have to force back my annoyance at not being able to pick up where I left off. BA – before Aventine – my arcade profile stored information and stats on my different avatars, progress through different games and dramatic scenarios.

But I've learned from this experience that it's less painful to start over with something new than to try to recreate what I had.

When I go down to the cafe for lunch the next day, a handful of couriers who haven't been sent out on assignment are already seated at the tables, chatting with one another. Almost imperceptibly, there's a short lag in the conversation as I cross the room. Grabbing the entrée salad I ordered ahead of time, I feel their eyes on me. Are they just sizing up the newest recruit? Or maybe they blame me for why half of us are benched for the day under the new security protocols Aventine's adopted.

I shake that thought off. I don't know what I could have done differently. Tahir even said so. I debate taking my suddenly unappealing salad back upstairs, but no, that would just mean I'd be in my room all alone. Rather pathetic all in all.

Dash and Bandit sit at a nearby table. They watch me with amused grins on their faces. At least it's not animosity. "What's going on?"

Dash leans back in his chair, arms crossed behind his head. "You tell me, M." Based on some things Kat has said, it sounds like he was a bit of a loner before signing on with Aventine. But now that he's among his own kind, so to speak, he's relished taking up the unofficial role of courier spokesperson.

"Just another day at Aventine," I say with a shrug. "Why?"

"Must not have gotten the good news yet," Bandit says with a smirk.

"What news?"

Dash just chuckles. "You got the short straw, newbie." He gives me a wink. "But it's nothing you can't handle."

Bandit gets to his feet. "Have fun on your walkabout," he says in a singsong voice on his way out of the room.

Walkabout? Another of Aventine's games? I stab my fork into my salad, skewering a slice of tomato.

Kat files in. "There you are," she says breathlessly. "I've been looking for you."

"What's with everyone lately?"

She exchanges a glance with Dash that has me grinding my teeth. "Have you spoken with Tahir yet?" Kat asks me.

I shake my head. "Should I?"

I'm just about to ping him when Dash says, "No. He'll be in touch soon, I'm sure."

"In touch about what? Everyone's being really weird today."

Kat fidgets with the edge of her glove. "It's just that–"

Tahir breezes into the room. "M, just the person I wanted to see." He heads for my table, his steps slowing as he takes in Kat and Dash.

I turn to him, completely fed up. "What's a walkabout?"

Dash holds out his hands and gives Tahir a beseeching look. "*I* didn't say anything. I swear."

Tahir levels a hard stare their way, but it's just for show. "Give us a few minutes."

Kat pings my implant. <<We'll talk soon, OK?<<

>>I'll hold you to that.>>

She flashes me a grin before the two of them disappear down the hall. Tahir settles into the seat across from me.

I push back my plate. "So what's this job that has everyone all twisted up?"

"One of the best ways couriers can protect the data they're carrying is to keep moving, right? Well, sometimes a client's uncomfortable holding onto the data and shifts the risk onto Aventine by having our couriers keep it longer than the time it typically takes to make a transfer. There can be a lot of reasons for this. Timing, logistics, and rare cases where a buyer's still being arranged."

"Why not just keep the data locked up at HQ or some other secure location?" I ask.

"Because the client doesn't want us to have that much control over the data either."

"They don't trust the network, but they don't trust us either?"

"Let's just say they are more comfortable with our couriers transporting the data out in the open where they can still monitor it."

"Sounds a bit more nefarious than usual jobs."

"Not necessarily. Sometimes it's simply a result of poor planning. Or a unique set of circumstances. We had one job last year where the client was moving offices, but the leases didn't match up. They'd been dealing with incursions from a competitor for months and didn't want to run the risk of them making another attempt to steal their data in the chaos leading up to the move."

"But a job where we pad out the time it takes to do a data transfer deliberately provokes the curdle."

"Yes. Sometimes it's necessary to hold onto the data for a couple of days. And the best way to protect it is–"

"Is to go on walkabout," I finish for him. Most jobs, the goal is to make the transfer as soon as possible, where time literally is money. But I guess occasionally there are jobs like this one, where finding constructive – and secure – ways to pass the time are just as important. "And since I'm the most junior courier…" Short straw indeed.

Tahir shrugs. "You want to go back out there, don't you?"

That he knows that much… "Yes, but…" I want the distraction, but not at the cost of courting the curdle.

He stands. "Finish your meal, and we'll get you briefed."

So much for a day off.

CHAPTER THIRTEEN

Leaving a modest office in the transitional Understory a few hours later, I can't quite quell my unease. Maybe it was the client's flustered actions when I showed up for the data transfer. I arrived on time, but they clearly didn't have their act together as they scrambled to get everything set up. Or maybe it was the blood. I've gotten better, but I did get a good eyeful before I had the presence of mind to turn my head away as the encoded blood was injected into me.

Either way, this walkabout's already pissing me off.

<<You know what to do?<< And Tahir's pestering certainly isn't helping.

>>*Yes*. They went over everything like six times before I was allowed to leave.>>

I keep my steps quick as I put more distance between me and the client. Have to make the drop somewhere on the other side of the Understory, but not until tomorrow afternoon. Holding the blood inside me until the end of day two is what makes this job tough. Then there's the whole walkabout piece. I'm pretty much on my own until I make the drop. No telling HQ what my plans are to pass the time. No making hotel reservations with my Aventine account. Or using the maglevs.

Tahir said less paranoid clients don't mind if couriers kill time on the trains looping round and round New Worth until we can unburden ourselves of our precious cargo. But that's a no-go for this job. At least I have a data stick from the client with untraceable credits. Enough for a hotel room and a couple of meals. Though I was told to check in and stay for no longer than eight hours. Then I'll need to be on the move again.

>>Also? This job's sketchy as hell. I thought we didn't do anything illegal.>>

<<*We* don't,<< he's quick to say. <<But our clients… who knows. We have plausible deniability. It's in our charter. Besides, a job like this can be quite lucrative. For you.<<

>>We need to have a conversation about my preferred risk-to-reward balance.>>

He laughs, creating a warm pressure on my chest. <<We would never take on a job we felt was unduly dangerous for our couriers, M. You're more than capable of handling this. Now, have you given a thought as to what you'll do?<<

Most definitely, but… >>I can't give you any clues, remember?>>

<<Fair enough. You know how to reach me.<<

I blink our connection to the background. Aventine *and* the client will only learn my route through the city as it unfolds in real time. Starting now, as I head to the closest bank of elevators.

Spangled sunlight fills the lift as the doors open on Level 2 of the Upper Canopy. My reward after braving the gloom of the Understory and climbing the towers of New Worth. With the sun tinting everything a soft orange, I almost don't mind being jostled by the other elevator occupants as we fight to be first to step onto the crowded concourse.

It's been way too long since I've had cause to be up here. The light, the fresh air, the ache in my chest at the loss of my old life. The work makes it easier to forget, but with only my own wits to manage the walkabout today, I find it that much harder to bury the old Emery down deep where she belongs.

I scan the crowds, perversely curious to see if I recognize anyone. But no, people pass by, absorbed in their own concerns, a bubble of obliviousness surrounding them as they're buffeted through the Canopy. When I turn off onto a smaller walkway, the air changes, the scent of orange blossoms beckoning me on. The Orangery, one of my favorite places in the Canopy, takes up a whole block, open to the glass sky. A path winds through the groves of trees and flowers, linking the two entrances, north and south.

A little after lunch, the gardens have thinned out. A young woman draws on her tablet in the corner underneath a bright patch of sun. Two men have an intense conversation on another bench, their takeout forgotten. Others drift past, some cutting through the Orangery to save time or to take in the sights. No one seems overly concerned by my presence on a bench where I can monitor both entrances, just in case. In fact, I doubt any of them even see me. Something I never would have noticed if not for Aventine and their training to pull the wool from my eyes.

Kat pings me. <<How's it going?<<

>>Ugh. Who would've thought killing time would be so *hard*?>>

She laughs. <<I always try to take advantage of all the things I can't do back at HQ on jobs like this. There's this one dojo in the Understory that lets me drop in whenever I want to spar with their higher belts.<< After her run-in with the police when she was younger, her parents got her martial arts training, thinking it might keep her out of trouble. She stuck with it, and was testing for her black belt when Aventine tapped her for service.

>>Believe me, I'm trying.>> I used to spend hours in the Orangery studying or synching with Rik. >>But I still have at least twenty-four hours to go before I can dump this blood and get on with things.>>

<<Poor baby. Dash says hi, by the way.<<

I smile, feeling slightly less alone despite the familiar surroundings. >>Hi back. Tell him he needs to annoy Tahir for me while I'm gone, all right? >>

<<I'll make sure of it. Oh, and if you find yourself near Belknap Towers, they have a taco stand that's fantastic.<< She sends me the Understory address and signs off.

If I sit here any longer, the Orangery's heavy, perfumed air will make me drowsy. Can't have that. My neck prickles as I get to my feet. Keeping my movements controlled and precise, I turn.

A young teen girl with no parental unit in sight is stationed along the path, holding up a digital placard that reads "Disconnects against the Dome." In the background, there's an image of a tree struck by lightning. She must've arrived in the time I've been sitting here, brazen enough to brave the upper Canopy by herself or groomed by her elders to make a political statement, given all the tensions lately.

Her gaze flicks toward me. No filter separates her from me. No data clogging her view, distracting her from her surroundings. No matter how skilled we get at using our implants, it's never as seamless as we intend.

Brita co-wrote her first article for the NW Signal a few days back talking about how the Disconnects are pushing to make themselves more *visible*. Not just through protests and demonstrations, but by moving up though New Worth, entering spaces they've implicitly been denied before. They believe that the upper levels are too far removed from their concerns. By making people *see* the Disconnects firsthand, putting a real face to the problem, they hope to move the conversation forward. They can't all be criminals or headcases who've had their implants revoked or religious nuts who abstain from all tech. Some are just mild-mannered teen girls looking for a better life.

And I know too well what that's like.

After lunch the next day, that dead feeling in my stomach arrives right on time, heralding the start of the curdle. Abandoning my half-eaten gelato I get up from the cafe table, pleased to find my lightheadedness isn't too devastating. At least not yet.

I fall in with the crowd and angle east, mentally willing the client to get their shit together so I can dump the data early and move on. A girl can hope.

I window-shop for hours until I can no longer stand looking at the items that don't fit into my life as a courier. I follow that up with an exhibit of impressionist art at a museum. Then a stroll through the biopark, oohing and ahhing at the displays of native species that comprise a handful of rooftops in the southeastern sector of the Lower Canopy. I walk the concourses of New Worth for hours and hours until I'm exhausted. Finally the destination comes through on my second circuit through the Understory.

<<There's been an unexpected holdup in getting the scrubbing kit to the drop location in Dalton Heights.<<

I roll my eyes. >>Why, Tahir, I'm shocked. You mean the client's constant delays have messed up the delivery window?>>

<<We're arranging for another scrubbing kit to be waiting for you in an empty apartment in the Terrestrial District a few levels below your current location, just in case.<<

>>Good. I'm ready to be done with this blood once and for all.>>

<<Won't be much longer.<<

I walk past a cluster of offices full of bland, unhelpful names that provide little-to-no insight into what the companies actually do. This part of the Understory's definitely on the more functional end of the spectrum, with hardly any plants to cheer up the storefronts and dreary apartment buildings. The slight pall that the sunlight simulators and mirrors can't seem to diminish doesn't help either.

But at least the offices of McKinley, Porter, and Santos show up right where they're supposed to be, though I'd be surprised if the paint was dry on the door.

"I'm here for Ms Santos," I say to an ancient receptionist, but I may as well be speaking to a robot for all the comprehension in his eyes.

A woman rushes into the room. She smoothes out her business slacks and beams a manufactured smile in my direction as she pings my implant. I can almost see the moment she relaxes when my signal matches the one she was told to watch for. "We have everything set up in the next room, Miss."

"Oh, this just arrived as well." The receptionist gestures to the nondescript briefcase I've come to know by heart. Must've come a few minutes before I did.

"Why didn't you say so?" The woman's face flashes with irritation before she gives me another forced smile. She takes the scrubbing kit from the receptionist and waves me toward the hall. "If you would follow me?"

A headache bubbles up behind my eyes. Let's get this over with.

The scrubbing's left me a bit twitchy. I feel like Humpty-Dumpty – not quite put back together again – as I return to headquarters. I can't tell if it's nerves or just the inevitable post-scrub malaise. Nausea, cramping, exhaustion all go with the territory. Less common are changes in blood pressure, resulting in the nosebleed that accompanied my very first curdle. Either way, it's still unpleasant as I ride out the sensations.

Kat sends me a synch request. >>There'll be a laserball tournament in the gym tonight,>> she says without preamble. >>You in?>>

I sigh. <<Maybe. I'm pretty beat though.<<

>>Oh, come on. Fleet's been trash-talking all day. We gotta show him up.>> I can just see him strutting around the common areas to drum up interest in the team-building activities the handlers put on every couple of weeks.

<<We?<< I ask as I carefully pick my way through the crowds.

>>We're on the same team, silly. Dash, Bandit, you, me.>>

<<You should've told me you already signed me up.<<

>>Well, now you know. Game's at 7. See you soon!>> Then she's gone, leaving a bemused smile on my face. She's no replacement for Brita, but it's good to have a friend at Aventine.

Crowds intensify the closer I get to Fountain Center. Angry chants float on the air. Way more people than implant signals mob the entrances to the city's administrative buildings. Just my luck. Another demonstration with all the hallmarks of the rallies that have popped up over the lower city. But this time the Disconnects have come to the upper levels to air their grievances. They don't want to wait until the time is right. Or turn over their fate to some lottery. They don't care about issues of infrastructure and orderliness. They just want to get away from New Worth and the implant-based society that has made them obsolete.

This close to headquarters, with an atmosphere of uncertainty that can roil into violence at a moment's notice, the demonstration's not a place I want to get caught up in as courier *or* as a citizen who enjoys being connected. An air of electric expectation charges up the people in the vicinity, regardless of what they believe about Disconnects, Emergence, or the future of New Worth. A breathless sort of awareness of something bigger than me threatens to take over, but I push it back.

I still have a job to do.

Whirling around, I bite back the impulse to run. Talk about blood in the water. That's the absolute worst thing to do in a situation like this. Showing I'm scared and drawing even more attention to myself and, by extension, Aventine.

I gather myself, my newly scrubbed blood pumping through my veins, as I stay on the edge of the crowds. I'll have to use an alternate route to get back to HQ. Lengthening my stride, I whip around the corner, colliding with something hard and warm. "I'm sorry, I–"

Oh no. Rik… Randall stands in front of me, a shocked look on his face. All the air in my lungs whooshes out of me. What is *he* doing up here? It's definitely him, right down to the inky black hair.

Randall stares down at me with dawning comprehension. Eyes wide, mouth parting wordlessly. "Emery?" He says my name softly as if he's afraid he's mistaken me for someone else.

And he has. I'm supposed to be M-37 now.

I had almost convinced myself I never needed to see him again. With Aventine's restrictions on outside contacts, who knows when or *if* I'd ever get permission to talk to him without subterfuge. But now that he's here, in the flesh, I can barely look at him. It feels too… intimate.

Tahir said in the event I run into someone from my old life, I'm to deny who I am. Or was. If that doesn't convince them, I'm supposed to report the incident to Aventine. What they'll do, I don't know.

I force myself to create a bland smile with my trembling lips. "Sorry, I think you have me confused with someone else." I step around him.

"It *is* you." His hand snakes out and grabs my arm. Static jolts between us, and he pulls back with a cry.

I inch away from him. "What the hell?"

"I'm sorry," he says, looking anything but. "But Emery, everyone thinks..."

"Look, I don't know who you think I am or what you want, but I'm this close to calling the cops."

"Wait. I..." His brow furrows. For a moment I see his doubt, wondering if he's misidentified me, then his jaw hardens in certainty. The longer I hang around, the greater the chance he'll wear me down. Which isn't fair to him. He's already grieved me, moved on. Meeting now can only dredge up that old pain. I try to move past him, but he shadows my moves.

"Don't run away. I don't care what ID you're broadcasting." His words wake me up. "Please."

I take a deep breath, unpleasantly aware of the evening crowds converging with the protestors that have already gathered. People going home from work after a long day. Heading to a restaurant for dinner or grabbing takeout. And our face-off with one another as the rest of New Worth eddies around us. "I'm not doing this here."

He glances around and leans in. "What, are you some kind of government agent?"

"Doesn't matter."

"It does. Whatever this is, it took you away from me."

I scan the concourse, on the lookout for someone from Aventine. A lump forms in my throat. "This isn't some arcade game. If my... work finds out about you..."

"Tell me what you're mixed up in, and we'll figure it out together."

Together. The word echoes through me. Bitter with promise. "Stop it. Just... stop. Forget everything you ever knew about me."

"Liv, wait."

My old handle on his lips sends ice through my veins. "That's not my name anymore."

He taps his temple. "Let me in, and you'll see the truth, I promise. These last few weeks…" His voice cracks, and tears prick my eyes. He takes my gloved hand in his, cradling the back of it. The urge to fit my data receptors against his is almost a tangible ache. "Liv, whatever happened doesn't change anything for me. I've missed you so much."

He's seen my mind, my face, and hasn't been scared off. But that may not last once Rik learns what I did that set me on this course. Or once Aventine finds out about us. Our meeting like this, no matter how coincidental, will look suspicious. And the risk of failure's too high. I don't want that kind of trouble for Rik.

You always had a choice. Just not very good options.

And they only get worse from here. My vision blurs as he places my palm against his. The heat of his hand is absorbed by my glove, preventing calibration. I wipe my cheeks and hastily pull away. I have to end this now, once and for all. I tell myself it's for his own good.

One day, I'll let myself believe it.

"No one can know about me. Not even you." Before he can protest, I continue, "Did you ever ask yourself why I didn't reach out to you after the party? I could have, you know. Any time."

I finally knew his real ID. It was just a matter of pinging him with a synch request. It would have tipped off Aventine, too, but that's not the point. Neither is the fact that I almost reached out to him through the arcade in a moment's weakness. "Remember how worried I was about meeting in person. That it would ruin our connection? Well, guess what. I was right."

He blinks as the meaning of that washes over him.

The poisonous words spew out of my mouth so easily, Harding would be proud. "Knowing who you really are just confirms that you're the last person I want in my mind."

Hurt flashes across his face – I'm nearly certain of that, even though Randall's all but a stranger to me. "You don't mean it," he finally says, but I can hear the lack of conviction in his voice.

"If you come here again…" I'll have to tell Aventine one way or another. I shake my head. "Just leave me alone."

I wait, half-expecting him to yell or crush me in his arms. I see only a shadow of what he feels pass over his face before it slams shut.

"If that's what you want, Emery." He sounds perfectly agreeable. "As you said, you know how to find me."

Then he leaves, taking with him my chance to be the one to walk away.

PART TWO
BLEED OUT

TWO MONTHS LATER

CHAPTER FOURTEEN

The work keeps me sane. That moment when Tahir pings me with a job is what gets me out of bed. While the fundamentals haven't changed, the variables do. Each data-rich blood transfer has a different character. Some lay heavy in my veins, not quite an ache but unignorable. Ice, fire... Others light and airy, almost effervescent. Tahir says it's all in my head, but *he's* not the one getting injected with secrets.

Between the clients' different data security preferences and my own latitude in how I get myself to each drop, no two jobs are the same. I've seen more of New Worth in the last few weeks than in all the years before I came to work for Aventine. So much of the city hides in plain sight. As long as I stay busy, I can push my old life down deep inside me in the wake of what's needing done. It's the days I don't get a job that are the problem.

For weeks after seeing Randall that day on the concourse, I jumped at every seemingly innocuous comment from Tahir. But either Aventine has no inkling of what transpired or they've done a killer job of lulling me into a false sense of security.

I finally decided I could either drive myself wild with worry they would send me packing to the Terrestrial District or save that energy for when I really need it. Especially in those quiet moments holed up in my quarters when I have no distractions left to keep me from remembering the wounded look on Randall's face or Brita's laugh. Or from wanting to reach out to my parents, have their consciousnesses fortify mine. I'd give almost anything for them to tell me everything's going to be all right as though I'm a little girl all over again. The rightness of wearing Emery Olivia Driscoll's ID again... all of it is incompatible with my role with Aventine, which is part of me now too.

It resides in a separate box though, compartmentalized and safe from the past, so long as the work keeps coming in.

Mid-morning, Tahir still hasn't contacted me with a new assignment. I hunt him down in the Crow's Nest, where he and the other handlers monitor jobs in progress. A jumbo-sized wallscreen partitioned into smaller ones flashes through different security feeds throughout New Worth. Set up in the corner, his station, a standing desk crammed with monitors, a touch console, and an old-school keyboard, faces the wallscreen.

At my entrance, he glances over and holds up a hand to forestall me as he finishes up his synch chat with whoever's out in the field. As I wait my turn, I try to see if I can identify the camera location on display before it rotates to the next feed. Finally, Tahir relaxes and acknowledges me with a nod. "What brings you here, M?"

"What's my assignment for today?"

"You don't have one. You're taking a break. Two days."

An eternity. Too much time on my hands left over for thinking. "Oh, come on. Send me out."

"No," his voice sharper this time. "Under the new rules, downtime's even more important between jobs."

Tensions with the Disconnects have yet to abate with only a week to go until the lottery selects the people who will be able to live at Vesa. If anything, the unrest has gotten worse, keeping us couriers on our toes. The areas in yellow on our maps that we're supposed to avoid when we're on a job have expanded, making navigating the lower levels tricky. The authorities have been trying to identify the people behind the movement ever since someone was killed at one of their pop-up rallies a few weeks back, but they haven't made much headway, according to Harding. As a result, the heightened security protocols are still in effect, making everyone at Aventine miserable.

"But–"

"Show me your arms."

"What does that have to do–"

"Show me."

Biting back a snarl, I push up my sleeves.

Tahir nods to himself. "Thought so." His gloved fingertip points out what I already know. Bluish stains along the inside of my forearms. Skin bruised from too-frequent data transfers. "Wound-heal can work wonders, but you need to give it time to catch up."

"But two whole days?"

"If someone knew about couriers and saw your arms, it'd be a dead giveaway. Even if they didn't, they might think you're addicted to something with all those needle pricks."

"Please. I don't look like a junkie."

"Looks can be deceiving. You should know that better than most."

I do, but... "I can't just stay here and do nothing."

He turns back to his station and sucks in his cheeks. "An excursion then. Up to four hours this afternoon."

A generous offer, but it's not enough. "You just want to foist me off on the unsuspecting public."

He laughs. "Can you blame me?" He gestures to his desk. "Some of us still have work to do."

Kat's handler, Miranda, looks up from her workstation. "K's around today. You can always practice together and work out some of your frustration."

"A wonderful idea," Tahir says, as if the matter's settled. I want to protest, but at the look on his face, I know better than to push my luck.

"You two are impossible."

Their laughter follows me out of the room and into the hall. Kat flashes me a bright smile when I join her in the training room a few minutes later. "Thanks for coming," she says. "The holos' feedback doesn't compare to sparring against a real person." She would know.

"No problem. Besides, I don't have anything better to do. Another day stuck in Aventine purgatory."

She groans. "Me too, but Dash lucked out and got an assignment."

I roll my eyes. "No kidding. You wouldn't be hanging around the training room with me if he were available," I say with a smile.

A faint blush appears on her cheeks as we meet each other in the center of the room. "We're not that bad, are we?"

"Only sometimes," I tease. "But seriously, I'm glad both of you let me be a third wheel on occasion."

"Well, we both know how hard the transition can be. Though you seem to be doing better."

I'm glad I've fooled *someone*. Readying my stance, I half-bend my knees, inhale deeply through my nose, and keep my hands out in front of me. I've learned the hard way it's better to stay on the defensive when sparring with Kat. She has the unerring knack of turning my every attack against me, capable of some truly impressive moves.

She feints left, jabs at me with her right arm. I block it easily with a wrist grab, and with that we cycle through different strikes and combinations. She eases me into it. I could almost let myself get lulled into a false sense of security with the punch-block-kick-counter rhythm we create if not for the persistent sensation that Kat, just like her namesake, likes to play with her food until she's finally ready to eat.

I strike out, expecting her to block as she's done countless times before, chaining moves together to create an opening in my defenses after a couple of seconds. Still haven't quite figured out a way to avoid it. Instead of her hand whipping out, her forearm blocking my strike, my fist meets her shoulder just as a sharp cry escapes her.

I pull back so I won't hit her with full force, but she still falls to her knees, hand at her temple.

"What's wrong?"

She blinks up at me, unseeing. "Something's happened to Dash. He's…" The color drains from her face.

Must be something bad. When Rik and I were connected, I had an almost never-ending awareness of his mental state floating in the back of my mind. For Kat to experience such a strong physical reaction, the emotional bleed must be overwhelming.

Our match forgotten, she lurches to her feet and hurries out of the room. I chase after her all the way to the Crow's Nest on the third floor.

The door doesn't open for us. They must have known Kat was coming. She bangs on the door. Miranda opens it a few seconds later, blocking the rest of the room from view. "K," she says with a frown, "this isn't a good time."

Kat kicks the door into her. Miranda curses, but doesn't fight Kat as she shoulders her out of the way. "You know the rules, K."

Kat's face nearly crumples at the rebuke in her handler's voice. "I know. And I'm not distracting him." She taps her temple. "I just want him to know I'm here."

Tahir's at his station, his hands making small movements as he controls the wallscreen's display, his eyes rolling through a barrage of eyecast commands. If I seek it out, I can catch snippets of his single-minded focus, but it's not directed at me, which is why I didn't notice it before. He croaks out, "Miranda," and she turns, rushing back to her position at another station.

"Shit," she mutters to herself, tracking the vids.

Scanning the screens, I finally make out the angular planes of Dash's face as he navigates the crowds milling around the Stadium during a football game at halftime. Four men pursue him, and they're not nearly so careful in weaving through the bystanders.

"They're not broadcasting ID," Miranda says. "Disconnects?"

Tahir doesn't answer.

Without breaking stride, Dash charges toward a set of stairs, leading to the upper deck of the stadium – high enough there'll be emergency exit access to one of the concourses. He'll be in an elevated section of the Terrestrial District, awfully close to an area Aventine says is now offlimits, but at least he'll have more options.

"How did he get routed into the game anyway?" I wonder out loud. The client's preferences perhaps? Or a desperate ploy to get rid of his tails, thinking the crowds would keep him safe? But I may as well have asked the question in my head for all the notice it gets.

A new camera angle snaps to Dash as soon as he comes into view. His steps speed up, the emergency exit beckoning. And, for the first time, we get an unencumbered look at him, and the dark stain along his right side.

"No..." Kat breathes.

"Get someone there now!" Tahir's voice explodes in the silence. Whoever he's talking to is in deep shit. I've never heard him sound so angry. His head twitches toward Miranda. "ETA?"

"If Diego's team leaves now, three minutes." Her gaze finds Kat's, something unsaid passing between them that curls

Miranda's lip. "I'll alert Harding." Then she's gone.

Tahir pushes back from the desk, running his gloved fingers through his hair.

Kat looks at him. "Tell me what happened."

With a grim set to his mouth, he turns back to the screens. <<M, I don't care how you do it, but get her out of here, *now*.<< Our connection vibrates with the command. I'm already moving before his words fade from my mind.

"Tahir," Kat says, "I have a right to know."

I give her arm a tug. "We should go. Let them handle it." The only thing she can do is get in the way.

She shakes me off her. "Tahir," her voice rising a hysterical octave, "tell me."

<<M!<<

Short of knocking Kat out – which, if our sparring sessions are any indication, is nigh on impossible – I don't know what to do. Casting about the room, my gaze lands on a med kit mounted to the wall by the door. There's an emergency kit in each room. I've never been more grateful for Aventine's paranoia. I open it, riffle past bandages and pill packets, and find a sedative. I yank off the protective covering and jam the autoinjector into the meaty part of her thigh. She sags to the floor before she even registers the shot. A wounded, accusing look is leveled my way before her eyes slide shut.

I run a shaking hand over my brow, telling myself she'll be better off. There were times when the emotional bleed between me and Rik and even me and Brita could spiral out of control, creating a feedback loop of negativity that devolved from commiseration into something far more destructive. When Rik's mother died, his grief rekindled mine after my grandparents passed away within weeks of each other a few years earlier. Our shared depressive bender had us both twisted up for months.

That's not what either Kat or Dash needs now.

"I'll get a med tech up here."

"No," Tahir says sharply, his gaze still affixed to the screen. "We need them right where they are for when they bring D-19 in."

Things happen quickly after that. Diego's team bursts onto the concourse. Two of them bundle Dash away, while Diego and another man give chase to Dash's pursuers. Tahir rushes downstairs to await Dash's arrival. I'm left there with the silent monitors scrolling through security feeds as though it's any other day, with Kat passed out at my feet. At least I can do something about that.

Bandit, who was sleeping in on his day off, helps me get her to her suite. We tuck her into bed. Her room's full of soft flourishes of her personality. Wall screens rotating through lush images of flowers, eclectic furniture she must've purchased herself, and an air filter adjustment filling the space with the fragrance of jasmine. Somehow she's managed to turn Aventine into a home. I force back thoughts of my own utilitarian apartment, nearly the same from the day I moved in. I do the work, get the job done. Isn't that what matters?

I debate sending Kat a message explaining what happened, but decide against it. I know firsthand how devastating emotional bleed can be. I also know how awful it is to be cut off from loved ones so abruptly. There's just no winning in a situation like this. With one last look at her suite, I go downstairs.

Dash has already been swept into the surgi-suite. I stand vigilant near the entrance to the med bay. In part because Kat can't, but also because Dash's my friend too. Until today, all of Aventine's warnings about the darker aspects of our work hadn't really registered. Sure, there's occasional weirdness on a job, but nothing like this since I've been here.

Tahir's muted our connection, but some of his anxiety leaches through, setting my teeth on edge. Forty minutes tick past in painful silence as I wait in the hall. Finola's lab techs peek their heads out every so often, looking for an update that has yet to come.

Without warning, Tahir barges out of the medical suite and sags against the wall. Before the door shuts, I catch a glimpse of Dash, prone on a hospital bed with all sorts of equipment hooked up to him, beeping steadily. At least he's alive, if unconscious.

"He'll be OK?"

Tahir's expression doesn't change, but the lines on his face deepen. "Eventually. If the team had brought him in any later..." He lets that hang between us for a long moment, then he meets my gaze, his eyes as hard and unyielding as I've ever seen them. "Simple mistakes can add up, Emery. Never forget that."

CHAPTER FIFTEEN

Kat's glower greets me when I visit Dash in the med suite the next day. She's pulled up a chair, her bare hand tucked in one of his. Even when I've caught her by surprise in our sparring sessions, she's never looked at me quite like this.

I almost turn myself back around, but then Dash gives me a friendly wave. I take a tentative step into the room. "Just stopping by to see how you're doing."

He's still in his hospital gown, propped up on the bed, looking wan but very much alive. He shrugs. "Doc says I'll be back at it in a couple weeks."

"That's great," I say. I mean it, too, even with Kat staring me down. "I was worried."

She stands abruptly, her cheeks mottled red as her hair. "Could've fooled me."

I hold up my hands. "Kat, Tahir asked me to–"

"I don't want to hear it. You know what we are to each other. If something were to happen…" She jams her glove back on, her movements violent yet precise. Then she exchanges a loaded look with Dash before stalking out of the room.

I turn back to him. "I should go. You need your rest."

"It's OK, M." He tips his head to the door. "And it will be with Kat too. She forgives easily. I should know," he says with a hint of his old grin.

He might be ready to forgive me, but I'm not. "She has every right to be mad."

He lifts a shoulder. "We both know Tahir has a knack of getting his way."

True enough. I gesture to the bed. "So what happened?"

He leans back with a heavy sigh. "Should've been a routine transfer with the drop in the Terrestrial District. Picked up a tail, though. Somehow they blocked all my implant's outgoing communications. When I tried to ditch them, another one was waiting along every alt route I tried. Thought I'd be able to lose them at the Stadium, but no such luck."

"Did Diego's team catch whoever it was?"

Dash shakes his head. "Nah, they disappeared into the shadows of the Terrestrial District. Client thinks it might have been a competitor, so they're looking into it too."

"Well, hopefully they'll figure it out so something like this doesn't happen again."

"No kidding." He gives me a wink. "But at least Aventine provides a nice disability bonus."

Three days later, Tahir summons me to Harding's luxe office on the third floor just past the Crow's Nest. Harding might appreciate the finer things, but I suspect it's more for the benefit of whoever he conferences with, considering the bells and whistles on the wallscreen mounted opposite his desk. Tahir said once that Harding's responsibilities include managing clients and finding new ones, and presumably this setup inspires enough confidence for people to turn over their secrets into our keeping for a few hours at a time.

Pushing back the automatic apprehension, I take a seat at the small table opposite Harding's desk. Tahir joins me, a slight crease to his brow that's been there ever since Dash was taken into the surgi-suite on a stretcher. Dr Finola sits across from him, a tired cast to her otherwise friendly face – she's been working double-time monitoring Dash and staying on top of her daily responsibilities. And Harding rules over all at the head of the table, synching with someone, somewhere, unconcerned with the minutes piling up as we wait for his attention.

Finally, Harding's awareness returns to the room, like a person in REM sleep woken suddenly. "Ah, M, thank you for joining us."

"Sure. Um... what's going on?"

Tahir's gaze drops to the table, the crease deepening, as Harding spreads his hands wide. "We have a special assignment for you."

"Not another walkabout, I hope."

Harding chuckles. "Not this time, no."

"One of our government clients has need of a data transfer," Tahir says.

"OK..." But that doesn't explain why I'm here. *Every* client needs a data transfer.

"D normally handled their data needs but..." Harding shrugs. "You're both similar in your abilities and habits on the job, and Tahir's familiar with both you and the client in question."

I bite my lip. It feels opportunistic, like I'm stealing away Dash's client or something. Once he recovers, I'm sure he'll be back in the field, no questions asked. But I guess that doesn't matter when there's business to be done.

"With the increased scrutiny from the public's interest in Emergence, our government clients have grown even more insistent on timely and secure data transfers," Harding says. "Until plans for staged development beyond the dome are finalized, it's, shall we say, a delicate time."

"Hopefully things will calm down once the Vesa lottery is over," I say. Once the citizens lucky enough to live at the new housing development are selected, the Disconnects will have to wait out the trial period along with everyone else.

Tahir and Harding exchange a glance. "Perhaps," Tahir says. "But no matter what happens, the government's still under a huge amount of pressure to make Emergence as seamless a transition as possible. Even with Vesa underway, Emergence for everyone is years in the making. If their plans, preliminary as they are now, were leaked to the public, it could lead to even more tension."

"More Disconnect unrest?"

Tahir nods.

"The Disconnects are one thing," Harding says. "But if everyone started to doubt, our whole way of life could destabilize, jeopardizing everything we've worked for."

"I thought I wasn't supposed to know what I'm carrying?"

"True," Harding says. "And you won't, not really. The specifics will still be unknown to you *and* us. We're only telling you this because you need to understand you'll be dealing with a different caliber of client than you've been interacting with up until now." Harding thumps the table with his palm. "So we'll take this as a test run since there are some non-standard elements to their request, in part because of D's unavailability."

"When do we get started?"

"Tahir said you are always chomping at the bit to get out there." He says it smugly, like the know-it-all he is. When, really, all I want to do is get out of this room.

"In two hours' time, we'll ascend to the Echelon," Tahir says.

"We?" I ask.

"You, me, and Dr Finola."

"Isn't that overkill?"

Before Tahir can answer, Harding clears his throat. "They have some very... particular needs for this job, requiring Tahir and Diane's presence." He closes his eyes, sending me directions up to the Echelon. "You've been given different routes to take to the pickup location. Plan for forty-five to fifty minutes' travel time." Harding looks at me. "Once there, you'll be briefed on the rest."

>>Why do I have a bad feeling about this?>>

Tahir's head twitches toward me involuntarily, but he makes no answer.

Dr Finola gives me a bright smile. "No worries, M. We just want to ensure this one goes smoothly."

I get to my feet. I'm actually glad I have an assignment after the last few days. Ever since Dash's job went wrong, there's been a slight pall over headquarters. Kat's still not accepting my synch requests, which also doesn't help.

Outside the briefing room, Dr Finola flashes me another smile. "See you up there," she says, before making her way down the hall.

I arch my brow at Tahir, falling in next to him as we take the stairs down to the second floor.

<<Everything's fine, M.<<

>>I don't believe you.>>

He glances my way, then stares resolutely forward. <<Harding and I disagreed on the dimensions of the assignment. That's all.<<

My steps slow. >>You don't think I can do it.>>

<<No.<< He shakes his head. <<That's not it at all.<<

>>Then what?>>

<<That's privileged information, M.<<

I scoff.

<<I mean it. Just trust we wouldn't send you out there if we didn't believe in your abilities.<< We split up, each heading to our respective quarters, but the connection stays open between us. <<Plus, you'll get to visit the Echelon. Ever been up there?<<

>>Once.>>

After my parents helped me move into my dorm room in the Canopy, the three of us traveled up to the highest reaches of New Worth, where the city's best and brightest made their homes. We knew we'd never have a chance at securing quarters in such exclusive company, even if I earned enough to move them out of the Terrestrial District, but it was fun to wander around the public areas and dream.

The memory tinges bittersweet. Tahir must feel some of it since he sends me the day's projected suncast for the upper levels. <<Supposed to be a beautiful day.<<

I smile in thanks. At least there'll be that.

All the things I like about the Canopy – the light, the fresh air, the flowering plants – are even better in the Echelon. With its unencumbered view of the land beyond the glass, green with promise, it climbs up the sides of the dome, surrounding Skychapel. Each residential terrace has its own theme, trying to be more awe-inspiring than the next. Lush desert, tropical paradise, secret woods. All things you can experience in an arcade simulation, it's true, but *this* is real. Or at least as real as it gets in New Worth.

I check my pace slightly, trying to absorb as much shimmery light streaming down as I can. This close to the dome, I can make out the slight tint to the glass thanks to the microscopic metal strengthening each panel. But the quality of light more than makes up for that.

Thankfully, my gawking fits right in with all the tourists up here, desperate for sun to warm their uplifted faces. But I don't have much time to take in the sumptuous sights as I stick to Harding's route, funneling me toward the most prestigious section of the Echelon where City Hall's tucked up against the southeastern edge of the dome.

The City Council's tasked with governing New Worth, setting policies that keep us all thriving under glass. The

Echelon houses special communications equipment that allows the Council to consult with other domed cities off-network, but ultimately each city must be a self-sufficient silo until Emergence. That was the only way to save humanity when the domed cities were first proposed. Now, with Emergence growing ever closer, I wonder how that will change.

Luckily, the Council isn't in session, so it's not nearly as crowded up here as it would be otherwise. Security's ready for me, and I'm able to bypass the line of visitors waiting to tour the building full of faux-colonial touches. I'm ushered deeper into the compound, down a hall warmed with wood wainscoting, and through a heavy door into an ornate conference room. I'm the last to arrive, based on the conversation that ends abruptly at my entrance between Tahir, Dr Finola, and an unsmiling black man in a suit who's not broadcasting ID. I'm guessing Harding planned that on purpose since he's the one who handed out our routes.

"This is our operative for this assignment," Tahir announces.

The suit frowns down at me as he takes me in, his eyes lingering on my face. "I thought you said the replacement was one of your best. This one's barely out of school."

"She *is* one of the best." A slight edge creeps in to Tahir's voice. "We wouldn't jeopardize our working relationship with anything less."

The man relaxes his stance. "Well, I suppose she isn't what anyone would expect." That's probably as close to a compliment as this guy can manage. He nods to himself. "Fine." His eyes flick back to Tahir. "I don't need to tell you what'll happen if something goes wrong."

"I assure you, she'll see this through." Tahir means it, which soothes the little part of me still bristling from the suit's disdain.

Dr Finola clears her throat. "I've brought our hemocrypt setup, as requested. I personally recalibrated it myself this morning."

"We'll be the judge of that."

The door opposite the one I came in opens, admitting a man of Indian descent, somewhere in his twenties. Must be a tech of some sort. Dr Finola backs away from the table as he snatches up the kit, a digital scanner in his hand. In a few seconds, he's dismantled everything, scrolling through his touchscreen's readout. He grunts and places all the pieces back in the kit without bothering to do it properly.

The tech and suit exchange a look, then he leaves without a word. "We'll be more comfortable using our own setup," the suit says to Dr Finola.

She shakes her head, appalled. "Aventine uses a cutting edge, proprietary process that I've spent the majority of my career perfecting. Whatever techniques you've developed are inferior."

"We've come a long way, Doctor, don't worry."

Dr Finola's eyes narrow. "I worked with Edward Boothroyd in graduate school. He's talented, but something like this is beyond his abilities."

"We're using our own encryption methods, and that's final." The suit doesn't raise his voice, but he doesn't have to – not with the quiet authority radiating from his frame.

Finola looks like she's going to say something else, then turns to Tahir. Their synch chat is fast and furious, then she breaks off in a huff. "Fine, but if your gear doesn't meet my inspection, I'm calling it off." She gives the suit a glare for good measure. "I have that authority, if I believe there's unnecessary risk to the courier or the data."

The suit merely inclines his head. "Naturally."

Finola's pique amplifies my own jitters. It's taken months to get used to Aventine's hemocryption, and I only just tolerate it now. I'm not mentally prepared for changes to the process, government-sanctioned or not. I prowl along the edge of the room, trying to banish the nervous energy swirling through me. Tahir catches my eye but doesn't say anything. He can't. He knows how blood affects me. But if I keep moving, count how many steps it takes to get me from one side of the room to the other, maybe I can convince myself there's nothing to worry about.

The tech returns with two more people. This time, he's carrying a computer the size of a small crate while the others bring an array of medical gear to the table.

>>Is the computer that big because of their heavy-duty encryption or because they don't know how to replicate Aventine's process?>>

<<It doesn't matter, if this is how they want to do things,<< Tahir replies after a moment.

Dr Finola's lip curls with derision as she looks over the gear. "Five years behind, with an encryption process that'll take an hour, instead of twenty minutes." She levels a glare at the suit. "Still think all this is worth it?"

So much for not worrying.

The suit doesn't answer, just waves to the techs to get started. Harding said Aventine started out as a government initiative before going independent, but I guess the government still needs their own way of securing data transmissions that don't involve a third party. Though why they need us today, I'm at a loss.

Under Dr Finola's watchful gaze, they link the computer up to the unit that will encode my immune cells, followed by another unit that'll duplicate the cells so there's enough of them to pump back into my body. Unlike the hemocryption kit which compresses all these processes together black box style, they have to do each step individually. Seeing all the different units laid out in a row makes it harder to ignore what's being done to me.

But there's no turning back, not after Harding picked me for this job. Even though I find myself going through the mental calculations necessary to escape the Echelon and put as much distance between me and the cumbersome hemocryption unit as I can. I force myself to breathe regularly, keeping tight rein on my emotions as I continue to pace.

The first tech turns to Finola. "The blood base?"

With a look that could curdle milk, she pulls out a bag of my blood from her satchel. The immune cells already programmed to self-destruct at the end of three days. Guess *that* safeguard the client couldn't replicate. The base is added to the Rube Goldberg setup and the mechanism whirs to life, sounding rather anemic and all wrong as it starts the encryption process.

"If you would?" The suit's voice whips out at me, and I freeze.

I rather wouldn't, but I take a seat at the table and roll up my right sleeve, trying to remind myself I'm supposed to be a professional. I jump when one of the techs hands me a medical cuff. Shaking, I fit it to my wrist. They take over. Just as well.

A few minutes later, the encrypted blood's flowing. It starts off cold, then warms up. A nearly unbearable stinging sensation radiates up my arm as though my blood vessels are being burned up from the inside out.

At my hiss, Dr Finola looks at my face and frowns. Then she whirls toward the suit. "Don't trust my gear, fine, but next time don't pad your blood with additives during the encryption process. It creates unnecessary discomfort for our couriers."

The suit looks at her like she's a pesky insect before she finally backs off. She turns to me. "The sensation should wear off shortly, but let me know if it gets any worse."

I give her a tight nod. Clenching my jaw, I stare at the far wall. >>Dash better recover quickly. I don't want to work for these jerks again. I don't care how much they're paying me.>>

Tahir's lips twitch, a smile or a frown, I don't know. <<I'll take that into consideration.<< But his calm presence in my mind helps stave off my anger and discomfort as the new blood pushes into my body.

>>Who do they think they are with all this cloak-and-dagger bullshit?>>

<<Now, now, you know the rules.<<

>>"Curiosity killed the courier." I know, I know.>>

A wave of… something floods the connection before Tahir clamps down on it. Maybe that was too soon since Dash's accident.

An eternity later, spent in awkward silence given the company, the encryption winds down with a slow wheeze as the last bit of blood flows into me. I happily disconnect myself from the gear and get to my feet, stretching out my legs after sitting so long.

Finola waves a sensor over my head, and once she's satisfied with my readings, she hands me a wound-heal patch for my arm. "Looks like she's tolerating it OK," she says to Tahir, "but I'll be making a formal protest that such crude measures are never used again." She gives me a smile that does little to mitigate the acid in her voice. "See you back at headquarters." She collects her abused hemocrypt kit with dignity and nods to Tahir before leaving the room.

The suit keeps his arms crossed, maintaining his silence until the three techs pack up the rest of their equipment and exit through the same door they came in. When it's just me, Tahir, and him, he clears his throat. "We'll have someone with eyes on you until you receive the next set of instructions for the drop-off."

"That won't be necessary," Tahir says. "You're welcome to monitor her progress, but we cannot allow any interference in the field–"

"We insist. I'm afraid this part's non-negotiable."

I exchange a glance with Tahir. Do they not trust me? Or are they worried I'll be a target once I leave the Echelon? Either way, I don't like it. But what can I do?

Tahir sucks in his cheeks. Frustrated, but not overly concerned by the request. "Very well. Just make sure your detail doesn't get in her way."

The suit inclines his head, then turns to me. "Descend to the Understory. No trains, no stopping. You'll be contacted once everything's in place."

And that, it seems, is that.

Tahir sees me out of the office. "There's a lavatory off the main lobby." I resist the urge to roll my eyes. He hasn't spent this much time hovering over me since my first job. But he took Dash's attack personally, so I guess his undivided attention's to be expected.

"I'll be fine."

"Don't delay getting scrubbed after the drop. I don't care how hungry you get, we clear?"

"One time I put off getting scrubbed, Tahir. One time. And it was way past lunch."

"Save me from your stomach!" Tahir smiles, but it doesn't reach his eyes. Our connection jangles with tension, even as he tries to reinforce it with reassurance. "Off with you, and be careful."

CHAPTER SIXTEEN

So many people are packed into the main lobby, I worry I've stumbled into another tour group. But it's actually much more interesting. Two men in body armor carry briefcases in their right hands. A loop of bone protrudes from their wrists, and a band of metal connects the bone to the cases. Armored guards tasked with transporting something extremely important, given the security agents buzzing around them as they make their way to the dedicated lift I took on my way up here from the Canopy.

I wait for the procession to pass before I slip away from the claustrophobic atmosphere of the City Hall, determined to enjoy my last few moments in the Echelon. Brita always talked about all the snooty bureaucrats, celebrities, and captains of industry who live up here. Her dad knew all the dirt. But that doesn't change how beautiful it is. Like so many of the other tourists, I meander toward the so-called Hanging Gardens that zigzag back down to the Canopy proper. They're the scenic route out of the Echelon, traversing different biomes – rainforest, temperate and tropical. In addition to the occasional glimpse of a high society home, the twists and turns and foliage will make whoever's job it is to tail me that much more difficult.

I can't help grinning at that as I pluck a leaf off a low branch. Twirling it through my fingers, I take in the sights, memorizing the smell of the green living things all around me. Pretty sure that'll be the only perk out of this particular job, so I may as well make it count.

An hour later, I'm a few blocks away from Fountain Center. >>Any word on the drop?>>

<<You'll be the first to know, M.<< Tahir's irritability hasn't eased up, though I can tell he's trying to save me from the brunt of it. <<But it sounds like they're scrambling to set up an alternate location since the first one's too close to a pop-up Disconnect demonstration.<<

>>Still upset about the lottery?>>

<<Yes, but this particular incident followed the announcement of an attack on a data storage facility. The pipe bomb used was linked to a group of Disconnects, but they're denying their involvement.<<

I scan the feeds for the preliminary reports. The government facility's high security and off-network. Probably where data backups or physical records are stored. >>What would anyone gain from the attack?>> And such an escalation in tactics?

<<No idea. But it does mean the client decided to make alternate plans instead of risking a run-in.<<

Which means I have time to kill. With a blink, I flick back to my city map. >>Then I'm going to hit up the Aquarium before it closes for the day.>>

<<I suppose that could work.<< I'm pretty sure he's smiling for the first time today. <<They *did* say no stopping.<<

>>That's right. And if it makes their observation detail's job harder, that's not my problem.>>

He sobers slightly. <<Still, I'm sending you the most up-to-date schematics we have for the facility. Just in case.<<

I've only been to the Aquarium once before, a school field trip when I was younger. I brace myself for the possibility of kids running rampant, but luckily the late afternoon crowds are rather sedate – mostly family units and a handful of individuals here to ooh and ahh over the sea life displays.

A freshwater exhibit's up first, talking about the region's natural waterways and habitats that were all but destroyed except for the preservation efforts of the Aquarium staff. The city's Biopark and Aviaries function the same way, all of them helmed by scientists tasked with rehabilitation, ensuring healthy populations of native species in anticipation of the day when it's safe for the glass to come down. I wonder how their responsibilities have changed now that Emergence is here.

In the next room, fish all colors of the rainbow dart through a tank roughly two stories tall. Each specimen's tagged, so I only have to zoom in on one to learn what it is and get a brief primer on their characteristics from my implant. One family's meticulously going through each of the dozen or so species on display. But I'm not interested in facts. I'm far more enamored with the play of color, the fish gliding to and fro, as seaweed floats along on a lazy current.

The hallway ends with another viewing chamber, this one a reproduction of a coral reef. My pace slows as I linger over the display. The frills of sea anemones, the clownfish that dart in and out of nooks and crannies of the coral, and the jellyfish that drift along the periphery, watching over all. A sudden thump shocks a school of angelfish into the depths of the coral reef. Near the edge of the display, two men grapple with one another, grunts and meaty sounds echoing off the glass and into the room.

Shocked murmurs propel visitors out of the way. A mother tugs her two children down the hall to the next exhibit, while a young man watches with open-mouthed interest, no doubt broadcasting the entire thing to his buddies via his ocular boost. I don't blame him. Something like this almost never happens in this part of New Worth.

An Aquarium employee pushes off the wall he was

dozing against, blinks at the men in surprise, and dashes off, presumably for reinforcements. With his slight frame, he wouldn't have a chance against these two, with their barrel-chested, muscular bodies that have been earned the hard way. The only difference between them is one's pale and brown-haired with cheaply printed clothes, while the other has slightly darker olive skin and black hair, wearing a tailored shirt and slacks.

I edge toward the exit. Maybe they haven't noticed me yet.

The brown-haired man slams the other against the glass. His dress shirt rides up, revealing a vest of body armor. Definitely not your average New Worth citizen.

I send their images to Tahir, then back away. It can't be a coincidence, can it? One of them must be my government tail, the other a competitor of some kind. But who's who? >>Do you want me to stay on course or use evasive maneuvers?>>

<<Stand by.<<

I could punch through glass. I have a head start. I could leave them both in the dust if he'd just give me the go-ahead.

The black-haired man pulls a taser out of his pants pocket, but his opponent bats it away, following up with a nasty uppercut that body armor won't protect against.

<<Client says the black-haired man is one of theirs.<<

Of course, he's the one getting his ass handed to him. >>Meaning?>>

<<Evasive maneuvers.<< He's silent a moment. <<Dammit, M, why did I let you talk me into the Aquarium, today of all days?<<

>>I wanted to piss them off for thinking they needed to watch me the whole time.>> He swears, and I'm blasted with all his nonverbal frustration as I slip into the hallway. >>Not helping. Besides, I got this, so just relax.>>

<<M...<<

>>Stand by.>> See how he likes it.

Ahead, the exhibits end at a food court that looks like it's built into the side of the coral reef display I've just escaped. By now about half of the shops are shuttered. Instead of funneling out of the only exit for visitors just beyond, I hop the counter of a burrito shop and crouch there, waiting for the thug to pass.

This is the first job where I've been confronted by competing interests. Something I've simulated dozens of times, but never faced in the field. He could want the data for himself or whoever he works for or maybe he simply wants to incapacitate me in some way, making a data drop impossible. Whatever his plans, I can't let him succeed.

Tahir patches me into the Aquarium's security system. I cycle through a trail of downed Aquarium personnel. A few seconds later, the brown-haired man appears on a camera mounted near the exit, cheeks pink from exertion, scanning the crowds with deliberation. Giving the food court one final look, he breaks into a jog for the exit.

<<You can't go out that way. If he has any sense, he'll be monitoring the exit from the concourse.<<

>>I *know* that. Just… wait.>>

I exhale, dispelling some of the tension that's collected in my limbs. I crawl along the length of the counter until I reach the door to the back of the burrito shop. Locked. Pulling out my Aventine-issued pick kit from my satchel, I make quick work of the lock, then slip past, closing the door behind me.

The air's scented with stale tortillas and chili powder. Moving past mixing and prep stations, the pantry and walk-in, I find the vendor access door. I unlock that too and follow a short hallway to the service entrance.

>>See?>>

Tahir doesn't congratulate me out loud, but I feel his grudging approval. <<Take the access stairs up two levels.

Approach the pedestrian mall that way. Lots of crowds, more options if you run into trouble.<<

>>Should I expect more complications?>>

He sighs, exasperation and frustration both. <<At this point, we should expect anything.<<

Two hours later, I'm still twiddling my thumbs as I move through yet another section of the Understory. It's market day, which means hundreds of people surround me, haggling for aeroponic produce, handmade clothing fashioned from smart fabrics, and limited-run gifts and wares. At this moment, there's nowhere safer I can be. That doesn't make pretending to browse the stalls with enthusiasm any easier.

>>Riot or not, I should've received the drop location by now.>>

<<I've already indicated our impatience to the client, M, but that's all I can do.<< Tahir's unease creates pressure in the pit of my stomach. Fight or flight kicking in.

The market's taken over a stretch of concourse between two squares suspended in the voids between buildings. I'm on my second circuit. I'll need to move on before the shopkeepers notice me. I linger over a rack of long-sleeved shirts in chevron and paisley patterns shifting colors and designs so subtly it feels like my eyes are playing tricks on me.

My implant chimes. Finally, the next set of instructions. >>Got 'em. For my eyes only, though.>>

<<Of course they are,<< Tahir says resignedly.

I start working my way to the edge of the market. In the crush, a woman knocks into me, her shoulder catching mine hard. Her shocked cry startles the people in our immediate vicinity. "Watch where you're going!"

She ran into me, but it's too crowded for me to do much more than shrug it off and keep moving.

<<I'll still be monitoring you from here. Stay alert.<<

>>Roger that.>>

I send my connection with Tahir to the background and open the message. A warehouse in the warren of buildings in Henderson Acres, a transitional Understory neighborhood. I place it into my map of New Worth, then frown.

They chose well. Half hour on foot to the nearest lifts, in the middle of the street block, so egress will take time. No intra-level access; maintenance access points few and far between.

I don't like it, but then I haven't liked anything about this job.

The lifts are the quickest way to descend and get this over with once and for all, even though it'll be a hike in to reach the actual drop location. I get off at Level 22. The buildings nearest the lifts are in fair condition, but the further I go, the more run-down things get.

One housing complex's taped off for mold remediation. I move to the opposite side of the concourse and hold my breath until I'm well past. Early-generation construction materials, while lightweight and durable enough to extend the pre-dome buildings higher and higher, aren't always reliable when it comes to managing humidity. Luckily the sectors of the Canopy and the central Understory where Aventine HQ is located have replaced and rehabilitated the outdated materials. Henderson Acres is due for a makeover, but with all the talk of Emergence, I wonder if it'll ever get done.

I turn onto a connecting walkway. The light dims slightly as the old buildings constrict around me.

<<Visual coverage is pretty spotty down there,<< Tahir breaks in.

>>Not much better in person, I'm afraid.>>

<< I'm having a hard time keeping you in frame, so your reports are going to be even more important.<<

>>Understood. The drop's not that much further anyway.>>

A couple of businesses have made a go of it down here, barely clinging to life, but more have shut their doors for brighter prospects elsewhere. The stench emanating from a twenty-four hour Asian fusion place reinforces the sickly vibe. As I walk past a building with a bank of street-level windows, a man from within looks up from his console with a glare full of that harsh animosity of people used to living in a bad neighborhood.

Everyone who comes here is suspect, including me.

The foot traffic thins out until I'm all alone with an early-generation cleaning bot. Needs some care – its casters keep getting caught on the uneven and cracked cement tiles. Only a few storefronts down, the warehouse at least looks clean, if in need of updating. A light buzzes over the entrance, dispelling the late afternoon gloom. As I head toward it, a flash of movement from the shadowed doorway opposite pulls me up short.

The brown-haired man who chased me through the Aquarium lurches into view, looking slightly worse for wear. I was so sure I lost him.

>>We have a problem.>> I hook Tahir into my ocular boost. >>I don't know how he found me.>>

He swears. <<Support team's seven minutes out. Deploying now. Your new goal is to play for time.<<

>>What about the client?>> They're theoretically closer and, given all their paranoia, must've expected something like this.

Silence across the line as he considers it. <<Stand by.<<

My new favorite phrase.

The man steps closer, bare hands raised, trying to appear non-threatening. "I can't let you do this. If you turn the data over to them, you'll plunge us into civil war."

I mentally calculate the length of his reach, at what point the vanishing distance between us becomes critical. "I don't know what you're talking about."

"The data you're carrying for Aventine." He steps closer, limping slightly. Right leg. "Oh yes, we know all about it."

>>You heard that?>>

Tahir's shocked silence on the other end answers my question but does me no good. No one's supposed to know about us, or, more importantly, me. Tahir won't admit it, but I could tell all the client's demands for this job bothered him.

And now this.

The man takes another step – the distance between us closing fast. I consider running, but he pushes up his sleeve, exposing a tattoo on his forearm. A tree cleaved in two by a bolt of lightning, the same one on some of the placards from the Disconnect demonstrations. "We know you're a pawn in all this. That's why we're giving you a chance to do the right thing." He pulls a taser out of the waistband of his pants. "But we're on a tight schedule."

<<The client's security force should be there by now,<< Tahir cuts in.

>>Well, I certainly don't see them.>>

<<What do you mean? They should be there. Five of them. Wait a minute. Shit!<<

Four minutes gone. Not nearly enough. "Why should I believe anything you say?" I ask the man, stalling.

<<What's your position?<<

>>Level 22. Northwest sector. Why?>>

<<Your signal places you on Level 36, the southeastern-most sector. Which is where the client expects you to be.<<

None of this makes any sense. >>But I was told…>>

The man's taser crackles to life. "Because deep down you believe everyone should have an equal opportunity on the other side of the glass."

It takes me a second to refocus. "What does that have to do with–"

He lunges toward me. Training takes over as I dart out of his way and sprint to the warehouse. Locked. I pound on the scarred aluminum door twice before the man's on me. I pivot, break his hold, knee him in the groin, and follow that up with a kick to his injured right leg. The taser skitters across the concrete, out of reach.

He lurches back with a cry. Instead of a subdermal implant, a centimeter-thick plate's mounted to his neck. Scrapped-together, obsolete tech. Only Disconnects desperate enough to–

<<M, report.<<

Behind me, metal scrapes against metal as the warehouse door opens. A twenty-something Latino man with enough muscles to make me nervous and a fortyish white woman with her blonde hair yanked back into a severe ponytail join us. But my relief vanishes at the sight of the illegal gun in her hands, rooting me and my opponent to the spot.

<<M!<<

>>Are my clothes bulletproof?>>

<<What are you–<<

>>Are they or not?>>

<<No. What's happening?<<

>>I–>>

My implant shuts off entirely. Tahir's gone. I'm completely unmoored from all things Aventine.

The woman pockets a small device. "Let's just keep all this between us, shall we?" Something about her smug, nasally voice sets my teeth on edge.

The man with the tattoo sags with resignation. But his eyes find mine, imploring. "If you go with them, Emergence will be for nothing."

The woman levels the gun at his chest. A small red dot bobbing along a sea of black fabric. She wouldn't dare fire. She only means to scare us, to–

She squeezes the trigger, and a sound like a shocked gasp erupts. The bullet rips through the guy, and he falls to the ground just like that. What the hell? She didn't even give him a chance.

The woman gestures to her companion to check on the guy, bleeding out on the street. Normally a prolonged interruption in a person's vitals will bring an emergency response team, but they've probably blocked his homebrew implant's signal, just as they did mine. Is it possible they hijacked my signal, sent me the wrong rendezvous instructions to get me down here? Away from the real client? If Tahir's right, and I'm at the wrong location for the drop, then these people are bad news.

But the gun already tells me that much. They were banned when people first decided to take refuge in the domed city. Given the close quarters, such weapons were deemed a danger to public health.

And now my own health's at risk.

No help for it. This job was bad from the beginning. Time to call it.

What's my exit strategy?

I take a step back, moving in half-time so I won't draw their attention away from the body. Then another.

The woman looks up, her cold gaze catching mine. "We have the equipment set up inside." She waves her gun in the direction of the warehouse as if nothing's wrong.

Another step. The cleaner bot whistles as it runs into the back of my knees.

"Stop blocking my implant. That's a breach of–" *everything, really*– "Aventine protocols."

"I couldn't let that man," she nods at the corpse, "do any more damage. Surely you understand that."

But not anything else. What I do understand, though, is this deal's off until I can get a better handle on what's going on.

"Come on. Time's wasting."

Something about her voice tickles the back of my mind but the gun's far more pressing. She won't shoot me and risk losing her precious data – at least not out in the open. As soon as my blood's exposed to too much oxygen, the data degrades automatically. Security feature. Which gives me some wiggle room. Besides, someone's bound to come by here eventually. It's now or never. I dash behind the bot and sling it toward the muscle. Its casters scrape across the concrete in protest.

The guy knocks into it with a heavy thunk. Pieces of the bot scatter as an internal component whines. Its lament follows me as I sprint back the way I came. The woman swears, her shoes slapping against cement as she gives chase.

What if there are more of them? Gotta figure a way out of this maze. I take the first side street, the woman and her lackey still too close behind.

The gun goes off again, hitting the wall above me. Grit explodes, and I shield my eyes. Shit! So much for *not* shooting at me.

"Get back here!"

I dash around the corner and find myself back by the Asian fusion place. I could retrace my steps to the lifts, but they'd anticipate that since they probably already know my route in.

As I gasp for breath, it hits me as the sour tang of fish sauce and grease fills my lungs. The restaurant's trash chute. All biodegradable trash is disposed for reclamation – filtered out into compost, graywater, fuel. Most restaurants have a pipe separate from the sewer lines that dumps into a processing plant in the Terrestrial District.

Descending's the only way out of this mess.

With a burst of adrenaline, I charge through the restaurant doors, an automated chime heralding my entrance. A young teen blinks up from the counter; his stack of fortune cookies topples. "Welcome to–"

I wave him off and stride into the kitchen. Shouts in Cantonese follow. Without my implant, I have no idea what's being said, but the tenor of the lone line cook's voice needs no translation as I bypass the kitchen.

I find the trash chute near the dishwashing station. Roughly three feet in diameter, the chute has a grate mounted over it to keep utensils and plates from accidentally falling into its depths. I pry it off, the fabric of my gloves sinking into the grime that's collected along the seam. With a sucking pop, the grating finally gives way, exposing the gaping maw of the city.

The stench's even worse now.

The woman's demanding voice trickles back from the entrance.

Can't chicken out now. I shove open the back door to the alley, triggering the emergency exit alarm. With luck, maybe they'll think I've moved on – at least long enough for me to regroup. I turn back to the chute.

Then I take a deep breath and drop in.

CHAPTER SEVENTEEN

The metal chute closes around me, humid, slick, and stinking, as I slide down countless levels. I keep my toes pointed and my hands tucked into my chest, forcing back nausea.

Blue sparks dance around me as my sleeve catches on something sharp. I get brief snapshots of welded metal and refuse in various stages of decomposition. Pretty sure I could've gone my entire life without seeing or smelling what surrounds me now.

The tube widens slightly as it intersects with others, and I'm dumped out onto a pile of garbage that dozens more chutes feed into. Air gushes out of me when I land – feet first, but my momentum flips me head over heels, and I roll a bit before I come to a stop on my back. Half-sinking into who-knows-what as my chest stutters.

Along the perimeter of the pile, garbage bots chirp as they excavate the mountain of trash. A fine wire mesh makes up the floor. Fluids are filtered through it, then siphoned off for processing elsewhere. The bots pick through the rest, routing the refuse to the appropriate channels. Compost, biofuel, incineration, compaction – each a separate opening in the far wall.

Gaining my feet, I teeter toward the edge. Ten feet to the floor, give or take. Before I can decide how to get down, my foot slips. I fall back, sliding on my ass all the way to the bottom.

I'm coated, but my clothes are still intact despite the rough treatment. Can't say the same for the rest of me. My hip's bruised, but it's not too bad as I step unnoticed past the garbage bots and find a maintenance door on the far wall. Unlocked, at least. After all, who'd come down here willingly?

I glance back at the garbage chutes. The muscle's probably too wide to fit, and I highly doubt that woman would come down here herself, no matter how important the data is. And that's assuming they've figured out where I've gone.

A short hallway leads to a small locker room for the bots' human minders. Empty. End of the workday? I don't question my luck as I start the shower, get in with my clothes on, and soap them up. Even though the Terrestrial District isn't the sweetest smelling of places, I can't risk attracting any more attention. Forgoing modesty, I strip down. Slime and grime spirals down the drain, leaving me as clean as I'm going to get.

Jimmying a locker open, I find a beige canvas jumpsuit. That'll serve me better down here than my sodden clothes, which still aren't clean enough for my tastes. My shoes are harder to salvage. I have to pry into a few more lockers before I locate a pair of work boots. Way too much space in the toe box, but as long as I don't have to run anywhere, I'll be OK.

I wad up everything into a spare trash bag from the janitor's closet and shrug into the jumpsuit. Have to roll the sleeves up a little, but it'll do until… What?

Should've known I'd end up back down here one way or another.

Breath gusts out of me as I drop onto a bench in front of the lockers. What *am* I going to do? As my heart finally settles into a steady thumping rhythm in my chest, the full reality of my situation hits me.

My implant won't reboot. In fact, it doesn't respond to any eyecast command I send it. If that's not bad enough, I've knowingly deviated from the standard operating procedures

Aventine's drilled into me since day one. The job's completely fucked. Even though that's not entirely my fault, the blame will fall on me, never mind the fact that Harding's fingerprints were all over this assignment. I doubt he'd set me up, but it doesn't change the fact that Aventine will think I've played them. As far as they know, I violated the client's instructions, and now I've gone completely dark. Could I look any guiltier? I'd like to think Tahir would be reasonable about things if I could simply explain the situation to him, but all the scenarios covered in training assumed the lines of communication would remain open between handler and courier.

I wasn't the most willing of recruits. I've thrown myself into the work, it's true, but they can't be sure I haven't been biding my time all these months for an opportunity like this. And with my implant out of commission... I'm so screwed. I need to figure a way out of this mess. I need an ally down here, someone I can trust to shelter me long enough to sort out what went wrong.

And how to fix it.

There's a chance friends and neighbors from my time growing up in the Terrestrial District are still around, but it's been years and not everyone was happy for me when I found a way to move up to the Canopy. Could I really trust them with this? I already know the answer to that.

Dammit. Why does everything have to come back to Rik?

I have to draw on every aspect of my Aventine training to not shock the people who pass by the bench I've commandeered outside Vector Agronomy's headquarters with my bulky clothes, my sodden hair, and bruises that scream domestic incident. But there are all kinds in the Terrestrial District, which is my only saving grace.

No matter how many times I try to talk myself out of it, Randall's my best bet down here. With my implant not working, I have no way of contacting him or finding out his home address. Aventine safe houses are too risky until I know where I stand with them. And then there's the whole botched drop. Whatever happened up there, it's big.

The streets grow more crowded as the end of the workday approaches. My gaze haunts the entrance to Vector, waiting for Randall to make an appearance. As the first wave of employees exit, I force back questions. What if he's not working today? What if he left early? What if… he doesn't want to see me? I can only blame myself for that.

Finally, he exits, chatting with a female colleague. Mid-twenties, tall with curly dark hair braided away from a tawny, heart-shaped face. Her shoulder brushes Randall's companionably as they walk by. My chest squeezes, and I remember to breathe again.

I ease myself into the crowds behind them, careful not to follow too closely. But close enough to hear the woman's bright laugh and see her playfully swat his arm. Their discussion continues for another block, then Randall's "friend" turns right, while he stays on the main throughway. Still too many people around to approach him directly.

My hands itch. Wish I had my gloves on instead of them all wadded up in my bag. At least I've put the jumpsuit's overlong sleeves to good use, covering up my unprotected hands with the excess material.

I stay with Randall through the next intersection where he turns left. Here, the crowds lessen. This stretch is actually nice, well lit and clean looking, with a number of air plants to soften the crumbling, industrial edges. Not giving myself the opportunity to think about all the reasons I shouldn't, I close the gap between us. Coming around his side, I disrupt his peripheral vision just enough to earn his notice. He glances over, then comes to a hard stop.

His disbelief's diminished by a flash of anger, quickly

dampened. "It really is you. What the hell, Emery?" He gives the jumpsuit a curious look. "What are you doing here?"

"I need your help."

He sucks in his cheeks and, for a second, I consider bolting. I was a fool to come here, to even consider...

"You could've messaged me."

I shake my head. "I couldn't. Not this time." I glance around. People swerve to avoid us. We need to get out of the open. And soon. "Just take me back to your place, and we'll... I'll explain everything. Please."

He's quiet so long I'm afraid he'll say no, but then he gives me one short nod and gestures for me to follow.

We continue down the walk lined with tidy shopfronts and cafes. A coffeehouse on the corner pumps out enough brew to scent the air, covering up the more unpleasant smells. Myself included. The neighborhood has a young professional vibe. Many of the people we pass have only been out of school a couple of years. As a result, it's a veritable oasis in the squalor that typically comprises the Terrestrial District. Randall glances over. "My place isn't much further."

I only nod, not trusting myself to answer verbally.

Randall heads toward a nondescript building, the entrance giving way as he approaches. I duck in behind him into a deceptively understated foyer so most people wouldn't give it another thought. That's one way to survive down here: not being too flashy about what you have.

The elevator responds to Randall's signal and takes us up three flights. His apartment's not much bigger than my Aventine-issued quarters, but with touches of his personality here and there to warm up the otherwise austere architecture it's a lot more comfortable. An envirosuit crumpled up in the corner must be from his last planting trip beyond the dome. A set of watercolors decorates one wall in the living room, the battered frames marking them as a family heirloom. A display case full of knickknacks...

Before I can fully process everything, Randall's voice cuts through my wayward thoughts. "You look ridiculous, and you smell even worse."

"Yeah, about that–"

He ducks into the bedroom and rustles through a drawer. He pulls out a pair of pants and a long-sleeved shirt, and waves me toward the bathroom. "Whatever you have to say can wait until after you get cleaned up."

I don't want to make things worse between us if I leave without explaining, but he's right. Despite my rinse-off earlier, I'm still rank. With a mumbled word of thanks, I shut myself in the bathroom. Under the hot water, I slather myself with Randall's soap and shampoo. Herbal, more medicinal than flowery, but at least it cuts through the layers of grime still clinging to my body. When the timer shuts off, I start it up again, lathering myself over and over until my wrinkled fingertips protest. He'll be docked some credits for excessive water use, but at the moment I can't bring myself to care.

I towel off and slip into his clothes. Still baggy, but not as bad as the jumpsuit. I brush my hair with his brush. Look at myself in his mirror. My hands are shaking. Could I be any more pathetic? I have no right to be here. To ask for his help. To assume I'd be welcome after pushing him away.

But I still need to unlock the bathroom door, cross the room, and give Randall the answers he's earned – along with those he thinks he deserves.

When I finally leave the sanctuary of the bathroom, Randall looks up from his seat on the couch. "Your clothes are being cleaned and will be ready in an hour or so."

"Oh. Um... thanks."

He stands, and some of that anger I caught a glimpse

of before is still leashed up tight inside him – making his steps jerky and forceful. "Well, you'd better start from the beginning."

"This morning?"

He makes a face. "No. The day you supposedly died."

Randall doesn't ask questions, just retreats deeper into himself as I talk in fits and starts. I'm so raw with it all, I hardly know what I'm saying anymore. When I reach the part with the gun in the Understory alley, his eyes flash, but he gets himself under control by the time I tell him about the garbage chute and my decision to find him.

I've run out of things to say so I look at my hands, still sore from the scouring I gave them. Infinitely more interesting than the dark look on Randall's face.

"Aventine set you up."

The conviction in his voice takes me aback. "What? No." At least I don't think so. Not until I know more.

"You said yourself they threw you into the deep end with a new client with trust issues."

"Yes, but catering to our clients' needs is what we do."

Randall shakes his head. "Then what about your handler? This is two of his couriers attacked in as many jobs."

"No. Tahir wouldn't do that." He was just as surprised as I was about the job being compromised, wasn't he? Calibrated emotions are practically impossible to fake. "If my implant was up and running, I could be more certain." But the damage my implant's sustained would be a red flag at any clinic in the city. If Aventine's not watching them, that woman from the drop certainly will be. Way too risky.

"And you have no idea what you're carrying?" Randall finally asks.

I shake my head. "Not supposed to. Security feature."

He sighs. "First thing we need to do is get that," he points to my head, "checked out." His eyes roll back into his head, then he nods. "Good. Charon will be able to meet us tomorrow morning."

"What? Who's that?"

"A friend who knows a thing or two about implants. Off the grid. After that, we'll pay a visit to one of my colleagues. She's into plants, but her background in genetics should help us figure out what you're carrying."

"Randall, stop. I just need a place to regroup, and then I'll be on my way. They'll be looking for me. It could be dangerous for you."

He shakes his head, mulish, resolute. "You came to me for help, so let me help."

"But..." It's already too late to not involve him, isn't it? "No one can know I'm here. Whatever contacts you have..."

Randall chuckles bitterly. "Don't worry, Emery. You'll be my dirty little secret. Besides, I scaled back my connections with everyone months ago."

"Really? Why?"

He shrugs with deceptive casualness. "I was a mess when Liv left." The blatant loneliness staring out of his eyes steals my breath before he blinks it away. "No one deserves being shackled to that."

You can be anyone or no one, but regrettably not yourself.

I can't be who he needs me to be, even if my implant *was* working properly, but I can't bring myself to say the words and add to the darkness he already carries.

He gestures vaguely to the bedroom. "Get some rest." He waits a second then adds, "I'll sleep out here, don't worry." His sardonic smile makes everything seem worse, but I don't know how to fix it... anything.

"Thank you. I mean it."

Something inside me twists tight and snaps away when he doesn't respond. I retreat to the bedroom. All this is just an exercise in agony. I shouldn't have come here. Torturing myself with a ghost from a past life. One that's no longer mine thanks to Aventine.

Back when Randall was simply Rik to me, things weren't so complicated. After *Partners in Crime* ended, we kept synch chatting. Wide-ranging conversations that moved past the confines of the game, no longer reliant on it as a communication crutch as we got to know one another better. Now we don't even have that to fall back on, thanks to me.

I've dreamed of this moment – I won't say I haven't – standing in Rik's room, with his scent everywhere begging me to inhale and hold it inside until I have it memorized. But it was never like this, where we're little better than strangers separated by more than the wall partitioning this room from the next.

It wasn't supposed to hurt.

When I wake, my clothes are laundered and hanging on the back of the door looking practically brand new. Even my gloves as I fit them to my fingers. I dress quickly and peek my head out before exiting the room.

No need for such caution. Randall's not even here. I feel oddly dejected at that, then freeze at the bag of croissants on the kitchen counter.

Part of me wants to ignore whatever this... offering signifies. I can't promise Randall anything, not until I know where things stand with Aventine, but the rest of me is starving. My stomach grumbles in anticipation as I take a bite, then another. Not as good as the ones you can get in the Canopy, but beggars can't be choosers, especially in the Terrestrial District.

I'm debating whether or not to eat the second croissant when Randall returns. His hooded gaze skates over me, lands on the pastry bag, then darts away with a guilty start.

Before I can ask, he says, "Had some things to take care of this morning. You ready?"

"Yeah, if we could stop at a drug store on the way, that would…"

He sets a small bag on the counter. "Got some toiletries. Didn't know what you'd need but–"

I glance inside. "No, this is great." A toothbrush, thank god, lip balm, moisturizer for my poor hands. The masochistic part of me was glad there were no items for overnight guests in his medicine cabinet even if it meant doing without. "I'll be ready in five."

I retreat back to the bathroom. When I'm done, Randall's pacing, but he comes to a halt when he sees me. "Let's go," I say as brightly as I can manage. It's early enough I have plenty of time before the curdle becomes a concern. Time enough to hopefully get some answers.

Randall's silent as we file out of his apartment building and trace our steps back to the main walkway we took last night.

"Your place is pretty decent," I say.

"For down here, yeah. Vector's housing allowance is generous enough I could afford a better place than what's customary." Capsule residences are often the norm for singletons right out of school unless connections or credits dictate otherwise. "I'm just lucky I got in when I did. A ton of places are trying to renovate but are tied up in litigation with current tenants." And while they fight it out, the Terrestrial District continues to crumble.

"It's nice that Vector rewards you for having to work down here."

"Nice has nothing to do with it. They're being competitive. No more, no less."

"Still. They must've wanted you to work for them very badly."

He shrugs, the action arrested by a frown as I dally at a street vendor's stall selling scarves and glasses. "You're on the run from your boss, and all you can think about is shopping?"

I count to three, concentrating on the weave of the different scarves, their patterns and colors. Then, channeling Brita, I beam at Randall as though nothing's wrong. "Buy one for me, won't you?"

His eyes widen. "What?"

"Pretty please?" I grab a blue one at random and shove it under his nose. "This one's perfect."

He hasn't quite erased the confusion from his face as he settles with the vendor.

I wrap my new scarf around my neck. I hold up one end, wave it back and forth, the gauzy material floating in the air, blocking my mouth from view. "Countersurveillance," I say after we move on. "Changing my appearance in response to my environment." Whatever that woman did to my implant, I have no idea if it extends to the tech under my face. Can't be too careful. I've learned that the hard way.

To make a point, I tuck my arm in his. His body turns to stone, but he doesn't fight the contact. I smile up at him and giggle into my scarf. "Do I look like a rogue agent on the run to you?"

He watches me for a long moment then looks away as if pained. "No."

I slowly put space between us once more. "We should stay with the morning crowds as long as possible on the way to your friend's place." If Aventine's looking for me in earnest, it'll at least make their job harder to find me in the crowds.

He nods, scanning the Promenade. I have the distinct impression he's avoiding my gaze. Finally, he faces me. "There's something you should know."

His apologetic look sends unease tricking down my spine. "What is it?"

"Charon's place is Underground."

CHAPTER EIGHTEEN

Underground. The domain of the Disconnects. Criminals even. People looking to get lost in New Worth. Or of such low status, the city wants them swept out of sight. And now me. Birds of a feather. I'm not sure which is more startling: that Randall knows someone who lives Underground or that someone down there can actually help me.

"I've learned a thing or two living dirtside," he says.

I want him to elaborate, but I'm not sure what I can ask him without opening myself up to more questions that must be festering under his skin as surely as the encoded blood I'm carrying is under mine. Quid pro quo can be a dangerous game. Especially for us.

Instead, I focus on our route to the Underground, doing my best to keep things compartmentalized. "How do we descend? I don't want to risk an official checkpoint."

To manage the flood of homeless throughout the Terrestrial District, the authorities have set up shelters in certain sections of the abandoned infrastructure that otherwise lies dormant underground. But they're heavily monitored by police. There's no guarantee Aventine will keep my disappearance quiet. If they alert law enforcement to help locate me, things'll get tricky in a hurry.

"Don't worry. I know how to get us down there undetected."

This time I can't hide my shock. He grimaces. "Look,

the people I work with... Not the scientists, but the actual workers? Most of them are Disconnects. They're not bad people – at least the ones working for Vector. A few of them even–" He shakes his head.

"*That's* why you were in the Understory that day. You're a sympathizer?"

He gives me a sharp look. "Don't say that word again. Not down here." He rubs his face and stops me with a hand on my arm. The touch is innocent enough before the heat of his fingers sinks into the fabric. "I'll tell you all about it when we can actually talk." He taps his temple with his index finger.

Our implants. My stomach swoops. Reconnecting with Randall. Having Rik's awareness filling me once more.

Something in Randall's gaze sharpens. "Of course, you can set the limits to our connection." The solicitousness in his voice is at odds with his eyes.

"Of course," I manage to say through the thickness in my throat. Once my implant is working again, there's no reason why we can't synch chat again, except for the pain I'm bound to cause him before this is all over.

He returns his attention to the street. We stay on the Promenade as it goes from stores and cafes to market stands and stalls. Crowds slow things down to a mere crawl. But I'm safer here, mired in potential casualties, if I'm being hunted.

The Promenade widens at a small square. On the opposite side, past a construction crew busting up a section of concrete with a painfully loud jackhammer, a phalanx of faux marble columns rises up four stories, embellishing the front of a casino.

Randall tugs me toward it, and I look at him in surprise. Unlike the ones that grace the upper levels, a Terrestrial casino's bad news. Rife with malware and the very worst of humanity, not beholden to New Worth's strictures for public spaces. As soon as you pass through the security gate at the entrance, you're subjected to the ever-changing house rules.

I shake my head and pitch my voice. "Don't know what'll happen if I go through the gates." Depending on what Aventine did to me, what alerts they put out, I could light up like a holiday tree on the security panels.

Randall gives me a smile, the first one since I dropped in on him. "Do you trust me?" His smile curdles. "Don't answer that." His eyes cross, synching maybe or otherwise using his implant. He nods to himself. "We'll take the third gate. Charon'll make sure we get through. Come on."

People drift in and out, business brisk no matter the time of day. Randall angles for the third security gate and I follow him in, breathing a sigh of relief when no klaxons sound or lights flash at my entry.

Brita had a birthday party at a casino in the Canopy a few years back. But two steps in, I can already tell this place can't command nearly a fraction of the gleaming glamour and ostentatious hospitality we enjoyed that night.

The casino floor's a logistical nightmare. Too many people and too few exits. This place would be off-limits for an Aventine op. Inside, strategically placed lights soften the devices of pure avarice. Slot machines, both old school and high tech, with their bells, whistles, and flashing digital readouts. Vid poker and other games requiring a physical uplink from a naked fingertip – the people at those machines must be truly addicted or desperate or both since all kinds of corruption can be mainlined through those interfaces. Clusters of the machines are positioned around the main floor, leaving long corridors for foot traffic between gambling areas, the on-site restaurant and lounge, and the various entertainment options – adult and otherwise.

Even the people are skewed toward extravagance. Body modifications abound – edgier than what's customary in the upper levels. And not just mods to present the body at best advantage. Ones that disrupt, perturb, and fascinate. The combinations limited only by the imagination.

One man has matte plastic scales protruding from his skin. A woman has printed hair – the only way she can have so much of it braided into ropes that dart in and out of piercings across her body – that doubles as clothing. A person of indeterminate gender has had their legs elongated and then wrapped in downy fur. Embedded LEDs or bioluminescent proteins grafted to the skin abound, as do bone spurs and ridges of cartilage that have been coaxed to extend outside the body.

And those are just the augmentations I can see. Who knows what goes on underneath?

I glance up at Randall, realizing the same is true for him. He tips his head toward the door to a small theater off the main room. "In there."

On stage, a magician tries to charm an audience that only half fills the rows. Bypassing the seats, Randall leads me down a small walkway, taking us backstage. I blink away the bright lights. Randall holds a silent conversation with a stagehand. Synching. Prudent considering the venue, but I don't like not having enough information to choose the next course of action. Makes me too dependent on Randall and whatever delicate negotiations are going on.

Beyond the curtain, half-hearted applause breaks out and strengthens as the magician executes a trick with unexpected skill. Randall and the stagehand break off their conversation. The stagehand rolls a wardrobe painted with whorls and arcane symbols that must be part of the magician's act across the floor, exposing a small hatch beneath it. He unlocks it, revealing a stairwell into darkness.

Randall gestures me forward. Aventine couldn't possibly know about this access point. I wonder what *else* they don't know as I lower myself down. The stairs lead to a short hallway, then another set of stairs takes us down, down, deeper into the bowels of New Worth.

Randall, a silent presence at my side, doesn't seem concerned by the feeble lights – too many burned out – or the slight humidity in the air that makes my clothes stick in all the wrong places.

"I never expected a casino to maintain access to the Underground, but I guess that's pretty naïve, considering."

He shrugs. "It's not naïve if you've never had cause to think about it."

Pipes and wires run overhead. Randall ducks underneath a large vent mounted to the low ceiling. "My friend has an... arrangement with the casino so he can monitor door security for people like us wanting to avoid attention while we descend."

"You've done this before," I say with certainty. "And this Charon? What's his deal?" The hard surfaces surrounding us distort my too-loud voice.

He gives me a sidelong glance and sighs. "Some people find their way to Charon to disconnect."

That takes me by surprise. To willingly give up your implant? They make modern life bearable.

"Don't look so shocked. Implants aren't everything. It's not a weakness to want to separate mind from machine."

Weakness maybe not, but definitely outside the norm.

We walk in silence for a little longer before Randall speaks again. "Anyway, Charon helps people 'cross over,' as he says. Lets me know when promising Disconnects come to him so I can help them find work at Vector."

"Couldn't you get in trouble?"

He shrugs. "Doesn't matter. Until our society has a better means of supporting Disconnects, they need help."

When Rik and I were connected, I had no idea. "I never realized you were so passionate about this. We debated about things, but..."

His steps slow. I turn back. His face stark, eyes haunted, unseeing. "You would have found out if we were calibrated."

He says it so plainly, I flush. I never should've given him an opening. "It was just an inperson meet. Anything beyond that was theoretical," I say, hating myself for the lie. I used to tell myself we would've lived happily ever after if it weren't for Aventine. That's not true, of course, but it makes for a better story. Now, though, after everything that's happened, I can't afford to entertain what-ifs with Rik, not with Aventine breathing down my neck.

"I know what Liv felt, and it wasn't theoretical." He gives me a long look. "But I don't know what you feel."

"Well, that makes two of us."

That surprises him into silence. We reach the end of the maintenance tunnel. A metal door grinds opens into a large subterranean chamber. Rusted metal girders span the ceiling. Cement blocks make up the walls. Water runs down one of the seams, creating runnels through old asphalt and dirt that seeps up through the cracks. This is all I can make out without my night amplification filter.

Randall steps beside me. "Can you see?"

"My parents got me a NAmp filter when we lived down here, but it's not working because, you know. You?"

"Vector paid for mine. So stay close."

As our voices fade, a scuttling along the periphery of my senses suggests we're not alone. It's so dark I bet even with the NAmp filter it'd be difficult to pick out the bodies creeping along the walls. Dark clothes, grime-covered skin, furtive movements. The air's thick with sewer gas and body odor.

"This way."

His face a mask, Randall wades into the middle of it all, heedless of the people who watch on, coveting our clothes, our relative cleanliness, our connection to the upper levels. At least I would be if I were stuck down here.

Further on, scavenged metal has been riveted together to create honeycomb structures – the Underground equivalent of capsule accommodations. Limbs that don't quite fit hang out over the edge. Scrap of a blanket here, a stocking-capped head there. Someone snores. Another's chest-rattling cough makes my ribs throb in sympathy. At an intersection, we pass an old woman hunched against the wall, muttering to herself. Her eyes track us, but she gives no other indication she's aware of our passage, her litany unceasing.

Randall either knows exactly where he's going or is doing a phenomenal job of faking it. He's perfected that confident stride that leaves no room for second thoughts. Another defense mechanism I recognize from living dirtside. At the third side tunnel, he turns, hunching his shoulders slightly at the lowered ceiling with a network of pipes running overhead. He stops in front of an area that's covered in scrap metal and particleboard. A barrier of some kind?

He raps against it. A haunting metallic sound echoes forlornly down the passage. A few seconds later a door creaks open, a feeble strip of light to welcome us.

A man in his late twenties with brown skin and slightly unkempt hair darker than the shadows around us gestures us inside. Charon's beady umber eyes are his most striking feature, refusing to settle on any one point for longer than a few seconds.

He lives in a little vestibule that's been fashioned from scrap metal and wood, floor to ceiling, but it's watertight and warmer than the slick chill of the public areas we passed through. The door's shut up again, Charon taking his time with the complicated set of locks. Whether it's to keep us in or someone else out, I'm not sure.

A small pallet is tucked up against the wall. A couple of shelves are welded above it, scattered with an array of empty wrappers, hand tools, cans of food, and pill packets. A large worktable fills the rest of the space, covered with computer components and a nightmare's worth of medical equipment and tools.

Charon greets Randall with a nod, then studies me with an intensity that raises goose bumps on my flesh. Randall doesn't say anything, but Charon's gaze flicks to him, and he snorts. Must be synching. I don't like how it leaves me out – something I never really noticed until my implant stopped working.

"Yeah, right, well, have a seat." Charon gestures to a stool in front of his workbench. He raises a diagnostic wand, and I flinch away automatically. "Don't worry. Just need to check some things out." He glances at Randall. "What did you do to her? She's as jumpy as a kangaroo." He might live Underground now, but he must've learned about life before the domed cities somehow – that's not always the case for people who live down here. Hopefully he's learned enough *other* things to help me out.

I force myself to relax. "Sorry. I've had a rough twenty-four hours."

He brings the wand up to the back of my neck where my implant lives, and whistles. "I'll say." He's about to set the wand down. "Hang on." He moves the wand back over my shirt, then down my pants legs. "Christ, you're tagged."

"What?"

"Your clothes. Each piece has a tiny transponder."

Randall starts. I glance at him, then back to Charon. Since they could track my implant, I figured clothing would be overkill. *In security, you plan for all outcomes, not just the most likely ones.* I should've anticipated this from Aventine. Stupid not to. "Range?"

He moves the wand over the one that must be embedded in my shoulder and looks thoughtful. "Well, they can't do anything from down here. Too much interference." Who knows how many feet of earth and infrastructure separates us from the civilized levels? He looks at Randall. "But they're probably able to get a signal from the Terrestrial District. Could take a while to triangulate, but still…"

Randall crosses his arms. "Can you deactivate them?" Charon nods. "Then do it."

I glance around. A crinkled shower curtain blocks off one corner of the room. "Is there a place I can change?" Into what, I'm not sure.

"Eh, it'll be easier if you keep your clothes on. We're not really set up for…" He makes a vague gesture toward me. I'm not sure if he means my particular issue or women more generally. "Right then." Charon plucks a taser off the table and whistles as he futzes with the controls. "Modified, of course. You'll feel just a pinch."

"Forgive me if I don't believe you."

He chuckles. I grit my teeth as his taser hums to life. He discharges a blink-and-you-miss-it blue spark and grunts in approval. He won't look me in the eyes. "Just a pinch, OK?"

Static slams into my right shoulder, rattling my teeth. Not enough to stun, but it still smarts. Charon brings up the diagnostic wand, casting it over the same area. "Good enough."

He turns to the one along my pants leg. More static wraps around my calf. He follows that up with my satchel, targeting a transponder along the front flap.

"All right, you should be good to go," he says a few seconds later.

"Check again. My clothes, my bags, and me." The modifications to my face, my forearms for the data transfers… Aventine could've embedded a tracker then. "*All* of me," I say at his raised brows.

"As you wish." He waves the wand over me just to double-check things, then pauses at a spot over my right hip. "Huh."

"What is it?" Randall asks.

"Not sure. Hang on." He twiddles with the controls and circles the area once more. "Shit. There's one under the skin."

"How deep is it?" I ask.

"Just a few millimeters under the skin. I could cut it out."

I flinch, but nod. "Get it out of me." Until I know what I've gotten myself into, I can't afford to be Aventine's property.

Charon meets Randall's glance over my head, then turns back to his workbench, shuffling aside metal components and clattering them against the hard plastic surface. He spins around. "Right, here we go. Randall, I'll need you to hold our girl still."

"You want me to stay seated?" The stool wobbles as I shift my weight.

Charon frowns. "No help for it. Unless you'd be more comfortable laid out on the floor."

I shudder involuntarily at the metal flooring, filthy-dark with grime. "No, this'll do."

Randall stares down at me for a moment, as though deciding how best to keep me in place. Avoiding my gaze, he presses against my left side. His arms loop around me, anchoring my arms to my sides. I breathe through my mouth, not daring to relax against him.

Charon gives me a wink. "It's going to hurt, so be sure to take it out on him." Charon lifts the edge of my shirt and works the waistband of my pants down to expose the curve of my right hip but no further in a bid to preserve my modesty, or what's left of it in this company. He swabs my skin with something cold. Antiseptic scents the air. At least there's that.

As Charon gets to work, I turn my head away, my cheek pressed against Randall's chest, and screw my eyes shut. I feel nothing, but I can hear the scalpel flense my skin and tissue away with a wet snick.

My body jerks involuntarily in Randall's grasp. "I can see

the bugger," Charon says from far away. "You got her?"

"I do." Randall at least sounds unperturbed.

The sensations change. Despite the local anesthesia or whatever Charon's using, I can feel him digging inside me. A sharp-needled pick in inexperienced hands. Screams build up in my throat. I press my face into Randall's shoulder and let them out. His arms tighten around me. He's saying something, but I can't hear it, just feel the slight vibration of his chest.

Metal pings nearby, and Charon whoops. "Hang on."

Flames lick down my side, then it's stoppered like a bottle. Charon pats me awkwardly as he fastens bandages to my hip.

I slowly release Randall; his arms fall to his side a heartbeat later. Blood rings my clothes and is already crusting against my skin. Too much. I force my gaze away with a grimace. "Where is it?"

Charon brandishes a small chip in a metal dish, no bigger than an earring stud. I move to take it, but he jerks the dish away. "Think of it as payment. I had to use my last capsule of muscle mend on you."

"But couldn't it be tracked here?"

"Not by the time I'm done with the chip." He gives it another lingering, no, *covetous*, look, then sets the dish on the far edge of the work bench. Finally, he pulls his attention away and claps his hands. "All right. For this next bit, I need to put you under, but I can't, see?" Charon gestures to his lab. "Down here, we have to make do with what we got. And you only got me."

"Understood. But before you bring me back online, there are a couple things you need to know."

Charon settles back on his heels, arms crossed.

"First, I'm probably going to show up as an anonymous user with no signal information." I give him a general overview of the modifications Aventine's made to my implant to help me navigate the city undetected. "Taking my randomized identities away is the first thing the... people I work for would do."

I'm grateful Charon doesn't ask any questions, only nods to himself. He must've dealt with all kinds down here: the good, the bad, and the desperate. "That's no problem." He spins back to his table, picks up a wire-mesh basket filled with data sticks, and sifts through them. "We'll get you a new ID, no flags, generous permissions that should hold up to," his gaze cuts back to me, eyebrows raised, "*reasonable* scrutiny."

"What about the tech under her face?" Randall asks.

"Hmm." Charon sets the basket down and picks the diagnostic wand back up. He waves it over my face, gaze glued to the digital readout on his screen. When he turns back to me, his eyes have a wild look to them. He's totally geeking out right now. He doesn't care about me. He's all about the tech. That in itself isn't surprising. It's more that he makes no effort to hide it. "I think... It's hard to say, but I'm pretty sure if the identity randomizer is turned off, your digital impressions will be too, but..."

"If it isn't," Randall says, "it'll be a dead giveaway at the first checkpoint she passes through."

"Hang on." Charon brandishes the wand at me, so close I flinch, certain the cool plastic will meet my skin. It doesn't though, and I relax my perch on the stool slightly. "There!" Charon taps the screen triumphantly. "There's a tiny transponder, see it? I can deactivate it so it can't be remotely triggered by your keepers. You'll be able to turn it on if you need to use it, but at least they won't be able to use it against you."

"Great. One more thing," I say. "Can you deactivate all my contacts?"

"Sure, no problem." He sticks a sensor to my neck, mounted right over my implant. He turns back to the console on the worktable, pulling up a map of my connections on his screen. "Showing five, one calibrated."

Randall stirs in the periphery of my vision. I tell myself I don't owe him an explanation. I force myself to look at Charon. "I want them gone."

"Should be able to dismantle them." His hands skate over the screen. "And… done," he says a few seconds later.

He sticks more sensors to my temples and another he instructs me to place next to my heart. As he bends his head, an ugly jagged scar is revealed along the back of his neck where his implant should be. Did he tussle with a scrapper? He straightens, and it disappears behind his shirt collar.

"All right. Now I need you to relax. This next bit won't be painful, not exactly, but it *will* be unpleasant. Can't be more specific than that, what with everyone's brains being different, OK?"

I nod and adjust my perch on the stool, my hip still numb. Over my head, Randall and Charon are synching again. Deciding their plan of attack? I grit my teeth.

Charon shuffles back to the console. "One, two–"

I gasp. My spine wrenches me straight, my head falls back, my eyes staring uncomprehendingly at the girders holding up the ceiling.

Someone stands behind me, supporting my arms and shoulders. Randall, Rik… he…

My head erupts. Screams fill my ears, my own voice harsh and panicked.

It's like my brain has been pulled into a long rope, malleable like taffy, stretched tighter and tighter until the gray matter snaps, rending one side of my mind from the other. My gaze wavers, and it's only later that I realize it's tears.

Feedback buzzes in the background. Static, snow, heat build up under my skin, underneath my eyes, inside the drums of my ears.

Then the five magical tones that herald the booting up sequence for my implant. The tension in my mind ebbs. The snow in my vision clears, the sounds dim accordingly.

"Emery, your nose is bleeding." Randall's voice is far away as I slowly drift back to reality.

My grimy surroundings come back into painful focus. Charon hands me a dirty handkerchief. I wipe my nose, try to avoid seeing just how much blood it collects. Sharp pain drills into my skull, as though the jackhammer the construction workers were using outside the Casino is now being applied to my head. Even the skin on my forehead hurts to touch.

But my implant's back online, which almost makes up for the pain radiating from my hip and my temples as I run through the config settings.

Randall grips my arm. "You OK?"

Too much touching too soon. I almost shrug him off, but I don't want to aggravate my injury. I give his hand a squeeze as I pull away from him. "I'm fine. Thanks." I nod to Charon. "Both of you."

Charon flashes me a smug grin, showing off a crooked front tooth. "If you ever find yourself down in the big bad Underground again, you know where to find me."

CHAPTER NINETEEN

With each step, fire lances along my hip, shortening my stride. And I need every bit of it to keep up with Randall.

He takes us a different way out than the way we came in. I'm hopelessly disoriented even with my implant back up and running. Not even Aventine has a map for the Underground.

My NAmp filter shades in the blanks I missed earlier. The constant moisture, the scurrying figures we move past, eyes impossibly wide to make out their surroundings. The aging infrastructure, the filth infecting the air. Dark mold insulates seams between walls and ceilings. Sewer gas chokes my throat. It's even worse than I imagined. But at least now I can better guide my steps around the more questionable refuse coating the ground.

Randall glances back and slows his pace. "We'll get you some painkillers once we ascend."

"No."

"What do you mean, 'no'?"

"Go home, Randall. You've done enough."

"I can't, remember? You had more bugs on your body than a corpse. They've probably tracked you to my place by now."

"So? Just say some random girl broke in and moved on before you–"

"Stop it, Emery. Just, stop."

I nearly run into him, an immovable, implacable presence

in front of me. My breath hitches, bringing with it a sharp pain up my side.

"We're in this together. Always have been, even before..." He shakes his head. "I'm going to take you to one of my colleagues next. She might be able to help us figure out what you're carrying."

That's right. A geneticist who might be able to uncover what was done to my blood. But that's assuming she'll be able to break the government's encryption. Finola wasn't exactly confident in their process, but that doesn't mean it'll be a breeze to decrypt either.

Randall glances around. We're in a tight corridor of corrugated metal, rusted and stained. No one's visible in the immediate vicinity, but looks can be deceiving, especially down here. Then he sends me a synch request.

It blinks impatiently in the periphery of my vision. I almost let it through, but something stops me as I focus on Randall's face, tense and waiting.

"It can't be like before." It comes out in a whisper.

Randall rears back as if I had slapped him. "This is the only way we can talk without being overheard. Not everything is about us."

"I know, I just..." I'm being stupid. But to open myself up to him again? That's not fair to either one of us.

Chastened, I close my eyes and accept the request. Immediately, Rik's awareness fills me. I nearly sob. Even on the default acquaintance setting, he's overwhelming. A piece I had almost convinced myself wasn't missing. My heart eases its frantic gallop in my chest as the shock wears off and an inevitable feeling of rightness returns after being gone so long.

He sighs a full-body sigh that travels his whole frame. Then he grimaces. <<A friend just sent me a request. Wanted to know what the hell just happened.<<

>>Thought you said you scaled things back?>>

<<I did, but emotional bleed doesn't always cooperate.<<

I flush at that, grateful for the dark. >>They can't know.>>

<<Don't worry. I'm handling it.<< His synch chat's brief. He stares down at me a moment later. <<Ready to go?<< I nod and minimize our connection in a desperate attempt to put more distance between us, but Randall wants nothing of it. <<You asked earlier how I knew Charon and my connection to the Disconnects.<<

I grit my teeth at the flatness of his tone. With this level of permissions, our connection's limited to thought-text only to keep appropriate boundaries between our minds. Nonverbals, emotional broadcasts, all prohibited. My mind wants to jump right in where we left off. But I'm not sure *I* can.

>>So you're part of some vast conspiracy?>>

<<Vast? No.<<

That throws me, and I give him a second glance.

<<When I started working with the Disconnects, saw the lives they were forced to live – that *we* forced them into… Let's say it was a humbling experience. So I decided to do something about it.<< Which is more than can be said for the majority of New Worthians. Myself included. Randall glances over at me. <<Don't look so shocked.<<

>>Not trying to be. But Charon's connected too. I saw you both synching. Though that scar…>>

<<Yeah, he used to live in the Terrestrial District with a job, partner, you name it. But he got divorced, and he couldn't adjust. He woke up in a hospital after trying to claw his implant out with his bare hands.<<

I shudder, trying to reconcile the version of Charon I saw with his past. Traumatic breakups or the sudden death of a confidant can wreak havoc not just emotionally but mentally as the mind relearns how to think on its own. Therapy can help, but that's often an unreachable luxury for too many who live in the lower levels.

<<At the time, he was upset it didn't work, but now, he uses his connectivity as a way to help the Disconnects stay competitive. Because New Worth's so dependent on implants, it's that much harder for them to do *anything* – things we take for granted with each eyecast command.<<

>>So the system's stacked against them.>> It's why my parents worked so hard to ensure that, whatever else, I was outfitted with the latest tech in the hopes I'd one day ascend. >>They're the ones who've rejected implants and the access they provide.>>

Randall sighs. <<It's not that simple. If you heard their stories and realized the extent of the shit they've had to deal with... Anyway, with Emergence creeping closer, their concerns are growing.<<

>>Why? Because they'd rather be the ones selected for the Vesa trial? They don't care the lottery's the fairest way to ensure *every* New Worthian has an equal chance of going.>>

<<It sounds selfish at first, I agree. But they've wanted to leave for decades. Ever since they saw the rehabilitation efforts led by Vector and other agro firms firsthand. Since they're more motivated than some random city dweller, they believe they have a greater chance of making Vesa succeed.<<

>>But Emergence is for everyone, not just the Disconnects.>>

<<True, but they're the ones being left out of the official planning for Emergence when their claims to the homes they left behind are just as valid as yours or mine. It's probably only a matter of time before the demonstrations turn even more violent.<<

My thoughts stall at his words.

<<What?<<

>>When I told you about the botched drop, I left out the part about the guy at the warehouse spouting nonsense about

Emergence, the possibility of civil war. I thought it was a ploy to sway me, but maybe there was more to his warning.>>

Randall stops. <<What you're carrying has something to do with Emergence?<<

>>I don't know. Whatever it is, it's important. And not just because of what happened at the drop. Even before that, the briefing and mission prep were out of the norm.>>

<<In what way?<<

>>You do realize everything I tell you puts you at greater risk?>>

<<I'm aware. Haven't changed my mind.<<

I worry the inside of my cheek. >>Data transfer took place in the Echelon.>>

He whistles. <<Corporate contractors?<<

I shake my head. The sulfur in the air's almost unbearable. >>I don't think so. We were dealing with the government directly. I'd bet money on it, given all the oversight.>>

<<And yet it still went bad.<<

Almost from the beginning. >>Yes.>>

<<Well, Geeta will help us f–<< A strange look washes over his face. "Get down!"

A light strobes overhead, momentarily shocking my NAmp filter. Randall grabs my shoulder and forces me to the floor. "What–" My knees hit concrete as a clicking sound echoes down the tunnel.

Randall shoves my head down and covers us both with his hands just as a whoosh and a rush of heat roars overhead. Fire dazzles my eyes. After a few seconds, it's all over. No more clicking sounds, no lights strobing.

Randall slowly gets up, holding out a singed gloved hand to help me do the same. "Sewer gasses. Have to burn them off periodically to keep them under control." Sure enough, the sulfur smell has abated somewhat, leaving the acrid tang of fire in its wake. "Sorry about that. It's one of the risks of this particular route. But the other option was to go through a settlement in an old subway tunnel. Didn't think that was the best choice."

I can only stare at him. He's apologizing for this? "It's fine. I would've made the same choice."

He gives me a relieved nod. "The good news is we don't have much further to go."

Ten minutes later we reach a set of steep stairs. Randall climbs up halfway and locks his legs as he lifts the hatch up a few inches. Whatever he sees must set him at ease since he opens it fully and disappears. I climb up after him. We emerge onto a quiet side street, the hatch covered with faux grating to make it look like an old runoff catchment. The dumpster blocks us from view of the street, giving me precious seconds to get my bearings.

Away from the claustrophobic Underground, the Terrestrial District's almost pleasant in comparison. The light, however feeble, reassures me we've returned to civilization. The air, thick with garbage and bodies, at least moves, banishing the slick chill from below. We're a good two miles from the casino we descended from. Thankfully my Aventine map of the city is still working. I've never been more grateful for their paranoia. They intended the local copy to be a more reliable version than what's on the New Worth network. But that also means they can't alter it remotely and route me into an ambush or some sort of trap to bring me in.

<<Vector's only a few blocks away from here.<<

Hopefully whatever Charon did to me is enough to keep Aventine off my back. They can't track me, and I have a brand-new identity. But… >>If Aventine's managed to trace me to your quarters, you'll fall under their scrutiny. Including your work with Vector.>>

<<You have a better idea?<<

I don't.

Randall nods to himself. <<Then we'll assume they haven't made the connection yet.<<

>>But–>>

<<I've already told Geeta to expect us. Come on.<<

Ribbons of different routes from our current location to Vector blink into existence on my city map. Randall more or less follows a path that'll take us to the back of the company's headquarters.

We aren't far from the glass perimeter and the only outdoor access point in this quadrant that's monitored by the authorities. We pass garage after garage filled with trucks with improbably large tires. For all the planting trips beyond the dome? Assuming I had the permissions, all I'd have to do is walk through the airlock, wait for it to cycle, then emerge into fresh air, big sky, and green as far as the eye can see. No longer would I have to rely on hazy views from the Canopy or digital renderings broadcast across the network.

When the first reports came out a few years ago that the air quality had improved, that it was no longer poisonous for short periods, people tried to go outside and see for themselves. They were turned away, but ever since then the police presence has had to be stepped up to deter the waves of curious citizens that usually coincide with each progress report. With the Vesa trial and the Disconnects whipping up renewed interest in what lies beyond the glass, there've been reports of violent confrontations at the entrances.

But the City Council has maintained, despite our strides to reclaim the land, too much is unknown to allow untrained, everyday citizens see what it's like. The grim stories about life before the dome – of deadly storms, polluted air, poisoned water and soil – carry such a psychic burden, the Council doesn't dare approve letting anyone out. When the domed cities were first raised many people made the migration willingly, but some had to be forcibly removed from their homes. Those who held out were never heard of again. With the troubles New Sacrament's faced still in recent memory, no one wants the sacrifices to build New Worth to be for nothing if we get Emergence wrong.

In the meantime, anyone can rent an arcade rec suite and select any number of simulations to recreate the outside world. Though how could they compare to the real thing? One day, maybe I'll have the courage to ask Randall what it's really like out there. Right now, I don't dare ask him for any more of himself.

He leads us toward the back of the Vector complex. >>Does Vector grow plants on site?>> I don't see any greenhouses, but that doesn't mean anything in the Terrestrial District where grow lights and vertical beds are the only way to cultivate anything in such cramped, dark conditions.

<<Some. But we're actually more focused on the soil's overall health. We test plants' interactions with soil from different regions, determine what the optimal conditions are, then outsource the actual plant husbandry to greenhouses and vertical farms throughout the city.<<

>>Such a coordinated effort must've taken a lot of time and money.>>

<<Absolutely. But can you really put a price on Emergence?<<

I don't answer. I don't need to. Emergence has always been the goal of living under glass.

<<Good. Geeta's waiting for us at the Disconnect entrance so I won't have to code in.<<

And alert Aventine to his whereabouts. A chill runs down my spine. I have to hope they're not paying attention yet. >>Smart. But we'll still have to do something about your signal.>>

Randall's profile is calm, edged with determination. He truly behaves as if there's nothing to worry about. At least there's that. He gives me a wink and pats his pants pocket. <<Charon gave me a new ID too, if it comes to it.<< He gestures to our surroundings. <<And if anyone inquires, I've been at work. Nothing suspicious.<<

>>Except you spent much of the day Underground.>>

<<So? I'll say I was on a planting trip beyond the dome.<< And the reach of the New Worth network.

>>It's a good story, but it won't hold up to scrutiny.>>

<<My team of Disconnects will vouch for me.<<

>>They'd really do that?>>

He gives me a tight nod as we approach Vector Agronomy's back entrance. A woman in a lab coat paces, a bored-looking guard watching her beyond a wire fence. The gates are open, but there's no security portal to log implants. A waste since Disconnects probably only use this entrance.

The woman looks up and gives Randall a wave. With a shock, I recognize her from the other day. The one Randall walked home with.

Before I've fully processed this, Randall's introducing us. "This is Dr Geeta Thompson."

"I wondered when you were coming in today," she says.

"Something came up." He gestures to me, and I give her a polite nod.

"Right." She looks me over, her smile cooling but not quite disappearing. She glances at Randall, synching.

I don't know why this infuriates me, but I do know I don't appreciate the gleam in her eye whenever she looks at Randall. My hands curl into fists at my sides. I straighten out my fingers and try to relax. Finally, the connection between the two of them eases.

Geeta flashes me a smile. "This way. We have much to discuss." Inside, the hallway takes us past locker rooms and laboratories. "Vector Agronomy prides itself on being at the forefront of the rehabilitation of the region around New

Worth. The initiatives we've spearheaded are what have made Emergence in our lifetimes possible," she says, as if I'm just another colleague visiting the site.

>>We'll need a quiet area, preferably away from prying eyes. Off the network,>> I tell Randall.

<<Relax. Vector didn't win a government contract for habitat remediation without knowing a thing or two about security.<<

Geeta flutters her hand toward two double-doors. Their glassed-in windows frame shelves of leafy plants. An onsite greenhouse. "We'll save a tour of the plants we're currently testing for reintroduction later," she says in a courteous voice as we turn down another hallway.

At the end, there's an elevator her eye scan allows us to access. My skin crawls as the three of us enter. Lifts are always logistically tricky. But Randall and Geeta are taking no small risk in bringing me here so openly. I have to trust that much.

The doors open two levels down. The sub-basement? I didn't think I'd be back underground so soon. We approach a small laboratory. As Geeta unlocks the door, Randall walks a bit further down the hallway, then turns back, satisfied we're still alone. Inside, Geeta switches on the lights and pulls a drop cloth off a table of lab equipment. Randall shuts the door behind me.

She glances up from an old console computer. "We can talk freely in here, don't worry." She levels another curious look my way. "I'll need to run some tests."

"I understand. And data security?"

"Nothing'll leave this room."

Randall gives me an I-told-you-so look. Got plenty of them playing *Partners in Crime*, and a real one's just as annoying.

Geeta glances at the equipment on the table. Some of it looks like early-generation versions of Finola's gear. "Hang on. Need to get one more thing." Geeta walks to the storage closet along the back wall and soon disappears among its dusty shelves.

<<You can trust her, Emery.<<

I stiffen and pull my gaze away from the closet as cavalierly as I can. >>Of course you'd say that.>>

He growls, and it's almost like the digital feedback I'd get from him whenever I frustrated him during our synch chats. Almost.

>>What?>>

<<You know what.<<

I cross my arms. >>No, I don't. We're on acquaintance settings, remember?>>

<<Bullshit, Liv. Besides, we can change that any time.<<

I stare at him, my mind suddenly blank.

Geeta breezes back over and gestures for me to take a seat on the lab bench. Gratefully, I comply. Even though she'll be the one poking me with needles, it's better than whatever *that* was with Randall. She pulls a catheter out of her purse, the wrapping on it carrying the reassuring brand name of a pharmacy chain. At least her equipment's in better condition than Charon's. I push back my sleeve.

She misses the vein and digs the needle back and forth in my arm before she finally lucks out. "Sorry," she says at my hissed breath. "My samples usually aren't living." No shit.

She siphons off a pint of blood and creates a set of slides, with different dyes and additives for each one. Then she settles down in front of a microscope. She cycles through the first couple of slides rather quickly, then whistles after taking a long look at the next one.

She blinks up at me in awe. "I heard this kind of thing was possible, but…" She shakes her head. "I'll need to isolate the data structure, then who knows if I'll be able to decipher it. No guarantees."

"I understand. Thank you." Rifling through her equipment, I find a needle and the tubing necessary to transfuse the remaining blood back into my body.

Beside me, Randall goes stock-still. Geeta gives him a concerned look. "What is it?"

He turns to me. "Tahir Ahmed wants to talk to you."

CHAPTER TWENTY

"How did he–" I cut that thought off. Tahir must've found Randall's apartment and reached out to him as a matter of course.

<<I haven't responded yet, but...<<

I know what he's asking. The utility's undeniable. To be able to sit in on their conversation, even interact if I want, would be huge. All I have to do is upgrade Randall's permissions. Let him back into my mind. Nonverbals, near-instantaneous sharing, practically everything we had before we were disconnected.

I close my eyes, take a breath, and let him in. I flush all over, very aware of Geeta's presence, as undeniable pleasure washes over me. Anger, resentment, from both of us, builds up, harmonic resonance almost a physical pain as we flash through the last few months. Then something snaps, and all is as it should be. Rik in my head. His hurt at being separated, the confusion and desperation when we found each other again, and the surprise at my real identity – all that swirls in the background, subsumed by the more immediate relief at being reunited.

<<Liv...<< The connection thrumming between us distorts his voice. <<What do you want me to say to him?<<

That jerks me back to reality. Slightly. >>Not sure yet. Link me in?>>

He does, though it takes me a moment to focus on it with all the competing information churning between us.

<<I repeat, this is Tahir Ahmed of Aventine Security with questions pertaining to a mutual associate named Emery Driscoll. Please respond.<<

>>Play dumb,>> I tell Randall. >>See what he has to say.>>

His agreement flashes through me. Then, <<Look, I don't know how you contacted me, but I don't know who–<<

<<Mr Iverson-Kemp, please,<< Tahir cuts in. <<I know she was in your quarters. Failure to answer my questions now will–<<

He's not using the royal Aventine we, but that's about all that can be said.

<<Someone broke into my place? Why didn't you say so?<<

There's a brief pause where I imagine Tahir's grinding his teeth.

<<Should I file a police report?<< Randall continues. <<I'm at work right now, but–<<

<<No. No, that won't be necessary.<<

<<You just said–<<

<<Where were you this morning? You didn't clock into work until an hour ago.<<

<<What are you, my mom?<<

I laugh, then immediately clap my mouth shut with my hands. Randall gives me a wink. Being able to see his face as we synch adds a whole new dimension to the experience. What happens when that's no longer enough?

<<Mr Iverson-Kemp, you have my contact information. Tell Emery she needs to come in. The longer she stays out there, the harder it is for me to protect her.<<

<<I told you. I don't–<<

<<Save it. This is a non-Aventine line. She can reach me here if something happens.<<

>>You mean like having the drop hijacked?>> I break in.

Randall glares at me, but I ignore him, waiting for Tahir's response.

<<M, thank god.<< Then, <<What the hell happened?<<

>>You tell me. The client's security never showed because apparently I was routed to the wrong location. That guy I picked up at the aquarium? He's dead. And I'm pretty sure I'd be too if I didn't run.>>

That throws him, but only for a second. <<We'll talk to the client, get things straightened out, but you need to come in, M.<<

Rik tenses. He's trying to be good, keeping his emotions in check to not confuse the connection, but his anxiety's contagious.

>>I can't do that. How do I know Aventine wasn't in on it?>>

<<We would never–<< Tahir stops abruptly. <<I can't help you out there, M.<<

>>Don't worry about that.>>

He's quiet for a long moment. <<You have no field support. No way to get scrubbed. And your implant's signal's completely dark. Let me meet you somewhere. I can bring–<<

>>*No*. Not until I know what's going on, Tahir.>>

<<M, listen. Please. People over my head are getting involved. If you don't come in soon–<<

<<We'll take that under advisement,<< Randall breaks in before he cuts the connection.

And before I can react to Rik's renewed presence, he does the same to ours. Not simply reverting back to the acquaintance settings, but severing our connection entirely. A headache crashes down on me, amplified by a slight twinge in my stomach.

"Why did you cut him off?" I nearly snarl.

"Your conversation was going nowhere."

"That was my call."

"He's trying to confuse you. Let your guard down."

I hold up my hand. "You don't know him."

"*You* don't either."

Casting about for a response, I remember Geeta. She watches us with a bewildered look on her face. "Uh, sorry about that."

She shrugs, trying to appear indifferent, but her wide, brown eyes give her away. "Don't mind me."

I exhale slowly. Clearly Tahir was able to connect Randall to me, but the question is whether he's disclosed that to Aventine yet. I'd like to believe he'd give me a chance to make things right, but after drinking from the hose of Randall's distrust, I don't know what to think anymore.

The laboratory walls press closer. We're too vulnerable if we stay here. I yank out the needle tethering me to the lab and slap on a wound-heal patch from my satchel. "I should go."

"Yes, *we* should," Randall says. "As far as we know, your handler could have Vector staked out by now."

I shake my head. "No. He would've told us that much." At least I hope I'd warrant a heads up. Besides, he'd have no way of knowing if I was here. All he knew for sure was I had a connection to Randall, incidental or maybe something more. He could guess we're traveling together or were connected somehow, but he couldn't be certain of it. Until I confirmed it for him.

Randall rolls his eyes and turns back to Geeta. "You got everything you need?" She nods. "Good. We're leaving. You contact me with what you find." His eyes close momentarily. "My real ID has worn out its usefulness, so use the one I just sent you."

He grabs a touchscreen from the table. "You don't have one of these in your bag of tricks, do you? Might come in handy."

I tuck it into my satchel. It's a good idea, and it can't be linked to either one of us, only Vector.

"But what about work?" Geeta asks. "What should I tell management?"

"Nothing. I left early today, and that's all you know."

"But–"

"We don't want you any more involved than you already are," I say. "The less you know now, the better."

"If you're sure..." She looks at me. "Will you be all right?"

"She'll be fine. She'll be with me," Randall says impatiently.

A wrinkle forms in her brow. "But didn't you tell him about the possibilities of rejection?"

Ah, crap. Before I can answer, Randall levels a glare at me. "No. She didn't."

The industrial neighborhood where Vector Agronomy is headquartered gradually gives way to housing developments and shabby storefronts the closer we get to the Promenade. Randall's brooding presence shadows me as I dart along the edge of the crowds. I send him a synch request, but he ignores it.

Guess we're going to have to do this the old-fashioned way.

"You're overreacting."

"The hell I am."

"We just have to figure things out before I can't function anymore," I say over my shoulder.

"You make it sound like it's no big deal."

"What can I do about it? Nothing. So we just have to take things as they are."

He grabs my elbow. "You should've told me."

I shrug him off me. "I was hoping it wouldn't be necessary."

"Then what's stopping us from getting you a transfusion or something so... *you know* can't hurt you?"

"The data's safer inside me than out."

The whole point of what we do is to obscure where the data is at any point in time. Not on the network vulnerable to attack. Nor copied to a datakey or card too easily stolen or corrupted. Instead, it's hidden in plain sight, underneath a courier's skin. *My* skin.

"Besides, we have plenty of time before we need to worry about the curdle." We've only burned a full day. Symptoms won't kick in for real until tomorrow.

He glances up and down the street. "Maybe we should go back to the lab."

"And what? Get in Geeta's way? Distract her from her work? Don't know about you, but I could use a break. Preferably not somewhere where we're sitting ducks."

"What if it's your symptoms?"

I cross my arms. "It's not." Even if it is, the stash of painkillers Geeta gave me as we left Vector will have to be enough to hold me over.

"But what if it is?"

"Still need to lie down."

Randall shakes his head, frustration welling up, but he pushes it back with a sigh. "Then where to now?"

Good question. I pull up my map of New Worth. Too many places are out of bounds with Aventine on the hunt. This sector of the Terrestrial District has a large Disconnect population. I skip over a section in yellow automatically, then realize my mistake. That's it: the areas Aventine has deemed too dangerous because of the Disconnect unrest. Places where they can't guarantee proper backup.

"The Bower."

"No way. You'll get eaten alive. Both of us."

I keep walking. "Doesn't matter. A den of Disconnects

is the safest place for us right now." I glance back at him. "Besides, you're the one who considers them friends."

He gives me a pointed look. "They've certainly proven to be more reliable."

If he's trying to hurt me, it almost works. "Well, *I'm* going. You can still figure a way out of this mess if you walk away now."

"Don't be ridiculous."

"Then let's go."

He mutters a curse, but at least he stops trying to change my mind.

The yellowed-out part of my map covers a wide swath of the Bower. The northernmost edge dovetails with a couple of blocks I canvassed when I was tailing Breck and some of the other scrappers. They were their hunting grounds for a reason. Lots of tight walkways, heavy Disconnect traffic, and a number of buildings and storefronts that have cycled through so many tenants, half are empty at any one time.

When we get close to the start of the Bower, I veer toward a clothing store. Randall swallows his objections when I pick out a hastily printed shirt for him and a zip-up sweater for me. Can't help the newness, but the disposable styles signal us as people who can't afford better. Randall purchases our clothes using his new ID. Before leaving the store, we slip them on over our clothes. Hopefully it'll be enough to blend in.

"Have you been in this neighborhood before?" I ask. The buildings constrict around us. Not even the mirrors get enough of the faint reflected light down here.

"Yes." He practically spits the word out, but whatever else he's thinking is hidden behind his stony demeanor.

"I grew up a couple of blocks away. Avoided the area for the most part even back then," I offer, trying to draw him out.

"They'll know we're connected."

Part of me wants to say no, they won't, but that's not true, is it? They'll figure it out eventually, even if we pass a cursory first examination. The eyes often give us away. The eyecast commands telegraphing our preoccupation with our implants. If not that, they could always get close enough to see the slight discoloration along the back of our necks. More obvious on someone like Randall with his pale skin than me.

"Then we'll just have to convince them we mean no harm."

"The whole city's ready to boil over, and you think you can convince them we have their best interests at heart?"

"We have to, if we're going to have a safe place to crash for a few hours."

His shoulders bunch, and I'm momentarily glad I'm not subjected to his unvoiced frustration. "Fine," he says flatly.

When we slip into the Bower, crossing an invisible line between relative safety and uncertainty, the quiet unease is similar to my very first job where the rally cut off my access to the lifts. But the sight of the checkpoints ripped from the corners of buildings, their dismantled entrails scattered across the ground or strung up overhead cheers me slightly.

Randall hasn't shed his discomfort, but, on him, he just looks pissed off which, thankfully, deters most people we pass. We have a tail though, a cocky kid in his early teens that picked us up as soon as we entered the neighborhood. If Randall's noticed, he gives no indication. Just as well.

We pass an old restaurant that's been converted into a shelter for Disconnects. The wide front windows reveal dozens of people in the well-lit interior. Families and individuals alike sit at the dining tables that have been arranged in a semicircle to face a man standing at an improvised podium made from dusty old computer towers.

Part-priest, part-politician, he makes a speech of some sort to the rapt audience.

Randall eyes the shelter carefully and sends me a synch request. <<You know what that place is?<<

I nod as we move past, not looking at it directly, but intensely aware of all the Disconnects inside. Gathering places like this one aren't uncommon for people who feel cut off from the rest of society. Sometimes they provide services for community members with mental and emotional issues – often ones who were denied implants in the first place. But after listening to Randall, there's a lot more of them, and reasons for disconnecting, than I realized.

>>When I was little, a friend took me to one of these places after school. When my parents found out her family were Disconnects, I wasn't allowed to play with her anymore.>> We still hung out at school, but after I got my implant and she didn't, we grew apart.

<<Early on, Disconnects were given more accommodations than they are now. At least that's what my colleagues told me.<< Tension lines Randall's shoulders as though he's personally burdened by their plight. <<But they've been left behind in a society that rewards connectivity, or, rather, exploits those who refuse it.<<

Some would go further than that. With the rallies, the network's been flooded with chatter about how the Disconnects are on an evolutionary track that diverged from the majority of New Worthians a long time ago. A contentious stance that's only added to the unrest plaguing the city. But some of the Disconnect hardliners are descended from those who fought coming to the domed cities in the first place. A while ago, I read a New Worth News feature profiling a Disconnect whose grandfather was convinced the domed cities were a plot to enslave the population. Such conspiracy theories must be enjoying renewed interest with all this talk of Emergence.

>>You make it sound like implants are a bad thing.>> After all, we wouldn't have found each other without them. Or be able to have this conversation right now in the heart of Disconnected territory if we were speaking aloud.

He's quiet so long I wish I knew what he was thinking. <<It's not that they're *bad*. More like their use and their impact on society goes largely unexamined.<< A pause, then: <<Did you or your parents ever question getting you an implant?<<

>>No.>> I was counting down the weeks until I was old enough for the procedure. I couldn't wait to feel connected to the city, my parents, my friends. It felt so grown up. A way to escape my surroundings. >>It's just what you did, what everyone does, if you're going to have a chance at succeeding here.>>

<<Well, maybe they should've questioned it. We all should have.<<

It's true connection has a cost. Just look at me and Randall. The messy infrastructure can barely keep pace with the demands implants place on it. Not to mention security risks, malware, and emotional bleed – the kind that incapacitates or breeds paranoia instead of bringing people together.

Drawbacks we blindly put up with in our search for efficiency and escape.

I guess the conversation's over because Randall disconnects from me again. As though he can't bear to be connected to me any longer than strictly necessary. I did come barreling into his life when he least expected it. And pushed him away before that. We can't exactly go back to the way things were, though I can't deny how good it feels to have him back in my head, even with the connection temporarily severed. But what kind of future can we have after this?

If that brief glimpse of his anger at me is any indication, I've done irrevocable damage to *all* my relationships. If Rik can't forgive me, how can I expect Brita, my parents, or anyone else from my old life to?

The deeper we venture into the Bower, the emptier the streets. Most of the franchises have shuttered their doors, the corporate honchos upstairs cutting their losses while they still can, maybe. A couple of places remain open, but with added security at the door – big burly guys who eye everything with suspicion. As we near a corner bodega, the kid tailing us whistles an intricate pattern, and one of the thugs manning the door comes out, blocking our progress.

"Just pretend nothing's wrong," I whisper. I put one foot in front of another as though I belong here. I'm not that rusty, and if these guys want to force the issue, my training will be the answer to that.

Randall stops me with a hand on my shoulder. "Brazening it out won't work."

"You have a better idea?"

"Just... wait a minute." Wait? While who-knows-how-many thugs join us? He closes his eyes with an eyecast command. "Trust me."

Every instinct in me tells me we're going to have to do things the Aventine way. But I wait, even as the guy from the bodega pulls out a knife, mimes slitting my throat. Is that what these boys do to people who dare to come here? I stare the enforcer down. If so, they'll be in for a surprise.

Randall cranes his neck, peering past the thug through the gloom. "Good. Just in time, too."

A young girl comes tearing out of a tenement building up ahead, darting in and out of the streetlights' beams. "Randall!" she shrieks as she hits him with a flying hug.

I'm not sure who's more mystified, me or the thugs.

The muscle relaxes his stance a fraction as Randall swings the girl around and around in the air. "How are you, Natalie?" he asks, finally setting her on her feet.

"I'm fine." Her blue eyes widen on me. "Who's that?" she whispers loudly.

"A friend of mine. I'll tell you all about her later. Your mom home?"

She gives him a solemn nod. "Uh huh."

Randall gives the thug a hard glare over the girl's head, and he slowly returns to his post in the store. "Then lead the way."

"OK," she chirps happily, pulling Randall along by his hand.

She's a year or two past the age where kids first get outfitted with implants. Too soon, and the brain's development could be affected. Too late, and some of the more sophisticated implant features are worthless. Early on, the stimulation overload takes a couple of years to get used to, but she's so obviously in the present, her steps practically buoyant, I'm certain she doesn't have one even without pushing aside the curly blonde hair along her neck to see for sure.

Our tail falls back, watching but not interfering as Natalie leads us into the building she came from. Randall gives me a wink that leaves me cold as we troop up a set of stairs off the main entry.

On the second floor, Natalie opens the door to one of the housing units. "Mommy, Mommy, guess who I found!"

A faded forty-something brunette greets us, her brow wrinkled in surprise. "Randall, what brings you here?" She glances around the room, a brief flash of embarrassment on her face. "If I knew you were coming..."

"It's all right. My friend and I happened to be in the area. Thought we'd stop by."

Two things I realize in this moment: one, the lie comes

easily to him. And two, being called Randall's friend carries more than some currency.

"Well, welcome. Michael's shift doesn't get out for a while yet, but..." She gestures to the room vaguely.

Natalie plucks at Randall's shirt. "Did you bring me anything this time?"

He hunkers down so he's at eye level with her. "No, I didn't. Sorry. But next time I'll bring you something extra special, OK?"

The woman's embarrassment grows more pronounced. "Nat, why don't you see if Maisy wants to play? Her mother's shift should be over by now." She practically shoves her daughter into the hall and shuts the door behind her. "Sorry about that. Kids that age are a handful."

Her eyes narrow on me. Not unkindly exactly, more assessing. I want to tell her that I grew up in an apartment similar to this a mile away, but Randall's right. She already knows I'm connected and, as such, I'm automatically suspect.

"What can I do for you?" she asks.

"We need a place to stay for a few hours off the radar," Randall says. "Not here, of course, but if you knew of somewhere else, I'd be grateful."

"Randall, we owe you for getting Michael a position at Vector, and for getting Jaxton into a good school but..." Her eyes slide to me again, the distrust palpable. She bites her lip and moves to the window. With jerky movements, she closes the blinds. Just simple strips of plastic with no other function. "The local organizer saw you coming. So did half the block. You may be a sympathizer, but that doesn't mean you're welcome here."

"I have credits." It's all I can offer, but the look the woman gives me says even if it were welcome, it's not nearly enough.

"You and the rest of New Worth think if you throw enough credits at a problem it will go away?"

"I just thought–"

Randall stays me with a hand on my arm. I fall silent as he gives her a farewell nod. "It was good seeing you, Jenna. Say hi to Mike for me, OK?" He pushes me to the door.

"Wait." Jenna sighs. "One of the residents was arrested last night. Lives on the fourth floor. You could stay there, but you'd better be gone by tomorrow. Things are heating up."

And the Disconnects are closing ranks.

"Thank you, Jenna."

She waves him off. "I just hope you two know what you're doing."

So do I.

CHAPTER TWENTY-ONE

Randall wrenches the doorknob and mutters a curse. "Locked."

"Here, let me take a look."

He backs away so I can attack the lock with my pick kit. "Where'd you learn– never mind." He glares up and down the hall as if daring one of the doors to open.

With a satisfying click, the lock gives way. The coast still clear, Randall and I hurry inside. Immediately, I regret my haste. The smell of trash overwhelms the tiny space, cluttered with a bachelor's carelessness. Old produce rots on the counter, cans and plastic meal packages lay where they were left, crusted with remains.

"I thought she said he was arrested yesterday?"

"His crime was being a Disconnect, not a poor housekeeper." Randall sweeps a couple of items down the trash chute in the kitchen and futzes with the air circulator's controls. "See if that helps." He heads for the lone window next, his hand reaching for the sash.

"Come away from there."

"Really think someone's looking for us here?"

"Your friend thought so."

He frowns but pulls down the crooked window shade. It's distinctly lo-fi. Even when I was living in the Terrestrial District with my parents, we had holoblinds in the living room. I miss the soft light they cast, the ambiance provided. "Well, there've been talks of a major demonstration in the next few days. One that'll make all the others look small in comparison."

"Violence?"

He shrugs. "They have a lot to be angry about. Being blamed for the attack on the government storage facility yesterday hasn't helped the situation."

Tahir mentioned something about that. "I thought Disconnects were behind the explosion."

Randall shakes his head. "Why would they attack a facility that stores their records? Well, *everyone's* records, but theirs are so much more vulnerable. They don't have implants maintaining all their personal, legal, and administrative information."

I check the feeds. "I don't see any reports yet about the extent of the damage."

"Probably because it's bad," he says grimly. "And the government's in damage control."

Whether it's true or not, a cover-up would be like dumping gasoline on a fire. "Just adding to the list of reasons for Disconnects to cut ties with New Worth once and for all. But you've been outside. You know what they'll face if they leave the city prematurely."

He nods. "I do. I've done my best to educate those who'll listen, but even if they could travel to their family's homes, it's been decades. They'll face damage wrought by the weather, war, and if not that, they'll need to clean up the pre-dome infrastructure that's surely failed by now. Not to mention the need for basic survival gear. Without water or a source of food, they'll be screwed."

"Guess it's telling they'd rather try their luck outside the dome than stay put."

Randall shrugs. "Some of it's rhetoric to push for fairer

treatment, the prospect of Emergence just the means. But in the process they've tapped into the hopes and dreams that have been instilled in us since birth."

We *all* want fresh air on our faces.

I cast about the room. Besides the window, the door's the only exit. Grunting, I pull the refrigerator in front of it. That way we'll gain a few precious seconds to decide what to do if we're found out. All out of precautions to take, I finally sit down. The lone couch crinkles underneath me, but I'm tired enough that I'm just glad to give my legs a break.

Randall drags a hard-backed chair over.

"There's room if you want." I scoot closer to the armrest.

"Nah, I'm fine."

Fatigue settles over me, overwhelming and undeniable. From here, I can see Randall up close. The slight bump on his nose, the small pox scar on his cheek, the shadow of his implant under the skin on the back of his neck.

He glances at me before I can pretend I wasn't looking. "You'll be able to sleep?" he asks.

"Think so; you?"

He stretches out his long legs and resettles his feet on the couch cushions beside me. "Oh sure. Even though we're camped out in the Bower, on the run from an organization I never heard of until yesterday, I should sleep like a baby." He tries to keep his tone light, but it's edged with anger.

"You've had plenty of opportunities to leave."

He scrubs his hand over his face. "I know. And you know I wouldn't do that."

Isn't that why I risked so much by going to him in the first place? I could have kept at it alone. That's what Aventine's trained me to do. But I was feeling vulnerable, frantic, and there was no one else I wanted to see more. Selfish of me, perhaps, but I can't deny Randall's connections have gotten me further than I could have managed on my own.

Aventine might have trained me, but the deck's been stacked against me since the beginning, hasn't it?

"I'm sorry things are such a mess."

He gives me a searching look. "Are you?"

"What do you mean? Of course I'm–"

"Or are you only sorry you've been found out?"

I knew we'd have to hash things out once and for all. I guess it was too much to ask that we'd be able to put us on hold till all this was over. Still, the vehemence in his voice takes me aback.

"You would've blithely done your work for Aventine, continued to keep the truth from the people who care about you, if this hadn't happened," he continues. "Do you deny it?"

I blow out a breath. "It would've made things easier."

"For you."

"No. For *you*. You, Brita, my parents." I beat my fist against my thigh. "Everyone who has any meaning in my life. Aventine could've–"

"They threatened you? Using us?"

"I couldn't risk it. Even if I got clearance to reconnect with everyone, there was no guarantee you'd want to do the same. The way we left things…" My throat's not working properly. "I thought maybe everyone would be better off."

"That wasn't for you to decide."

"Maybe not. But I was trying to protect you from Aventine–"

At the name of my employer, something in his face wavers and breaks, fragile as glass. I fall silent, wanting desperately to make him understand, but I don't know the first thing about the stranger before me. Before Aventine, I could simply *show* him what I felt, and eventually all would be made right again. But we've regressed so much, sniping at each other like we did throughout much of *Partners in Crime* when we were newly acquainted and still figuring out how to work with one another.

Biting the inside of my cheek, I lean forward, reaching out with my gloved fingertips. Randall freezes as I find the implant along his neck hiding under the skin. Then I take his hand and press it against my implant, his gloved fingers cool but warming as they settle against me. "That brief glimpse of your mind… Tahir's call. It's messy and confusing right now, but you must've seen, you must know what I feel. And I know what you feel, despite…"

A slight tremor works through him. He squeezes the hand touching his implant as if he can't decide whether to hang on or pull me off him.

"So why aren't we synching right now? What's keeping you from–"

He jerks away, and my hand falls. "I had to figure out a way to live without you. It was the hardest thing I've ever done. To let you back in… How do I know you won't run away? Or that Aventine won't make you disappear? What if I have to figure out how to live without you all over again?"

"You think it wasn't hard for me?" I ask in a dangerous tone. I knew I was throwing away any chance at a future together that day on the concourse, but I did it anyway. To protect *him*.

He sighs. "I don't know what to think any more, Emery."

And I can't make up his mind for him. I settle back against the couch, cross my arms, and try to remember what really matters here. "Then I'll make it simple for you: help me get through the next day, and I promise I won't trouble you again."

He stares at me for a long moment, but I have no idea what's going on behind his unreadable face. "Get some rest." He sounds ancient as he says that, collapsing back in his seat as if suddenly exhausted by the whole thing.

"If anything happens…"

"Don't worry," he says. "You'll be the first to know."

• • •

"Geeta just contacted me." Randall's voice is a gunshot in the dark, wrenching me from sleep.

I flail about, ready to fight the shadows, until I remember where I am. It's a little after three in the morning, the tenement building finally quiet around us. But the bustle above, the slamming doors, the heated conversations through plastipaper-thin walls, didn't keep me from sleeping.

He glances over, his face illuminated by the touchscreen he took from Vector. "How are you feeling?"

"Doesn't matter."

He sits down on the couch next to me with a grimace. The call to Geeta's relayed through a half-dozen network access points just in case. "Ready?"

I nod, trying to shake the cobwebs away.

Geeta answers almost immediately. Dark circles rim her eyes. Looks like she's still hunkered down in Vector's basement lab. "Isolated the data structure from the blood sample, but still haven't cracked the encryption. There are a couple more things I can try, but without knowing more–"

"No, you've done more than enough," I say. It was a long shot to think this would work. "Thanks for trying, though."

"We need to figure out how you can hand off what you've managed so far and destroy the rest."

I turn to Randall in surprise. "What? Why put her at risk?"

His hand tightens over the touchscreen's casing. "Maybe if you saw the data yourself it might spur some idea of what we're dealing with. That's your background, right?" To her, "We can't come to you, so you need to come to us."

"Just keep piling on the collateral damage," I mutter.

"I don't like it either," Randall says. "But you know we can trust her, which is almost as important right now."

Geeta looks like she's about to argue, but she swallows the impulse. "Meet me at my place in an hour."

"Where–"

"*Randall* knows where it is." Then with a significant look at him, "Be careful," she says, as though I'm just a temporary accessory in his life. And maybe I should be.

"You too." He sets the touchscreen down on top of my satchel with a sigh. "She lives in an apartment near the top of the Understory."

"Didn't take up Vector's offer for housing?"

"Her family didn't want her living down here." And must have the means to keep her close.

"What about yours?"

His shoulders pull back slightly. "I can take care of myself." He was doing a pretty good job of it before I entered the picture, too. The sooner I can get his life back in order, the better.

"Before we go, we should contact Tahir, see what he's been able to dig up on his end."

Randall's eyes widen. "No way. I can't believe you'd even suggest that."

"He's just as upset about this situation as we are."

He scoffs. "He only wants to cover his ass."

"Look, I don't expect you to understand, but Tahir and I–"

He holds up his hand. "He's the one you're calibrated with, isn't he? Did he force you? As part of the deal?"

The insinuation in his voice already tells me what he thinks. "It wasn't like that. Our connection's supposed to help me on jobs. Situational awareness, problem-solving, things like that."

"Bullshit. It's just another way for them to control you, by creating a psychological bond with your handler."

"To foster communication." But even I can hear how weak that sounds.

"They alienated you from everyone you know, forced you to calibrate with a stranger, and kept you isolated."

"They didn't *isolate* me. I had to go through some serious training and couldn't be distracted."

Randall challenges me with his gaze. "Tell me, when did they let you return to the Canopy?"

"What do you mean?" I had a couple of missions that took me up there, but now that he mentions it I never had an opportunity to go there until my walkabout a couple of weeks in when I could actually *choose* where to go. So many of my early jobs were Understory or lower. Ostensibly to get me used to operating dirtside because of my history. But what if they were actively not assigning me jobs in the Canopy? "You think they were deliberately keeping me away?"

"I wouldn't put it past them. I know how much you love it up there. Even if the Law of Digital Recency holds, they probably couldn't risk sending you up there so soon."

I stand, stretch out my legs, walk off some of my annoyance at this conversation, at Randall, at Aventine. Everything he says makes sense. I also know Aventine has a reason for their methods. Ones I accepted, even if I didn't totally believe in them all. "Listen, everything you're saying, I've asked myself at one point or another. But at the end of the day I belong to Aventine. And they made it very, very difficult to walk away."

He shakes his head. "You never should've been put in such a position to begin with."

"It's a little late for that. I've done the best I could. The sick thing is I actually *like* it. Not the shady parts. But learning how to be a courier, being able to see the city in a different way…"

"It doesn't take a genius to figure that out from your arcade history. They're probably using that to their advantage too." His posture relents slightly. "Look, reaching out to your handler now doesn't make sense. Even if you *could* trust him, you certainly can't trust Aventine. Given all the ways they tried to track you, they must have just as many to track him and his communications."

A small voice inside me protests Randall's assessment of Tahir, but what if it *is* just my lingering loyalty to him from being calibrated? No. All those times he gave of himself, to help me out on missions when I was confronted by blood or my past in the Terrestrial District. You can't fake those kinds of interactions. He might work for Aventine, but he's always tried to do right by me.

"Maybe so. But I still trust him."

"Give me one good reason."

The most obvious one, Tahir's help in tracking down my attacker, I can't give him. I'd have to explain what happened to me and what I did about it. I can't afford his estimation of me to plummet any further, not until I see this job through.

"Forget I mentioned it, all right?"

He reluctantly nods. "Before we go, do I need to disguise myself or anything? I don't have pixel scramblers embedded under my face like you do."

That Randall would be willing to go to such extremes, just for me… I blink back the sudden urge to cry. When this is all over, I hope I can make it up to him somehow. "*No*. Don't. I've been poked, prodded, and modded enough for both of us."

"You sure?"

I nod, and leave it at that. I may not be sure about a lot of things, but I'm certain about this.

CHAPTER TWENTY-TWO

A few steps from the tenement building two thugs coalesce out of the shadows across the street and fall into step behind us. I send a synch request to Randall. He doesn't answer. Instead, he throws a look over his shoulder. It's early enough that whatever light filters down from the Canopy has yet to make an appearance. Buzzing streetlights and luminescent graffiti are our only defense against the darkness.

Randall's steps quicken. I want to tell him it's a dead giveaway we're running scared, but our connection's still severed. Stubborn jerk. We'd be doing all right if another man and a woman hadn't emerged from an alley up ahead, blocking our path forward. In training, Tahir hammered into me over and over confrontation is to be avoided. It's time wasted, risking injury or worse, when I should be focusing on getting far, far away. At least between Aventine and the arcade I know how to defend myself.

"You two look lost," says the man in front of us. In the dark, it's hard to tell what he really looks like, even with the NAmp filter. A scar bisects his brown cheek from an injury that he was either unwilling or unable to have treated. "Why don't you let us help you get on the right track?" Unkind laughter follows as the others join in.

The woman, lanky with tight, bleached braids on one side of her head, pulls out a knife, while the two men behind me loosen their stances, ready if we kick up a fuss.

<<What do we do?<<

>>Oh, so *now* you want to talk?>>

<<Well?<<

>>Let them approach me.>>

He looks at me in alarm. <<What?<<

>>Do it. On my signal, run through the bakery and out the back.>> I shrug off the pullover we bought yesterday and toss it aside. No need to hide who I am anymore. >>Then turn left and wait for me.>>

The ringleader with a shit-eating grin on his face circles around me. Randall edges away, moving closer to the panaderia. The guy lunges for me. I feint left, then right, then left again, taunting the bull until the man's hands clamp down on my shoulders.

Up close, I'm able to see that exact moment when his triumph fades as blue electricity jolts through him and throws him back three feet.

>>Now!>>

Randall's off and running. The remaining two men check on their fallen compatriot while the woman slashes at me with her knife. I knock her wrist away. She makes another grab at me. This time, only a weak burst of energy flares up from my clothes at her touch. I follow that with a well-placed elbow to her midsection and then sprint after Randall. We slam through the bakery's emergency exit, turn left at a run.

Randall puts on a burst of speed, his long strides outpacing mine. Despite my training, the curdle's creeping ever closer, sapping my reserves. I won't be able to keep this up for much longer.

<<Where to?<<

>>The Ridgmar Market. We'll lose them in the crowds and take the lifts.>>

<<But that's blocks away.<<

>>I know. Just stay close.>>

We reach the boundary between the Bower and my old haunts, but there's no perceptible change in the flaking buildings around us. Luckily I don't need my map to know where we are.

Only a few months ago, the building beckoning at the end of the street was rebar and I-beams, excavated until just the barest skeleton remained. Breck used the construction site as the locus of his operation, giving him nearly 360 degrees of access to the surrounding streets and buildings. Now it's largely rebuilt, though progress must've stalled, since the windows looking out on this level are boarded up instead of fitted with glass. Old notices for utility tie-ins have darkened with age.

One of the boards has been pried off, leaving a gap big enough to squeeze through. >>In there!>>

I fit myself into the window frame and the dark room beyond. Randall follows with a grunt and curse. Can't blame him. The rank smell of unwashed bodies is pretty terrible. Squatters have used this place, and recently. Though it looks like they've cleared out for the time being. Probably chased off by the cops on a regular basis, but not so regularly they can't crash here for a couple of hours at a time. A delicate balance, that.

On one wall, the same symbol of a tree struck by lightning has been plastered on the cement in glowing paint.

Holding a finger to my lips, I sidle up to the window we clambered through to get a look at the street. I try to quiet my body, straining to hear our pursuers. Hard footfalls echo off concrete, but they're already fading. Hopefully they'll give up and return to the Bower.

Adrenaline from the chase drains out of my body, leaving me with too many memories of my time down here.

<<You've been here before.<<

It's not a question. >>A lifetime ago. There should be a way to cut over to the next block.>>

<<It's more than that though.<<

It is. If I let it, that frantic helplessness creeps back as if it never really let go of me in the alley that day. Where I was attacked is not nearly far enough away from here.

I can still see the knife that was only supposed to threaten me into submission. How it slipped when I fought back, somehow finding an empty beer bottle to slam against my attacker's head. The moment when the stinging nick along my neck suddenly turned into a fount of blood. *My* blood.

<<Liv!<<

Seeing his eyes widen in panic as my blood coated his shirt – he never figured on that – I knew in that moment he wasn't invincible. I also vowed no one would make me feel that way again. His departing footsteps echoing off concrete is the last thing I remember before I woke up in the hospital.

I still don't know his name. Tahir gave me the power to put a name to what happened that day. But–

Rik grabs my shoulders. "Liv, snap out of it." He smoothes his hand over my cheek, his solid bulk grounding me in the here and now. With him in my head, in my space, it's easier to push back the sensations. To remember that scrapper can't hurt me or anyone else. Not anymore.

I take a step back. "Sorry."

Rik, no, *Randall*, doesn't move, but he keeps sending me reassurance through our connection. How… His permissions. I upgraded his permissions during the call with Tahir and never changed them back.

<<Every now and then – before – I'd get glimpses of…<< he makes a vague gesture with his hand, <<whatever *that* was, but… I didn't understand. What happened to you down here?<<

For a moment, I teeter on the edge of my emotions.

Conflicting, contradictory… the urge to run away combined with the desire to drown myself in Rik's consciousness. But at least I have the presence of mind to downgrade his permissions, giving me a bit more breathing room.

His mouth purses at the loss of my nonverbals and emotional color to my words, but he stands at attention, all of him focused on me.

>>When I lived down here with my family, I was attacked by a scrapper. I fought back, and when his knife nicked my neck he panicked and ran off.>> I turn away from him. >>This was before we met. Ancient history.>>

<<But it explains so much. How long it took you to open up to me, some of your reactions over the years, all those rules… And why *Partners in Crime* and the other arcade scenarios were so important to you.<<

It's not so much a criticism of my behavior, more acknowledgment of something that puzzled him about me, but it still sets my teeth on edge. >>I can't help who I am.>>

<<Of course not. That's not what I'm saying.<<

>>Then best not to say anything at all.>>

<<Not all of us are pros at bottling everything up inside. This shades in so much of who you are. How can I pretend it didn't just happen?<<

"We need to keep moving."

He sighs, his gaze, once open, now shuttered. I've gotten better at reading him, but that doesn't mean much compared to what we had before, so attuned to his every mental state. "That *is* what you do best."

And with that, he cuts the connection. Again.

The neighborhood Geeta lives in is one of the more insufferable parts of the Understory. The storefronts we pass on our way to her apartment must take turns rotating through the latest fads exported from the Canopy. A mod parlor specializing in trendy skin transparency and frame extension therapy. A vapor bar catering to only those who've augmented their olfactory glands. Branch locations for the big fashion houses located in the Upper levels. But it feels premeditated, almost predatory, considering all the status-seeking souls who live here. All Canopy pretension, but none of the charm.

Though they do have a glimpse of sky. I'd probably feel pretty smug about that too if I lived here.

The apartment complex centers around a thin sliver of dome glass, the different buildings oriented just so to take advantage of the vertical crack of natural light.

Daytime, we only have to worry about passive security measures that log our aliases' entry into the complex. I keep my head down, pretending to sneeze until we're out of the range of the cameras. Randall leads me to the third apartment down flanked by planter boxes full of prickly succulents and evergreen shrubs.

Geeta answers as we reach the door, clearly expecting us.

After a prolonged moment of silence, I realize she and Randall are synching furiously. I take a few steps into the spacious apartment, giving them the chance to work out whatever it is that's sprung up between them. There are no words of accusation, no shouts. That makes everything worse, knowing they're synch fighting, and I'm just supposed to pretend nothing's wrong.

Swallowing my curiosity and another emotion I refuse to name, I take a seat on the couch. Finally Randall sits down stiffly beside me. "Everything all right?" I ask.

"It's fine," Geeta announces curtly as she joins us. At her hand gesture, a light screen resolves out of the air opposite the couch. Her eyes roll back into her head as she pulls up a window streaming with nonsense characters. "This is what the raw data looks like. At least one layer of encryption, maybe more."

"The data originated from the government, so at least one layer's probably theirs. But there's no guarantee–"

"Really? I got my hands on a government key when my boss accidentally sent me a file encrypted like this…" She gives Randall a sheepish shrug. "One of those reports documenting the rehabilitation efforts of the other domed cities. We were using it as a benchmark against our own work."

"Can't hurt to try it," he says.

Her hands are a blur on the projected keyboard that accelerates whatever she's doing. "Ha! It worked. But this is…" She shakes her head. "Here's what I've got so far."

I pore over the new display. The decryption's cleaned things up, but without any documentation or other identifying info to help us out… "It looks like a file executable or something, but… Can you scroll down?"

She does, revealing rows upon rows of raw data. "A couple hundred records, maybe." In my data curation classes, we were tasked with all sorts of assignments where we had to determine what we were looking at based only on the contents of data fields. "That line of code there is a command to update a database with this information."

"So this file's some sort of patch to a database that's already out there?" Randall asks.

"Looks like. The question is which one."

"Some of the data fields contain names. Let me see if I can compare them with the public registry," Geeta says. A moment later, she pulls up the live database that feeds into practically every administrative portal in the city. "This is what this record looks like right now in the registry."

My fingers twitch toward the screen. "I know how to compare the two–"

"I got it," Geeta says sharply, her hands not pausing in their work. She frowns down at her interface. "Huh. A bunch of fields from the patch line up pretty well, but there are definitely some leftovers."

"Those are probably hidden fields we can only see with the right permissions." Every citizen has an entry in the database, tracking all sorts of demographics, education and work history, place of address, account balances, and other secret markers we can't access through the public interface.

Randall catches my eye. "So presumably your government client wanted to update the registry with the information in the patch. And whoever ambushed you must've wanted to prevent the update from happening."

"Makes sense, but why the registry?"

"And why is everyone working so hard for it to be kept secret?"

Geeta toggles open a new window. "Here's a record I was able to reconstruct by pattern-matching the registry's fields and populating it with the patch's raw data." The patch's data fields overlay the live database.

"Huh. Not obvious what the difference is. Maybe the big changes we can't see because of the hidden fields."

Randall leans forward. "Weird. If the patch's updating the live version, then someone must have compromised the public registry in the first place."

"Or maybe the government's the one compromising the integrity of the registry with this patch," Geeta offers.

"They could be," I say, "but my money's on the people at the ambush being up to no good, not the other way around." The government took a lot of precautions with this job, it's true, but the folks at the ambush were playing for keeps. "Just wish we could access the hidden fields to be sure."

"There's something else," Geeta says. "Look. Most of these records are for known Disconnects. We might be looking at a small subset, but that can't be random, can it?"

Randall swears. "That explains your Disconnect tail at the drop. They must've gotten wind of the transaction somehow.

They've always feared their records could be tampered with. Now it looks like someone made their fears reality."

"And then there's that attack on the government storage facility. You told me yourself it contained valuable information," I say to Randall. "Maybe the explosion was targeting the originals kept there."

He nods. "Without proof, it'd be impossible for them to fight the changes."

"But why now?"

"With Emergence and the Vesa trial shaking things up, maybe someone saw this as an opportunity to make the changes to the registry. Or not. Without knowing more, all we really know is the government's patch is focused on updating Disconnects' records. And there're at least two other interested parties. Not counting your work."

"All right," I say, starting to pace. "Let's say the government's trying to fix the registry. How was it compromised in the first place?"

Geeta looks thoughtful. "Well, whoever did this would need librarian permission, but to pull this off without notice?"

Randall starts to pace. "They'd have to go slow. Say, a record at a time?"

I nod. "Probably wouldn't be enough activity to draw notice." I feel sick to my stomach. But this time it's not the curdle, at least not wholly. That someone could do this and get away with it? Unthinkable.

"But aren't there protections in place to ensure data integrity?" Geeta asks.

"Of course. Log-ins, permissions, file redundancies…" I tick them off on my fingers as though taking an oral exam. "Curators take provenance very seriously. Standard data practices dictate data never leaves the network servers – that way the access logs capture any and all activity. But clearly they can be forged with enough time and effort."

Randall whistles. "So whoever did this could reasonably assume if they managed to change the live database, circumventing the standard data practices in place, no one would be the wiser."

"Law of Digital Recency." The words pop out of my mouth. No one would look closer at the data if there wasn't any reason to, allowing whoever masterminded all this to fly under the radar.

"This is bad, and we don't even know what the changes to the registry actually do. But just the hint of manipulated records combined with all the unrest…" Randall shakes his head. "This'll be the last straw for the Disconnects. Enough to galvanize the fence-sitters and the pacifists into action." He would know.

Geeta holds up her hands. "All right, you two are seriously creeping me out."

I turn to her. "If we're right and the registry's been compromised," I gesture to the screen still hanging in the air on pinpoints of light, "then I'm carrying the only accurate version in my blood. And someone's working *very* hard to make sure no one finds out about it."

"So you're some kind of secret agent?"

"No," I say at the same time Randall says, "Yes." He catches my eye, and I have to turn away at the challenge in his gaze.

Geeta raises a brow. "Uh-huh."

"Look, it's complicated, OK? But you've been an amazing help. There's no way we would've figured this out without you."

"So what do we do now?" she asks.

"You turn over the data to us and disappear for a few days. Call in sick to work, whatever you have to do," Randall says.

"We don't want you caught up in this any more than you are." I glance at Randall. "We'll figure out the rest."

"It's a bit late for that, don't you think?"

"No one knows about you," I say. "So long as it stays that way, you'll be fine. Randall will be in touch when it's safe to resurface."

She sighs. "If that's what you think is best. Good thing I'm too tired to argue."

"Then we'll get going." Randall stands, and I follow suit.

"Yes, of course," Geeta says, and turns to him. "But I'd like to talk to your *friend* here before you go. Alone."

I don't know who's more surprised, me or Randall. But he dutifully goes to wait outside, leaving me alone with his colleague who's suddenly dropped all pretense of friendliness based on the dark look in her eyes as she stares me down. "I've already destroyed all the physical samples," she says in clipped tones. "The decrypted database patch is all that's left. You still have the touchscreen?"

"Yes." I dig it out of my satchel and hand it over.

Geeta transfers over the patch and holds the touchscreen out to me in return. She doesn't relinquish her grip, even when my fingers close over the casing. "I should hate you for what you've done to him. You must be the infamous Liv. The one who nearly singlehandedly sent him into an emotional tailspin a few months ago. The only one who could put him up to all *this*."

"I... guess so." It's as accurate a description as anything else.

Her face wavers with old pain as she finally lets go of the touchscreen. "When you pulled your disappearing act... Well, let's just say it was rough going for a while for *everyone* in his life."

And she was on the front lines. Randall said he'd scaled things back with all his contacts after Aventine severed our connection. The emotional bleed must've been overwhelming regardless of what level of permissions she had. "I'm sorry. Please believe me when I say I had no choice."

"I figured. Whoever could do that to your blood has a long reach. But even though you've magically reappeared, Randall's still miserable." She gives me a pointed look. "And so are you."

"There's just a lot going on right now," I say dismissively, ready to bolt.

She snorts. "Both of you look like you're dying from the inside out."

"Aww, thanks. When I'm not running for my life, I'll look into that." I turn to go. There's nothing she can say that I haven't already blamed myself for.

"I mean it. You're supposed to be *everything* to him, and yet–"

I swing back to her. "What? Is this the part where you tell me I don't deserve him? That you'd happily step in? That's why you've been oh-so-helpful this whole time, no matter the risk to your career, right? Because it was Randall who came to you. Well, don't worry." I don't bother to hide my bitterness. "When this is over, he's all yours again. I screwed up, and there's no going back to what we could've had. So you can just relax."

Saying the words out loud is surprisingly more painful than just thinking them. But it isn't as if our connection hasn't been on life support this whole time. I guess dreams are harder to kill off.

Geeta presses her lips together, composing herself. "He's made it clear he's only interested in my friendship. And I respect that," she finally says, albeit stiffly. "But when you left, I lost him too, up here." She taps her temple.

"Join the club."

"He's considering having it removed." She's dead serious, her voice even and deliberate.

"You're joking," I say, even as the cold bite of fear creeps up my spine. Randall would never get rid of his implant, would he?

"He has a friend in the Underground," Geeta continues.

"Charon." When I was in his workshop, he treated me with inexplicable familiarity. At the time I thought it a character quirk. But he must've known all about me if Randall told him why he was thinking about disconnecting.

"If you hadn't popped up again when you did, he would have done it. Said it was the only way he could cope with having you gone." Her hands flutter helplessly. "No one could convince him otherwise."

"I didn't realize. I thought..."

No, I was only thinking about me, my own pain and insecurities. I always assumed Randall would be better off without me. That thinking's what got me through each day I spent working for Aventine. But I never dreamed he'd go to such lengths to forget what we were to each other and what we could've become. He must've known Disconnects who'd done the same and were better off for it. Our relationship might be permanently damaged, but if coming back has stayed him from making such an irrevocable decision, I can't regret that, no matter what happens in less than twenty-four hours.

"Well, now you know." Geeta's unflinching gaze roots me to the spot. "And now I want to know what you're going to do about it."

CHAPTER TWENTY-THREE

Randall detaches himself from a wisteria-draped column. "All set?"

Nothing in his face hints at the curiosity he must feel at being excluded from my conversation with Geeta. Or the devastation that drove him to seek out Charon to disconnect. But if I go back through my cache, focus on those bright brief moments when our connection was restored, I can pick out glimpses of his anger and hurt that leaked through, suggesting more lives beneath the surface. What does it cost him to even be in my presence?

We file out of the apartment complex. "We need some place to plan," I say. "Maybe a public workspace, or we could camp out in one of the gardens..."

"Or you could come with me."

I'm more accustomed to hearing the familiar voice in my head whenever I'm out in the wild. My steps slow as I scan the concourse, suddenly afraid of what I'll find.

Tahir detaches himself from where he's been standing in the shadows of a restaurant awning, and despite my better instincts I freeze. My brain tells me to run, but the rest of me is inordinately glad to see him. Even if I can't tell from his closed expression if things are about to go from bad to worse.

"What's going on? Who is this guy?" Randall asks.

"He's my handler."

Tahir strides over, clearly expecting us to follow him without fuss.

Randall clenches his fists but otherwise keeps his reaction under control as we join the current down the concourse. Morning crowds bustle around us. <<We could lose him if we leave now. Just say the word.<<

I battle back surprise at Randall's sudden synch message. I wasn't sure when or if he'd try to reconnect, but I'm grateful, even if it's out of an overabundance of caution when it comes to Tahir. >>No. He's come to help, I'm almost certain.>>

Rik eases back on the emotional filter, letting me know just what he thinks about that.

>>I didn't bring him here, I promise.>>

His disapproval eases to just a prickle along the back of my neck. But that he willingly resumed our connection gives me hope. Maybe we can fix things between us, in time.

Just not right now. Not with the way Tahir's surveilling the concourse, regardless of how discreet he's being. "How are you feeling?" he asks, deceptively casual as he leads us out of Geeta's neighborhood to a set of escalators that will take us to the level below.

"Forty-two hours and counting." I catch his brief frown. "How'd you find us–"

"I've been monitoring your *friend's* contacts just in case." Which led him to Geeta, and now to us. He glances over at Randall. "You're Randall Iverson-Kemp? You've changed your ID. Good."

"Did you come alone?" I barely restrain the urge to glance back the way we came.

Tahir chuckles and uses the motion to scan the area. "That was my intention. Not a guarantee. Turns out what you're carrying's pretty important."

"We know," Randall says, looking angry and anxious all at once.

Tahir grimaces. Catching my eye, he tips his head toward Randall. "Can you trust him?"

I don't look at Randall when I say, "With my life."

"Hmm." Tahir turns right and directs us toward a grubby, half-empty diner. We slide into a booth near the back, away from the windows overlooking the concourse. As if he has all the time in the world, Tahir orders coffee and eggs, using the table's menu console. Finally, he looks up. "By the time I'm done eating, a government taskforce will have arrived on the concourse."

I nearly jump out of my seat.

"Relax, M. We have a few minutes. And I still have a few more tricks up my sleeve."

"You have to understand. Those people at the drop were all wrong." I tell him about how they cut off my implant, the gun, how cavalierly the woman shot the man with the tattoo. "How could I have stayed there?"

He puts his elbows on the table and tents his fingers. "You did the right thing, M. Up to a point. After reviewing the footage, it looks like this job was much bigger than we were led to believe. In fact, they even set up two decoys to throw whoever was watching off your trail." The guys with the surgically attached briefcases I saw leaving City Hall. "When you were in the market, someone got close enough to mimic your signal somehow, which is why I thought you were miles away from your actual location. The client was fooled too."

"What do *they* think happened?"

Tahir frowns. "They aren't saying, at least not to me out of concern for where my loyalties lie."

Me versus Aventine. Guess I shouldn't be surprised it's come to this.

Tahir's gaze flicks to Randall, then back to me. "But I'm guessing the data's related to the Disconnects somehow." Randall stiffens in surprise next to me, but he should know by now that Aventine only takes the best. "It's the only thing that explains that man at the Aquarium," Tahir continues. "But as to who was masquerading as the client? I don't know. But if they worked that hard to get their hands on the data the first time, you can bet they'll try again."

Randall's gaze goes to me. <<Then the question is: are they trying to keep the changes to the registry a secret or do they want to expose the truth?<<

>>And if it is the second option, is it out of the goodness of their hearts or do they want to see the city implode?>>

Questions without answers, including what Tahir's intentions are. He taps the table with his index finger. "If you come in now, you'll be disciplined for aborting an op, and your blood will be scrubbed, regardless of what you're carrying, per Aventine's terms of service."

"Disciplined? Does that entail wiping my implant and leaving me to rot in the Terrestrial District? Because that's not much of an incentive."

"No. You have my word on that, M."

"She's not coming in. At least not yet," Randall says quietly, but the menace in his voice raises the hairs on my forearms.

Tahir turns to him, assessing as always. I almost wish Tahir and I were connected again, just to get a hint at what his impressions are. "Obviously, it's not an easy decision. But if you're going to... What *are* you going to do?"

Randall inhales sharply. "It's probably best not to tell you, what with that government taskforce and all..."

Tahir grimaces. "Right. Well, keep in mind the client's fighting us on the automatic destruction of the data, which means..."

"They want it back?"

Tahir nods. A waitress brings over his breakfast. My stomach lurches as the smells wash over me. "However, the curdle needs to be your primary concern, regardless of *what* you decide to do with the data." He takes a luxuriant sip of coffee and dabs his mouth with his napkin. "Remember your walkabout?"

How could I forget? Even though I've completed dozens and dozens of jobs for Aventine, that one's still relatively fresh in my mind. Pickup in the transitional Understory, data drop two days later. There was some confusion on how I'd be scrubbed because the kit hadn't arrived on time. Aventine arranged for a kit in an empty apartment for afterwards, but by the time I got to the drop the original scrubbing kit had been delivered thanks to the perseverance of the New Worth mail service, and everything that followed went as smoothly as it could.

Well, until Randall showed up.

Tahir waits for me to puzzle it out. My eyes widen. "How did you manage *that*?" Normally a secure scrubbing location would be decommissioned after use, but since it ultimately wasn't needed, it wasn't dismantled. And with Tahir pulling the strings, maybe, just maybe, the rest of Aventine lost track of it.

He gives me a wink. "After all this is over, perhaps I'll tell you."

"If you two are done reminiscing, we really should get going," Randall cuts in.

Tahir ignores him, and I half-expect Randall to reach across the table and throttle him. "Funny story about the woman who owns this place," Tahir says. "Back when I was a detective for the police force, I helped break up a fight." He points to the corner. "Right over there, in fact. Nearly took out her front window. To thank me, she invited me to her quarters upstairs. Lovely studio apartment with a terrace backing on to one of the largest vertical farms in the city. Recently suspended operations because their workforce went on strike, so I understand."

Randall nudges my shoulder. “Emery, this isn’t the time to walk down memory lane. Seriously, let’s get out of here.”

I hold up my hand, cutting him off. I search Tahir’s face, but there’s no deception, just honesty and exhaustion that lurks about his eyes. I’ve worried him, terribly. “Thank you, Tahir.”

“Be safe. Be smart. I won’t be able to help you again.”

Randall practically jumps out of the booth. My eyes burn as I follow, leaving Tahir to the rest of his meal. Randall scans the concourse, but I shake my head. >>Not that way.>>

<<Then where are we going to go? Your beloved handler set us up.<<

>>No, he didn’t. Weren’t you listening?>>

<<What do you mean?<<

Think in three dimensions.

>>Upstairs.>>

The hall to the bathrooms includes another door marked “Private” that’s unlocked. Randall and I go through, shutting the door softly behind us. Stairs take us to the apartment over the diner, just like Tahir said. The entrance recognizes my signal and opens without protest – another present from Tahir. Musty perfume and cat hair scent the modest apartment, thankfully empty. With the heavy taxes on companion animals, the diner’s proprietress must be making a killing serving up greasy food.

“To think Tahir got it on with whoever lives here back in the day,” Randall says, his voice surprisingly loud in the stillness.

“Ugh, did you have to point that out?”

Past a tidy living area, a small balcony overlooks the tight alley separating this building from the farm. The woman’s made an effort to fix it up. In addition to a small bistro table and chairs, ivy claws up the external walls. Planters full of bright flowers line the railing. The farm reaches into the

Canopy, a column of windows illuminated by grow lights running down its side.

"What now?"

I pull up my map of New Worth. The vertical farm spans dozens of levels, with a dedicated freight elevator that goes all the way down to the Terrestrial District. Distribution centers are on our current level, as well as Level 24 and Level 6, to make it easier to ship out fresh produce to all strata of the city. All we have to do is cross the four-foot gap separating the terrace from the start of the facility.

"We'll have to jump."

"You're kidding."

"Nope."

"And then what?"

"We'll use their freight elevator to bypass this level's security. Should dump us out in the Terrestrial District."

Randall processes that, tingling awareness across our connection giving way to relieved approval. Like aloe smoothed across singed skin.

A big exhaust vent extends from the building, then it's two stories to the walkway below. Just have to hope it will hold. Swinging myself to the other side of the balcony railing, I take a moment to catch my breath, pushing back a wave of vertigo. *That's* new.

Randall squeezes my shoulder. "You OK?"

I swipe my damp forehead. "Yeah."

"Here, let me go first." He launches across the gap before I can protest, landing with a metallic thud. The exhaust vent groans ominously as he shifts his weight. "If I can do it, you can." He flashes me an encouraging smile just as the vent creaks again, a high-pitched whine that makes me suddenly furious at how weak I've become.

I jump across the gap and land sure-footed despite the way my stomach and my brain war with each other. The vent protests, a loud pop as one of the rivets bursts from the concrete wall on a wave of dust.

Randall sidesteps over to the next ledge underneath a window, his careful movements not quite quick enough for me as the exhaust vent shifts under my feet. "Window's locked," he says.

"Hang on." Wedging my right hand in the small mortar gap between bricks, I reach across him with my left. "Close your eyes." I press my palm against the glass pane. With an eyecast command, my glove emits a short static burst, sending shards flying.

"*Wow.*"

"Don't get excited. Won't be able to do that again for another couple of hours at least." A police siren sounds, followed by panicked shouts and a couple of screams from the concourse near the front of the diner. The government taskforce Tahir warned us about. "Come on."

We carefully clamber down from the window onto the distribution center floor. Inside, I can barely make out an automated voice telling people this is not a drill, would you please submit to a security scan, thank you and have a nice day.

The words fade as we pass automated carts lined up in rows, some stacked with boxes of vacuum-sealed produce, others empty where they sit in the semi-darkness. Packets of veggies lay abandoned on conveyor belts angling up from the floor below. Guess things were shut down in a hurry.

We find the stairwell. "The freight elevator should be accessible the next level down." I pull up the police frequency. While officers can synch with one another freely, transparency laws require them to announce decisions and report actions and findings on a public channel. Rumors have always swirled that much is left off the official channel, but then there are always rumors of what goes on behind people's eyes. Chatter about another Disconnect demonstration in the Terrestrial District's followed by an alleged sighting of a female fugitive in the Darlington Heights neighborhood of the Understory. "They're setting up a canvass for this sector."

"Think they'll come in here?" Randall asks, as we trundle down the next flight of stairs.

"By the time it occurs to them, hopefully we'll be long gone."

"Gone where?"

"Markley's Terrace. That's where Tahir said I could find a scrubbing kit. You know, for after." After *what* is still the question.

Randall doesn't answer, but his acceptance of this course of action comes through. That he's sharing his nonverbals with me again… I don't know what the reversal signifies, but I know I don't want to draw attention to it, if it means he'll just shut me out again. There will be time enough for that when this is all over.

The final flight of stairs leads us to the plants. Running the length of the building, rows of fruit and vegetables climb floor-to-ceiling shelves. Each one's climate-controlled to evoke the conditions best suited to the crop. Water vapor, the scent of warm growing things, and the tang of nutrients fill my nose. Not unpleasant, but so different from nearly every other place I've been in the city. Even the gardens I love to spend my time in don't smell like this, the scents diffused almost immediately.

Growlights mounted to the bottom of each shelf provide the only illumination as Randall and I cross the room. Our footfalls echo on the metal grating, open to the floor of plants below us. Overhead, harvesting apparatuses dangle down from the ceiling like dormant mechanical spiders.

All the green runs together, looking so different from the items that actually make it to my plate. "You know what all this is?" I whisper, not wanting to disturb the plants. A silly impulse.

"A few. Different kinds of lettuces, beans, and herbs. But some of them are trickier, the roots hidden from view." He shrugs, not nearly as impressed by the farm as I am.

"You said Vector contracted out places like this to grow the groundcover and native plants for outside, right?"

He nods. "Whatever we do can't impact the city's food supply, so we've found a way to create rapid-spreading, hardy plants that are supposed to remove generations of impurities from the soil, which in turn create the biomass needed to restore the original ecosystem."

The freight elevator's at the opposite end of the floor. Randall hits the button and it opens with a soft rumble a few seconds later. "At least the power's still on."

Large portholes in the elevator doors give us a ghostly view of the plants still growing without help from their minders as we descend level after level. I've never been in a place that was so quiet, yet so obviously full of life. If that's what it's like living outside the dome, no wonder people are impatient to see Emergence come to pass.

My ears pop, clog, and pop again by the time we reach the bottom. Plastic tubs and glass bottles full of a library's worth of nutrient mixes line the walls. Tools for planting and harvesting are hung on hooks, automated carts piled high with bags of fertilizer. In the next room, we find a loading dock that must lead to the Terrestrial District. Randall heads toward it.

"Chances are they'll have door security and cameras monitoring the exit."

He turns back to me. "So what do we do?"

"We pretend we're anything but who they're looking for." At his blank look, I continue, "Who'd come here, with the farm shut down? Young punks looking for trouble, homeless people needing a place they can rest a few hours without being harassed by the cops, people desperate enough to steal food." I cast about the room. "We can't avoid the security, but we can *control* what they think they see."

I point Randall to a set of lockers lined up along the wall. "See if anyone left a shirt, hat, something."

While he searches, I braid my hair, two plaits draping down either side of my face to hopefully obscure a head-on facial rec scan. The changes Charon made to the scrambler under my face are still holding up as far as I can tell, but I don't want to take any chances.

Randall comes back with a dusty cap and a handheld stamper that punches the farm's logo onto packages and crates. I pull the cap out of his hands and jam it onto his head, swiveling the brim until it sits low over his forehead, shading his eyes.

"Perfect." I take the stamper from him as well, testing its heft. "OK, we're going to pretend we broke in here for fun. If an alarm sounds, we laugh like we're drunk, and I'll use the stamper thingy on the walls like any other graffiti artist. Then we bail. Got it?"

He nods, looking far too serious for what we're about to do. Or maybe it's just the hat. "Like that time we went undercover in *Partners in Crime*."

"Except this isn't a game." Taking a deep breath, I approach the exit next to the loading dock. I shove aside any misgivings along with the door, stumbling a bit to complete the picture.

I take a few steps and turn back to Randall, hold a finger to my lips, and give him an exaggerated "Shh," as we creep forward.

Chain link encloses a small yard. Still no one, but a camera mounted to the entrance locks onto us. Show time.

I wave Randall forward, giggle into my hand. Along the wall, I line up the stamper and pull the trigger. A high-pitched whine sounds for a second as the device warms up. Then a satisfying thunk follows, leaving the farm logo emblazoned on the wall in prismatic color.

I whirl toward Randall; he's closer than I expect. I brandish the stamper at him playfully, smiling so hard my cheeks hurt.

For a second, his stiff demeanor and wide eyes give him away. Then his frame melts into a more languid pose, a grin tugging up one corner of his mouth as he tries to make a grab for the stamper. "My turn."

I dangle it away from him as he takes another swipe at it. Ducking under his arm, I'm suddenly breathless as I set the stamper against the wall again. He comes up behind me, and I block him with my shoulder as I pull the trigger. I do it again and again. This would be fun if it weren't so necessary to maintain our cover. No sirens have sounded but I've no doubt video evidence of our delinquency's being scrutinized somewhere.

Holding the stamper out to Randall, I pretend to giggle. "All right, fine. You can try it."

His fingers brush mine as he takes it from me, slow and deliberate. He glances around the lot and gives me a wink. He stamps the wall once, twice, then tosses it to the ground. "This is boring. I thought you said this would be fun." He's angled himself so his face is in the camera's range. If they're capturing audio or have lip-reading analytics, it's a nice touch.

"I guess we could try the arcade. I know a guy who always lets me play for half-price. Come on." I tug his arm toward the fence. So far so good. Even if an alert went out to the local police station, we still have time before one of their officers can feasibly get over here. "Up and over."

We make our way onto a small street paved in crumbling asphalt. Not populated enough for my tastes, but it'll open up in a couple of blocks. I swipe Randall's hat off and throw it into a trash receptacle. I undo my braids. My hair's an unruly mess, but it can't be helped. As the distance between us and the farm lengthens, my adrenaline wanes, leaving the dead feeling in my stomach at the forefront.

Randall nearly comes to a complete stop. <<Shit. Security guards, two of them, coming this way fast.<<

>>Probably sent to check up on the factory.>>

<<What do we do?<<

>>We–>>

A wave of dizziness crashes into me with the force of one of Kat's punches. He looks down at me in concern, then back up to the guards heading our way at a hard trot. They're still a couple of buildings out, but not for much longer. Randall veers toward an alley up ahead, bringing me with him. I force my body into motion. He props me up against the wall, and I lean back, trying to press all my fatigue into the concrete bricks.

Randall crowds around me, not quite touching, his arms on either side.

>>What are you–>>

<<You said people would see what they want to see, right?<< He leans in, blocking my face from view. His mouth hovers by my cheek, before slipping down alongside my neck.

My breath stutters. Too close.

<<They gone?<<

What? The guards. I wasn't even paying attention. >>I… I think so.>>

He eases back slightly, then stops, his gaze intent on a spot on my neck. I can feel his questions, just as surely as he can feel my sudden discomfort. <<This is where he cut you.<< A statement, not a question, full of restrained fury.

I can only nod. My mind, my voice, both unable to answer properly.

His gloved fingertip traces the nearly invisible line that spiderwebs across my skin, thinner than the nib of a stylus.

A hiccupping breath escapes me as he looms closer. But this is Randall, my Rik. I should know by now I have nothing to fear from him.

Tension rolls down my spine, dissipating somewhat at the interplay of emotions brimming between us, amplified by Randall's fervent gaze. Full of helpless anger – the most destructive kind – before it gives way to tenderness, warming me from the inside out.

<<Did they get him?<< His hand settles against my collarbone, heavy yet soothing at the same time.

It's too much. >>Eventually. Sentenced to penal labor and had his implant taken away, turning him into one of your precious Disconnects.>> Tahir said the case and sentencing were fast-tracked, another favor he called in for me.

Randall hisses but doesn't back away, which is what I want. Anything to make it easier to breathe, to find enough separation between us so I won't drown. But no matter what I do, everything leads back to him.

<<Vector has a strict vetting policy for Disconnects. So do I.<< He gives me a long look. His emotions stutter slightly, but I can sense his disappointment. <<But you already know that.<<

Because he picked me out of all the noise on the New Worth network, just as surely as I picked him, before everything got so complicated.

<<If I thought it'd do any good, I'd kiss you right now.<<

Everything between us sharpens, narrowing into this one unbearable moment. The sweep of his eyelashes, the angle of his head, his pupils impossibly wide. And me, vibrating with anticipation and fear in equal measure, our connection dizzy not only with competing impulses but the limitations of our current configuration that restrain and compel, magnets being forced end-to-end.

<<I want to, and part of you wants it, too. To finally see if

this is the way it's supposed to be between us.<< He pauses, waiting for my denial that doesn't come. <<But until you decide what you want from me–<<

He stoppers that thought with a slow breath, a grimace fracturing his features. <<We should probably move on. In case those guards circle back.<<

CHAPTER TWENTY-FOUR

I'm still adjusting to the shift in topic as Randall straightens and turns back to the street. Just people going about their business, oblivious to our little drama. "How are you feeling?" he asks as we move out of the alley.

"I've been better."

"The curdle?" I don't answer, and his mouth flattens into a grim line. <<What's the best way to get to that place where Tahir left the scrubbing kit?<<

>>It's in an elevated section the next sector over.>>

<<After we get the kit, we'll get you scrubbed.<<

>>No.>>

<<What do you mean? You can't keep going like this. You've been popping painkillers practically every hour.<<

I wince. Guess it was too much to hope he hadn't noticed the way I've been burning through Geeta's supply. >>We still have time.>>

<<For what?<<

The million-credit question. >>Something Tahir said, about the client disputing the automatic destruction of the data that typically happens in a situation like this.>>

<<They need it back.<<

I nod. >>So we'll bring it back to them. We take this to City Hall.>> The Echelon, where all this started, but this time I'll deal with the city councilors themselves. >>It's the only way I can clear my name and prove I wasn't in on the botched drop.>>

Randall remains silent. Doubtful. Reluctant. Like the worrying of a hangnail.

>>Don't you want to help the Disconnects?>>

<<Of course, but–<<

>>Then let me do this. I can't undo all the wrongs I've done to you. Or the risks you've taken in helping me. But I know how important the Disconnects' cause is to you. So let me deliver this data to the people who have the best chance at fixing this mess.>>

He wants to protest. A wave of despair-tinged anger, like metal in my mouth, tells me that much before he clamps down on his reaction. <<It's a long way to go, all the way up to the Echelon.<<

I hear what he's not saying: it's a long way to go with both Aventine and whoever they've recruited to help bring me in. I pull together a short message explaining how the scrubbing process works. With a clumsy eyecast command, I blink it on its way.

Randall takes a deep breath. <<I'm not going to need this, Liv. Promise me that.<<

>>Just in case, all right? Does that make you feel better?>> He doesn't answer, which I take as a good sign. >>Then let's get going.>> I force myself to stand and tap my temple. >>Implants from here on out, OK? We can't risk being overheard.>>

He gives me a grim nod. <<Understood.<<

Thirty minutes later, we reach Markley's Terrace. Most elevated sections of the Terrestrial District are a weird mix of platforms and scaffolding that scale the facades of buildings, multiplying the space available for living areas and businesses. Neighborhoods like this are often afterthoughts, cobbled together in the last decade once people realized room was running out in the upper levels. But they look down on the Terrestrial District, often blocking whatever light makes its way here, putting them in high demand.

A set of escalators brings us to a sleepy section suspended over the throughway below. We're a couple of levels below the office I completed the data transaction for on my walkabout. The apartment where Tahir said I'd be able to find the scrubbing kit is above a half-empty Middle Eastern restaurant. >>That's it. Should be in Room 207.>>

Randall frowns as he inspects the building. <<Seems awfully quiet.<<

>>Maybe we caught a break.>>

The neighborhood *is* quiet, he's right about that much. But I can't let that deter us, not when the kit's so close to being ours. The quiet persists as we go up to the second floor, but it only feels sinister because Randall pointed it out. At least that's what I tell myself.

I make quick work of the door lock. Randall surveys the tiny apartment, empty and ready for a new tenant. I don't want to think about how many credits Aventine's burned keeping this space available.

"Check the cabinets. We're looking for a briefcase of sorts." Disappointed it's not immediately visible, I wander toward the small bathroom off the main living space. Thankfully, the scrubbing kit's wedged underneath the sink. I pry it out, relishing its familiar weight. I'm never going to let it go.

<<Liv...<<

>>Just a sec.>>

A nagging sensation from my connection with Rik almost distracts me from a soft grunt from the other room. "*Emery.*" Randall's tone raises the hairs on my arms. I retrace my steps and find him immobilized in an expert hold that's only a few degrees away from dislocating his shoulder, a cut over his left cheek.

All courtesy of Kat.

CHAPTER TWENTY-FIVE

Part of me is happy to see her. But then I remember the way we left things, her refusal to talk to me, and now this, both of us on opposite sides of Aventine. The scrubbing kit in my hand suddenly weighs a hundred pounds, shackling me to this room.

Kat watches me expectantly. "Emery, huh? Such a *pretty* name."

"Let him go, Kat. Please."

She cranks Randall's arm higher. He winces. "Is he the one who forced you to go on the run?"

"*No*. He has nothing to do with this."

She clucks her tongue. "Not nothing. He knows your real name. That makes him rather special, doesn't it?" She shakes her head, suddenly serious. "You should've come in, M, and none of this would've happened."

She makes it sound like this is all my fault when I've done everything in my power to do right by the data I've been entrusted with. "What I'm carrying? It's bigger than Aventine." I take another step toward her. I'm two arms' lengths away, with more maneuvering room than where she's backed up against the kitchen counter. Not that that's ever helped me in the past. "Whatever they told you, it's not true, I swear it."

She wrenches Randall's arm again for good measure, then

shoves him away from her so she can face me head on. "You broke the rules."

"Yes, but I would've died if I didn't."

She flinches, covering almost immediately as Randall gingerly rotates his arm.

>>You OK?>>

He grimaces. <<I'll live.<<

I'll take it. "Can we talk?" I ask Kat. I tap my temple. "Alone?"

Her posture relaxes fractionally. "This whole sector's been spotty with network outages of late. Didn't you know?" She gives me a wink, and for a moment it's just like old times. "But I can't guarantee they don't have other ways they can listen in," she says with a significant glance to our surroundings. It's an Aventine safe house, after all.

Better make this quick then. >>I was set up from the beginning. A special job for one of Dash's clients who couldn't wait for him to recover.>>

At the mention of Dash's ordeal, her lips flatten. Still upset, but at least she's listening to me. <<You think he was taken out so you'd get the assignment?<<

>>I don't know. But I *am* the most junior courier.>>

<<Probably thought you'd be easiest to intimidate.<< She gives me an appraising look. <<Guess you proved them wrong.<< She relaxes her stance, crosses her arms loosely over her chest. <<So you think Aventine's behind this?<<

>>I don't know. But clearly whoever did this had tabs on our internal processes somehow.>>

<<We're supposed to be an independent unit.<<

>>Or is that just what Harding tells us?>> She grimaces. >>He gave me this assignment, Kat. And now he's the one who sent you after me, right?>>

<<A number of us were sent out to bring you in before you got hurt. Though we were left to our own devices how best to

do that.<< Her gaze flicks to the scrubbing kit held tightly in my hands. <<Figured you'd be getting desperate right about now with the curdle.<<

>>You're not wrong, but I still need to see this blood through.>>

<<But that's not how it works. In a case like this, you're supposed to be scrubbed no matter what.<<

>>And whoever did this is probably counting on that. That's why I can't come in, Kat, not yet.>>

She throws up her hands. <<And when Harding finds out I let you go, what then?<<

>>I don't know.>> I really don't. I'm figuring this shit out as I go, praying I'm not making things worse. >>If there was any other way…>> I'm the biggest hypocrite, expecting her to stray from the company line when I took her out when Dash needed her most.

Kat puts her hands on her hips, the look in her eyes contrary and calculating at the same time. <<And him?<< Her gaze flicks toward Randall. <<What does he have to do with this?<<

>>He… He's the one I told you about, the one I left behind. He's helped me, when no one else could.>>

Lips pressed together, Kat's face closes up so I can't tell what she thinks about Randall, the situation, or what's going to happen next.

She rolls back her shoulders. Unease trickles down my spine as she takes a step to my left. Automatically, I hand the case off to Randall, mirroring her movements like it's sparring practice all over again.

"I've always enjoyed fighting you, Emery, but you've never been very good at *offense*."

Why bother when she can lay me out at a second's notice. She flinches toward me, and I dart back, sluggish in my movements. Too close to the full onset of the curdle.

<<This would be about the time you hit me, M.<<

Randall tenses, unsure whether to defend me against her or not. I wave him off. >>It's OK. At least I think it will be,>> I tell him.

She circles around again. <<Give me *something* so I can convince them you got away fair and square.<<

I almost stumble. >>Kat, I don't know how to thank you.>>

She shrugs. <<Make it look good, and make the rest worth it.<<

>>I will.>>

She comes at me again, just like practice, but this time when I strike out, I make contact with her midsection. I follow up with a punch to her jaw she makes no move to counter. Hard enough to knock her out. When she collapses to the floor, she stays there.

I can't tell if she's faking or not. The impulse to check on her wars with the clawing need to get out of here. *Now.* I point Randall to the door, and hastily we rush down the stairs and back onto the walkway. He hands over the scrubbing kit for safekeeping in my satchel.

<<What now?<<

>>We need to find a way to the Echelon.>> I consciously shake off the sensation of being watched. Even if the backup team's not closing in, thanks to Kat, knowing Harding sicced some of the other couriers on me isn't remotely encouraging. Aventine's bound to be watching the lifts and trains too. I close my eyes momentarily and focus on the sector map my implant projects into my field of vision. >>We'll take the Fairmont Stairs.>>

<<You're kidding.<<

>>Nope. It's not well patrolled, and they haven't fully updated the cameras there.>> It helps that it's shaded in yellow on my Aventine map too.

<<It's also a crime scene waiting to happen. We'll attract

too much attention from the locals.<<

>>Better them than the police.>> Or Aventine.

<<Even so, you're in no condition to ascend.<<

>>Doesn't matter.>>

<<It does to me. Surely there's some place we can regroup before...<< He leaves the rest unspoken.

>>All right. We can afford a break.>> A maintenance hatch isn't too far away. >>Come on.>> I position Randall so his bulk blocks me from view as I get to work. It takes longer than I'd like to override the lock.

<<What is this place?<<

>>You ever wonder where all the cleaning bots go when they aren't cleaning?>> This one's small, with only a few older bots charging along the wall. The dedicated trash chute stinks, but enough cleaning fluid scents the air to make it bearable.

I back Randall onto a small cabinet full of supplies and replacement parts for the robots. "Let me take a look." He tips his head back. The good news is the blood's mostly dried, only giving me a small wrench of unease as I look him over. Kat got him good. His cheek's already starting to swell. I rustle around in my satchel and pull out a wound-heal patch. I use the edge of the bandage to wipe away what blood I can, then smooth the patch over his face.

He winces, and I catch a bit of pain reverberating through our connection, but he remains still until the patch has set. "Should be all right in a half hour."

I step back, but he captures my wrist. Rusty brown blood stains the fingers of both of our gloves.

"Where'd you get all this stuff?"

"Standard Aventine complement."

"They think of everything."

"Never had to use most of it. Until now."

His thumb swoops under the edge of my glove and across

the inside of my wrist. "I'm glad for that."

"Yes, well, not all couriers are so lucky. One girl busted open her knee when she fell on a crowded concourse during rush hour. Another had to deal with a compromised exchange. They roughed him up before a protection detail could reach him," I say, thinking of Dash's ordeal.

"But the way you talk about it... And earlier, seeing you fight those assholes in the Bower. You like it."

I shrug off the accusation in his voice. "I do. Whatever else Aventine's done, they've given me that much."

"Given you? From what I've seen, they've *taken* practically everything from you and somehow managed to convince you you're better off for it."

"That's not true. They also kept me out of jail."

"What are you talking about?"

I gesture to my scar. "The guy who did this to me? I did everything I could to hunt him down when the police gave up looking for him. I targeted scrappers operating throughout the Terrestrial District, hoping to find him... I never did, but I helped put others behind bars."

"Liv..." I want to strangle the sympathy out of his voice.

"I'd do it again, too. Even knowing what happens. Sorry if that destroys your idealized image of me, but better you find out now." He doesn't flinch away, mentally or physically, and my defiance fizzles out. "Anyway, Aventine found out and decided I fit the profile. Tahir even helped close my cold case." A hot wave of hatred shudders through me. Still. Even knowing my attacker's been punished for what he's done. "Then Aventine continued to build on my skills and experience, making me into the monster I am today."

"You're not a monster." Randall watches my face for a long moment. "They blackmailed you."

I shrug. "I never had a choice. It was either do the job and try to enjoy it, or do the job and be miserable. And just hope when my ten years of service was up, I'd earned enough credits to retire in peace."

"Did you think you could just walk back into our lives?"

"No, but what else could I have done? I had no one." He drops my hand. "I had to start over, and I've tried to make the best of it." I don't know what else to say to make him understand.

He processes my words, his face unnaturally still, but between the emotions that swirl around his eyes and the slight tension along our connection, I know looks can be deceiving.

"If it helps, I wanted to reach out to you. I even set up an alias in a stupid plan to send you a message through your arcade account, but I chickened out. I hoped–" I cut myself off at the spike in our connection.

"I haven't logged any time at the arcade since… you know. But that day in the Understory. You still pushed me away."

The "why?" is implied, demanding an answer.

"You didn't deserve to be chained to a data vampire who's better off dead. I might have to live with Aventine's restrictions, but you don't."

"What will you do when this is all over?" he finally asks.

"What do you mean?"

"Will you still be a courier?"

I snort. "I doubt I'll have a choice. Things'll get cleared up one way or another like Tahir said. And with all the time left on my contract, Aventine'll figure out a way to put me to use."

"I don't want you putting yourself in danger."

"What you want doesn't matter. Besides, you're a fine one to complain about danger when you're mixed up in some kind of conspiracy with the Disconnects." Geeta's words come crashing back down. Randall must feel some of it, because he gives me a questioning look. "So much so, you considered becoming one of them."

I touch his neck, the shadow of his implant. With my fingertips at first, then the whole of my hand. Randall's pulse speeds up. The urge to bolt warring with the desperate desire to lean into my touch. "You wanted to get rid of it." Of *me*, my mind shouts.

He doesn't deny it, and that somehow makes everything worse. "Liv, when you were gone..."

He cut himself off from his contacts, stopped going to the arcade, and threw himself even deeper into the Disconnect cause. All because of me.

"You were supposed to go on, live your life, not..." Obsolesce and roll back to a cruder version of himself.

He turns into my hand and presses his face against my gloved palm and inhales. "I thought if you weren't coming back, it wasn't worth being connected. I couldn't imagine sharing my mind with anyone else. Once I realized that, everything about implants seemed unnecessary. I wanted a clean start. Maybe that way I could..."

I bite my lip. "And what do you think now?"

He eases up on his emotional damper. Too many feelings rush in to identify them all, but I recognize enough of them. "You already know how I feel."

What we both feel. And it still hasn't changed despite everything. I tremble, sweat beading across my brow.

He takes both of my forearms in his hands. "Are you OK?"

"Yeah, just give me a sec." I close my eyes and plead with my body to hang on. Just a little bit longer. The tremors gradually subside, but my brow's still clammy.

Randall watches me patiently. Then he raises his right hand. An offering. A promise. Just like before, except this time Aventine doesn't stand in the way.

All I have to do is reach out and–

My stomach wrenches, and I bolt to the other end of the room. Vomit – bile streaked with blood – coats the floor. I run a shaky hand over my face. But I feel better. Marginally.

"Not quite the reaction I was hoping for." Rik comes up behind me and gives my shoulder a squeeze. Then he sees the mess. "Shit, Liv. How can you still function?"

"Because I have to."

CHAPTER TWENTY-SIX

The Fairmont Stairs beckon beyond a shuttered restaurant and a consignment shop in one of the earliest sections of New Worth. Now it's a rundown relic, from a time when movement between levels was welcomed before society grew so striated by elevation and entrenched in status. Left behind in New Worth's march toward progress.

My joints complain with each step, but Rik's moving with the same ease he had when we started. Unlike access stairs, the Fairmont Stairs are open to the city. So you can look up and marvel at the buildings all around you. Must have been something at the time it was first built, but now dirt and grime mar the once-pristine surfaces. Air scrubber residue coats one building, leaking from the ledges like a runny nose. Handrails are worn down to nubs at the landings. Back in the day, this was a place to see and be seen, the stairs folding back over themselves as you go up, like an MC Escher print. Now it's a path through New Worth for those who can't afford the nominal train fees. A haven for Disconnects and criminals alike.

For us, it's simply a means to an end. And thankfully, the end's almost in sight.

Rik glances down at me and frowns. <<Let's stop here.<< He guides me to a column propping up the sixth landing from the bottom.

I lean back, my head thumping against concrete. >>We're nearly there.>>

Rik doesn't answer, his gaze turned back the way we came. No, Randall. It's getting harder to keep them separate. He swears. Then he shares with me the feed from his ocular boost, already trained on a figure near the bottom of the Stairs, moving too fast to be a typical New Worthian. He's built like my tail from the Aquarium. All muscle and thinly disguised body armor. Could be one of Diego's new recruits or a member of the client's security team, but either way, there's guaranteed to be more of them.

>>He won't be able to catch up with us before we reach the top.>>

<<Still. If they know we're here, they know where the Stairs end...<<

Randall doesn't say under normal circumstances I would've already figured that out. But there's nothing normal about the curdle.

>>Hang on. Let me think.>> I can almost hear Tahir clucking his tongue. *What's my exit strategy?*

Dammit. I push off the column and lean down, head between my knees. The pounding in my temples eases slightly even as the gray and white marble checkerboard landing swims before my eyes. Another deep breath, and I pull up my map of New Worth. There's not much. Concourses feed into the Stairs at each landing, but between levels you're pretty much stuck. With a half-blink, the city's infrastructure overlays my map. Water, electricity, air, sewage...

>>There.>> I send Randall the schematic of an old mechanical floor connected to the landing above us. Skyscrapers have designated floors every dozen levels or so for all the machinery needed to keep them operational. This one was decommissioned at some point for upgrades, but even if it was closed off, it's still there. It has to be.

He frowns up at the landing where it should be located. <<Can't get a visual. Too many people in front of that spot.<<

>>We have to try.>>

His frown intensifies, but he nods and guides me back to the stairwell. The first step trips me up, and he catches me under my arm.

>>Sorry. Clumsy of me.>>

<<Stop lying, Liv.<<

I don't reply, just redouble my concentration as I fit my leaden feet to the step in front of me. And the one after that. And the one after that.

<<Ah, shit.<<

I follow his gaze to the landing where the access to the mechanical floor should be. A homeless woman has set up a makeshift tent in front of the wall. She watches us with hooded eyes as her brown hands move quickly, knitting something out of thick, ratty, reclaimed yarn. Two feral-looking children sit nearby, legs slung out over the edge of the landing. The boy's blond with green eyes; the girl, darker than I am. Both come armed with the same suspicious stare. A family unit of convenience? No, necessity.

>>We'll just ask nicely.>>

<<Let me handle this.<< Randall pushes a manufactured smile onto his face. "Would it be possible to examine the wall behind your… setup?"

The woman stiffens, her dark brown eyes narrowing as she inspects us both. "What's it to you?" she asks in a harsh voice. "This is my spot, fair and square."

I step forward. "There's an old mechanical access area behind here. And we need to, well, access it."

Her defensiveness shifts into something darker, calculating. "You're lying."

"I'd show you if I could," I say, tapping my temple.

She growls, and Randall glares at me. <<Are you trying to

piss her off?<< To her, "She doesn't mean to be rude. We're just in a bit of a jam," he says.

The woman whistles at the boy – ten, eleven at most – who snaps to attention. "What's it worth to you?"

I open my mouth to answer, but don't know what to say in terms she'll understand. What *is* it worth? It might not even be accessible, walled over by concrete.

Randall shifts his weight, then rolls up his shirtsleeve. The woman coils into a sudden crouch, removing a UV wand from underneath her blanket. A small tattoo glimmers in its light along Randall's forearm. The ghostly outline of a tree being struck by lightning. Where did he–

"You may pass," the woman says to Randall. She turns her glare on me and pulls out a surprisingly new credit transfer device from the folds of her knitting. "Fifty credits."

My mouth falls open. "You're kidding."

The woman just arches an eyebrow. Randall steps forward and places his naked fingertip on the pad, authorizing the transfer. The woman waves the boy toward the tent, and he holds the flap open for us. "Corey'll show you the way."

"If anyone asks," Randall says, "we exited the Stairs on the next level."

The woman snorts but doesn't object as she returns to her knitting. The body odor intensifies as I duck inside the tent. The kid bypasses three sleeping nests and a small cook stove and unfastens a panel along the back. Someone has cut through the mortar and concrete.

Crouching, I follow the boy as he nimbly crawls into the darkness and waits for us on a rusty metal catwalk. Dusty control panels and abandoned meters flank the walls.

"You knew about the access point?" he asks in an awed voice.

"It was on an old schematic."

"No one's ever figured that out before. Except you." He grins and scrambles across the catwalk with fearless grace. In the dark below, transponders hum ominously. Like the precursor to goose bumps on my skin, never-ending, surrounding us on all sides.

"On my map, the tunnel leads to the northwest sector, elevated section."

The boy shakes his head. "We're not going that way. Too dangerous."

For Disconnects like him? Or us? A prickle of unease works through me, and Randall gives my shoulder a squeeze in response. "So where does this lead?"

"The Graveyard."

That's back in the Terrestrial District. The opposite direction of where we need to go. Tahir said once the best path's rarely a straight line. But my optimism at reaching the Echelon in time sinks with each step we take.

The mechanical floor runs the length of the building. When we reach the other side, the kid waves us into a hole someone cut into the grating under our feet. A slight rumbling shakes the building as the kid jumps down beside us with ease. We're in some kind of access tunnel that runs along the maglev tracks.

"How did you find this place?" I ask.

Corey frowns. "Had to. Needed a place to hide from the police."

"But–"

<<Leave it alone, Liv.<<

I give Rik a startled look.

<<There are caches like this all over New Worth. Pockets between the aging infrastructure and the new, where people have taken advantage because they have to.<< I'm still thinking over all the implications of this when he adds, <<People like us have no idea what it means to live off the grid.<<

>>That doesn't mean we shouldn't try.>>

<<Absolutely.<<

>>Then why shut me down, when all I'm asking–<<

<<You haven't earned the answer yet.<<

I whirl around. Push up his shirtsleeve. Ignore his shocked breath at my touch. >>Then have I earned the answer to this? This is the same tattoo on the guy at the botched drop. What does it mean?>>

<<It means that I'm an ally. That I'm someone who's willing to help the cause. They deserve so much more than what society's granted them. I may not understand what it means to be disconnected, but–<<

My stomach plummets. >>Did you tell your Disconnect friends about me? What I'm carrying?>> He never left my sight, but that doesn't mean anything with implants.

<<No. How could you think–<<

>>You were ready to join up, ditch your implant. Telling them about the potential changes to the registry would prove you're one of them.>>

<<I don't need to prove anything to them. Just to you.<<

The hurt and barely concealed anger radiating off him gives me pause. >>I'm trying to keep us safe from Aventine, the government, and whoever else has been sent after me. I don't need Disconnects making my job harder.>>

<<Liv, I haven't told anyone anything.<<

>>Yet.>> I gesture to his arm, the invisible tattoo that lurks there.

<<That's not fair.<<

I hold up my hand, and our connection quiets. Corey glances back at us impatiently. >>If there are any more secrets you're keeping from me, now's the time.>>

He shakes his head. <<I have no more secrets, Liv. You know everything.<< The look in his eyes hollows me out. <<What you see is what you get.<< Whether that's something

I want he leaves unspoken.

"You guys coming?" Corey asks.

I force myself back into motion. This tunnel runs parallel with the maglev tracks, but we're underneath them, at the place where the tracks are anchored to the buildings. Air whistles through the metal panels – all that separates us from the gaping abyss between buildings. Except for the occasional tremble when a train passes overhead, the only other sound is our footsteps along the corrugated metal floor.

>>Sorry I overreacted. Guess the pressure's getting to me.>>

Rik's quiet for a long moment. <<It's all right. I know trust doesn't come easy to you, between what Aventine's put you through and...<< He means my past. I bristle at that, but he's not wrong. <<I just don't know what else I can do to prove to you once and for all I have your back in all this. If we calibrated, became confidants...<<

Like we were so close to doing in the maintenance hatch. Raw desire warring with my weakening body. Even if we did, it'd do us no good. >>Aventine would just take you away again.>>

"Won't be much longer," Corey says cheerily as he scampers under a low-hanging I-beam.

I'm not nearly as graceful as I stoop down and nearly clock my head.

Rik's concern flashes through me. <<How many hours has it been?<<

>>Need to know.>>

His frustration builds up behind my eyes. I grit my teeth, digging my hand into my churning stomach, begging it to behave a bit longer. We've come this far, which is pretty amazing, considering. It doesn't matter that I'm half asleep, that I can't feel my arms...

Randall comes up next to me, trying to get a good look at

my face. <<How are you doing? For real?<<

>>Just a little light-headed.>>

<<There's no way you're going to make it to the Echelon…<<

I certainly feel like shit, but that doesn't mean we can stop now. >>We have to try. What else can we do?>>

He gestures to my satchel, the scrubbing kit inside. <<We get you healthy, then we'll worry about the rest.<<

I'm already shaking my head. >>No. Too many things could go wrong once the data's outside my body.>>

The feedback along our connection practically rattles my teeth with his disapproval. <<Liv, you aren't responsible for the city's sins.<< To emphasize his point, Rik blasts me with enough nonverbal frustration to water my eyes.

>>Stop making my job even harder.>>

He wants to protest – almost a tangible mental twinge – but he lets the matter drop. After traveling downward for a half hour, Corey veers toward a section of wall and pries a metal panel back. No marks or anything I can see. He must have the route memorized. He waves us into another tunnel and replaces the panel, leaving whoever does come down here to maintain the maglev lines, robot or human, unaware of our presence. The heat and humidity in this section of the tunnel suggests we're near industrial hot water pipes, but I'm having a hard time pinpointing our exact location. Must be too embedded in the city's infrastructure to get a signal.

Corey's suddenly standing in front of me. "Stay here, all right?" Without waiting for our answer, he wades into the darkness and taps out an elaborate pattern on the hatch up ahead.

After a long moment, a slow groan of metal results, followed by a crack of anemic light that gradually strengthens. Corey exchanges a few words with a rough-looking man with light brown skin and closely cropped brown hair. Corey returns, waving us forward. The kid doesn't realize we can see better than he can down here with our NAmp filters.

Unlike the reclamation center I found myself in two nights ago, the Graveyard's where machines go to die. Factory equipment, building materials, motorized carts and bots left here to be picked over, recycled or smelted down, the rest to rust and flake into oblivion.

I'm so busy taking in the towers of junk, I'm slow to focus on the man who's manning the other side of the secret tunnel. His arms are crossed, his face puckered as he looks us over. "Pay up." He pulls out another fingerpad.

"We've already paid the toll," I say.

"That was to get in. Not *out*."

"But–"

"No problem," Randall cuts in smoothly. He depresses the pad, not breaking eye contact with the man. <<There's something wrong with my credit limit,<< he tells me a second later.

>>They could've frozen the accounts of anyone detected on the Stairs when they spotted us there to try and slow us down.>> Even the dummy accounts Charon gifted us.

<<But you know where we are?<<

>>Yeah.>>

<<Good. When I tell you, you run.<<

>>What–>>

Randall gives the man a smile. "Sorry, must not have lined it up right the first time." He presses his finger down again. <<Now.<<

Two days ago I would've questioned him further. But now, everything in me responds to his voice. I bolt.

"Hey!" the man shouts. His voice transforms into a sharp cry as Randall punches him.

Then Randall's bounding next to me. So not fair. I had a head start. Stupid curdle.

Behind us, an intricate series of whistles pierce the air. All around, the skeletons of rusted machinery animate. Shadows shift. More rough types – four that I can see – emerge from the flaking husks of ancient enterprise. Of course. The gatekeeper has a crew.

Randall leaps over a metal strut. I'm a second behind him with an awkward little hop, but at least I don't lose my balance as we sprint down the aisles of junk.

A teenaged boy angles toward us, trying to cut us off. He vaults over a wall of compacted scrap metal and lands only a few feet away from Randall. Without pausing, Randall lowers his shoulder and drives into the guy's side, knocking him back. His spine slams against the metal wall, and he sags to the ground.

>>Through there.>>

Ahead, an abandoned maglev car rests where it's been picked over for salvage. Randall adjusts his course slightly, and we dart through the doors, permanently splayed open like a dissected corpse, then out the other side. He lets me go first, keeping an eye on the way we came. My head throbs with each step, but I lengthen my strides, trying to increase the distance between me and the salvagers.

I send Rik the best route for getting out of the Graveyard and back on course.

<<You go on. I'll try to draw them off you.<<

>>*No*. We stay together.>>

<<Liv–<<

I turn my head – to yell at him, look at him in disbelief – I don't know. We didn't come this far to split up now.

A man swings down from the overhanging crane and almost knocks Randall off his feet. He recovers quickly enough to block the man's follow-up swing.

They grapple with one another – neither particularly skilled – though Randall's opponent's surely had more practice as his fist glances off Randall's jaw. *No*. Randall's stunned for just a second, but it's enough for the man to be able to punch him in the gut unchallenged. My vision flashes white.

I reach out, already calculating how to take Randall's opponent down – a swift jab to the ribs followed by a punch to his throat – when hands grab me from behind. My clothes fizzle in weak protest. Kicking back, I find someone's shin, and they grunt in pain. I whirl around, using my momentum to swing my satchel against the man's head. The scrubbing kit inside connects with his cranium, and he drops in a boneless heap. He's still breathing – I make sure of that as I pant. Then I remember Randall.

He eyes me with disbelief. He's finally downed his opponent, writhing around in the dirt. <<Jesus, Liv. Maybe *you* should be protecting *me*.<<

I roll my eyes. >>Let's go. Don't know how much more gas I have in the tank, if you know what I mean.>>

His face hardens. <<Right.<<

We jog along the perimeter of the Graveyard. The gate where equipment gets dropped off leading into the Terrestrial District isn't much further, but a dozen people block our way, not a single implant signal among them.

Randall swears next to me.

"Friends of yours?" I ask between gasps. "You promised me–"

"I didn't do this."

A familiar face resolves out of the crowd. Brown skin, black hair, eyes constantly in motion. Charon. That he's on terra firma and not skulking in some dark corner below tells me something big's happening, but I don't have the first clue as to what that could be.

Randall moves in front of me, his face unreadable as he stares down the Disconnects. Behind us, someone pelts closer, the head honcho manning the Graveyard. I tense, unsure who I should focus on, as I ease the touchscreen out of my satchel.

Charon inclines his head toward the leader of the Graveyard. "Sorry if these two gave you trouble."

The man eyes the group of Disconnects carefully. Not overtly hostile, but definitely calculating as he relaxes his stance. "Didn't pay the toll."

Charon nods. "They don't know how things work down here, but I'll vouch for them."

>>What's going on?>>

Randall's head flinches toward me, but his gaze never leaves Charon's face. <<I don't know.<<

Not at all reassuring. I call up the database patch Geeta decrypted for us and delete it from the touchscreen. Then slide it back into my satchel.

<<Did you just do what I think you did?<<

>>Can't risk the data falling into the wrong hands. You should know that by now.>>

<<But we're running out of time. *You're* running out of time.<<

"And what good is your word, Ferryman?" the man asks.

Charon tosses a datastick at him. "That should be enough to smooth over any… unpleasantness they've caused."

The man grimaces as he stoops to pick up the datastick. His cheek is already starting to bruise, courtesy of Randall. He then turns on his heel. A sharp whistle tells his crew to do the same.

>>I thought Charon was supposed to be your friend.>>

<<He is.<<

>>Does he make a habit of tracking you down?>> Somehow he must've been monitoring the aliases he gave us.

"You keep saying you're one of us, Randall," Charon says, pushing up his sleeve. Baring the tattoo of a tree cleaved in two by lightning in vivid color. "Time to prove it." He nods to me. "Convince your girlfriend here it'll be best for all concerned if she comes with us."

CHAPTER TWENTY-SEVEN

"What's going on?" I look from Charon to Randall to the two Disconnects brandishing stun guns.

Randall's silence as he stares down Charon sends unease tripping along my spine. Our connection isn't reassuring either, full of churning conflict and competing loyalties. He committed himself to the Disconnect cause long before I was in the picture. How can I expect him to side with me now?

His gaze cuts to me. <<You should know better than that.<<

Charon waves forward two Disconnects, and they take up position on either side of us. "The whole city's after you. This is for your own protection."

Guess Aventine decided to officially call in the reserves. I pull up my map but blink it closed a second later. Even if I could find an alternate route away from here, I'm in no condition to go on the run. Not again.

"Why do you care?" I ask.

Charon's jittery stare settles on me for a long moment. "Because anything getting *that* much attention from the upper levels is of interest to us."

I shrug. "Just a misunderstanding with my employer. It'll blow over soon." One way or the other.

"Then in the meantime, I suggest you avail yourself of our hospitality. In exchange for our goodwill, I think it's finally time you tell me about your business at the Henderson Acres warehouse the other day."

<<I never told him about that, Liv. I *swear.*<<

And this time I believe him. Randall's just as shocked Charon knows as I am, a breathless sort of disbelief pressing up against my ribs. >>How did they figure it out?>>

Before he can respond, the rangy black woman standing next to Charon stamps her foot impatiently. A heavy braid drapes over her shoulder. "We need to get out of the open."

The Disconnect closest to me discharges his stun gun. A test burst, but I still flinch away, angry with myself for reacting to the taunt.

Putting myself beyond the authorities' reach *is* appealing, but to turn myself over to the Disconnects? That's almost as bad, but what other options do we have? The Aventine playbook doesn't have any answers for me. Not this time.

Reluctantly, I face Charon. "If you want to know about the warehouse, then you need us – *both* of us – in good working condition to learn more."

"Of course." His gaze darts to the empty space hanging above us. There's no skybridge overhead for levels, but Charon still hunches his shoulders as if he doesn't quite trust being out in the open. "Let's go."

The Disconnects swarm around us as we leave the Graveyard behind. The industrial fringe of the Terrestrial District gradually gives way to cramped residential neighborhoods.

We don't get far before Randall leans over, gesturing to my face. "Your, um, nose is bleeding."

"Oh. Thanks." I fumble with my satchel and stem the flow with a tissue.

Charon eyes me speculatively. "Looks like you've had a rough time of it."

"You have no idea," I say, trying hard not to think about the blood leaking out of my body.

Randall's concern burns the back of my eyes before he's able to tamp it down. <<Liv, we can find another way.<<

It's a bit late for that, surrounded by Disconnects with the curdle barely held in check by sheer force of will. >>Not seeing a lot of other options.>>

He makes a subtle gesture toward the satchel again. <<I mean the data. You can't keep going like this.<<

>>Doesn't matter. The data's my responsibility. I can't risk turning it over to a proclaimed enemy of the client.>>

<<You think the distinctions matter at this point? Let's say we do get the data to the Echelon and prove your innocence in this mess. As far as Aventine's concerned, you still deviated from protocol.<<

>>I'm not doing this for Aventine. I'm doing this because it's the right thing to do.>>

He sighs. <<You're taking this martyr complex too far.<<

>>That's way out of line.>>

<<Really? You hunted down how many scrappers so they couldn't hurt anyone else, putting your own safety at risk. Same with Aventine, working for them in a misguided attempt to protect everyone else in your life. And now this.<<

>>It's not that simple.>>

<<No?<<

The woman with the braid passes out facemasks to everyone. We're close enough to a quarantine zone, my palms are sweating. Guess it was too much to hope we'd be avoiding that area. But my immune system can't take much more with the curdle coming on. I fit my mask over my face just in time as we pass into the zone, my implant flaring with warnings until I acknowledge them all.

Rik sighs when I don't respond. <<Don't worry. You won't get sick – it's just a ploy the Disconnects cooked up to keep people out.<<

Creating a safe space where they can avoid interference

from the authorities while they plot against the upper levels. I marvel at the ingenuity of turning the city's protections against illness to their advantage. Just because they aren't connected doesn't mean they aren't smart. They've been underestimated for too long.

I force my legs back into motion. My stomach trembles. My eyesight dims. At first I think it's just my booster not adjusting to our surroundings as we speed through a series of twisting alleys. They do need recalibration sometimes. But no. It's me, the curdle coming on strong. My world narrows, until there's only room for me and Rik and each step we take.

>>Tell me what it's like outside.>> In case I don't get another chance to ask. In case I don't get fully scrubbed in time.

His flash of surprise at my question fades as quickly as it appears. <<The first time I left the airlock, it was so bright, my eyes watered despite the polarized glass on my helmet. You could see the scars left on the land, but things were growing. Green stubborn shoots as far as the eye could see. And beyond that, trees that my colleagues before me had planted. In that moment, I'd never been happier.<<

Vaguely, I'm aware of the Disconnects' alarm at our shambling pace. I must look a sight. Despite the dark scowl on Rik's face, he keeps talking, his voice in my mind where it should be, a balm on my brain.

<<Some of the planting trips lasted for weeks. All day we'd toil in the earth, then sleep under the stars. The sun's amazing, but the night sky is what makes me feel just how small we are. A tiny speck in a larger pattern.<<

My shoulder rams into a pillar that I didn't realize was there. I catch myself on the knots and whorls carved into the concrete tree trunk, buttressing an elevated section.

"Shit." The next thing I know the street's upside down as Rik bundles me up over his shoulder in a fireman's carry.

I have Rik in my head and Randall around me. If it weren't for the curdle, I'd want for nothing.

"What's wrong with her?" Charon demands.

"We've been on the move for forty-eight hours. She's worn out," Randall says, as if it should be obvious.

Charon grudgingly returns to the front of the procession, and Randall's arms tighten over me. <<You're doing great.<<

>>Haven't thrown up yet.>>

<<That's my girl.<<

I close my eyes. On my city map, little blips of light representing me and Rik move through the Terrestrial District. A wave of nausea crashes over me. I clutch Randall's shirt and battle it back, breathing through my mouth.

The thumping of my blood in my ears subsumes the ambient noise. My world narrows some more. No more pattering of feet on concrete. No rustling of clothes and satchels, the jingles that blare from the storefronts. Just my blood and Rik's thoughts. Just...

<<Liv!<< Randall clutches my shoulders. "Liv." Rightside up again, I find Rik's face staring down at me in alarm. "You passed out." I feel a huge weight slip off away, but it's just Randall easing the satchel off my shoulders. "Easy now."

"I'm OK," I say for the benefit of the Disconnects watching.

His frown deepens as he loops his arm around my shoulders. <<We may not be calibrated, but I still know when you're lying.<<

"The break did help." I take an experimental step forward, Randall hovering beside me. So far so good.

"Can't be much further," he says. We're taken into a rundown bar occupying the corner frontage of a building that rises all the way to the Canopy. The lone bartender doesn't react to our entrance as she polishes the concrete bar top with a rag. Bypassing the front room, we're led down a short hall, then a set of stairs. My headache flares at all the screens depicting different feeds across the city, covering the basement walls. Most of them are centered on areas in the Terrestrial District and the Understory, places that have seen high Disconnect activity the last few days.

Homebrew tech litters the tables, along with touchscreens full of schematics, old computers, and data sticks. At our entrance, the four individuals manning the room look up. They eye me and Randall curiously, then shift their focus onto Charon. One of them hands him a touchscreen, and he scrolls through the readout with interest.

>>I didn't realize your friend was such a big player in the revolution. Before today, I'd swear he's never left his underground home.>>

<<Me neither. I thought he was just another sympathizer, but you've seen his skills. Guess he decided to put them to use.<< He nudges my shoulder. <<How are you holding up?<<

I don't answer, tired of lying to him.

"You were in the Understory where our colleague was killed," the woman with the braid says without preamble.

The room quiets around us as though everyone's holding their breath. I raise my hands, palms out. "I didn't kill him."

"But you were responsible for his death."

"No, that would be the woman who shot him."

"Could you identify her?" someone else asks.

"I was more focused on getting out of there alive."

"Come now." The woman taps her temple, making a mockery of the gesture. "You want us to believe your implant didn't identify her?"

"She did something to my signal and wiped my cache." I give Charon a significant look. "As you already know."

Charon exhales loudly. "Denita, I think we should just lay everything out on the table."

Her eyes widen at his interruption. "She isn't one of us."

"Doesn't matter. Not any more." He turns to me. "Emery – can I call you Emery? When you met me before, I was simply doing Randall here a favor. That's what friends are for." His smile dims. "But then I realized Aventine's missing courier and you must be one and the same. Luckily I put a tracker on you both when you swung by my place. Just in case."

An aura of pain haunts my vision at the news. We've been screwed since the beginning.

<<Shit. I never thought–<<

>>It's OK. You couldn't have known this was all tied together.>>

"You were told to deliver a dataset two days ago," Charon says. "Our operative was supposed to *encourage* you to not attend that meeting, but there were some unanticipated complications. How am I doing so far?"

I resist the urge to look at Randall. It's my call, whether we deal straight with Charon and his allies or continue to go it alone. I know I wouldn't have gotten this far without Randall's help. Just as I know we're running out of things we can achieve together, when each hour the curdle makes me weaker. The temptation to set down the burden I carry in my blood blurs my vision. But I have to remember these people wouldn't have much sympathy for me if I didn't have something they so desperately wanted.

Charon waits for some reaction from me, but I bite the inside of my cheek, keeping my expression as neutral as possible. Charon's gaze flicks to Randall, but he stays silent as well.

The woman steps toward me, a knife suddenly in her hand. "If you think we won't cut the information out of you, you're mistaken."

Charon rolls his eyes. "I already told you, Denita, she's clean. I checked her out myself before I knew who I was dealing with."

Rik's bemused relief filters across our connection. <<They know about the data, but not the way Aventine transports it.<<

>>And it needs to stay that way.>>

He disagrees, but I don't have time to address it before the woman whirls back to me. "Then where's the data?"

She slashes at me shallowly, trying to scare me into talking, but I'm not having it. Grabbing her wrist, I dig my fingers into the hollow place between her wrist bones. It's all I can manage at this point. She winces at the havoc I'm wreaking on the pressure point there and drops the blade. Everyone who isn't Randall or Charon reaches for a weapon.

"It's someplace safe," I say. "You think I'd just let *anybody* have it after what happened?" The woman wrenches free of my grip, sucking her teeth. Gradually the tension in the basement drops low enough that civil conversation's possible again. "Besides, I have no idea who or what the data's for. I'm only supposed to deliver it."

"That'll be hard to do with the entire city hunting you."

"Doesn't matter. At this point, my employer's security protocols mandate that the data's destroyed, regardless of what it's for. We also have reason to believe someone high up in the government's working very hard to keep the situation from coming to light."

Charon frowns and snaps his fingers. On one of the wallscreens, the woman who masqueraded as the client at the botched drop appears. I'm there too, but my face is pixelated into obscurity. "This was the last image our operative was able to broadcast before…" Charon points to me. "Look familiar?"

"If you want to blame someone for the death of your colleague, start with her," I say.

Charon crosses his arms. "She's Joan Sheridan. She's been an aide to the secretary of Economic Development for years."

My gaze flies back to the screen. "There *has* to be some mistake." Her hair's styled differently, her clothing crudely printed, compared to the buttoned-up woman I remember from my first job with Aventine... That's right. There was something about her voice that seemed familiar. But I didn't make the connection at the time, not without my implant to help connect the dots.

"You know her?" Randall asks.

I blink rapidly, trying to ease the ache building up behind my eyes. "Early on I did a job for them. Data transfer for a housing development in the Terrestrial District struggling to make a go of it since they wouldn't rent to Disconnects. But how this relates to everything…" I shrug.

"It may not," Charon says. "But what we do know is entries in the public registry have been tampered with. But we can't prove it, not after that attack on the records facility the other day."

"But everyone thinks you're behind the attack." I shake my head, then regret the corresponding throb in my temples.

Randall nudges my shoulder. <<You OK?<<

Wordlessly, I acknowledge his concern, but keep my attention on Charon.

"We make a good scapegoat. We've always made a good scapegoat." For a moment, he loses his manic energy, and a flash of weariness clouds his eyes, stoops his shoulders. "Anyway, once we get our hands on the data, thanks to you, we'll have a better idea what we're up against."

I stare into his gaze, for once still and fixated on me, but his fathomless eyes hold no answers. "I can't let that happen," I finally say.

Denita tenses, along with the other Disconnects.

I raise my voice, ignore the cold sweat on my brow. "But I won't turn the data over to Sheridan or anyone else at the Department of Economic Development either. The fairest way forward is to bring it to the City Council. Only they have the authority to handle something like this."

Denita shakes her head. "Unacceptable. They'll bury it like everything else."

Rik presses a tissue into my hand. My nose's bleeding. Again. <<Liv, you can't put this off any longer.<<

>>The data's supposed to come first, not me. This isn't negotiable.>>

I tremble as I face Charon and the others. He watches me carefully. "You won't help us?"

"I'd be helping *everyone* if you'd let us go." My voice's slightly muffled as I blot at my nose.

He scoffs. "Why would the City Council suddenly start caring about us when they haven't bothered for decades?"

"The data breach potentially affects everyone, not just you."

Randall steps closer, a steadying hand on my arm. I'm losing it. <<But it's only affecting *you* right now. You have to get scrubbed. No more excuses.<<

I blink a few times, marking the worry on Randall's face. "You promised." My voice sounds broken, along with the rest of me.

"I lied." Heedless of the stun guns pointed at us, he gently steers me to the nearest chair as though I'm made of glass. I'm too wiped out to fight him, all my reserves burned up in my face-off with Charon. Rik pulls the scrubbing kit out of the satchel and lays it on the table.

Charon waves off the guns and hovers over Randall's shoulder as he sets things up. "*That's* how they do it?" He eyes me with newfound appreciation. "I *knew* you had more secrets." He gives Randall a pointed look. "You've been holding out on us."

Randall ignores him. He gestures to the kit. "Does this look right?" he asks me.

"Mostly. Hand me that medical cuff." He does, and I point to the small button. "You press this to locate the vein." I move on to the needle slot, hand shaking. "This is where my blood will enter the tubing for scrubbing."

I take a deep breath, my vision darkening for a long moment. >>There's no guarantee the kit'll be able to crack the government's encryption, so you'll need to collect a pint of my blood just in case.>> The encoded immune cells already make up a small portion of my blood, and they've been self-destructing for hours. >>That way you'll have enough of a sample to decode.>> Though recalling Finola's professional disgust of their methods, maybe we'll luck out. The universe owes us that much.

<<But you're already so weak.<<

>>Doesn't matter. You know that.>>

Randall fits the medical cuff to my forearm. When it chimes, he siphons off enough blood to fill the collection bag halfway. Not as much as I instructed him, but I'm too exhausted to tell him otherwise. Charon watches on in silent fascination. "Just hang on. We're almost there," Rik says as he hooks me up to the scrubbing kit.

Wordlessly, Charon gestures to his nose. My nose. More blood drips from it. Everything wavers as I contemplate all that red staining my fingers. It's dictated so much for so long.

And now I'm throwing it all away. Aventine, the life I thought I had to give up. All that sacrifice, meaningless.

<<Liv, stay with me.<<

Rik takes my shoulders, and my head falls back to stem the flow. The basement dims around me as though there's been an outage. The screens strobe, making it hard to focus on Rik and the desperation radiating off him.

Newly scrubbed blood finally starts looping back into me. But instead of the slight buzz it usually brings, clean and full of oxygen, it can't fight off the curdle. >>I'm sorry...>>

<<You can't give up now.<<

Pretty sure I can. Pretty sure I have no choice. >>I'm sorry about *everything*.>> I reach for him, my hands clumsy as I find his neck, the implant living below skin. >>Whatever you do, don't get it removed. Not until–>>

<<Liv!<<

Leaving behind smeared blood like a brand, my hand drops away. Along with everything else.

CHAPTER TWENTY-EIGHT

As consciousness drifts back into my mind, part of me wants to stay in slumbering darkness. No pain, no exhaustion, no more responsibilities.

The rest rushes into waking, heedless of the full-body fatigue that anchors my limbs and weights my head against the pillow. I don't have to open my eyes to know that Rik's with me. His anxiety leaches under my lids and tugs them open sooner than if I were left to my own devices. I'm on a small, makeshift pallet in the bar's storage room.

Randall's on the floor, his back against the wall. "You were asleep so long," he says, "I thought you wouldn't come out of it." A rusty brown stain rings his collar. I stare at it, puzzled, until I remember it's my blood, marking him. And blood means data.

I push into a seated position, hating how drained I feel. "Did they decrypt it?"

Randall's gaze drops to the floor. "Yeah. All of it. They were able to confirm the database patch targets the same Disconnect records Charon and the others say have been tampered with."

"So the government *was* trying to fix things." Even if covertly.

He nods. "When we examined the patch with Geeta, we couldn't see what was going on in the hidden fields, right?

Well, Charon built a backdoor into the registry to make them visible. That's where all the big changes are, just like you suspected."

"What did they find?" I'm almost afraid to ask.

"Land claims, primarily. Whoever's behind the data breach tried to reassign ownership of parcels owned by Disconnects."

"Why would…" Then it hits me. Erasing claims, positioning people with more valuable plots in the lead up to Emergence, and no one would be the wiser. "I can't believe it. This would be the biggest land grab in recent memory."

Randall gives me a grim nod. "That's the only thing I can think of that's worth killing over."

"Whoever did this must've thought between the Law of Digital Recency and the destruction of the physical records, no one would be able to prove the registry was changed, assuming they noticed the discrepancies in the first place." I flop back down on the pallet. My head hurts with it all.

"And they're still analyzing the database patch to see what else it does." Randall's silent for a long moment, long enough for my outrage at being forced into getting scrubbed to rear its head. "I'm sorry," he says softly.

"No, you're not." I tap my temple. "I can tell."

He grimaces. "I couldn't stand by and let you sacrifice yourself. Not over this." His fear and fury at the situation matches my own; our connection practically seethes with it.

"It was my call, not yours. If I had more time, I would've negotiated a way to get us out of here. Now, any bargaining power we had is gone along with the data."

"It was *killing* you." My stomach lurches in remembrance. "I already sat through one of your deaths," he says, face tight with anger. "I won't do it again."

"That's not–"

Denita barges into the room without so much a knock. "Come with me."

Randall holds my gaze for a beat longer then looks away as though I mean nothing to him. Still angry, but more at the helplessness he felt watching me deteriorate, rekindling all the old hurts when we were forcibly disconnected the first time by Aventine. I follow Denita and Randall back into Charon's makeshift headquarters, chin held high in a shallow attempt to mask my fatigue.

If the bar's basement was crowded before, now it's filled to bursting with more operatives in the Disconnect rebellion. Charon claps his hands when he spies me and Rik. "Excellent. Now that all the players are assembled, we can get down to business. Based on our intel and the data so kindly provided by Emery here…"

Charon gestures to me with a flourish, and I can't help but cringe as people's gazes dart toward me.

"…it looks like the government stumbled onto the changes in the registry and wanted to fix them, wonders of wonders. To do that, they enlisted Emery and two decoys to transport the data to the city's network file servers in the Understory where the original version could be restored, leaving the public none the wiser."

He points to himself and the other Disconnects. "*We* wanted the data as incontrovertible proof that our records were tampered with, putting a stop to yet another government cover-up." He points to the screen, Sheridan's image still displayed there. "This woman or the people she works for are either behind the original data breach or saw the transaction as an opportunity."

"An opportunity for what, though?" someone asks.

"Blackmail, extortion, who knows?" Denita says, dismissively.

"Maybe," Charon allows. "But think about the people she works with. Business sectors across the city. Industries all over New Worth are facing uncertainty as to how their business models will change once Emergence becomes a reality. Some simply won't survive outside the dome." His gaze jitters over the crowd. "I believe the Department's colluding with these businesses so they'll be better positioned once the glass comes down, and they're stealing our land to do it."

A current of dismay runs through the crowd.

"There's another registry field the patch's supposed to roll back, but no one can figure out what it's for," Denita says over the murmurs.

"But the fact that someone secretly put it there can't be good," Charon says.

Whoever did this has gone against everything Emergence stands for. I catch Charon's eye. "Now do you see why we need to get this information to the City Council? Keeping us here just makes our job harder to convince them they need to act. As it is, there'll be questions because you broke the chain of custody."

"And you think they'll believe you? A disgraced courier?"

That stings, but I try not to show it. "I'll have a better chance, yes."

He shakes his head. "This is just one injustice in a long list of injustices we've faced. But this time, they're going after our homes, our futures, a life not tied to this broken city. How can you ask us to trust in a system that has everything to gain if they simply look the other way?"

"I have to believe–"

"Even if the Council ruled in our favor, it doesn't change the fact there's a very powerful faction who'll do *anything* to get what they want. All that's left for us to do is escape the tyranny of this city once and for all." An impromptu cheer goes up.

Charon looks at Randall. "And good ole Randall here's going to lead us home." Outside, beyond the dome, fresh air on our faces.

Rik's surprise filters through. Whatever he was expecting, it wasn't this.

My mouth falls open. "You can't possibly think–"

"We are tired of being passed over, the lies, the manipulation," Charon continues. "Time for us to take back our lives. Start anew."

Randall crosses his arms. "You can't be serious. Besides, there's no way out that isn't monitored."

"Ah, that's where you're wrong." Charon gestures to the room. "We've been working on an exit strategy for years, and we won't wait any longer."

"It's too dangerous," I say. How many times has Rik said the Disconnects are fools for wanting to push outside prematurely?

"That's why we need Randall. How many planting trips have you gone on for Vector? You're the only one who can lead us to sanctuary beyond the dome."

Randall shakes his head. "I won't do it."

Charon pauses, his stare almost unbearable as he looks from Randall to me, then back again. "Then it's a good thing you don't have a choice." He points his chin at me. "Unless we've misjudged your attachment to Emery here."

"He's not doing it, no matter what you do to me." I step in front of Randall, as if by blocking him from view I can keep any of this from happening. >>This is all my fault. I never should've gotten you involved.>>

<<Liv, it's OK.<<

>>No, it's not. This whole situation's what I've tried so hard to protect you from.>>

Randall's quiet, along with the room around us. <<Then let me protect you for a change.<<

>>Rik–>>

He meets Charon's gaze. "I'll do it."

• • •

The bar's basement has a trapdoor leading into a humid Underground tunnel. Before we're forced into it, Charon fastens a metal and plastic collar around my neck that immediately snuffs out my connection to Rik. He gets a collar as well. "No more secrets, you two," Charon says. For a moment, I wonder if Randall's going to punch him. Charon must worry too since he steps away, looking guilty.

Whenever Rik vanishes from my mind, I feel like I lose another piece of myself, and this time's no different. But I relax slightly at Rik's calm face. He gives me a wink and makes the hand sign for *trust me*. Remembrance washes over me at the signals we used in *Partners in Crime*, a combination of sign language and military hand signs. Like putting on a long-forgotten outfit and realizing it still fits perfectly. We might be our analog selves once more, but at least we'll still be able to communicate right under the Disconnects' noses.

My relief's short-lived once we enter the tunnel. It's so dark I can barely see, let alone sign. Taking a deep breath, I close my eyes to acclimate the best I can to the crawling dark around me, the press of humidity, and the never-ending droplets of water – at least I hope that's what they are – that trickle down from a crevice somewhere.

When I open my eyes, I can't quite stop the squeeze of panic at the near-complete darkness my unenhanced vision can barely make sense of. The walls of the tunnel slowly resolve, my white gloves outstretched before me, as I make out phosphorescent paint along the ceiling, marking our path past abandoned subway lines and unused maintenance access points that run parallel to sewer and water pipes. The skeletons of pre-dome infrastructure transform into what looks to be a natural cavern of sorts, though the silence here feels more alive than the manmade areas we passed through earlier.

The natural cave opens up, illuminated by generator-powered lights. Over the hum of the machinery, voices bounce off rock. More of Charon's followers have gathered here, the heart of the Disconnect unrest, the same people who've thrown New Worth into turmoil. But I can't blame them, not after learning of the forces working against them firsthand.

Denita parades us through the cavern, which looks more like an improvised shelter than a staging area for our exodus outside the city, before leading us to a small cell carved into rock. "We move out in a couple of hours." Then she locks us in.

"Your friends aren't much better than mine," I say with a look at our temporary prison. A small cot, a sink, and a bucket. Lovely. "But the accommodations leave something to be desired."

"It's not funny, Emery."

I draw back at the frustration in his voice. He only calls me Emery when he wants to put distance between us. "No, it's not. But I don't know what else to do." My Aventine training can't help us. All the arcade scenarios I've completed over the years are child's play compared to the stark reality of leaving the city behind along with everything I've ever known.

Panic unfurls in my chest, pressing against my ribs. "I don't know what to do," I say again, my voice cracking.

Our prison's dim enough, I only see his gloves ghosting closer until they settle on my shoulders. Then the rest of him comes into view. I still startle, a reflex so ingrained I can't stop it, not even for him. He grimaces, as though pained by my reaction, but he doesn't let go. Doesn't pull me closer either. Just lets the weight of his hands sink into my bones, letting me know I'm not alone.

"We'll figure something out. Once Charon's satisfied, maybe we can come back–"

"Like that'll happen. Besides, in a twisted way isn't this what you wanted? To help the Disconnects? Become one yourself?"

His hands tighten, as though he can't decide whether to hug me or shake me.

"Yes, I wanted to get my implant removed, all right? Because I couldn't stomach a future without you in my mind. But now..." He shakes his head, fighting with himself over what to say. "Knowing what we could have if we didn't have to worry about anything else, I'm not strong enough to give you up a second time."

If we were synching, he'd be able to make sense of the snarl of emotions swirling through me, at what I can't put into words. We'll have to start over, learning a new language composed of looks, speech, and subtle movements to get through whatever comes next. A tremor goes through me at the thought. "But it's too late, isn't it, with the collars..."

"This is how we started, remember?" He holds out his gloved hand, and I take it as though it's just another checkpoint in *Partners in Crime*. "We'll have to go back to basics. Except this time you're the rookie."

And just like that, everything is easy between us.

"You're still mad the AI determined I had more experience to play the lead detective? I don't believe it."

He smiles, his teeth flashing white in the dark. "It was a blow to my pride some random girl could outclass me in an arcade game. But now that I know you're a courier with the actual skills to back it up, it doesn't sting quite so much." He turns serious. "I meant what I said, though. I've been dealing with the Disconnects for a lot longer than you have."

"And yet you never suspected Charon?"

"I mean, I knew he was a true believer. We've been working together for months to find Disconnects decent jobs throughout the city. Beyond that... I'm not exactly surprised.

Just wish we weren't caught up in their rebellion."

"You and me both." I'm quiet for a moment. "Do you think they can do it? Get all these people outside without getting caught?"

"There's a good chance we're already on the other side of the glass, actually." That makes sense. The bar was on the outskirts of the Terrestrial District, and we must've walked for a good hour to reach the cavern. "We'll have to tunnel further out to avoid the proximity sensors running along the perimeter of the city. They'll alert the authorities if they're disturbed, making a quiet escape impossible."

"So if they manage all that, we'll be in the clear."

"They don't have a death wish. You saw the supplies they have. They must've been planning for months, maybe longer. Plus these tunnels didn't just appear overnight."

"And you'll help them." It isn't a question.

His gaze drops to the floor. "If it'll keep us both safe, I will."

I roll back my shoulders, force myself to smile. "Then it's a good thing I've always wanted to see what it's like outside."

A strangled chuckle escapes him. He still hasn't decided what to do with his hands, so I decide for him, stepping in close, looping my arms around his waist.

Before the face-to-face meeting at Brita's party, before I knew who he was, before I knew *him*, I was so worried we wouldn't click physically, killing any potential between us. Such shallow fears seem so foolish now after everything we've been through. He's the person I constructed in my mind, externalized. The wry humor, the way he forces me to confront my own assumptions, his dependability no matter the situation. All those things are still there, wrapped up in a package I can hold in my hands, not just my head.

It's as simple and complex as that, and I'm still learning how to adjust to Rik-as-Randall. Rewriting stimuli. I have to trust in the weight of his gaze, take comfort in the steadiness of his frame under my hands, and the intent of his words, even though our connection is blocked, stripping away nuance and emotional context.

It's an imperfect system. But trapped Underground, with his steady heartbeat underneath my ear, his arms anchoring me to his chest, maybe it's exactly what I need.

CHAPTER TWENTY-NINE

Later, sometime after I collapsed on the cot, still drained from my bout with the curdle, a loud explosion rumbles through our cell. I jump out of my light doze and seek out Rik, sitting crosslegged on the floor next to me. "No turning back," he says.

"That's been true for a while now."

I'm rewarded with a brief grin. The blast must've cleared our way to the surface since a few minutes later there's a brisk knock on the door. Denita escorts us back to the main chamber. "Grab a pack and join the others." We select ours from a motley assortment of supplies in the center of the room.

Just about everyone else has lined up with at least one bag. A handful of people have stolen automated carts loaded down with more supplies. Some of the Disconnects look serious, others hold an air of expectation about themselves with Emergence finally within reach. Then we start moving forward, down the tunnel of blasted rock. I don't know how long we walk, slowly but surely climbing upward. The path gets more difficult, rocks only partially cleared away in the Disconnects' haste to leave the city behind.

Shouts of joy filter back, and the people in front of us quicken their steps, scrambling through the rubble. Rik leans down, his voice finding me in the rush to the surface. "This is it. Ready?"

I am. Despite everything that's happened, I'm eager for my first lungful of unfiltered air.

We finally emerge from the tunnel, blinking over and over again in the bright afternoon light. All my trips to Skychapel didn't prepare me for the immediacy of having the sun overhead. No glass refracts its rays before it reaches me. The pure light renders the foreign landscape in vibrant color – plants in the Canopy desaturated in comparison.

Rik sheds some of the tension from his frame as he takes his first breath outside. I do the same. He's right. There's *nothing* like it. The lightness of it, scented with strange growing things that I desperately want to familiarize myself with. It's hard to explain. All I know is I want to keep breathing it in, chasing suitable descriptions with each inhale that can encompass all this… feeling.

I'm not the only one slack-jawed at our surroundings. Wild, rugged green, not carefully manicured city parks, continue as far as the eye can see. Trees, shrubs, and spiky grasses radiate out from the dome, reflecting so much sunlight I can't look at it properly. Turning away from New Worth, I find Rik's gaze on me. "What?"

"I wish…" He shakes his head.

"What is it?"

He taps his temple. "I wish I could feel what you're feeling right now. The first time's special." He steps closer, our bulging packs pressed up against one another. "Your face tells me only some of the story." He reaches out, places his palm against my heart. "The rest I can't access," he says wistfully.

The feel of the sun's warmth on my skin, the clarity of light that makes everything sharper somehow, the unreality of being out from under glass for the first time… Things too new and wonderful to put into words.

"Before…" Before we left the city, before Aventine, he means, "I could always tell when you were near one of the city's parks by the joy that leaked across our connection. Because I felt the same thing on my planting trips."

I lean into him. Watch his face, realize I want him to kiss me despite the dozens of people around us. Wonder if he feels the same pull between us. Without my implant it's hard to be sure.

Nearby, one of the Disconnects sneezes, shocking us apart. He sneezes again more violently. Randall turns toward him, concerned.

"What is it?" I ask.

"Probably nothing."

The man sneezes again, this time clutching his chest.

Randall swears under his breath. "Hey!" he shouts. "Can we get some medical supplies over here?"

Someone does, as Charon stands with Denita and a handful of others who eye the horizon impatiently. "What's wrong?" Charon calls out, as Randall sorts through the supplies. Despite the air of authority in his voice, Charon still hunches his shoulders, unused to having the space to stand tall.

Randall doesn't answer, not until he slams an autoinjector full of epinephrine into the man's leg. "He needs to go back," he finally says with a nod to the man, gasping for breath.

Charon trudges over. "Why?"

"He's allergic. Seen it before. Won't be able to live comfortably out here, not without a constant supply of antihistamines, maybe even more heavy-duty meds."

"We have supplies."

"And he'll be a constant drain on them until he dies," Rik replies harshly. "You told me you read up on the risks."

Charon rears back. "I did."

"Well, *this* is one of them. If this exodus is going to work, your followers need to be able to tolerate the environment."

"But it's not his fault." Charon's sweeping gaze takes in the pristine landscape. "Something must be out here that doesn't belong."

"Not necessarily. Living under glass for the last couple generations, maybe *we're* the ones who've changed." Randall shakes his head. "It's a kindness to send him back."

Charon stands there with his arms crossed.

"You wanted my expertise, Charon. I'm giving it to you."

They glare at each other for a long moment before Charon finally relents. Two of his followers volunteer to help the man return to the city back the way we came. When no one else exhibits a violent allergic reaction, Randall gives Charon the all-clear.

"What's our heading?"

A remoteness shrouds Randall's features as he faces his one-time friend. "East, northeast. If we hike until nightfall, we should reach a good place to camp."

Charon nods. "You heard the man," he says to the others. "Onward!"

Low voices and laughter hover over our makeshift camp spread out under the stars. We walked as far as we dared before daylight abandoned us. Rik seemed pleased with the group's pace. It helps that everyone's motivated, excited at being outside, beyond the city's reach.

He's been run ragged, though, overseeing all the preparations for the evening, pointing out plants to avoid, the right way to stake tents for the less experienced – all things he must have done countless times on his trips for Vector. He scarfs down the lumpy, dehydrated vegetable stew we were given for dinner that I can barely stomach. He's still fielding questions between bites.

After I hand him the rest of my portion, a man comes running into camp. I don't recognize him, but that doesn't mean much. There's at least a hundred of us, and I overheard Charon saying there are even more people from the Underground who'll be joining us once they find an appropriate site to start over. The man heads straight for Charon and Denita who sit at a folding table near one of the solar-charged lanterns struggling to beat back the encroaching shadows. Charon's face contorts at the man's hasty, indistinct words, then he's on his feet shouting for Randall.

Rik groans. "What now?" We make our way over, past haphazard rows of tents.

"There's been a change of plans," Charon says as soon as we get near.

"Why?" I ask.

Charon hands me a touchscreen preloaded with the latest news stories from New Worth. They are all variations on the same thing: the Vesa lottery winners have been chosen, and everyone who was selected lives in the same two blocks of the Terrestrial District in the Bower. Claims the lottery was hacked are rampant, with Disconnects the prime suspect. After all, they're the ones who want to leave the city by any means necessary. But without proof, the government's in a quandary: let the manipulated results stand or start over. Supporters for both outcomes have been demonstrating non-stop in the time we were gone.

And I thought things were bad *before* we left.

Rik frowns. "I'm guessing that wasn't part of your plan?"

"We didn't hack the lottery, if that's what you mean," Charon says.

"Then who did?" I ask.

"I don't know." Charon rubs his face. "But what do you want to bet it's the same people behind the registry breach?"

"The Department of Economic Development? But why? We must be missing something."

"Agreed. That's why I want Randall to lead us to Vesa. Maybe we can get some answers there."

"Or we could go back and bring all this to the City Council. Let them sort this out."

Denita rolls her eyes; Charon just shakes his head. "We're committed to leaving the city behind. But we're close enough to Vesa we might as well check it out."

"Why, when you're just going to run away?"

Rik gives my forearm a squeeze, begging for silence. "Vesa's fifteen miles west of here, give or take. The rough terrain might slow people down though," he says with a nod to the tents around us. Families with small children make up a significant portion of the expedition.

Charon waves that off. "Only a few people, then. Recon. The others will stay here, keeping the lines of communication open with my operatives back at the dome." Like the runner who brought him word of the lottery results. He looks over the camp, grim but resolute in the lantern's light. "We'll leave at dawn."

I'm not sure what to say as we trudge back to our shared tent, just a simple tarp set up over trampled grass to cushion our bedrolls. I kick off my boots and collapse onto the blanket. Rik follows me in. He removed his gloves at some point today to make his work easier. I watch his hands as he smoothes the flap of the tarp closed and hunkers down beside me. "Well, tomorrow just got more interesting," he says wearily.

I sit up slowly. "Whatever's going on begins and ends with Vesa." The courier job gone wrong, the changes to the registry, the hacked lottery, crooked government officials, and the Disconnects. A rats' nest of possibilities, and none of them good. "Since we're stuck out here, we might as well see what all the fuss is. But after that…" I shake my head.

"What?"

"It's just we could be working with the authorities to bring the registry changes to light right now instead of playing house in the wilderness."

"Maybe, but try convincing Charon and his guards of that."

"I know," I say with a sigh.

"But you're not wrong." He pulls something out of his pants pocket and presses it into my hands. A datastick. He must've grabbed it earlier when he was given free rein of the Disconnects' camp. I'm rubbing off on him. "Tomorrow, at Vesa, there'll be less people to worry about. I'll create a diversion, and you can return to the city."

"But what about you?"

"Doesn't matter."

"It does to me." He closes his mouth, his Adam's apple working. "Whatever happens tomorrow," I say, "we stay together, all right? We've been through too much to give up now." My career with Aventine, the emotional cruelty of popping back up when I did in Rik's life, the physical toll of the curdle. I get a fleeting smile before it's gone as though he's too tired to maintain it. "I mean it." I unbutton my right glove.

Immediately, I have his attention as I push it down my forearm, work it off my hand, fingertip by fingertip. "I know I hurt you. I know was too stubborn and scared before, and it won't make a difference out here now." My words rapid so I won't lose my nerve, I start on the second glove, set it aside, and reach for him. "But it's always been you."

Implants blocked, miles away from the nearest node of the New Worth network, there's nothing the data receptors can really do, but the zing of feedback as they align still steals my breath. Experimentally, Rik pulls back his hand, then lines it up against mine once more. Heat and sensation and something more as our fingers knot together, even as subdued as it is without help from our implants.

With my free hand, I trace my fingertips over his heavy brow, the line of a shadowed cheek, the slight bump on his nose, hesitating to smooth them over his lips. He turns into my hand, pressing a simple kiss to my palm that would turn my legs liquid if I weren't already sitting down. "Liv…"

"Yes?" I say unsteadily.

"You're driving me wild."

Relief spreads through me at the admission. Without my implant, I've been secondguessing my intuition. Too reliant on our connection to tell me what to do, what to say. Too scared without it to risk getting it wrong. I shift my hand to the pulse in his neck just below the horrid collar, fluttering madly just for me.

"I can see why Brita likes this."

"What do you mean?"

"All body, no brain. Just feedback from our data receptors when... you know."

"Like this?" He tightens his grip on my hand, sparking our receptors again.

I nod, mouth suddenly dry, imagining what it must feel like when we're connected for real. Our implants thrumming with emotion, the shared intensity creating a feedback loop taking us higher together than we could achieve on our own. Though even now, unenhanced as I am, what I *can* feel is already devastating.

He reaches for me with his other hand and cradles the back of my head, pulling me close. I rise on my knees, meeting him halfway as our lips fit together. Awkwardly at first, then he makes an adjustment that sends my blood roaring, a flush spreading across my skin. I gasp against his mouth, our hands clasping each other over and over again, electricity building up under my skin.

All that energy needs to go somewhere. And we figure it out, together.

When morning comes neither of us is ready for it, but Charon doesn't care. He bellows for us to prepare for the hike to Vesa, a frenetic intensity to his words. With a groan, I disentangle myself from Rik. He gives my hand one last squeeze before I put my gloves back on and shoulder my pack.

Charon's assembled eight other Disconnects to join us, and Denita makes twelve. After a hurried breakfast, we make our way west, Rik dutifully stopping every now and again to check our progress against the map as we march. With fewer people and supplies, we're able to move more quickly through the scrubby brush and fragrant grass that disguise the terrain.

A couple of hours in, trees surround us on all sides, filled with a stately beauty the columns in New Worth's Canopy can't touch. "You did all this," I say to Randall.

"Well, Vector did, along with dozens of other agro firms over the course of many years."

"Still..." I gesture to all the plants and shake my head when I can't find the words.

"This region was rehabilitated maybe a decade ago. You can tell by the height of the trees. These are ash trees, modded to grow quickly to get established. That trait will fade in subsequent generations." He affectionately pats the trunk of one of the trees we pass, and my heart wobbles. "My team was responsible for an area south of here. Prepping the soil for a rollout of native plants, then monitoring them as they grow and mature."

"What for?"

"All the old pre-dome buildings and infrastructure didn't just disappear, even if the elements battered them up pretty good. We had to break them down using chemicals and microorganisms and incorporate them into the topsoil, creating nonreactive filler essentially. Then, modded plants are introduced that'll help break down the materials further and filter out contaminants."

"Leaving pristine land behind."

He nods. "That's the plan, at least."

"Looks like you're succeeding. No wonder the Disconnects have been eager to leave."

He deflates slightly. "It looks good. Hell, it smells good too. But it's still dangerous out here. Without my equipment, we have no idea what's underfoot. Some plants are here to filter out specific substances from the soil and groundwater. Lead, mercury, arsenic, radioactive particles..." He tips his head toward Charon at the front of the column. "They don't know what they're in for once their supplies from New Worth run out."

"Let's hope it doesn't come to that."

Well after midday, the trees start to thin out, and the soil grows sandy. Murmurs gain momentum as a lake of shimmery blue-gray water appears in the distance with Vesa spread out on the opposite bank. It's just as picturesque as it was in the news feeds. Five cream buildings face the lake, like a diamond sparkling in a ceramic setting.

Charon cocks his head, eying Vesa with curiosity. "I couldn't find much about it on the network besides promo. No specs, no reports, nothing."

"If they're hiding something, we'll find it," Denita says.

We march around the lake, two scouts sent ahead to ensure there are no New Worth officials lying in wait. But the complex is empty. Charon instructs the others to rest for lunch while we take a look in the first building. Living quarters as advertised with offices and common areas on the main floor, smelling of fresh paint and new carpet. Waiting for the picture-perfect family to walk in the door.

The next building is a different story. Charon goes first. I almost run into him when he stops stock-still. Then I see why. Rows and rows of bunks. Past the cramped aisles, a line of communal showers and a crude trench in the ground.

"Underground shelters are more humane than this," Randall says.

"Maybe this is where the workers stayed?" I say. "They probably used prison labor for the project to keep it out of the news feeds until they were ready for the reveal."

Charon nods slowly. "Maybe."

The three of us walk to the next building in silence. But the same sight greets us. Barracks-style accommodations with cesspit-like bathroom facilities.

"They said Vesa would have the capacity for hundreds of families," Charon muses.

"But they made it sound like they'd be getting one of those shiny apartments in the first building not… this," Randall says. "There's no way they can house all those people here."

"It's a scam," I say, disbelieving at first, then with greater certainty. "It has that too-good-to-be-true vibe some of the predatory housing developments have in the Terrestrial District. Everything's faked for the advertisements to get people's buy-in, then… gotcha!"

Randall's brow furrows. "Not everything's fake. They've figured out a way to power this place. But what about water?" He sketches his hand over the pipes that run from the shower nozzles into the floor.

Charon shrugs. "There's a lake."

"No way," Randall says. "I wouldn't bathe in that stuff, let alone drink it."

"What do you mean?" Charon asks.

"Even if that's an aquifer lake," Randall explains, "it's guaranteed to be polluted with contaminants caught up in run-off from all the aging infrastructure in the area. There could be algae blooms or some sort of Frankenfish in there too. That's why the plants are supposed to filter that crap out from the soil and groundwater."

Charon frowns. "We brought water and sterilization units with us, but I thought…" They'd find an uncontaminated water source and live happily ever after.

A joyous whoop reaches us through the walls, followed by a muffled sound almost like a slap. "Wait. You hear that?"

The same sound, but this time I hear it for what it is: water splashing, slapping against skin. In the heat of the afternoon, that lake would be awfully tempting. "You don't think–"

"Shit!" Charon runs to the door, Rik on his heels.

The three of us retrace our steps at a hard trot.

"I thought you warned everyone about the water out here," Rik says.

Charon grimaces. "About drinking it, yeah. I didn't realize they'd be so foolish as to get *in* it."

The rest of our party has set up camp along the lake's shoreline. Some people lie out on blankets, faces to the sun. A few flirt with the water's edge, their pants pushed up to their knees, frolicking in the shallows. Two others are farther out, swimming in their underwear.

Randall swears as Charon flags down Denita standing at the shore, chatting with another person. "Get out of the water!" Charon shouts. "Get out this instant. We have no idea if it's safe."

With a confused look on her face, Denita relays Charon's words to the others and waves everyone back to land. They groan and grumble but do as they're told. I almost don't blame them. With the sun's warmth like a soothing hand on your shoulder, it's too beautiful here for something to be wrong with the crystalline water.

"No one sets foot on this shore again, we clear?" Charon demands. People reluctantly gather up their stuff and move to an area further inland. Charon swings back to the lake and kicks a rock into the water. It disappears into the depths.

"You see what's happening here, don't you?" I say. "Vesa's not the exciting new initiative it's made out to be. At best it's some sort of labor camp. At worst, it's a one-way trip into the wilderness. What do you want to bet someone figured that out and manipulated the lottery to send people from the Terrestrial District here? Those changes to the registry could've been a part of that plan." Charon doesn't turn around, but the angle of his head tells me he's listening. "They may not all be your followers, but you can't deny whoever did this is targeting the Disconnects who live in the Bower."

"It's a win-win situation," Rik says. "If the lottery results stand, they silence a large number of opponents. If not, they use the hack against you, further damaging any credibility the Disconnects still have."

"They're already doing that," Charon says tonelessly.

"We have to go back," I say. "The people of New Worth deserve to know the truth about Vesa, the lottery, everything."

He shakes his head. "No. We keep moving. Start over." He finally faces us. "We can rejoin the others by nightfall–"

A woman's scream bounces across the lake. Charon's already in motion, moving up the hill. Rik and I follow him to a woman nearly beside herself at the bloody welts crawling up and down her legs. She was one of the people wading in the shallows.

Charon gathers everyone who was in the water together. Some have the same oozing welts, though not as pronounced. "Did any of you drink the water?" He eyes the two young men who were swimming.

The shorter one cringes under Charon's stare. "Maybe a little." He elbows his companion in the side. "Holton dunked me."

"How do you feel?" Charon asks.

The guy quails a bit at all the attention. "I don't know, OK? It seemed fine at the time."

After a whispered conversation with Denita, Charon turns back to us. "You lead us back to the others," he says through clenched teeth.

"You saw that woman's leg," Rik protests. "We need–"

Charon holds up a hand, and Rik falls silent. "Right now, we need to march."

We do as he says, though the woman, Rosa, needs to be carried toward the end. When we finally reach the other camp, the evening meal's underway. A handful of tents have been cordoned off in the time we've been gone. Quarantine. That can't be good.

Charon waves Randall over after a whispered conversation with one of his lieutenants left in charge of camp. "Says a group of people got sick after digging a trench for the latrines."

Randall's already shaking his head. "No, no, no. I told them to make composting toilets from our supplies. If they dug past the new soil layer, they could've disturbed whatever nasty chemicals were left behind out here."

"That explains why everyone got sick," I say. "Who knows what they were breathing in."

Tension fills Randall's frame. "They've put everyone here at risk."

Charon waves him off. "Doesn't matter. We're moving camp in the morning anyway."

"That's not enough," Rik says, a new layer of steel to his voice. "Your people have no idea what they're in for. It's irresponsible to–"

Shouts go up. Charon shoulders past us, joining a knot of followers that have converged on Holton. "He's convulsing," someone says. Rik and I watch on as they work to stabilize him with whatever medical supplies they've brought along, but he soon falls unconscious. Charon leaves orders to be notified if Holton's condition changes, then retreats to his tent. One of his lieutenants tries to tempt the onlookers with the prospect of dinner, but no one's hungry. How can they be?

I clench my fists. "This has to stop." I cast about camp. "I need a touchscreen."

With everyone distracted by Holton, pretending to eat dinner, or sick in their tents, I find a screen in someone's unattended bag. Rik blocks me from view as I hide it underneath my shirt. We get our own tent assembled, and once I'm safely inside I waste no time connecting the datastick Randall swiped to the touchscreen. I pull the list of names from the lottery and compare them against the patch's record set, as though this is just another exercise from one of my data curation classes. Not only are they all a match, but that mystery field that Charon and the others flagged shows the same code for each record that ended up being selected in the lottery.

"So someone deliberately inserted that data field to skew the results," Randall says over my shoulder. "If it wasn't the Department of Economic Development, then at least they wanted the corruptions to stand long enough for the lottery drawing." Otherwise why would they bother chasing me away from the real drop?

I lean back against him, for a moment letting his strength fortify my own. "Not only did they take their land, but they ensured no one would find out about it, assuming that the people who were selected for Vesa wouldn't notice before they left the dome."

"And by then it'd be too late."

"We can't sit on this any longer."

"I know."

"I have to find a way to tell everyone…"

"We will." He takes a deep breath. "Charon's not an idiot. Maybe in a few days–"

"*No*. No longer." I'm tired of running away, skulking in shadows, turning my back on others. We can't turn away from this. "We have to talk to him now. Come on."

Heedless of everyone else at camp, I stalk towards Charon's tent, Rik at my side.

Denita steps in front of me, blocking my way forward. "He's not to be disturbed."

"Bullshit. You already know what we have to do," I say, pitching my voice toward the tent. "We have to go back."

Moments later, Charon throws open the flap of canvas and scowls at me. "Keep your voice down."

"Why? I think everyone's already figured out we're screwed. Or at the very least far less prepared than they thought they'd be."

He pinches the bridge of his nose.

"You know we're right," Rik says softly. "If we go back now, we can get your people the medical attention they need. If not that, at least let us return to warn the others about Vesa."

I thrust the touchscreen under his nose. His eyes skate over the confirmation of the skewed lottery results being a direct result of the manipulated registry, but instead of anger or a return of his frenetic energy, Charon just scoffs, shrinking into himself. "You think they'll just let you waltz back into the dome and dismantle all their secrets?"

"We have to try," I say.

"The magnitude of their lies..." Charon shakes his head and hands the touchscreen back to me.

"It's the right thing to do," Rik says resolutely.

"The cycle stops now if you let us tell the truth." I hold my breath as Charon stares at both of us.

His posture relents after a long moment. "All right. All right."

"We'll retrace our steps using the tunnels," I say.

"Which works so long as the authorities haven't found them yet," Rik interrupts.

"My operatives would've told us if they've been compromised," Charon says. "But even if we get back into the city, what then? Aventine and the authorities will still be looking for you."

"They can capture us or not," I say, "but we can't risk the database patch and evidence of Vesa falling into the wrong hands."

Charon snorts. "Good luck with that."

"That's why we need to bring the data in the same way I brought it out. In my blood." Rik and Charon just stare at me. "Think about it. This is the biggest conspiracy to hit New Worth in living memory. We need to ensure the data stays safe and secure until we decide what to do with it."

Rik takes my arm. "Are you sure about this?" He knows what the last job cost me. But this'll be different. It has to be.

"No, no, she's right," Charon says, professional enthusiasm finally giving way. "Once they get their hands on her, she'll be debriefed by the highest levels of government. They'll examine her inside *and* out to make sure we haven't tampered with the goods, so to speak."

"That's right. And even if I'm captured, I'll end up in Aventine's hands one way or the other. I still have allies there." At least I hope so. "They'll help me – help us – tell the truth." I wait for Rik's reaction, but for once he doesn't jump at the chance to criticize my employer. "But that's the worst-case scenario."

"Let's hope it doesn't come to that," Charon says.

"Can you do it?" Rik asks Charon. "The blood encoding?"

"Not with all the bells, whistles, and autodestruct capabilities, but, yeah, the general concept, I think. But not out here. With my gear in the Underground." His gaze goes off into the distance. "My whole life I've been looking for something to believe in." His fingers skate over the jagged scar at the base of his neck. "It wasn't implants or the society that built them. I thought Emergence was it, a chance to start over, but even that's tainted now." He whirls back the way we came.

Despite how long we've walked these past few days, New Worth's still visible, a glass sentry over so much green, the dome sparkling in the sunset.

"We'll make them pay."

CHAPTER THIRTY

We return to the dome the way we came, the tunnels thankfully untouched in our absence, though the mood's much diminished from when we first set out. Exhausted, Rik crashes in the bar's storeroom as Charon and the others gather the supplies necessary to secrete away the data and the images of Vesa in my blood. Rik needs the rest more than I do after the last few days.

I try to answer as many of Charon's questions about hemocryption as I can, wishing I paid more attention to the process. But as with everything having anything to do with blood, I blocked most of it out.

"Won't be able to replicate their process exactly," Charon says when I run out of things to tell him. "But we'll encode the data onto your blood cells, unencrypted."

"That'll be good enough. And then we'll make things right. I promise."

Denita snorts, not bothering to look up from one of the consoles. "What good's the word of a Canopy brat?"

I try not to react to the dislike radiating off her frame. "I lived down here until I was eighteen."

"Bet you couldn't wait to escape."

"No, I couldn't. The only things we have to sustain ourselves are the implants and thoughts of Emergence. Don't judge me for taking one of the few avenues available to me, and I won't judge you for refusing it."

She rears back, ready to fight, I'm certain, but Charon waves her off. His gaze drifts to the collar around my neck. "I'm guessing you'd like that gone."

"That would be nice," I say, as diplomatically as possible.

He produces a magnetic key of some kind that unlocks the collars. "Back to normal, though you should probably only use a secure channel. No telling what'll happen when your signal shows back up on the city's network, all right?"

"Right. Thanks."

While they work, I join Rik in the storeroom. Sleep now softens the apprehension that's lined his face ever since I showed up on his doorstep. He doesn't stir as I remove his collar using Charon's key. The full weight of our connection settles over me, familiar and full of longing.

Not knowing when I'll get another chance, I let myself really look at him in this unguarded moment. At the messy dark locks that sweep down over one eye, begging me to tuck them back into place. At the relaxed jaw I've too often seen firm in annoyance at me or in resolve at what needs to be done.

After everything we've been through – after everything I've asked of him – he's still here, at my side. I've taken so much from him. I'll find a way to make it up to him, no matter what happens today.

<<Charon finally relented? Good.<<

Blinking back consternation, I realize Rik's looking at me from underneath his bangs. For how long? >>We'll need the implants up and running if we're going to have a chance.>>

His eyes momentarily drift shut again. <<*Sure*...<< He doesn't let on what sensations he was able to detect from me, but I can imagine. <<Though that wasn't what I was referring to.<< His lips curl up in a teasing grin as I watch, unable to look away. His drowsy amusement strengthens into something I can only guess at before the limitations of our connection kick in. <<Tell me you didn't miss this.<<

The easy camaraderie, the slight friction promising more. I want to deny it – an automatic defense mechanism to keep him at bay, especially after the other night. But… >>I… can't.>> What good has pushing him away ever done for me? I've learned that lesson too many times to count.

He nods as though I've confirmed something for him that he's known all along. His gaze finds mine. Our connection zings with reverb – him watching me watching him – reinforcing the fact that although I now know his face in concert with his signal, something's still missing. Something we found outside.

"Liv–"

A curt knock announces Charon. "We're ready for you, Emery." We join him, Denita, and the other Disconnects in the main room. Charon waves me toward a chair near a nightmare apparatus of tubing and circuitry. "Not as scary as it looks."

"I sure as hell hope not." I take a seat. Eyes shut, I focus on my connection with Rik to help ground me as Charon hooks me up to his equipment. If Finola thought the government's tech was behind the times, I can only imagine what she'd think of this. Once the gear starts humming, I finally open my eyes. "All right. The City Council's chambers are in the Echelon. If we stick to access stairs and areas with spotty surveillance, we just might have a chance."

Charon's already shaking his head. "Not the Council."

"But I thought we agreed–"

"Can't trust they'll do the right thing in time. We need to find another way."

"Then I guess that leaves the media," I say.

Charon frowns. "We don't exactly have the best relationship with them. All the local offices down here get skittish with the tips we give them."

"That's because you've manipulated them one too many times to advance your cause," Rik says.

Charon just shrugs. "Desperate times."

"Then I'll need to go alone to New Worth News headquarters in the Upper Canopy," I say. Won't even bother with the satellite locations – they're technically closer but aren't nearly as secure as the flagship location. "But no matter what route I take, it'll still be tricky with the police hunting me."

Charon's gaze darts around the room, unsettled, thinking. "What are you suggesting?"

If you can't avoid attention, then try to set up an unwitting decoy.

"You need to flood the Canopy with protesters. Another rally protesting the lottery results will be our cover." His followers weren't too happy at having to return to the city. We can put that pent-up anger to use. "You get us close enough to the New Worth News headquarters, and I'll do the rest."

"Anything else you need?" Charon asks.

A chuckle escapes me. "A way to keep Aventine off my back once I'm out there. But I think that's something beyond even your abilities."

Charon's eyes narrow. "Don't be so sure."

A few hours later, a good twenty of us spill out of the bar onto the street, Charon leading the way. >>I don't know how you do this,>> I tell Rik.

<<What do you mean?<<

>>Return to the Terrestrial District after each planting trip.>> The filth, the cramped streets, and the claustrophobia of the rest of the city looming overhead. My memories of being outside are being corrupted as we speak.

He laughs. <<Just makes the next trip that much better.<<

More protesters join us, emerging from the buildings closed off from the fake quarantine.

>>I don't know if I could be that patient.>>

<<I've had lots of practice learning to be patient for things that are worth the wait.<<

Suddenly we aren't talking about being outside any more.

We head east, toward the center of the city. Commandeering a maglev car isn't really an option to ascend all the way to the Canopy since a group this large will immediately alert the authorities. The lifts and the lines they're famous for are bound to be monitored as well. That leaves the access stairs.

"Are we heading toward the northeast stairwell in the next sector?" I ask.

"You'll see." Charon gives me a wink, but it does nothing to ease my anxiety or that being broadcast by Rik.

Overhead, the weight of the city crashes down on me. So many levels to climb, I'm dizzy with it all. Every block, someone new attaches themselves to our little procession. When we don't take the turn for the stairs, I scan our environs in earnest. The only possibility in a square mile is this sector's air handling structure.

Even in the early days of New Worth, when poisonous clouds blocked so much of the sun, heating the dome was never a problem – not with so many bodies trapped under glass. Same with energy, thanks to the molten salt reactor powering the city. But air conditioning, keeping all the public areas at a livable temperature, was a huge engineering hurdle. To clear it, each sector is outfitted with a skinny building that rises from the Terrestrial District into the Canopy, dedicated to pumping cool air out to counteract the dome's inherent greenhouse effect.

And ahead is the one for this sector. No windows, just a plain concrete façade decorated in holographic projections and digital billboards, their shimmery LEDs dispelling some of the gloom.

I catch Charon's eye. "We're using the air handling structure to ascend?"

He nods. "It's in the process of getting an upgrade. Most of the crew are Disconnects. So it's just a matter of *convincing* the supervisors to let us borrow the construction elevator."

A group of ten or so people take the first carriage, led by Denita. Five minutes later it returns for us, and we file on. Not as fast as the lifts, but I'm still impressed at the Disconnects' ability to use the city against itself.

As the elevator doors open, Charon shuttles us past a bewildered staffer surrounded by Disconnects. They've zip-tied his hands together and mounted a metal and plastic collar to his head to block his implant. As least they didn't kill him outright.

Ducts thunder overhead as cold air's pumped into the Canopy. The vibrating cacophony lessens slightly as we move toward the exit. The concourse's crawling with enough Disconnects already in position that our arrival is quickly swallowed up by the whole. Rik takes my arm and maneuvers me into the center of the chanting mass. The protesters close ranks around me and Rik, our faces blocked from view by the protesters' signs and digital placards.

Following the concourse, we move deeper into the city. Our escort scares away anyone who gets too close. Denita elbows me and gets into my face, plucking at my gloves. Ah, shit. She's right – it's a dead giveaway.

Rik's already had the presence of mind to ditch his gloves. I rip off mine and drop them to the ground, where they're swallowed up by the churning feet below.

The protesters sweep us along on their convictions. More people join the march at each intersection. The energy from so many bodies whirs through me like the aftermath of too much caffeine. The concourse takes us to a wall of escalators leading to the uppermost levels of the Canopy. I duck my head as we crawl up them, avoiding the checkpoint overhead. This is the most exposed I've felt, what with the Echelon just beyond, scaffolding the sides of the dome, staring me down.

A ripple goes through the protestors at the top of the escalators, now getting off. There are so many of us any impediment of traffic could transform the rally into something more ominous. But looking at Charon and the others, at the anger barely banked in their eyes as they chant, they're probably counting on that. Riots, mass panic in the Canopy… Sure to draw the attention of the news feeds and the police, if it hasn't already.

Rik and I near the top of the escalator, Charon and Denita right in front of us. We join a writhing mass of Disconnects and sympathizers. The distinctions disappear in the wake of so many people in one place, their voices united in shaking the very concourse and the surrounding buildings to their foundations.

A woman with the same glossy brown hair as Cache moves through the crowds. A man blocks her from view, and I lose track of her in the crush. Damn.

Rik catches my eye. <<What's wrong?<<

>>Thought I saw an old friend.>>

<<Aventine?<<

I nod. >>We need to find an opening – or make one – in case we need a quick exit.>>

Someone's enhanced voice rattles the concourse. "Disconnects against the dome!" Then they pause, the crowd joining in with "Lottery lies!" before the sequence repeats, call and enthusiastic response.

Rik's doubt trickles through, like ice between my shoulder blades. <<How? We're completely surrounded.<<

>>Which won't do us any good once the police get here.>>

As soon as I think the words, sirens peal, momentarily drowning out the chants. "People of New Worth, we're at capacity for this sector. Please vacate the area in an orderly manner." The chants grow louder to combat the police presence, each battling for sonic superiority. Even adjusting my implant to help filter out some of the sounds, it's still deafening.

Charon turns back toward us. "Well, we got you this far," he practically shouts. "Now it's time for you to do your part." Over his shoulder, a dozen protesters away, there's no mistaking Dash's grim face, his gaze trained on me.

"Citizens, please disperse. Capacity is at unsafe levels."

Someone screams. Frantic voices bounces off pristine floors and buildings. The echoes transform the charged crowd into a roiling mass. A swell of protesters slams into our little group, nearly knocking Denita off her feet. Her shoulder slams into mine, but Rik keeps me standing.

"You wanted a distraction. You got one," Charon says.

"There's just the small problem of my employer."

"We've got you covered." His eyes roll back into his head with a flurry of eyecast commands, and the Disconnects in the immediate vicinity pull out a crudely printed collar they fasten around their necks. With the press of a button, my face is projected onto all of theirs, along with a facsimile of my implant's signal as they fan out into the crowds.

Dash's eyes widen as he's shouldered aside by a protester. More couriers have to be around, but between the police and the protesters, hopefully Charon's ploy will pay off as the rally tips over into riot. Rik pales at the agitated crowds, and Charon and Denita exchange a panicked look. But for the first time today, I relax. As a courier, navigating the inevitable New Worth crowds is my bread and butter.

Time to go to work.

Shouts and protests continue, but now they're interspersed with screams and the police's automated voice still commanding us to disperse. Then the crackling sound of a stun gun ripples through the area. The atmosphere buckles into hysteria as people start pushing.

Charon's nearly swept away by the tide. Another protester knocks into Denita, and she curses. The next wave pulls me bodily away from Rik. >>Whatever you do, don't fight the current.>>

I'm pushed past Dash, struggling to get around a wall of protestors. He slogs after me, against the flow, as I duck, weave, and position myself so the crowd pushes me roughly in the direction I want to go. Which is away, first and foremost, then to the edges, and, after that, the spillways off the concourse intersections. At this point, it doesn't matter which one.

Dash's incoherent shouts reach me, and I turn back. His wild gestures draw the eye of a police officer who's waded into the thick of things. People back away from both of them in fits and starts, and the crowd slowly gives way. Then the current's dragging me along again, bringing me closer to the edge of the concourse, where I'll have a fighting chance to escape the clusterfuck once and for all.

A police officer's stun gun gets knocked aside by a protester, and her shot goes wild, static slamming into one of the checkpoints mounted to a girder overhead. Fireworks cascade along the wires connecting it to the rest of the security system.

Screams echo through me as the sparks and smoke flutter down onto the panicked masses. I'm nearly body-slammed into the front window of a cafe. The workers and remaining customers have barricaded themselves inside, watching on with bewilderment as another woman who isn't so lucky thumps against the glass and slips to the ground, unconscious.

The familiar nausea rises up at the blood oozing from her temple as I jump over her, intent on getting myself to the next intersection just a storefront away. I can't afford to stop for her or my stomach.

>>How are you doing?>> Rik's still on the concourse, but he's closing in on one of the arteries away from the heart of the rally. I send him the location for a gift shop down a connecting walkway. >>We'll regroup here.>>

Someone knocks into me, dragging me the rest of the way to the intersection. I keep my feet moving, despite the breakneck pace and the loafer I stomped on accidentally a few people back. Scraping my shoulder along the wall, I maneuver myself past a woman helping a man with a broken nose.

Rik's waiting for me in front of the store. "The police set up a barricade. There's no way to reach the New Worth News offices."

"Then we'll have to bring them to us."

He blinks down at me in disbelief. "How are we going to do that? We don't have a lot of time, and I'm not sure what we could say that'll convince them to come."

"Brita. I need to talk to Brita." I pull up the directory with an eyecast command. Aventine severed my link with her so I have to do this the old-fashioned way.

"What does she–"

"Her dad runs New Worth News. She can convince him to get a journalist with enough clout to help us." When anyone with an implant can record events, the big stories have to be vetted by a bona fide journalist with press credentials. I could upload my story to the network myself, but it would just be one signal in the competing noise. Not strong enough to effect the change the city needs in time. "A team's probably already been dispatched to cover the rally. Maybe she can get them redirected to us. Ah, here we go."

After sending her account a synch request, I get an automated rejection. Unsurprising but annoying. With millions of implant users across the city, you quickly learn to block anyone you don't already have an established relationship with. But desperate times.

I send another request. |||Brit, it's Emery. I need your help.|||

Her reply's instantaneous. |||You twisted fuck. Can't take no for an answer? Reporting you for abuse.|||

|||Wait. Please, it's me. I swear. You have a leaf tattoo on your shin to disguise a scar.||| Crap. That might not be enough. |||You told me once you were the only story in New Worth your father wasn't interested in.|||

No response, but she hasn't reported me for abuse. Yet.

<<Em, is it really you?<< She has me on the most restrictive setting, but her guarded voice is a ray of sunshine.

>>It's me.>>

She upgrades the connection, allowing me access to her nonverbals, gifting me with parts of herself I thought I'd lost. <<I don't even… How *could* you?<<

I wince at the relief and fury competing across the line. >>Long story, but it'll have to wait. I need you to convince your dad to send a press team to my location. We have information that needs to get out there. Like, right now.>>

<<Wait, we?<<

>>Rik, I mean Randall, and–>>

<<*He* knows you weren't really dead?<<

>>Only recently.>>

<<I don't believe it. You can't be Emery because surely my best friend wouldn't hide the fact she's still alive.<<

>>I know it's a shitty situation, OK? And I'll spend the rest of my life making it up to you. But I need you to do this for me.>>

Silence. She has to feel my desperation – those kinds of things can't be faked. And yet, the seconds tick past between us.

<<I can't get you New Worth News. But I can get you someone from the NW Signal.<<

Shouts and sirens echo down the concourse as a team of paramedics jog in the opposite direction. Rik gives the concourse a nervous look. "We can't stay here much longer."

He's right. Too many protesters are scattered around. Injured, angry, and on the run. Bound to bring police with them. Or worse. >>Fine. We'll meet the press team at Skychapel,>> I tell Brita. >>It isn't far from our current location.>> But far enough away from the blockade.

<<Wait. You're a part of that demonstration?<<

>>Kinda. It's hard to explain.>>

<<Well, you'd better try. I'll be there in ten.<< Then she's gone.

I groan.

"What's wrong?" Rik asks.

"Brita's going to meet us herself."

"She's a reporter?"

I'm already pulling up the staff listings at the NW Signal. She's listed as an assistant to one of their senior correspondents. "Not exactly." But she's written a couple of articles for them these past few months. Gotta start somewhere, I guess.

"I thought you said–"

"I know. We'll just have to make it work somehow."

"Where to?"

"Skychapel."

"Guess some things don't change." The tail end of his chuckle reverberates through me.

"It's a public space," I reply, feeling the need to defend my choice. "We'll find a quiet corner and tell the truth."

"It does have nice symbolism to it."

"Hopefully Brita will appreciate it." If nothing else about the situation.

Thankfully Skychapel appears largely untouched by the chaos only a few buildings away. I lead Rik to an area off the main path with tightly manicured hedges, providing the illusion of privacy. Inhaling, I hold the fresh air in my lungs, imagine it diffusing through my body, displacing the filth from the lower levels. The Canopy's the only place in New

Worth where you come out cleaner than when you entered, though it's lost some of its sheen after being outside.

<<I'm almost there,<< Brita announces. She sounds more eager than angry, thank goodness.

>>We're on the southernmost corner, near the…>>

Hasty footfalls rush toward us. I have only a second's notice before Rik and I are surrounded by stun guns. Not police. Government. Rik goes deadly still beside me at the sight of Joan Sheridan leading the charge.

>>Shit! Stay back. We've got–>>

Sheridan presses a button on a small device in her hand, and my implant's blocked. No ingoing or outgoing messages. Rik steps closer to me, his shoulder brushing mine in silent support.

"Miss Driscoll, you're a very hard person to find." Sheridan watches me with an almost expectant intensity, neither angry nor annoyed. "I hope you don't mind, but I'd like to have a *private* conversation with you."

CHAPTER THIRTY-ONE

Now would be a perfect time for a witty comment, but for once I come up empty.

She chuckles. "You know, part of me thought we should just wait it out when you didn't come in quietly. The body of one young woman who's already alienated from her friends and family? What would it matter? But the curdle clearly didn't take you out, so here we are."

Rik practically growls, but Sheridan only gives him a dismissive glance. "Of course you must be one of Tahir's," she continues. "He always manages to find the ones with backbones."

Brita cautiously comes up behind Sheridan's security team, partially hidden by an overgrown peony bush. I catch her eye, and she gives me a quick thumbs up. What is she up to? She's too far away to listen in, but if she gets any closer her implant will be jammed too, which won't do us any good.

"You wanted the most inexperienced courier, didn't you," I finally say to Sheridan.

Her nod's almost imperceptible. "You must have some idea of what you're carrying, otherwise you would've run back to Aventine with your tail tucked by now."

I give her a lopsided shrug. "Can't trust them with this after what happened. You know too much about how we operate. How did you manage to get Harding's buy-in?"

She clucks her tongue at me as if I'm just a wayward child. "I didn't need him, not when I helped create the courier program to begin with."

That's right. Early on, Harding said Aventine started out as an initiative of the Department of Economic Development. It explains so much. How she was able to subvert our operation. Why she's standing in front of me now.

She flashes me a picture-perfect smile. But after watching her kill someone, well, there's no expression she could make that I wouldn't be able to see through to the monster underneath. "Like a good soldier, Harding's just trying to clean up your mess. I thought that'd be enough. But clearly we underestimated you."

"Why are you doing this? Who are you working for?"

Her security team tenses, then I hear it too. Feet, lots of them, tramping toward us. Charon, Denita, and four more Disconnects halt in front of us, each one matched to a member of Sheridan's personal force. Denita has a bruised cheek, and some of the others are sporting shallow cuts, but they appear otherwise unharmed by the riot as they brandish their own stun guns.

"Didn't take you long to find yourself in trouble again," Charon says to me. He turns to Sheridan. "Sorry, but we can't let you detain Emery here."

"You *have* been busy," Sheridan says to me. "Leave, now," she tells Charon and his Disconnects, "and we won't leave you gift-wrapped for the police."

Denita's hand tightens over her stun gun, the others following her lead. "Let's see you try it."

Sheridan crosses her arms. "You must know the odds of you getting out of the Canopy after your display this morning are rapidly vanishing the longer you stand here, wasting my time."

"We're not going anywhere," Charon says. "We have evidence you and others like you in the government are working together to destroy everything Emergence stands for."

Sheridan just raises an eyebrow. "What nonsense is this?"

"You had to know the public registry's been tampered with – that's the only reason you'd be so interested in what I was carrying for Aventine."

"I was merely concerned with what another arm of the government was doing. Call it professional curiosity if you will."

That's probably how she's managed to stay relevant for so long at the Department of Economic Development despite all the rotating appointments for secretary. Sheridan *is* the Department. The one with the institutional knowledge and the backroom contacts to get things done.

"You killed one of ours in cold blood. That's not curiosity," Charon says in a hard voice. "You were protecting your plans to destroy the future of hundreds of Disconnects by erasing their land claims and then sending them to Vesa to silence them. Why?"

She chuckles. "Surely you have a ridiculous motive to go with the rest of this wild story."

"We'd like to hear it from you. We have proof. It's only a matter of time before it all comes falling down," I say.

"It's so sweet you believe that," she says with an infuriating smirk.

"We already know Vesa's no prize. How can the government essentially send people to their deaths?"

"People have been wanting to leave the dome for ages. We're merely giving them what they want."

"On your own terms," Rik mutters.

She glares at Charon. "Thanks to certain subversive factions, a large percentage of citizens think the New Worth government is lying about the habitability of the region outside the city. It doesn't matter what the research says or reports on the news feeds. People can see the green horizon in the distance and are growing impatient."

I inhale sharply. "You *want* Vesa to fail. A demonstration like New Sacrament to keep us complacent in the dome."

"Want? No. But that doesn't change the fact that it probably will, if the compromised health of the construction employees we contracted out to build Vesa are any indication. That's when I knew we had to make alternate plans."

"No matter the cost?"

"Please. Emergence's the dream this city was founded on. But have you really thought about what that means? The dismantling of our way of life. Decades of living under glass, wanting for nothing."

"Folks in the Terrestrial District would beg to differ," Charon counters.

Sheridan gives him a quelling look. "Everything we've achieved here to ensure our longterm survival requires a delicate balance until Emergence – true Emergence – is a reality."

"And in the meantime, you'll plot and conspire so you and the businesses you represent are positioned to best advantage when the glass comes down," I say.

She lifts a shoulder. "We only get one chance to set the foundation for our society."

"You have a narrow definition of society," Charon counters.

"You think you deserve a say in all this when you spurn our way of life?" She taps her temple. "Proven over and over again you're beyond rehabilitation? I've watched Department secretary after Department secretary try to clean up the Terrestrial District, only to meet resistance by small-minded individuals like yourself. We cannot let you or anyone else dictate the terms of Emergence, not with the entire city's wellbeing at risk."

"Wait." I'm still processing the awfulness of what I'm about to say. "That's why you went after the lottery too. You *wanted* all those people from the same blocks to be chosen, just like with the land claim consolidation. To make it easier to secure the permission to redevelop their neighborhoods."

All those buildings in the Terrestrial District that couldn't get updated because of holdouts and lawsuits. The never-ending infighting between government leaders, businesses, and residents, while the lower levels molder around them, inviting crime and desperation. No one's been able to make good on the promises to clean up the Terrestrial District. But Sheridan's found a way to make it happen.

Healthy roots, healthy city. When, not if, Vesa failed, it would renew interest in the city's infrastructure and overall health. And Sheridan and the businesses she represents would be ready to pounce.

Rik sucks in a sharp breath. "You knew the Council would be pressured to let the results stand once the protests started. That's…"

Diabolical. Such twisted calculations go against everything I've ever been taught. Denita swears. Charon's dark glance grows even darker as he stares down the secretary.

"Cleaning up the Terrestrial District has been a goal for years," she replies. "Sending people outside, creating space in the lower levels for redevelopment… It's an opportunity I couldn't ignore."

"That's a cleansing, not a cleaning."

"Semantics. And in any case, it doesn't matter anymore." She nods to the nearest guard. "Now, we're about to have a messy security incident, I'm afraid. Harassment of a public official, threats to my personal safety… leaving me no choice but to defend myself."

For a few tense seconds, blood pounds in my ears, the only sound in our little clearing.

"If I may interrupt, I've taken the liberty of evacuating the park." Brita, brave foolish Brita, approaches us, buying us time with the borrowed press badge hanging from her neck. Hopefully that'll be enough to protect her from the stun guns suddenly aimed her way.

"Allow me to introduce Brita Cruz with the NW Signal," I say. Sheridan's face goes stony in recognition of Brita's last name. "She was able to record our conversation for posterity." At least I hope so.

Brita pales as the focus shifts to her, but she courageously faces Sheridan and the others down. "My colleagues are packaging it up back at the office as we speak. *Daddy* taught me the importance of carrying backup recording gear in case something ever happened to my implant," she says with a brilliant smile. "But since I have your attention, would you mind answering a few more questions?"

Police sirens sound, cutting off Sheridan's reply. Scores of police officers in riot gear surround the Disconnects and Sheridan's security detail. Harding and a group of government agents, based on the suits and body armor, join in. Brita did way more than just evacuate the park.

A few seconds later, my implant's back in action. Harding watches me with a wintry gaze as Sheridan and her security detail are arrested. But the police don't stop there. Charon, Denita, and the rest of the Disconnects are rounded up as well. Denita resists an officer, earning the butt of a stun gun to the head.

"Emery, you promised," Charon shouts, struggling with two officers.

I start toward him, but Rik holds me back with a hand on my shoulder. <<He'll be all right. It's the next part I'm worried about.<<

Convincing the authorities of the conspiracy. If they realize Brita's not here in an official capacity…

I send a synch request to Harding, but he ignores it.

Deliberately, he turns away from me and talks to one of the suits. Freezing me out?

"Sir, you need to step away from her right now," a government agent tells Rik.

I give her a sharp look. "No, he stays with me."

It's like I don't even exist to her. "Come away now. We won't ask again."

Rik ignores her. Behind him, Brita's talking fast and brandishing her press badge to the expressionless police officers.

The agent gets behind Rik and grabs him by the shoulders.

"*No!*" I say. "I told you–"

Rik wrenches free. I try to catch Harding's eye – surely he has the authority to call them off – but he's still in conversation with the lead agent. The woman and another officer try to drag Rik away. *We stay together*. I reach for him, finding his fingertips first, then, our bare hands clasp one another.

The calibration works despite the chaos around us. Our data receptors align in the most intimate of handshakes. No hesitation as skin meets skin. As Brita and the rest of New Worth looks on. And all that follows?

<<Liv Liv Liv<<

>>*Yes.*>>

My eyes open wide as Rik crashes down around me, in me, in vibrant spirals of light and feeling. What we had before was a mere shadow of our connection now. No filters, no restrictions. His mind and mine, fitted together in newfound harmony.

Even as fatigue bears down on me, slightly dulling the sensations. Even as he's dragged bodily away from me. Even as Brita's shouts and the sirens grow louder, so loud my ears must be bleeding.

<<They might keep us separated, but we have this now.<<

>>I won't let them. I won't–>>

Someone puts their hands on me, and I react, Aventine training taking over. "Don't touch me." I land an elbow in someone's side, my foot finding someone's shin. "Leave him alone! He's not–"

A bolt of lightning sizzles into my chest. My body seizes up from the stun gun blast, lungs sputtering.

"Liv!"

I thought I'd lose myself in Rik, that he'd overwhelm my sense of self. Instead, I've found–

<<Stay with me.<<

–I've found so much.

<<Stay with–<<

>> ... >>

>> … >>

>> ... >>

CHAPTER THIRTY-TWO

Turns out getting zapped's almost as debilitating as the curdle. Exhaustion and anxiety and phantom pain battle it out in my brain as I drift. Rik's concern filters through, a lifeline as I slowly shrug off unconsciousness and drag myself back to reality.

But he's not at my side in the small bedroom full of beeping medical equipment. Where…

<<I'm here.<< In our connection, so vivid and alive between us, I can't focus on all of it at once. Like staring into the sun. <<Just not there.<< In the flesh, which I want almost as badly. <<Figures the one time I leave, you'd wake up.<<

>>You're OK? The last thing I remember…>> The police roughing him up in Skychapel.

<<I'm fine. Brita and your friends at Aventine helped straighten everything out.<<

>>The calibration… it worked?>>

A pause. I strain for an answer, but this time it isn't verbal. Our connection thrums with the sensation of his hand squeezing mine in an echo of the calibration handshake that made us confidants. Mentally, I reach out to return the gesture, tentative and clumsy as I adjust to the new settings. So many more options linking me to him. So many more emotions, full of color and nuance. Relief, affection, and…

<<That too.<<

"Christ, Em." Brita's strident voice demands my attention as she enters the room. "Do you have any idea what a crazy brave thing you did? You nearly died."

It certainly feels like it. A stun gun blast to the chest can be dangerous. I push myself into a sitting position. "How long have I–"

"Two days. Since the story broke, New Worth's been turned upside down."

Panic tightens my chest. Aventine, the authorities, and, thanks to Brita, citizens throughout the city will want answers. I have to–

<<Breathe, Liv. You've played your part. Time to let someone else handle things.<<

"The data?" I croak out.

"It's safely secured at New Worth News' headquarters," Brita says.

"But I thought you worked for–"

"I'll get to that. Two city councilors have been forced to resign while the rest of the Council has set up a taskforce to investigate."

"And Sheridan and her cronies?"

"There've been some arrests. Sheridan, some prominent business leaders, even a few government aides." She ticks them off her fingers.

Brita gets in my face, staring into my eyes as though she can see all the way to the back of my skull. "Hi, Randall." She may as well have dumped a bucket of water on me. She straightens and puts her hands on her hips. "I guess there's no point in asking *him* to butt out so we can really talk. You're a package deal now." At my blank look, she adds, "You two finally did it."

My mouth hangs open. "What?"

She waves me off. "Not *that.* I mean calibration. I'm impressed it worked, considering all the chaos back there."

"Me too. Sorry I got distracted." It was only for a handful of seconds, but enough of a tell for her. It's hard to muster up any embarrassment, though, when Rik's focus on me works better than my IV full of painkillers. "I'm still getting used to splitting my attention."

"Well, you might want to dial back the fidelity until you adjust. You have some guests that have been desperate to see you. And something tells me you'll need to give them your full attention."

Aventine. I glance around the room. Designer furnishings, far more luxurious than my family's quarters or Aventine's. "Where am I, anyway?"

"A New Worth News safe house, courtesy of good ole Dad."

The bitterness in her voice reminds me of the terrible position I put her in. "How–"

"When he heard his daughter landed the big scoop, well, let's say it gave me enough leverage to finally convince him to let me work for him. Turns out he's a big fan of initiative."

"I'm really glad to hear that."

She watches me a long moment as if she's trying to decide something. Then she rolls back her shoulders. "I wish you felt you could have told me the truth, Em."

"Brit–"

"I heard what happened, don't worry." She perches herself on the side of the bed. "Next time, don't forget your friends. I may not be all the things Rik is to you, but I'll always be there."

"I'm sorry."

She gives me a hug. "I know you are, silly." She pulls back, and she's her breezy self once more. "Besides, it's not all bad. You handed me the story of the decade on a silver platter."

"More like in a red vial."

She snorts, then stills, a fleeting frown on her face as her eyes roll through an eyecast command. "Your visitor's getting impatient. Are you up for seeing Tahir?"

I nod. Might as well get it over with.

"Don't look so glum. I'll still be here. Technically, you're my informant. That makes you *my* responsibility." She winks and leaves the room.

For a moment, I simply sit there, relishing the changes to my connection with Rik. He's everywhere I am, subtle and secure or as immense and immersive as I let him be. Still working on that part. Becoming confidants has been the goal for so long, I haven't really thought through what's supposed to happen next.

>>Where are you?>>

<<Nearly there. Was helping Geeta move into her new place.<<

>>She moved?>>

Rik frowns, and for a split second, anxiety squirms in my chest. Something bad happened. <<A gas leak at her apartment a couple of hours after our meeting.<< Sheridan's handiwork, no doubt, trying to tie up loose ends. <<She's OK. Luckily, she had stepped out for an errand.<<

Thank goodness for that. Even if their relationship complicates things.

<<She's just a friend, Liv.<<

>>I didn't *say* anything.>>

Brita returns with Tahir, and it takes a moment to regain my focus, like swimming against the current. His face is a mask as he approaches the bed. "M, glad to see you're awake. How do you feel?" Brita lounges on a couch tucked against the far wall, feigning disinterest.

"Like I've been run over by a maglev. How bad are things with Aventine? No, don't answer that. But you understand, don't you, why I did what I did?"

"I understand," he says shortly.

"Does Harding?"

Tahir crosses his arms. "He… does, and he regrets the situation you were placed in, even if you deviated from protocol–"

The door opens, cutting off whatever else he was going to say. Randall, my Rik, out of breath and for a second so in need of reassurance my chest aches. His frank gaze lands on me, heedless of Tahir and Brita's presence.

I'm suddenly very glad I haven't tried to stand yet as he looks at me inside and out.

>>Did you run the whole way?>>

I'm rewarded by his smile and the corresponding warmth that floods my body. <<Can you blame me?<<

Brita arches her brow. "You two are going to be impossible, aren't you?"

"If this is impossible," Rik says, finally sparing her a glance, "then yes."

Tahir makes a displeased noise in the back of his throat, and with effort I turn back to him. "As I was trying to tell you, you've been suspended." He holds up his hands. "Don't worry. It won't stand for long, not after what happened. What that barbarian did to your blood…" He shakes his head. "Well, we now have an opportunity to talk about what your role with Aventine should be."

"I'm still a courier?" I wasn't sure that'd be possible once the dust settled.

"No, but you still work for us."

"What does that mean?" Rik asks.

"Even though you're capable of carrying data-encoded blood, the level of notoriety you've garnered thanks to recent events makes that impossible. Luckily, I have something else in mind for you." At my questioning look, he says, "How does being a handler sound?"

"You really think I'm a good fit for the job?"

"I think you could be. Eventually."

More training, but that doesn't sound so bad. Not after this last job.

"How long's my suspension?" I ask.

"Three months, but we can get that cut down. Before we make it official, though, there's the small matter of your implant." Déjà vu, so nauseatingly intense, fills me as I remember my first day with Aventine. Rik looks at me in alarm as I brace myself for Tahir's next words. "I assume you're still synching with Mr Iverson-Kemp here?"

<<Why does he make it sound like a dirty word?<<

Tahir and I may no longer be connected, but he knows me too well. I shake my head. "I gave him up once for Aventine. I won't do it again."

Tahir's silent for a long moment. "Then we'll start the vetting process right away. Normally, you'd need to disconnect from him, even suspended as you are, but given his role in your return to us, we'll let that go for now."

My relief and Rik's twine around one another until any remaining tension pours out of my body. But I'm not quite ready to relax just yet.

"And Brita?"

"Background checks are already underway, at her insistence."

"Damn right," Brita chimes in.

"My parents too."

"Them as well," Tahir agrees.

Warmth fills me. I've been so focused on protecting my friends and family, I nearly forgot how much I need them to bring any meaning to my life. But I won't have to be alone any longer.

Rik's hand closes over mine, and I jump at the feedback. Even with our gloves on, the pleasure of touching and being touched magnifies until it reverberates between us like a live current. Overwhelming, and at the same time, something I never knew I needed.

Tahir notices, then looks away, embarrassed. I try to dampen my reaction, but it doesn't help, not after Rik's unrepentant grin from behind Tahir's back. "I'm surprised Aventine OK'ed the safe house," I say, struggling for normalcy.

Tahir arches his brow, his gaze finding our linked hands once more. His lip twitches. "It's too risky, bringing you back to HQ right now, considering all the attention. But we aren't abandoning you completely. K will be keeping you company."

"Did you give her a choice?" Last time I saw Kat it felt like we came to some sort of understanding, but that was *before* I knocked her out.

"She volunteered. Something about brushing up on your sparring skills."

I fight back a smile at that.

"Kat's great," Brita says from the couch. "What?" she says at my questioning look. "Someone had to fill me in on everything since you died, and *you* weren't available."

My nightmare's complete. I can only imagine the stories they've shared with one another.

She gets to her feet, a mischievous smile on her face. "Oh, Tahir, I forgot. Got some questions about the press conference and the New Worth News exclusive you've promised us, now that Emery's awake. We should probably discuss them in the other room." She waggles her eyebrows. "Like, right now."

Tahir starts guiltily at that. "Oh. Well, I expect the doctor would appreciate the opportunity to see you as well," he says to me, drifting toward the door after Brita. "I'm glad you're OK, Emery. Be safe. I still have things to teach you."

"*After* her suspension's up," Rik says.

"That'll be up to M," Tahir says, fighting to keep his tone mild, his face neutral. Then he shuts the door, finally leaving us alone.

I turn to Rik. "He's really not that bad."

"He didn't force you to calibrate with him again, but that's about all that can be said."

"When I go back to Aventine..."

"I know. I get it. I just want to keep you to myself for a little bit longer, that's all."

I flush at his proprietary tone. "Will it always feel like this?" I don't need to explain to him the exhilaration, the sense of rightness, and the promise of more.

"I hope so. I guess we'll find out." Together.

In the past, he's always been able to help battle back the dark thoughts that sneak up on me. Now that we're confidants, being so exposed and vulnerable to his consciousness, the loss of control's terrifying. >>If it gets to be too much...>>

<<Whatever boundaries you want to set, just say the word.<<

I already know the answer, but it can't hurt to be sure. "You don't mind taking things slow?"

"I've learned to become incredibly patient when it comes to you," he says with a grin. Well, not exactly. Only the corner of his mouth tugs up. But the sensation of him grinning comes through with perfect clarity. Like an iceberg – there's so much more going on under the surface. Things I can now access since we've become confidants.

Our connection gives me a split-second warning of his own question for me. One that needs to be spoken aloud. "What happened in Skychapel, this – *us* – it's what you wanted?"

For a moment, I don't understand what he's asking, then I think back to how things went down from his perspective. Me trying to keep him from being taken away by the police, the calibration an accidental side-effect at best, a mistake at worst. He should know better. We're partners in this, partners in everything.

I take both of his hands in mine. "The only thing I wanted in that moment was you." The line of his shoulders relaxes, accompanied by a corresponding quickening across our connection that warms me from the inside. "So I'm afraid you're stuck with me." I poke him in the chest with my index finger. "*All* of me, including Aventine."

"Pretty sure I've already proven myself in that regard."

I slip off one of my gloves. "Doesn't mean we can't practice."

He takes in a shuddery breath, some of that rawness from earlier creeping back into his gaze as he struggles with the button on the edge of his wristlet. "No. No, it doesn't."

ACKNOWLEDGMENTS

I wrote this book in scattered bits over a number of years, with many false starts and much uncertainty whether it would ever move out of my head and into yours. Many people helped me reach this point, and they have my unreserved thanks:

To my agent, Lana Popović, for her tireless support and guidance on this project. To the entirety of Team Robot for helping me bring this book to life: Marc Gascoigne, Phil Jourdan, Mike Underwood, Nick Tyler, Paul Simpson, and Penny Reeve, who cheerfully held my hand from beginning to end.

To Lori M Lee and Laura Snapp who have been with me the longest on this journey and have always had my back.

To my fellow Bruisers for all their feedback and sage advice: Nicole Feldringer, Chris Gerwel, Kelly Lagor (especially for her help in designing the hemocryption process), Sara A Mueller, and last but never least, Fran Wilde.

To the members of Critical Mass who have given me a writerly home in the high desert: Emily Mah, John Jos. Miller, MT Reiten, SM Stirling, Janet Stirling, and Sarena Ulibarri. And special thanks to the late Victor Milán, whose support and encouragement over the years was deeply appreciated.

To Christopher East, Christopher Cornell, and Catherine Schaff-Stump for their feedback on an early draft of this project.

To the baristas of my favorite Satellite Coffee in Albuquerque for keeping me well caffeinated as I handwrote the bulk of this book on your couches, overstuffed chairs, and at your cafe tables.

To my parents for fostering in me a love of reading and learning. One of you thought I could do anything. The other feared for me if I failed. Neither of you are here to see this moment, but I hope you both knew it would come one day.

To my family and friends and colleagues who have supported me in big ways and small over the years. I am grateful you are in my life.

To my husband Eric, my partner in crime and in anything else the world throws our way. I don't want you in my head, but I want you always by my side. And to my daughter Brynn who is still too young to understand why I am so distracted all the time. Thank you in advance for your patience.

And to you, reader, for joining me on this ride into one of our possible futures.